RED ORIGINS

THE COMPLETE SERIES

BY

KENDRAI MEEKS

BEAUTY
AND THE
BETRAYER

RED ORIGINS
BOOK ONE

ONE

Even as Gerwalta trailed her eldest sister down from the keep, the silver in her had pooled and transformed, changing its contours with the whims of her mind. Though the outer bailey walls cof Schloss Wolfsretter would bar a werewolf's entry, the sword she'd visualized into being would be a critical weapon if the beast came looking for a fight.

"West gate, and hurry," Helga directed.

Gerwalta doubled her pace. Even lacking time in the field to intimately predict lupine nature, she deduced that a single wolf, alone and wearing his laymen form, willingly approaching the sacred fortress of the House of Red, wasn't looking for a fight. Unless he *wanted* to die, in which case his wish would be granted forthwith.

"A short sword?" Helga looked back over her youngest sibling's shoulder to inspect the armament she'd shaped. "Explain your rationale."

Why did all her sisters treat her as if she were still in the midst of her training? Even her sole brother, Maximilian, criticized her, despite her natural superiority as a woman. Gerwalta had claimed her fire six months ago, under the light of the Snow Moon. She was a righteous hood now, blessed with the ability to wield silver and a recognized wolfsretter of the clan. Even if Helga was ten years her senior and the heir apparent to their mother, *she* was not Matron yet.

Tradition demanded Gerwalta show respect to her elders, even if said elders annoyed her with the constant reminder that she was the baby of the family.

"He comes alone, in the form of a man. He does not bellow and he does not brood." Gerwalta had seen as much from the tower where she'd been tasked as the lookout when first he'd approached. "He exhibits no signs of open hostility. His gate is steady, his mannerisms gentle. Tentative, even. He will speak gently, drawing us near. If a weapon is called for, the conflict will be in close proximity. The short sword will allow me lethal force with maximum maneuverability."

"Might you not raise tensions by bearing a weapon upon his arrival?"

Gerwalta pulled ahead of her sister, keeping the sword at her side. "Speak not to me of tensions when a werewolf is at our hearth."

The Schloss Wolfretter was a proper castle, if a small one, it did not have the moat her cousin's in the Rhineland did. Given that the west wall sat precariously perched on the edge of a cliff high above the forest valley, how could it?

The wolf must have sensed their approach as much as they recognized his presence halfway across the outer bailey, but he did not turn. *What curious behavior*, Gerwalta thought, *to keep an eye to the woods and not to the enemy at your back.*

"Wolf!" Helga pushed her little sister aside, forcing Gerwalta to flank her. "Speak and declare by what gull or gullibility have you come here uninvited."

"I wish to present a petition to the Matron."

Gerwalta clicked her tongue. "Only the konigswolf may petition my mother."

His body shook with silent laughter as he pivoted. "Is that so?"

When his amused gaze met hers, Gerwalta realized that the supplicant did not need his fur to be a threat. Most wolves had dark features, but this one bucked that expectation. Blazing green eyes, and hair neither blonde nor brown, but a smattering of both. God had taken great effort in molding the clay of his anatomy. Tone, lithe, long-limbed. He used his lupine eyes as weapons, letting them fall upon her figure. And what sharp blades they were; his stare pierced Gerwalta deep within, making her weapon hand slack. The sword sunk to her side, as did her hostilities.

She'd been told some wolves could be devilishly handsome, but no one had said as handsome as the devil himself. His crooked grin melted her metal. *An animal nature, raw and unrefined, that speaks to our own,* the Matron had said, adding, *but never forget, they are the animals, and we, the masters.*

She'd expected ragged clothing, for the wolves of their

territory were merely farmers and didn't claim the wealth the wolfsretter did. His clothes, however, were quite fine. Not made from exotic fabrics as her formal attire was, but still, dignified.

And they fit him nicely. *Ever* so nicely.

"He *is* the konigswolf." Helga turned biting words on her younger sibling, forcing Gerwalta back to the moment.

"Though only recently so. You can be forgiven for not knowing, Fraulein." The king of the pack paid no mind to Helga, keeping his gaze fixed on Gerwalta. "You must be Fourth Daughter, the one who does not come to the packlands."

Helga ignored *him* in turn, also talking to Gerwalta. "Notify the castellan to raise the gate and send word to the Matron that an official audience has been requested. And, for the sake of St. Peter, stop staring at him, silly girl!"

"There's no call to demean the child, Frau Helga," the wolf said, leaning into the iron bars of the castle gate. "Let her look all she likes. It's only by accepting our ignorance that we can correct it, and the Matron has chosen to let this child remain quite ignorant."

Gerwalta sneered. All he had to do was open that pretty mouth to reveal his ugly inner nature. "Keep your silence, wolf, unless I should be forced to make you whimper."

The wolf's grin widened, setting Gerwalta's blood boiling. Ah, yes, there it was. Vanity, assumption, familiarity: all vices that wolves held in spades. Oh, he was dangerous, but he didn't need claws or teeth to be so. All he needed was that intoxicating, seductive smile.

Silver was in no short supply here, nor was its acquisition difficult. While owning the mines had made the wolfsretter wealthy, it had not, as with others who dug at the veins, deformed them. The righteous needed no pick or ax to pull the ore from the earthen holds below ground. All she needed was her power, her awoken supernatural ability to wield the precious metal and command its obeisance. In Gerwalta's hand, a chunk of silver could become an arrowhead, a dagger, a needle, a shield.

In this moment, as Helga's power fell over the metal grated to her hands in the form of gauntlets, it could be used to form manacles.

She held them up at eye level. "You know our procedure."

The wolf, taken aback but also visibly stealing himself, nodded. "I do."

"And you agree?"

"Mark my words, Frau Helga, I would not readily suffer such torture without need." The wolf presented his hands, fingers caked in dirt. "I submit to your hold."

The manacles again became liquid, pooling on Helga's open palm. As she pushed her hands through the grating of the iron gate, the metal began to siphon off, wrapping itself around the wolf's wrist. Searing flesh bubbled and baked. To his credit, the konigswolf merely winced, although the pain must have overwhelmed him. Even now, Gerwalta could see the tortured flesh under the metal weeping blood. Gerwalta back walked from her vantage point, wondering what in Christ's Kingdom could provoke one of his kind to endure so excruciating torment. She, for one, would never be able to stomach it.

And certainly, never for the "privilege" of being in the Matron's presence.

TWO

Schloss Wolfsretter had never fallen to a foe's attack. It was guarded from the world of man by a tightly-woven forest lattice the laity called the *Schwarzwald*. Inside the Black Forest, the House of Red had built their fortress at the edge of a cliff, high above the valley floor. Only the west and south gates permitted entry, even the paths leading to those so narrow and treacherous, it was customary to tie blinders to the horses pulling the carts that would occasionally traverse the road, lest they panic and fall off the trail as it clung to the edge of the mountain.

In ancient times, a massive tree had grown on the cliff. It was said that, under its branches the first red Matron, Hlin the Conqueror, slew the Konigswolf Kroon, establishing the clan's dominion. The compound had grown around the tree, and even now, hundreds of years later, the base remained, carved to seat Hlin's progeny. This throne, a twisting upheaval of wood and antler melded by metallic threads and embellishments, sat at the back of the third inner chamber. From it, Gunda Faust presided over both her family and the forest with a silver fist.

The Red Matron, they said, never smiled but in private moments of pleasure and in the execution of slaughter. No exception would be granted for the wolf who groveled before her now, pleased though she must be with such an act of obeisance. With a nod, First Daughter laid a hand on his human shoulder, forcing him to the ground.

"Andreas Baron."

Frau Gunda Faust pronounced his name like a slur, as she had the several times they'd encountered each other since Andreas had risen as king. He thought, it must please her that he should have to accost her here, in her own castle, surrounded by the trappings of her station, wearing the pelt of one of his ancestors.

"Speak."

At the Matron's command, Andreas touched his forehead

with the fingers of his right hand before covering his chest and dotting the floor with his brow. He then lifted his head only enough to show his eyes.

His rough voice bore witness to the pain induced by his silver manacles. "I would make a petition, Matron, if you would hear it."

"*If* I would hear it?" she barked, bringing herself to the edge of her throne. "Are you suggesting that I would be reticent in my duties as Matron? Do you question my competence to rule your pack?"

His eyes cast downward as his palms flattened on the floor, leaving him fully prostrate. "I did not mean to imply such. As you know, I am only in the third moon of my kingship, and still unfamiliar with the ways of court. Please overlook any gaff of protocol."

"You are on your knees, and that is a start. Look up, Konigswolf." She waved a hand dismissively. "Proceed."

He did as commanded, bringing his bound hands up, steepling them into his chest. Blood from his veins burned by silver trickled down his forearms and soaked into his darkening sleeve. "I request permission to leave the Schwarzwald, to reclaim one of my pack who left last night."

That brought the Matron to the front of her throne. "A rogue or an exile?"

"I'm not certain, Matron." Andreas shifted, shying his eyes away. "As I said, I am still learning to properly wield my power as Konigswolf. In anger, I neglected to recall how my words can bind action. I cannot recall my exact wording, if I gave an order for my brother to leave, or merely suggested it. In any case, I could not intercede ere Stephen had departed. If I *did* command his departure, he'd be powerless to return unless I seek him out and remove the obligation of the edict. I must have my brother in my pack; you know his value to me."

"Your pack's situation is not without remedy. We have discussed this. Why not wait for him to return? Brothers quarrel, men take respites to let rows clear."

"Matron, I'm afraid it is more than that. You see, the reason we quarreled was that Stephen informed me that he wishes to wed a member of the laity. Ordinarily, I would entertain such considerations, but the object of his desire is a member of the imperial court in some way. Exposing a bride of status to our world comes with consequences.

I fear that he has set out in some rueful attempt to claim her, against my wishes." The wolf licked his lips before adding, "The moon grows fuller by the night."

The Matron's skin went white. "He would reveal our kind to the world, to man, church, and emperor."

"I know your veiled interactions with the court are of great import to your wealth and power. I say this not to judge. I merely wish to acknowledge that his retrieval is critical for both the prosperity of your clan and the sanctity of my pack."

"Not to mention for the continued secrecy of our kind." Andreas had never seen the Matron so red-faced. "So newly a king, and already, you have let lambs go astray. It puts your leadership in question, Herr Baron. Even that you allowed your own kin to become entwined with a laywoman..."

"That sin falls to my predecessor." Heat fringed the edges of his words as he dared cut off the Matron. Realizing his mistake, he resumed groveling. "Apologies, but we are of the same mind in this. I beg, permit me leave to pursue Stephen and retrieve him. I vow that I shall return with my scoundrel of a brother forthwith and that he shall be immediately mated on my orders to one who will anchor him to the pack."

The Matron fanned a silver coin through her fingers. Where had it come from? Her command, of course. Moments before, it had been a ring on her finger. "And if your brother proves to be beyond your reach?"

The wolf faltered, losing three shades of color. "I shall do what's needed."

"Really?" Amusement made the Matron's tone suddenly light. "You would kill your own brother? Even if you think you mean that, Herr Baron, I do not believe you capable, when nip comes to bite. Your words failed to deter him, why would your maw be any different?"

"If the good of my pack must come before the viability of my bloodline, then it must. Would you not do the same, Matron? To secure your clan, would you not shed your own blood?"

That comment brought the Matron to her feet, a sudden burst of movement that made the konigswolf flinch. But it was not to attack that she rose, but to draw attention to her family's presence.

"Helga." The Matron descended from her dais, brushing the cheek of each of her children in turn. "Gretchen. Zelda. Maximillian," and pulled back just enough to abstain from touching the youngest. "Gerwalta. My five children are like the fingers of the hand which clutches my sword. Should one become diseased—" She paused, lacing the fingers of her hand around the youngest offspring's throat, squeezing just enough to make Gerwalta flinch. "It would grieve me, but yes."

Andreas couldn't believe his eyes, or his ears. Nor, did it seem, could Fourth Daughter, whose anger flushed her cheeks ere she lashed her head aside. The konigswolf became heartsick when he thought it may be his fate to end his own brother, but his brother was responsible for his own downfall. But to end one's own child?

And *they* considered *him* the animal?

The moment passed, and the Matron turned again on the supplicant. "Is your second prepared to mind your pack until your return?"

"Yes, Matron. Angser is a capable wolf who believes in firm discipline. He can be counted on to keep peace until my return."

"He must, or I will dispatch him without consultation," the Matron assured. "You are right insofar as saying your brother's revelations would affect us both. Thus, I too have a vested interest in either his return, or his destruction. I will grant your request to seek him... under the condition that one of my clan accompany your journey."

Silver slicked over the weapon hand of many a wolfsretter as a growl curdled in the wolf's throat. His mouth bore witness to his condition, his teeth growing long and pointed.

"I do not require a minder. I am *konigswolf.*"

The Matron descended upon him with bladed fingertips crowned in silver. She pulled back a hand before letting it fly forward, the metal burning marks into the wolf's cheek. "This is my condition. Accept it, or I will send *two* of my clan in your stead, with orders to kill on sight. If you want a chance to save him, you will take what I offer."

To his credit, Andreas did not whimper. With eyes closed, he ate the pain. "Frau Helga and Frau Zelda know Stephen's face best."

"Helga is with child. She cannot leave the forest." The Matron turned back to the dais, where each of her brood remained in quiet obeisance. "Gerwalta will accompany you."

Andreas sneered. "She is but a child."

"She *is* young, but righteous nonetheless, and my own blood. Though she lacks experience of overseeing your pack, she is a capable warrior. Should retrieving your brother prove troublesome, she will dispatch him posthaste. Prepare yourself, then. You leave at sunrise."

THREE

"This is preposterous."

Away from court, where cousins, visiting wolfsretter of other clans, the families of her siblings, and select trusted laity always lurked with open eyes and contagious tongues, Gerwalta could share with her mother her exact thoughts.

"What do we care if one wolf has gone chasing after a laymaiden?" the youngest Faust bemoaned. "When full moon comes, he will take his wolf, ravage whatever poor village or hamlet he finds himself in, and be killed for his misdeeds posthaste. The problem solves itself."

"And let innocent laity die?" Gunda dropped a few more pfennige into the purse at her daughter's waist before tucking the pouch of coins behind the dark green folds of skirting. She'd travel with silver, of course, but the lower denomination could be used to avoid attention. "The primary reason for our existence is to protect them from the wolves. I would have dispatched one of your sisters upon learning of Stephen Baron's intention for that reason alone, even if Andreas had not sought to retrieve him. And that is the primary mission you are to undertake: protect the laity."

"Primary?" Gerwalta repeated the word as though having just learned it. "What other task would merit this journey?"

"You heard the konigswolf. Stephen's beloved travels with the imperial court. Mayhap your travels will take you into the sphere of power, where I would have you... *listen*."

Gerwalta narrowed her eyes on her mother. "For what?"

"For some indication of why favor has turned from us."

Incredulity crept into Gerwalta's tone. "Who else besides us could supply the crown with silver at such low cost, or match our craftsmanship?"

Gunda sharpened her gaze, giving her youngest the kind of

drawn-out silence that demanded her to reassess her conclusion. Gerwalta combed memory, myth, and the moment for evidence that could weigh against her supposition.

"Precisely the question to ask, daughter." The Matron let her chin dip once. "The Ottomans may have let Vienna slip through their fingers, but their campaign brought more than laymen soldiers to the empire's borders. When the Grand Turk withdrew, his remaining footprints filled with the consequences of his quest."

"But you couldn't possibly believe the Emperor's court would conduct business with the House of Black, or vampires, even." Her mother nodded. "But… they are Saracens! How could the *Holy Roman Emperor,* the great defender of the Church, favor Muslims over Catholic subjects?"

"Profits change men's allegiances faster than gods. But that is not what's bothering me. What I wish to know," Gunda paused, examining the silver bands that encircled her wrists, "is what the black hoods are trying to achieve by selling cheap silver to the crown. If they are merely raising funds to return home, let them make haste. If they are settling in with intents to settle west… Well, then, we'll need to plan accordingly. This is why I chose you to be my emissary on this mission. Even though your experience with lupines is limited, your training in laity court procedures and politics is more thorough than your sisters'. You are my progeny; you will always be a wolfsretter first, but what I need on this mission is a daughter who can spin intrigues as well as silver."

"Then, you would like me to let Stephen Baron make it as far as court?"

"Just be certain he is not there come full moon. As soon as he's made it far enough to provide an excuse for visiting the emperor's court, do away with the lone wolf. Keep up the illusion that you are merely an overseer, for the moment Andreas Baron understands we are using this crisis to our advantage, he will either turn on you, or turn away from you. Neither serves our purposes."

The young hood bowed, the grin carved by pride barely hidden. "Understood."

"Good. Keep your wits about you. Never let that wolf from your sight, and do not hesitate to strike him or his brother down should they pose a danger."

FOUR

They left at dawn, at an hour in which both would rather have taken to their beds than dragged themselves away from home. Gerwalta hoped her brother was right. As a man, Maximillian was often called upon to conduct the family's business with the laity, a vulgar race who thought women the weaker sex. As such, Max often had to adapt the rhythm of his duties to day. "Sleeping at night, and waking *with* the sun instead of the moon..." he'd said to her as he helped Gerwalta pack her sack. "It feels wrong, but after a day or two, one learns to tolerate it."

Halfway through the sun's arc across the sky on this first day, doubts festered. Gerwalta prided herself on her dutifulness; she would *not* let the konigswolf from her sight. She *did* wish, however, that Herr Baron would slow down. As was custom among wolfsretter, Gerwalta tracked the wolf-like prey, but from the safety of the treetops. She nimbly leaped from oak to pine, trailing the wolf, but keeping him in sight. He drove forward with a veracity that had her weaving through branches like a needle through cloth to keep apace. His stamina... where did he get it? It might be easier to walk on the road beside him, but Gerwalta didn't feel it proper, acting as though the wolf were her equal.

Nonetheless, when Herr Baron paused to rest shortly past midday, she *almost* thanked him. Was he oblivious to her observation from the branches above, or indifferent to it? Her body tingled with the innate gift of her kind: the sense of knowing when a lupine was near. Did wolves have the same ability? How had it never occurred to her to ask that?

"You'll have a difficult time as we descend into the next valley."

His sudden words drew her from her reverie. By whatever means, he at least knew she was within earshot, it seemed.

She sat down on a branch. "I will endure."

"Not up there, scurrying like a squirrel in pursuit. The trees are younger farther on, unlikely to bear even your graceful form."

Her form's bearing on the trees was hardly the issue, but he need not know the particulars of why. Not even her own mother had been able to learn that piece of knowledge, and Gerwalta well intended that the Matron should never become aware of the secret her daughter hid.

Herr Baron settled onto a large boulder, making a show of unpacking his food stores. He ripped into a hunk of bread (she smelled cheese too, if she wasn't mistaken), his jaw working hard to consume what even now must be beginning to lose its freshness. "Do you think, Fraulein, that I am merely waiting until we are a goodly distance from Schloss Wolfsretter to turn and rip you, limb from limb? I assure you, I haven't the slightest intention. Not to mention, it is midday. I am never weaker in the passage of time. So why not come down, already?"

"Do you think that you can command my presence, and I'll obey?"

"I will never command anything of you. An honorable wolf does no such thing; he offers what he is happy to give. Even if you are a wolfsretter and in any other situation, I wouldn't be concerned at all with the way you go about doing things. Walk all the way to Ulster on your hands and wearing a bell, for all I care. But you were tasked with accompanying me, and I know you obey your Matron like my wolves obey my order."

"A poor comparison, given our quest."

The jibe dented his demeanor, and she observed with glee as Herr Baron grimaced. Nonetheless, he pressed on. "If I attempt to escape you, it will have ramifications for my pack. We are stuck together on this sojourn, no matter that either of us would under any other circumstances eat a salad of hemlock than spend time together. I must make haste to retrieve Stephen as quickly as possible, which means that *you also* must make haste to keep up with me. Since I'm obligated to stay on two feet, not four, the road delivers us to my brother fastest. Already I have slowed too much to allow you to keep apace, jumping from tree to tree, but no more. Please, come down, partake of your stocks, and rest. We'll be underway again soon enough. You have my word, I will make no attempt to harm you."

She dropped from the trees in a squat, her cloak pooling around her, a length of two klafters separating them. As a wolf, he could have crossed the distance in two bounds. As a man, he'd first have to struggle to his feet, giving her time to leap away should he try.

"A sword can always injure, even when it is rusty."

His amused smile annoyed her. "Is that what you think of me? Nothing more than a warmonger?"

"You are a wolf."

"I am a man."

"You are both," she snapped, rising to her feet. "And a man, while less deadly, may be of no better intent."

"Speak from experience?" He dusted the last crumbs of his meal from his lap. "You seem so young to have felt the pain of a man's deception."

"I have encountered as yet no man who would dare deceive me." Ire bite into Gerwalta's words, and she knew from countless lessons that one must keep emotions in check when dealing with a wolf. "I would not flaunt seniority over me when you have little ground to claim it."

"The number of moons between us may compare, but I am a konigswolf, and you, merely a fourth daughter."

As he stood, raising a hand, she took a step back. Only after a moment did she realize he held a skin of water. Hers had run out earlier in the morning, and so intent was she with keeping up with him, that she hadn't had opportunity to deviate from the road to replenish it as yet.

"Go on, drink," he encouraged, raising the skin higher. "You're far too loud when you move, and you lack grace in your leaps."

She made to spit back his venom in kind, but he cut her off.

"I do not criticize to spite you. I'm only pointing out that it's causing you to lose strength too fast. I can hear how breathless you've been, hopping from tree to tree in an effort to remain both hidden and in position. The tactic is a good policy when pursuing a wolf in a limited space. It does not adapt well to sustained, long road journeys. You've not imbibed in nearly an hour; you must be parched."

How infuriatingly presumptive he was. "As I said, I will endure."

"You will fall ill," Andreas retorted. "And if I miss an opportunity to save my brother because I had to stop and nurse you back to health, I would ally with your mother in her anger. Drink, and when we start off again, save your energy by walking with me. Your mother bade mind me, but she did not say it had to be done covertly. That is an improvisation of your own design."

The speed with which she snatched the skin from his hand must have shocked him. Herr Baron's eyes widened with wonderment as she tipped the vessel and poured the water down her throat. Gerwalta had only begun to ease her posture when he spoke again.

"Remove your cloak."

Gerwalta lowered the water skin to find his hungry eyes focused on her throat where a rivulet of water, having overflowed her mouth, trickled into the fabric of her dressings. "How *dare* you?"

"By my fang, are all wolfsretter as vain as you?" The wolf shut his eyes, exhaling. "The common laity do not wear such brightly-colored cloth. You will give yourself away as a wealthy woman and they will conspire to rob you."

"I am a wealthy woman, and you speak as though any layman could get the better of me."

"I am quite certain they could not. But here, young ladies— at least those of proper learning and some social standing— do not conjure silver spears and impale those attempting to take advantage of them." Andreas pulled the skin from her hands and tucked it back into his satchel. "Remove the cloak, for my sake, if not yours. We can hide it in your sack, or if that proves insufficient we... can... Oh, my."

The wolf's words died in his throat as Gerwalta's red cloak turned to dust and flitted to the ground. Even a mythic beast as he was, as *they both were*, he marveled.

"You simply made it disappear."

Gerwalta inspected herself for defect before cawing a laugh. "Do not tell me you were unaware of our ability?"

"Should I have been, would I be in such awe?" He ventured closer, hunting for evidence of what had been there moments before and trying not to make her flinch. No good; three steps had her pulling back. "Can all wolfsretter do this?"

"Only the righteous. And I do not know why it should surprise you. Do not you conceal fang and fur in the light of day?"

"As is evident, Fraulein." Andreas held out his arms wide, calling far too much attention to a body she shouldn't appreciate so much. "Can you make all your clothing disappear?"

He barely managed to step back in time to avoid her smack, holding out his hands in supplication. "That came out wrong. My apologies. Only... witnessing such craft does birth a number of questions to a curious mind."

She paused a moment, as though weighing her next words. She knew the fundamentals of her kind's practices, and by consequence, many facts about lupines. Still, as the youngest child of a fearsome Matron, her curiosity had never been encouraged. Perhaps Herr Baron would prove a more willing tutor than her older siblings.

"I, too... have questions."

His frame eased. "I would attempt to answer them, if I can."

She couldn't stop her grin. "First, why have you not taken your wolf for this journey?"

"Do you not recall? The matron bade me travel as would a layman."

"She said *sleep* in times as would they. *That* interpretation is an improvisation on *your* part."

She didn't like to admit that a thrill ran through her when, turning his own words back on him, the wolf grinned.

"Surely you would travel much faster with four legs in place of two," Gerwalta continued.

"Do you not recall the farms we passed in the last valley?" He pointed back up the road they'd traveled. "No doubt word has reached you, as it has my pack, of the recent attacks on livestock in this valley? Natural wolves, of course; all my pack except my brother are accounted for, and he could not have done so much damage and in so little time. No, Fraulein. A farmer out this way would see a wolf in the light of day as no welcome thing, and as full moon approaches, I do not know that I would resist."

"But, *you* are a farmer."

A line creased between his eyes. "Indeed, and what of it?"

"Well, I mean… How is it that you do not slaughter your own stock when in the throes of your animal nature? And how do the animals you keep not bolt from your presence? I can smell your wolf nature even now. Surely, the pigs can too."

"I'm certain they do." A smile grew across his face as he placed a blade of grass nipped from the ground between his teeth to gnaw. "But our animals are reared knowing our scent. Can I say for certain whether or not they are confused by my two forms? I don't know. But as we make no vicious movements on what we ourselves depend on for our civil existence, they pay us no mind. We slaughter no more of them than do any farmers. They have no special need to fear us either as laymen or wolves."

That still left her to wonder. "But on a full moon night…"

A scowl flashed across his face as he offered her bread. "No, not then. When the moon is full, we barely recognize ourselves for what we truly are."

Gerwalta took a step closer, broke off a small piece from the loaf for herself, and gave the remainder back. "Lupines?"

Herr Baron shook his head. "Men, Fraulein. We begin and we end as men." Spinning, he took to the road with a vigor that forced her feet to move swift in time. "A fact I dearly hope that Stephen recalls."

FIVE

She slowed him down, and it was becoming annoying.

When Gunda Faust had given Andreas permission to leave the forest and chase after Stephen, he wondered if his predecessor's condemnations of the Matron had been misguided. If she could so easily grant a petition that took not only a wolf, but the konigswolf himself, out of her jurisdiction, surely she was a woman of civility or, at the very least, practicality. But when the proviso of an escort had been added, and who that escort was, Andreas knew that Gunda Faust was the type of Matron to add insult to injury and sell it as a blessing.

Fourth daughter to the Matron was a position no wolfsretter would envy. Gerwalta Faust had never even been out the to packlands, let alone been trusted to police any of his pack. Certainly, Gerwalta would have trained in combat, and being righteous she'd have control over silver, but the role of a fourth daughter was primarily diplomatic and, for lack of a better term, *domestic*. The youngest Faust was hardly better than one of Andreas's breeding sows. She'd be married off to an ally or potential enemy soon enough, likely a distant cousin who'd assure the Red bloodline wouldn't dilute. There her role would be to procreate, and to listen. Forget love; wolfsretter didn't consider matters of the heart in their matchings. While lupine pairings could have political aims, at least the mating bond assured that the relationship between husband and wife was one of joy. Fraulein Faust's future was one of disregard, utility, and indifference.

It *almost* made him feel sorry for her.

Then again, she was trudging along at such an intolerable pace...

"Are you ill, Fraulein?" Andreas spoke over his shoulder.

Gerwalta stopped and stood straight as a rod. *With the rod of indignation running up her backside,* as his mother would have said.

"Of course not."

Andreas stopped, turned on heel, struggled to keep his voice tempered. The last thing he wanted to do was suggest to this untested wolfsretter that he had any bad intentions where she was concerned.

"Each of your sisters—even your brother—are able to keep apace of me even on a full moon night. Being of the same bloodline and education, I would think your capabilities equitable. Yet, here we are, two days into our journey, and you appear to be slowing, even though we are walking down a well-worn road, not careening about pines and rocks all around the *Schwarzwald*."

Conflict warred in her features, as though she were equally relieved and insulted that he should broach the subject. Finally, after a moment, the lines around her jaw loosened and she let her arms fall to her sides. "There is some matter of my boots."

"Aye?"

"They were new only last week, and not worn in a manner befitting a long journey."

He took two steps nearer, pleased to see she did not retreat this time. "Are you telling me, Fraulein, that your *boots* have not been conditioned for endurance? That if you need not trudge in them, you may speed your feet?"

"It is not my mother's intention that I should be fielded. What are... Folly, wolf! Folly! You put me down this instant!"

Her tiny fists could sure pack a wallop. Lack of training or no, her blows landed on his back with the full ferocity of her breed. If she had actually intended him mortal harm, his back would well be broken. As it stood, he'd be black and blue from this temper tantrum of hers, but the amusement he drew from swooping up the wolfsretter and throwing her over his shoulder balanced out his pain.

"Fraulein, I am doing what I can to hurry along our journey. We both wish it over as soon as can be had."

"If you do not release me, *your* journey will be at an end. How dare you manhandle a Faust!"

"Have you no interest in seeing out this task with haste?"

"Of course, but—"

She huffed when he put her back to her feet over the rise of the next hill. Before she could manage to make meat of their faceoff, he drew her attention to the sight laid out in the valley below them. "Do you see the village?"

The confusion of such a question turned her from her ire. "My eyes are every bit as good as yours in the day."

True, if annoying to think they were equals in any way. "We are at the edge of the forest now. Up until this time, I have been able to follow Stephen's scent."

She blinked. "But he was two days ahead of us."

Andreas drew his eyebrows up high. "Have you not detected his scent ere we've traveled? Or is your nose not as good as mine, day or no?"

"I…" Gerwalta's eyes closed as she inhaled, pulling the aromas of the glade deep into her lungs. Her tongue clicked the top of her mouth as though she was sampling a taste, and Andreas wondered if his wager, placed on his good humor that he could give her arrogance a comeuppance, might not pay out after all.

Then, the wolfsretter's eyes flew open. Gerwalta huffed as her muscles went taut. "There is no scent of lupine here. Other than yours, which turns my stomach!"

Andreas grinned. Oh, he was enjoying her anger a little too much.

"If you are doing this to mock me then—"

He pressed a finger to her lips, stilling her rebuke. "It was only idle curiosity, Fraulein. It is not often I am able to communicate so intimately with one of your kind. I'm eager to partake what lessons I can."

"Nothing *intimate* shall pass between us." She bore her teeth, and in doing so, forced a curl of confusion over the konigswolf. "Except, perhaps, a blade."

"Injured pride is hardly a slay-worthy offense." Andreas dropped his hand and reclaimed his thoughts. "In any case, his trail here ends. Stephen didn't proceed on foot from here. Either he begged a ride on someone's cart, or was provided with a horse."

"So close to the village?" He saw the threads of theory weave behind her eyes. "If his stamina is anything akin to yours, it seems unlikely he'd waste good coin to secure a ride for such a short distance."

"My thoughts as well."

The wolfsretter balanced her chin on a fisted paw. "Whoever provided him assistance must have been expecting him. Someone with an interest in encountering him *before* he made it as far as the village. Though, to what end?"

"Stephen was my middleman for brokering the pack's goods to market. He may have had contacts in a town such as this, friends willing to offer him a night's rest. But who? At some point, he must have tread ground again, but even such a small village has many possibilities. I'll have need to scratch around a little, and that will take time. As you cannot help in this, I propose we find an inn for you. Maybe you'll be more quick-footed with a few hours rest."

She ground those very same teeth, but he could also see the battle behind her eyes. She *was* tired, and accustomed to sleeping in luxuries of which he could never dream. The past two nights they'd bedded in the cradle of nature. The thought of a proper bed on which to rest her weary body must be far too tempting.

Gerwalta's eyes dropped to the ground. "If we must."

She remained tight-lipped after that, until, outside the village's small inn, Andreas paused, leaning down to a boy of perhaps eight or ten years, engaged in some sort of game involving sticks and rocks.

"Have you labor to offer, child?"

The brown-haired boy popped up at that, rubbing a sleeve over his besmirched forehead. "Yes, sir. I can carry messages. I can tend horses. I can even see to provisions, such as Unsbach can offer."

The konigswolf drew a pfennig from a sack tied at his waist, before depositing it in the wee lad's hand. "You'll wear the lady's boots and walk about town in them to break them in."

"He'll what?" Gerwalta's indignation returned, and with it, the increase of both pitch and volume in her voice. "I am not giving such quality leather over to a village pauper! These boots came all the way from Mainz!"

"Unfortunately, not on someone's feet, or we'd not have this problem." He pushed Fraulein Faust into a chair that sat outside the inn. "Off with them. When we continue, I'll not have your sore feet slowing us down anymore."

She hesitated only a moment more, finally letting go her objections for practical truths. "It will hurt *his* feet, though," Fraulein Faust said, pulling off first the left and then the right boot. "And they'll come up over his knees. How will he walk?"

"So concerned with the comfort of the laity, now?"

They could use that word here with freedom, at least, for the wealthy were known to refer to the common folk that way at times.

"I am concerned for any creature that undertakes a discomfort in my stead. It gives me a certain level of responsibility to return the gesture in kind."

Andreas disguised his smile with a quick turn, proffered boots in hand. The boy put them on posthaste. Indeed, the result was comical, but as he trudged off to keep up his end of the transaction, Andreas knew it had been a wise decision.

"Then you give him the additional pfennig from your purse ere he returns."

By the time Herr Baron returned to the inn and Gerwalta sensed his approach, the sun had already given up the sky.

In his absence, her lack of utility burned soft embers, every hour left useless adding fuel. *A short tarry*, he'd said. It had been an entire day and then some! By the time the lupine passed into the room he'd arranged for her, Gerwalta burned as red as her hidden cloak.

"Where in the Lord's green kingdom have you been?"

The irritation crashed into him, actually making Herr Baron step back. The konigswolf, however, proved capable of reciprocity. He dropped the bag lugged over his shoulder to the floor and let loose his reprove.

"Where do you think? I've been sniffing every alley and byway, tracing Stephen's trek, while I've graciously allowed you to rest your delicate frame here – and all on my pfennige!"

Gerwalta pushed herself off the bed and grabbed the bag of coins normally tied at her waist. "As if I could not have paid!"

"No, you could not have, for you are a woman."

Red became molten. "How dare y–!"

His massive hand pressed against her mouth, silencing her as he negotiated the closure of the door with his foot. She should have drawn the silver grafted to her torso out and conjured a blade, but injuring the wolf would have caused the same difficulty he must have been seeking to avoid now: unwanted attention. Instead, Gerwalta recognized the need for diplomatic engagement, in lieu of more violent pursuits. She closed her mouth and softened her repose. When Herr Baron seemed certain she wouldn't bite, he lowered both his hand and his voice.

"We are no longer in the *Schwarzwald* and the dominion of Schloss Wolfsretter, Fraulein. This is the world of the laity, and here, a woman of good social standing does not let a room at an inn with a man in tow unless she is a very certain kind of woman, and he, a very general sort of man."

Thinking out the implications, she realized what it must mean. "How precisely did you put our names to the register, then?"

He grinned. "Mr. Wolfe and wife."

When she burst out laughing, Gerwalta wasn't sure if it was because the idea of lupine and a wolfsretter was so ridiculous, or that the false name he'd given hardly did much service in obfuscating his nature. Confusion stood between them for only a moment, before Herr Baron threw back his head and joined her.

"Now that cooler heads have prevailed," Andreas continued, "I would tell you of my findings." He held out a hand to her. "Are you hungry?"

She hesitated a moment, staring at his fingers as though they might nip her. But then, a brilliant thought struck her that if plied with ale, the wolf may dispel the ways of his kind to her more freely.

"Quite." Gerwalta slid her hand out from her costmary leather gloves, and gave her bare fingers to the wolf, allowing him to pull her toward the door. "Feed your *wife* well, Herr Wolfe. A wolfsretter left unsatisfied is a dangerous thing."

Gerwalta had not the keen ears of her foe, but they still bested those of the laity. She didn't miss, therefore, how Herr Baron's pulse quizzically quickened, nor miss the darkness in his eyes when he turned back to her. A queer pulse emanated from her belly into the sacred parts of her frame, a longing to tighten her grip on his fingers that didn't have a rational purpose. Even without the ability to see herself, she knew her innate powers had been called upon, and didn't doubt that her eyes gave off their faint silver gleam.

"Herr Konigswolf, if I have offended you in saying something foolish—"

"No." He shook his head, crossed to the door, and opened it. "You said nothing wrong. I only listened erroneously." He looked at her feet then, as they stepped into the hall. "The boy returned your boots already?"

"Yes, though do you know what that clever boy did?"

"No, what?"

"He filled them with hay and put them on a cow. I had decided to be angry with him, but the hay absorbed the odor and the boots are now so much more comfortable. It was a brilliant idea, Herr Ba... Herr *Wolfe*."

He grinned at her on the end of his arm. "I shall mark this day in my memory of when I received a compliment from one of your kind. And the pfennig?" he continued. "Did you give him one, or should I find him out and pay up?"

"I gave him two."

"Two? Why?"

"Well, the rate, I figured, was for a pair of feet, and three pairs ended up involved in the transaction. He seemed most pleased."

Herr Baron turned his beaming gaze to the ceiling. "No doubt."

The innkeeper greeted them with a loaded smile, one Gerwalta read into easily. He saw them as newlyweds, lovers who had no doubt just come from their marriage bed to catch a nibble. Gerwalta found herself blushing, despite having no cause.

Their hosts stayed only long enough to tell them what the larder could offer, and to receive their request, then skittered off.

Within moments of their food being set before them, all the awkward spirits drifted away. Both made due with stew and crusty brown bread, grumbling even as they did that fresh meat would have been the best salve for two and a half days on the road.

"So your search for the trail?" Gerwalta asked when again she felt they could speak with some measured liberty. The other patrons of the inn, likely weary from a full day spent traveling, took to their beds, leaving them alone by the fire. "Was it successful?"

He waved a hand dismissively through the air. "I found his scent in a few places, but only a step or two, as though he avoided touching anything except when unavoidable. Likewise, I could find no trace of his scent on any path leaving town. Either he's still here – which he is not, as I would be able to sense *and* smell him – or he found a way to mask his trail when he departed as well."

She looked to the empty bones of the fish still setting on someone else's table. "How likely is that?"

"If he is traveling by coach or by horse? Not difficult." Herr Baron paused to draw drink. "But it still prompts questions. In whose coach, or by what horse? I suspect we'd find his scent further up the road if we were to investigate, but there is rain tomorrow. It will wash away any evidence of his footfalls in short order. We wolves will ride short times in a cart or mounted, but it's against our nature. We are compelled to stalk ground before too long."

"So water can mask a scent?" There was a piece of knowledge that had not been passed to her. Gerwalta pointed to his left. "Where do you suppose the innkeeper acquired such fresh fish?"

"I'd imagine from the local fishmonger." The wolf chuffed at her seemingly distracting question. "After all, there is a river that runs through town and—" The realization made his eyes bright. "The river."

Gerwalta grinned. "He must have taken a boat, mayhap specifically because he knew you'd be tracking him."

Andreas muttered an oath. "I don't know which disturbs me more, Fraulein: your summation of my brother's actions, or the smile you get when you've figured out the logic of a wolf."

"I may have little experience in policing of your pack, but I am well educated in lupine nature," Gerwalta continued, almost believing she spoke the truth. "The only question that remains, then, is, once he reached the river, did he head east or west?"

"East." The quickness and surety in his voice left no room for doubt. "I overheard someone speak of it today; the emperor's court is on the move again, many of his retinue having passed this way not too long ago en route to Nuremberg. His lady love travels with the court, so shall he pursue them. The quickest way for us to catch him up is to travel the same way."

"We'll not catch a boat this night." Gerwalta stood, dawdling over to a basin to wash her hands. "We'll need to wait until morning. After being about all day, you'll have want of rest, even if the moon has risen."

"My inner wolf wishes to say he can endure, but our journey is long, and pride will not speed it." Herr Baron, too, took to his feet. "I would say that you should make use of the night for your own purposes, but again, here, among the laity, I wonder what that might not suggest."

"I'll remain in the room. My mind can find occupation, even when my body cannot."

SIX

The innkeeper could have signed his own execution papers.

When they'd set off on this trip, Andreas had had no doubts about the troubles traveling with a wolfsretter would bring, the least of which was normalizing the intrinsic feeling of her proximity. The pull in the base of his stomach when one of her kind neared was born of an ancient power, one meant to warn a wolf of danger. The longer he kept company with Gerwalta Faust, the more he feared the familiarity, and failed to feel compelled by the immediate threat she represented to flee.

One thing he had not anticipated, however, was the need to defend the lady's honor. As the innkeeper took Andreas's coin to settle for the extension of their room, the scent of the man's arousal setting eyes upon the young wolfsretter, coupled with honeyed eyes and a whispered suggestion of how the blankets could be removed if Andreas had a better way of warming himself through the night, put the konigswolf on edge of taking his fur. How easy it would be to rip away the man's throat, but then, how would killing this laymen help him find Stephen?

Despite it only being a few hours past sunset, a time in which he should have either taken his wolf, or passed a good meal with his pack, all Andreas wanted to do when they'd managed to return to their room was lay his weary body down and sleep.

Fraulein Faust closed the door behind them. "You can use the bed. I will tary on the floor."

"That is very kind of you, Fraulein." He placed the candle on the nightstand and went to work divesting his feet of boots before taking off his jacket and pulling his shirt over his head. He'd just managed to pull off his belt when he felt the weight of her stare. Andreas looked up to find Fraulein Faust glaring at him, gap-jawed.

He paused, his hand clutching the brass belt loop. "Is something a matter?"

"You are..." Words failed her, as did her hand a moment later, when it dropped from pointing at him to her side.

Oh, dear. A bashful wolfsretter. Who would have thought it possible?

"I am a wolf," he said as plainly as he could imagine, hoping to inspire her indifference. "And I sleep as such. You would know it if you stayed closer when we slept the last two nights."

"I know. That is, I don't know. Of course not, how could I know your manner of sleeping, but what I mean to say is..." Gerwalta tapped her tongue to the roof of her mouth. "You are undressing."

Though he couldn't understand why, he blushed. "Of course I am, else I would turn all my clothing to threads when I shifted to fur. Surely you knew this is a preference, wherever possible, to remove our clothing peacefully before we take our fur. What happened to your claim to be well-learned on the nature of wolves?"

Gerwalta continued to stumble for words. "I suppose I must have known, only, I never thought through the implications. I've never... I've never seen a naked man before."

He actually laughed as he finished off his belt and let his trousers fall, leaving him in nothing but his skivvies. "I assure you, we are nothing to marvel at. The lupine form is much more refined. The male laymen body is quite silly, if you ask me."

Her eyes glowed silver, and caught the candlelight as she looked everywhere but at him. "I wouldn't say it's entirely silly."

How foolish of him, to demean the fact that her kind would never know the grace and joy of being in a wolf form. Still, he had a right to his own prerogatives.

"This is the only pair of underclothes I have with me on this trip, and I've no intention of rending them simply for you to retain your eye's innocence. Look or do not; I honestly do not care."

Her mouth fell open and her gaze became unfocused. A moment later, Fraulein Faust broke from her reverie. "Perhaps if you'd allow me a moment to blow out the candle..."

"We both know you don't need candlelight to see me this close in a darkened room."

"But it... *you* will be less distinct that way." Her hands laced over her eyes, and for the first time ever, a wolfsretter beseeched *him* for kindness. "Please, Herr Baron, being here with you is already peculiar enough to my senses. Do not upset my sensibilities as well."

He did not blow out the candle, but what he did do was nearly as compromising. If she was not to sleep, she had no need of the bedclothes. The wolf pulled off the coverlet from the mattress and made himself a cover-up, tucking the loose end of the linen in at his hip bone, before sliding off his underthings effectively out of view.

"Open your eyes. I'm quite proper."

She did, and the look she gave him when her eyes fell upon him... Silver did not capture the brilliance with which they'd shone. All wolfsretter's eyes were capable of glowing, but as brightly as this? Andreas changed his mind. Swiping the candle off the table, he blew it out and collapsed to the floor. He should take his wolf; he'd be more comfortable, but as the darkness fell and Gerwalta shimmied on to the bed to find her comfort, he hesitated. Why? Was it because he'd wished she'd still talk with him, and he could not answer her in a way she'd understand if he were in his wolf? If so, he refused to acknowledge the irrational hope.

After several silent moments, on the edge of sleep, her voice recalled him.

"You must love your brother very much to tolerate me with such kindness."

"Despite what I predicted, your presence is not nearly as intolerable as I feared." He smiled despite himself. "I *do* love my brother, but there is more riding on his return than familial and pack obligation. I need to keep him from wasting his mating bond on a laywoman."

"But if he loves her without the bond..."

"Is a *wolfsretter* suggesting the validity of a love match?" Andreas rolled over, catching the Fraulein watching him through the dark. "I do not doubt his heart, but he and I are the last of our line. If the blood of my konigswolf heritage is to endure, he must take a *proper* mate."

There she found a hold in which to needle an argument. "Or *you* could take a mate. Aren't you already of an age that you should?"

"I'm only three months into my rule, Fraulein, but rest

assured: I *will*," Andreas returned, rolling over. "Just as soon as I find a shewolf worthy."

"Are the females of your pack so inferior?"

"No." The answer was as certain as it was sudden. "Do not misunderstand; I am not saying that they lack in any way, nor that they would not make good mates to any wolf. I, however, sense a change in the winds. The age of war is passing; an age of reason approaches. I wish a wife who shares in that understanding."

"The age of war will never pass until the minds of men are stronger than their desires for power."

"Precisely." Andreas wondered if her eyes widened at his concurrence. "Until they become more like a lupine. This is our existence and always has been: the animal battles to dominate our rational human mind, but we are its master."

After a few minutes of silence, no doubt in which she ruminated a retort to reframe lupines as the barbaric, godless creatures she *knew* they must be, Andreas supposed she had fallen asleep after all. Instead, when she rolled over and spoke again, her words reflected rumination on another matter.

"Will you want to fall in love with her first, or just decide she's the right kind and take her immediately to your bed?" Even through the dark, his sensitive eyes saw the blush of Gerwalta's cheeks. "Forgive me, I did not intend to be so vulgar, but I've always been curious about that aspect of your society, and have only ever been shushed and ridiculed for asking."

"I do not believe one's earnest attempts to seek knowledge are ever vulgar, Fraulein Faust."

Encouraged, she continued. "I know your bonding will induce love, but I once overheard Helga chastise your kind for wishing to fall in love *before* dedicating to the bond. It seems a foolish expenditure of the heart on something guaranteed by the deed."

What drivel these wolfsretter spoon fed their young. Though if doomed to an arranged marriage to enhance the power of the bloodline, he supposed it did have a certain ring of logic. Still, he could sweeten the truth to counteract their poison.

"Love is not the only need for a lifetime of happiness. For that reason, where possible, we encourage a meeting of hearts before a meeting of... *other* parts of the body. Yes, when I find my mate, I will love her exclusively and excessively—even before we give each other our mating bond. I do not want to dominate my mate. My queen will be able to read, write, conduct diplomacy, and be my equal if not my better."

The pillow Gerwalta held to her face failed to silence her laughter.

"What is so silly?"

"What you're describing is a wolfsretter, Herr Baron."

Embarrassment struck him to his core. "I said no such thing."

"Mayhap not intentionally."

"Certainly not. Beyond the obvious, a wolf could never be *with* a wolfsretter; *she* would never accept me to be *her* equal." He measured the wisdom in sating his curiosity but rationalized his boldness in the fact that he'd likely never again have such an opportunity. "And what does a wolfsretter desire in her future husband?"

Her tone flattened. It was as though Gerwalta were repeating back lessons drilled into her memory by the silver tip of her mother's blade. "A wolfsretter desires nothing. Desire begets passion, and passions misguide the soul. A wolfsretter is paired to ensure the strongest progeny, and to consecrate bonds with other clans. My mother will choose my mate, and I will honor whomever she deems appropriate."

Andreas refused to yield to sleep lest he speak his mind, even if through a yawn. "You will not die alone, but you will not live happily."

"Because my marriage is set before me, a thing done?"

"Yes, *precisely* because of that."

"Is it any different from what you're planning to do to your brother?"

The truth slapped him hard, but a king wolf knew the need to make such decisions were merited. Besides, it was not an apt comparison. "Yes, I will force Stephen to wed, but the mating bond ensures fealty and love follow."

"Then what is the point of having a heart if it is forfeit to the actions of the marriage bed? Why bother with romance at all?"

"Forgive me, Fraulein, that I do not know a better way to put this, but it's because the hunt is a hell of a lot of fun."

Gerwalta scoffed. "Fun? Whatever does that have to do with marriage?"

"For your kind, little, it seems." He pulled the sheet up over his chest. "Sleep, now. I think we've reached the end of our understanding on this subject, and you would not like it much if I were to teach you."

Only, as he fell into slumber, part of Andreas couldn't help but wonder if Gerwalta, in fact, *would*.

SEVEN

A wolf was near.

Gerwalta awoke with a start, and only in having done so, did she realize she'd dozed off at all. Could it be Herr Baron rousing her instincts, some aspect of her nature triggered by the fact that she'd been asleep? A moment more of consciousness, and she had her answer. This was a different wolf, its energy tinged with anger. Hatred. *Regret.* She'd have asked the konigswolf if he could illuminate the situation, but given the weariness with which he'd return to the inn, Gerwalta behooved stirring him.

Not to mention, as she looked at the pile of man and linen on the floor, one very naked leg, concealed just in the nick of time by the sheet he'd wrapped himself in earlier, stuck out. Didn't he say he'd take his wolf to sleep? Did a lupine shift back to his lay form whilst slumbering, the way they were said to do after death? More questions to save for later.

The proximity of the second wolf remained unchanged for several minutes as she sat in the dark, listening for movement. Either he, too, was asleep—unlikely given the nocturnal nature of one who had *not* spent the day canvassing a village for the scent of a missing packling—or he lay in wait. Only, in wait for what, and who exactly was he?

Gerwalta slipped on her boots and managed to make her escape seamlessly. Taking a moment in the shadows, she summoned her cloak, the red cloth cascading down her shoulders and enveloping her from head to toe. It was better like this; anyone she'd encounter would need to look closely to know for certain if she were a man or woman.

A short walk from the inn, her silver eyes turned on a figure lurking near a cart. One breath in, one breath out...

He bolted.

Empty streets in the wee hours of morn let them both break

speeds that would make members of the laity dizzy. The wolf crossed the river via the footbridge, the common square, and soon made the edge of the forest. Even as the trees thickened and the wolfsretter weaved, he managed to stay one step ahead, then two, then more. Soon, Gerwalta lost sight. Then, hope fled as well. The wolfsretter leaned against a tree, racing to catch her breath, when the man's voice found her.

"Leave me be, Red. I have committed no crime."

She didn't spare a moment to wonder who this wolf may be. Coincidence played no role in the supernatural world. She'd hadn't forgotten her mother's edict, but she would not forgo an opportunity to assess Stephen Baron's plans and motives if present.

"You left the *Schwarzwald* beyond the capacity allotted by the Matron and without the permission of your konigswolf. I could have your hide for those reasons alone, but I will grant clemency if you return to the inn with me unopposed. Refuse, and I'll be forced to take appropriate measure."

"You'll grant clemency?" Stephen laughed. "A fourth daughter who's never even seen the packlands, let alone tussled in a real battle with one of my kind? I am of Asena's bloodline, father of all wolves, you pitiful waif. You think you can best me? You couldn't even catch up to me. We wouldn't even be speaking had I not changed form to face you."

Gerwalta's eyes fell over the wolf. She could not kill him; then she'd have no cause to follow him to the emperor's court. She also couldn't just let him go without displaying the bravado a wolf would expect; they were animals, but not *stupid* animals. Stephen would suspect plots afoot if his escape came too easily.

She must restrain him, act as though she were taking him to face his brother, then conveniently let him feel he'd taken advantage of her to get away.

Gerwalta concealed her silver like a skin, grafting it around her torso, hiding it from both potential thieves and her traveling companion. She called on it now, pulling with her power, teasing its state and shape. The liquid metal obeyed, streaming up the valley of her breasts, pooling down her arm, and melding itself into the shape she visualized.

The chain that formed in her hand was hardly a weapon, but

she could use it to bind him.

"Last chance. Return to the inn with me now or suffer the consequences."

"No, wolfsretter. It's *your* last chance. Release my brother, or the consequences will be *yours*."

Gerwalta wobbled out of her crouch, knocked dumb by the words. "Sorry?"

"You heard me. Release my brother from your hold, or I'll have your throat."

"It's not..." Was that all this was? Some grand misunderstanding? "What reason would I have to imprison the konigswolf?"

"Since when does one of your kind demand reason? Your precious Matron must have known my purpose in seeking Court. I'm certain my brother blabbed that, for he advised me against it. Andreas is a weak king, one who refuses to allow wolves to see out the width and breadth of their potential."

"As king, it is his prerogative to do so. As a packling, it should be your obligation to obey."

"If Andreas truly wanted my obeisance, he'd need only invoke my heeling, and I'd have no choice but to comply. Instead, he sent me forth in the passion of his rage, only to regret his decision if your precious spit of a mother learned what I intended to do. Now, Gunda Faust's proxy uses my brother as her bloodhound to track me down."

Gerwalta knew a wolf, separated from his pack, began a rapid fall into madness. Had Stephen's senses become so addled in the space of two weeks?

"You've been misinformed. Your brother came to *us* looking for help."

But that wasn't why she was really here, was it? Andreas merely sought permission to go himself *alone* to retrieve his brother. Her accompaniment had been her mother's condition, one for which the wolf had not been at all eager.

Stephen spat. "Why would a lupine need a wolfsretter's help? Once we are free from your yoke, it is wolves who will save this land."

That threw her for a loop. "What are you talking about?"

"Vampires." Stephen pointed behind her, as though one might be standing right behind her. "They have allied with the Ottomans. Openly."

"That is a matter for slayers to discern. Vampires attack neither your kind nor mine."

"The world is changing, Fraulein. We must ally ourselves with the laity, or die at the fang."

"Enough nonsense!" Gerwalta suddenly belted out, resuming her fighting stance once again. She fought the instincts telling her the wolf spoke the truth. Hadn't her own mother suggested vampire involvement on the eastern front? "You've exhausted my tolerance for prattle."

"Oh, it's not prattle. I only felt it my obligation to tell you why I am willing to bring down the wrath of the House of Red by killing you. If werewolves are to survive, we must align against the true enemy. Your kind has become no more than a distraction. Goodbye, Fraulein."

As quick as a clap of thunder, he retreated into his wolf, rippling with fur and fang. His pure silver fur was interrupted by a distinctive patch of brown fur behind his ear. Stephen's size overwhelmed her; she couldn't have anticipated his magnitude relative to his laymen frame. Massive, vicious, snarling, and powerful, he charged at her. A wave that would crush her. A storm that would kill her.

Gerwalta turned to run, but three steps in, the earth rose up to meet her back, knocking both wind and reason away. Colossal paws pinned her to the ground. The chain! Where was the chain? Her hands in his maw, every ounce of her strength went to pushing back his assault. If only she could turn her head and see the silver, then she could reach out to it and...

And what? Wrap it around him? His fur would protect him, unless she was lucky enough to touch flesh. No choice now; she'd need a blade, and she'd have to strike to survive. But then what? Trot back home to a victor's welcome, dragging Stephen's limp lupine form? Her mother would lash into her for failing the mission. She still needed Stephen to get as far as court. There she could slay him, skin him before the sun rose to reclaim flesh, and take the wolf's hide back to Schloss Wolfsretter.

Only, how would she explain to Herr Baron that his brother had been made into a hat or a stole?

And why did she care what he thought?

No sooner had the thought occurred to her than the weight lifted away. Gerwalta wasted no time. She flew from the ground and scrambled for her weapon. It took only moments for the truth to become clear, but it would take a lifetime for the ramifications of that moment to do the same.

The view of him stopped her heart. Regal, terrifying, awe-inspiring, stalwart, massive. Especially massive. She'd never seen a wolf as large or as fierce. Herr Baron's lay form already impressed. Now, wearing a mosaic of tan and russet fur over his back, his white chest rising and falling with each breath, and baring knife-like teeth, no one would question that *this* was a konigswolf. He dominated Stephen, making his younger brother seem no more than an insolent pup.

Silver pooled in her hand for one brief moment, the chain collapsing in on itself before obeying her command, taking on the form envisioned in her mind's eye. Where there had been links, now there was a sword, one the length of her arm and sharp as an Archangel's blade. Gerwalta drew back her arm, ready to assault the smaller of the siblings should the konigswolf gain too much of an advantage. No longer in fear of her life, the grander scheme snapped back into place. She needed Stephen to get away, needed him to lead her to the imperial court. Fate balanced at the end of her sword as Herr Baron pinned his brother to the forest floor.

I'll throw my blade and injure the konigswolf, she thought. *I'll claim I was aiming for Stephen, that I thought the battle would swing the other way. An accident. An unfortunate mishap. Maybe if he's hurt enough, I can convince him to allow me to continue the pursuit alone.*

A good plan. A simple plan. An *efficient* plan.

But her hands refused to obey the order to throw, even as the konigswolf's maw latched on to Stephen's exposed throat. Or did it? No, Gerwalta realized. It was merely a symbolic show of dominance, proved further when Herr Baron hesitated. Stephen's neck was exposed; Herr Baron could end him there, ripping his throat away with his dripping jaw. A wolfsretter would. So why didn't *he*?

Suddenly, she understood. Emotion had gotten the better of him. He was not pure animal, for if he were, the fratricide would be complete.

Andreas hesitated *because* he was not an animal.

As did she, because she did not want to be one.

The momentary reverie into which she allowed herself to slip was all it took for peril to take advantage. Stephen's body writhed, somehow managing to set the konigswolf off balance. In a moment, their roles had reversed, and Gerwalta suspected Stephen would not stop himself at a mere display.

Gerwalta drew back her weapon, aimed for the smaller wolf's heart and...

Collapsed to the ground as Stephen Baron threw the entirety of his weight backward.

"No, Stephen, no!"

Only fragments of the remaining conflict came into the line of sight. Andreas, in his lay form, using his body as a battering ram, knocking the attacking wolf from her. The sounds of guttural grunts and ghastly growls. A curse the king let out, begging his brother to come to his senses. The breaking of twigs and shifting of earth as the wolf readied an attack. The feel of the silver in her hand as she pulled her arm from the ground, readying a strike to save the wolves from destroying each other.

The press of the king's weight as he placed himself between Gerwalta and death, and one final yip.

By the time she'd come to terms with what had happened, Stephen had made his escape.

Andreas remained.

Naked.

And laying right on top of her.

He held both her hands over her head, even as the silver she still gripped rubbed across his thumb, scorching its likeness into his skin.

"How dare you?" Even with the voice of a man, he still

seemed to growl. "How *dare you* try to attack my brother?"

Gerwalta employed all her strength, thinking to kick the man atop her off. Herr Baron, however, anticipated her next move, and straddled her at the hip, pinning her down, limiting her leverage. Good thing her cloak had bunched up when he toppled her, or she'd be looking directly at his wolf's bane.

"What better way to award his disloyalty than to end him?" she pressed. "You were only attempting to do the same."

The corners of his mouth quirked up, though not in a way that made his grin look gleeful. Rather, it looked garish.

"Attempting the same?" He laughed with bitterness. "I was protecting *you,* you insolent, arrogant wolfsretter. Stephen was trying to kill you!"

The claim stilled her body, though it only propelled her mind forward. Herr Baron could not have been near enough to hear Stephen speak the words, could he? "How did you know?"

"Because we still speak words you cannot fathom. Our minds remain sentient." His grip loosened slightly when the threat of her giving chase abated, and though he drew back his hands and released her wrists, he still did not remove himself from her person. "He was downwind on the river when we arrived today. He returned thinking you had somehow taken me prisoner, only perpetuated when you stalked out in the middle of the night without me at your side, for what right woman would venture into the dark of night without a chaperone unless her fellow traveler was held under duress?"

"That's silly, a wolfsretter female is not a..."

"Wolf!" Andreas cut her off. "Fraulein Faust, your Matron has done you a great disservice. So concerned was she in raising a bride, that she forgot to educate a warrior. You are all passion and fury, without any discipline or wisdom. The first rule of defeating your enemy is *sympathy* not *apathy.* If you cannot think as a wolf does, you will always be bested in conflict, just as you were today. Twice."

He stood, and Gerwalta's chin swung to the left so fast, she feared she'd knock herself out should a stone be beside her. Suddenly, a thought came to her: she could still use these events to her advantage. Did he truly think that was all she was good for, to be a bride? Then that's where she'd manifest his unintended injury.

Even if this plan was against her mother's orders, Gunda Faust had never foreseen the dangers of her traveling with a wolf.

Namely, that she began to see Andreas beyond his fur.

"Hypocrite!" She scrambled off the forest floor, determined to take the level of her eyes safely out of harm's way. "Do not you see what you've done? I could have easily slain your brother, and this whole matter would have been solved. Instead, you'll try to reclaim him as one of your pack, and if you do, the story of how I was toppled will echo throughout the Schwartzwald. How well are my marriage prospects then, if I am a wolfsretter who let two wolves overtake her in as many minutes?"

She turned on heel, crossing her arms over her chest. "It would have done better to let Stephen rip out my throat. Now instead of aiding you in your quest, I must end his by any means necessary."

When he reached for her, a curious pang struck her: a desire to round on him and apologize for her initial misstep, but pride cauterized the wound before it fully healed. Instead, she jerked away and began to find her way back toward the village.

"You must stop thinking we are enemies, Gerwalta."

The use of her given name boiled her blood. "But we are."

"No," Andreas cautioned. "Wolves and wolfsretter are, but you and I are just two people. I had begun to think we were... learning to exist beyond that. Please, reconsider. A woman traveling alone in the world of men is..."

This time, *she* cut *him* off. "Is better than a wolfsretter traveling alongside a konigswolf. I wish you luck, *Herr Baron*, in finding your brother. Best pray that you're able to do so before I do."

And with that, she left.

EIGHT

Mass served a lupine well—except when in pursuit of a smaller, more agile wolf or when fleeing from a pursuer.

When had Stephen gotten so fast? He made mincemeat of the tightly-covered trees, weaving and bobbing about hill and dale with a ferocity Andreas could not manage. Or was it merely that Andreas had slowed, his steps weighted with irrational worry about what would become of a wolfsretter he despised?

But did he despise her? Try as he might, Andreas couldn't convince himself it was so. His thoughts lingered on their last moments together as, defeated, he trotted back toward the village before daybreak. Had she really been at fault for anything? Other than not waking him when first she'd sensed his brother nearby, for surely she must have, he could not think how. Gerwalta was merely giving in to the instincts with which she was born, following a rogue wolf when it gave chase. Though it would have pained him to lose his brother, she would have been justified in defending herself once attacked. She'd created a chain, not a blade, with her silver. At least, at first. That restraint had earned her some consideration in his eyes.

By consequence or conscious, perhaps Gerwalta Faust was not a typical example of her species.

By the time Andreas had broken from the forest, dawn stretched its rosy fingers across the valley. Without the cloak of night, sniffing out Stephen's trail in his wolf form would be impossible. The konigswolf resigned himself to return to the inn. He'd slept some before he'd awoken, feeling suddenly free of a wolfsretter's presence, but not much. It would be wise to rest before resuming the chase. This was no longer the Schwarzwald; both he and Stephen would be obligated to continue on two feet, not four, and would both suffer from the restriction. One advantage Andreas held was the newfound knowledge that Stephen's mind was already beginning to turn. He'd heard it echoed in his words and thoughts during their skirmish. Reason would soon be unable to germinate in the garden of his thoughts. Stephen would be a creature of pure emotion. Emotion would turn to instinct. Then, with the setting of the third full moon, passion would surrender to the beast within.

The innkeeper nodded to Andreas when he entered. "I'm usually the first up around this way, Herr Wolfe. You must have passed some night to drive you out before dawn."

"Sleep and I do not often break bread at night." Andreas shifted his weight, trying to find comfort in the stolen clothing he'd ripped from a fence behind one of the farms on the edge of the village. "I would take it by the reins now for a spell, though, if you would not object, ere I depart."

"Of course not. Late mornings are the privilege of the newly-wedded."

Andreas paused in his turning. He'd forgotten the artifice under which he'd entered their names in the innkeeper's book. The thought of Gerwalta's amusement at being branded "Frau Wolfe" drew a smile across his face.

Which the innkeeper mistook for humor of another sort. "Cherish these days, boy—the ones in which your wife turns to you with gentle eyes and open arms. Once the babes come and the moons fly past, they become fewer and fewer."

"Babes?"

The konigswolf found himself unable to wrest his imagination before it leaped into its flight of fancy. What would a child look like, if he and Gerwalta were to mate? A boy, strong in heart and in body, but gentle and tender in manner. A girl, with hair like her mother's, the color of the cherry's first blush, and skin that would look like milk in the moonlight.

In a turn of a moment, Andreas's face soured. His stomach dropped as the word crept into his thought, guilt branding his soul.

Traitor.

What thoughts were these? A wolf and a wolfsretter? It was more than improper, it was abhorrent! A base daydream that belied some sort of defect in his character. What kind of konigswolf could keep the loyalty of his pack, should he take the enemy as his bride?

The innkeeper reflected the reversal. "Oh, Herr Wolfe. Forgive me! I didn't mean to be overly informal. It's only... Seeing you and your missus reminded me of happy days long ago when me and mine were green in years. I see in the way you two kept to yourselves at supper last evening that same fervent passion. I meant no offense."

"No, there was no offense..." A band of sweat glistened across his forehead. Had he caught a chill? But who had ever heard of a wolf with grippe? "Thank you, Herr Innkeeper. I'll... *We'll* be on our way midday."

Back in his room, Andreas landed on his bed, breathless, dizzy. He was getting sick. He must be. What else could explain such a sudden turn in his humors? Perhaps lunacity, the madness that took over a wolf when too long he stayed from his pack on full moon, was contagious. Perhaps in tussling with Stephen, Andreas himself had become infected, for what else could explain...

Lightning touched his brain as clarity invaded. The room was still drenched in her scent, and nowhere stronger than on this bed where she'd lain half the night. Andreas's body had alerted, his animal instincts rearing at the most inconvenient time. He closed his eyes, pulling her essence from the bed and the echoes from his memories. When Andreas had shifted back to his lay form in the forest and lain atop her, quite consequentially and with no other thought than to save Stephen, mind, but, oh, how it had nonetheless stirred his—

No! It wouldn't be done. He was a wolf. *He was a wolf.*

Andreas sat up in bed, ripping a stranger's clothes away. They would smell like her too now, having laid himself down where she'd lain. Departing was no longer something he could defer; he had to leave this place where she'd been posthaste. He *must* rid himself of the illogical pull he felt. The konigswolf rolled his coins inside a cloth and tied it with some twine to a thin iron chain he wore at his throat. Then, he let the animal within him out. He needed to run.

And so he did, out into the hall, and into the commons, and out the door into the street.

NINE

She arrived in Ulm with little money and less hope.

In the forest, a wolfsretter had little difficulty in moving about. The trees leaned her height and their brush and canopy, cover. Had she a keener sense of direction, Gerwalta would have bypassed the roads and made her way across the undeveloped mountains, lousy with pines as they may be. Reality, however, proved a difficult master. Other than the fact that it would increase the time it took her to catch up to Stephen Baron, there were other issues turning her from such actions. She'd been taught to pray and hunt, but not to navigate, and as Herr Baron had predicted, the open roads—and the men on them—were not kind to a woman traveling on her own.

The first time she'd had to fight off the wretched creatures had been mere hours after leaving the konigswolf. At daybreak on the riverfront, she'd talked with one of the traders about booking passage. Then, right out of the sight of town, he and his three crewmen gathered on her, demanding twice the agreed amount. When she refused, they'd taken it from her purse by force. She'd wanted to fight back. Of course, she did, but Gerwalta also knew the consequences of drawing attention.

When one tried to take of her body, however, she'd filleted him.

She'd barely made it to shore fast enough to find safety. Unfortunately, it came at the cost of most of the silver she'd used to conjure her blade. Fighting time and tide, she'd let go her weapon once in the water.

Gerwalta's hand went to her throat, pulling the last bit of the metal that remained unmolested. The blood-claimed medallion, a gift bestowed by the Matron when Gerwalta had taken rites and joined the righteous, gleamed in the sunlight. The token was considered sacred by her people, a piece of silver only once wielded when emerging from the sacred fires that awakened their gifts, then never shifted into another form again. Blood-claimed in the light of a full moon by the wolfsretter presented it, *this* silver would obey only her.

Gerwalta tucked the medallion back under her shirt. She was far from death.

But she did need to eat.

At least she'd been fortunate enough to come into town on market day. On the edge of the market square, she wished away her red cloak. Herr Baron, wolf though he was, had been right on that matter; it was a dangerous beacon, especially now that she was alone. Moving freely through the streets, Gerwalta may have been any of the local folk if not for the particular fashion of her dress; the style revealed her Black Forest origins.

The smells—not all of them pleasant—assaulted her from all directions. Animals held in crates or pens throughout the thoroughfare cawed, clucked, and grunted. Chickens, geese, ducks, pigs... Even a few goats and one small cow. Supplementing the menagerie were spices, the aromas of dyes used on a variety of clothes, flowers picked in the late blushes of summer... In one stall, freshly baked breads twisted in knots and sprinkled with peppercorns whetted her appetite. On the far end of the square, she found a set of vendors offering baskets, fabrics, and rudimentary tools. The bounty overwhelmed. Back home, it was only her father and brother who went to the Freiberg market the first few days of every month. Her mother had told Gerwalta that a righteous wolfsretter born fourth daughter did not require marketing skills when she'd beg to go. "The purchase of sage and the bartering of beef do not aid in the birthing of children," had been Gunda's exact words.

"Fraulein?"

Gerwalta turned to see a small, round woman wrapped in a gray woven shawl, sitting in a stall offering root vegetables. Gerwalta had never cared for their starchy taste in isolation, but admitted they paired well with mutton and its drippings. What she wouldn't give for a roasted leg of lamb now. Her mouth watered at the prospect.

"Carrots? Parsnips? Onions?" The vendor began to hold up her stock in turn. "A few of these?"

The wolfsretter eyed the small, brown curiosity. Something that looked like the result of an egg mating with a river rock. "What is it?"

"They call them potatoes." The jolly woman rolled the thing around in the palm of her hand. "Not much on its own, but mightily able to absorb flavors, thicken stews... Can even be used as a base for breads and pies. Does particularly well when roasted with meats."

A slice of ham or a slab of beef. Either would make her utterly giddy, but even this meager tasteless thing, this *potato,* was more than she could afford at the moment. "Thank you, no."

She turned to go, but the vendor called out. "Is it because you don't have no money, love?"

The truth ensnared her, an act that the vendor took as well as confession. The woman ducked out of the booth, taking a small sack from a place hidden out of sight. When she stood before Gerwalta, she thrust the sack in her hands.

"Mind, these are all on the edge of spoiling, but a few always get nicked and minced on the way into town for market. You'd want to eat them right quick before they go to rot. Won't be much taste without good cooking, but I reckon it will do you a might good to get 'em down all the same."

"I... You don't need to..." Such kindness as this? Who did these things? A wolfsretter did not ask for that which she needed; she either foraged, fought, or ferreted. Here, without even a humble beg, a woman offered up kindness, compassion, and *food*? These were the simple, evil laity her mother so ridiculed for their lack of civility?

First the manners of wolves, and now the way of men. Why had the Matron painted the outside world for her in such colorless and fallacious hues?

Gerwalta rummaged about her pocket for even a single coin but found none. The medallion's weight on her neck tripled. Surely, for such an act of kindness, lifting a few tiny drops wouldn't be unfounded. And who would notice? A smudge of silver's value far exceeded that of a pfennig or two.

The wolfsretter called on her power as she lifted her hand slowly. Three drops of silver collected into a coin just large enough to pinch between one's forefingers. It would still leave most of the medallion intact, and the small bit she lost would be more than worth incurring debt to a laywoman. Done so smoothly, the vendor didn't realize the magic performed before her eyes, focusing instead on the prize it delivered.

"My word, is it really?" The woman snapped up the offering, raising it to eye level to examine its details. Gerwalta did not worry over an emergence of suspicions; her silversmithing could counterfeit the stamp of any coin of the realm. "Wait a minute, Fraulein. Let me give you some of the fresh vegetables. For this amount, you should get something better than half-rotten throw-aways."

"No, please, don't..." Gerwalta's voice faded as she saw the efforts to quell the laywoman's kindness and excitement came too late. On the edge of the crowd, two men who fit every conception of "highwaymen" she'd heard spoke into their shoulders. Two men who were making plans. Two men with eyes on her and a hand on the knives sheathed at their waists.

Gerwalta thanked the vendor but cut off any further pleasantries. She hid away the vegetables behind a nearby vendor's barrel. She could return for it after she'd dealt with these two brigands. With wizened eyes, the wolfsretter took survey of the scene before her. They wouldn't attack until she was out of sight of the crowded market. Laying arms to her here could lead to others lending her aid. They'd need to wait until she was somewhere they could have her alone.

They wouldn't have to wait long. Gerwalta had no intention of delaying what seemed inevitable. She'd best them easily. They didn't know that, and for the moment, that was a huge advantage.

I go to town to confess, and I go to town to shop, but never both on the same day. Heinrich Faust, Gerwalta's father, rarely found himself lacking for an explanation when his young daughter had asked as a child what kept him in Freiburg for three whole days when the market lasted only one. On a market day, few would be inside the chapel.

Gerwalta may be of the country, but she knew how to conduct herself in the church, even if its size far surpassed the modest chapel her family traveled to for holy days in Triberg. To the right of the entry sat the baptismal font; a quick dip of her finger before dotting holy water in the sign of the cross about her person played into the illusion of virtuous intents. The men trailed her, likely scoping the chapel interior for witnesses. She'd managed the feat in half the time, using both a wolfsretter's hearing and eyes to look deep into the shadows.

They were alone, a trinity before the altar.

Lithe footsteps drew near as she lowered herself in a nave dedicated to St. Ailbhe. Stone buildings proved useful when relying on one's ears to also serve as eyes. The smaller of the two men went wide and right, while the larger one pulled a dagger from its sheath and approached her from behind. No matter, their weapons would become hers soon enough. Gerwalta worried not about the odds, but it would require waiting for just the right moment.

Three more steps...

Two more steps...

His last step...

"Bloody... hell!"

Hands on the floor, feet kicking out behind her, Gerwalta pushed herself back, only to shoot up again. Now the larger one's back was to her, the maneuver executed so swiftly, the thug's head whipped from side to side, trying to figure out where she'd gone.

"Behind you, Nico!" his compatriot called out, pulling his blade as well. "She's a devil, this—Oy!"

With a roundhouse kick into his stomach, he doubled over, grasping. No time to gloat; turning on Nico, Gerwalta found the man with his weapon ready, balancing it at the height of his shoulder. He wasn't trained in any way. The position would force him to stab down, at best getting her in the shoulder or chest, and without much control over which.

"Now, now, girlie. No need for all this. We just want that pretty piece of silver you got dangling around your neck. And maybe a wee nip at the body beneath it. Nothing to lose your life over."

Gerwalta steadied herself, lowering slightly to give herself bounce. "And all I want is your dagger."

That made Nico guffaw. "Oh, I'll happily give you my... *dagger*. As will Hans, right after I'm done with you."

Hans let out a wet cough. "I'll give her my own dagger, thank you much."

Nico leaned to the left, peering around Gerwalta. "Not what I meant, you—*oof.*"

Never take your eyes off an opponent. Untested in combat as she was, that had been a lesson ingrained into all wolfsretter. The second Nico looked away, Gerwalta drove forward, grabbing his weapon hand and twisting his arm behind his back, forcing his grip to loosen. No sooner had she caught the handle of the blade than she shifted to Nico's weak left side, pushing the tip of the weapon into the bottom of his chin.

"If I press this up here, it won't kill you, but it will leave you without a tongue."

Hans fought the conflict through a tight jaw and jutting stop-and-go movements. "Hands off him, wench, or I'll—"

"Hans, you bastard." Nico sounded on the edge of tears. "Don't you see? She's one of them, like the lord. She's a…"

"A wolfsretter?"

With a voice that froze the nave, the man who'd spoken from the back of the church came upon them silently, undetected. He brushed aside his lengthy red cape to show the long sword secured at his side. A *silver* sword. Noble, tall, his hair was the color of winter hay, and his eyes the brown of tree bark. At his hip, a weighted purse pulled heavy. A wealthy man. An affluent man. For every step he took forward, the two thugs took a half step back. Soon, Gerwalta found herself alone in the middle ground, looking up into the churlish grin of her would-be savior.

Or more likely, the savior of the two thugs she would have momentarily dispatched.

He reached out, his gloved hand finding the chain that hung from Gerwalta's neck and pulling its counterweight into view.

"Your medallion seems smaller, Walta."

Tongue-tied. Gerwalta was utterly tongue-tied. Not a new phenomenon, by any means. The only born son of the vicematron of Ravensburg had always knocked the words of out of her mouth.

Gerwalta palmed the medallion. "Perhaps it is merely that I've grown," she bantered.

Bernard threw his arms out wide. "Come now, cousin. Embrace your kindred."

TEN

The last time Gerwalta had been so stuffed had been at her elder sister's wedding two years before. What a feast it had been! Suckling pig and quail stuffed with cherries. Venison served with walnuts. And wine! It had been the first time Gerwalta had been permitted to drink, the Matron herself pouring the sweet liquid, telling her fourth daughter that she ought to note her older sister's actions during festivities, so that when she herself wed, the night would not overwhelm. After that, Gerwalta had tailed her sister with a deftness befitting the righteous. When the time arrived for Zelda and her bridegroom to consummate, Gerwalta learned what precisely that word meant, all that wine and food betrayed her, landing in the hedges outside Schloss Wolfsretter's keep.

As leaves sprouted, grew green, then turned red and fell, only to renew again when the snows of winter were reclaimed by the land, Gerwalta's objections too had fallen away, curiosity and a smidgen of anticipation growing in its place. The sounds that escaped her sisters' rooms several times a week didn't inspire fear. She was in her twentieth year, after all, and old enough to take a husband. Every full moon, her body reminded her that it longed for union.

Now, here in this parlor, Bernhard became her full moon, every laugh, every smile, every twinkle in his eye causing a sensation of pinpricks.

"And my men thought they'd take you on!" Bernhard laughed, refilling her glass. "Mind, I was tempted to hold back and see if you'd run them through or merely rough them up, but then I recalled how much their services cost me and I didn't want my investment spoiled!"

Gerwalta threw back her head and hooted. "Good thing, too! I am out of coin and would have had no means to pay you back."

Bernhard's goblet paused on his lips. "How in God's kingdom does a woman who can stamp her own coinage with a passing thought find herself without funds?"

She sat a little straighter, letting the comment roll down her lest she pick it up and be bitten. "I know you're of my mother's mind on this issue, but I have never believed I have divine rights to *other people's* silver simply because it speaks to me."

Her cousin reached down and jiggled the pouch tied at his hip. "Good thing I am, else we'd have no way to pay for this meal and I'd force you to fight the innkeeper to ensure our safe retreat."

"Well, I am stronger than you." Gerwalta raised her goblet in recognition, reviving their mirth. When silence fell upon them again, she finally broached the obvious question. "Why are you in Ulm?"

"I was curious when you'd finally ask." Like a child caught in mischief, he froze. "I'm on my way to Ansbach."

"Ansbach?" It was a well-known town, but not one of any notoriety, and not one where the Ravensburg Wolfsretter conducted any trade of which she knew. "Why there?"

"For the last few weeks, we've been receiving reports of livestock attacks." Bernhard pulled another hunk of pork from the diminishing animal on the table before them. "There is word of a wolf who's been terrorizing the region. It may be an unreported rogue."

Gerwalta's stomach became a stone sinking into her feet, even as she efforted to still her tongue, which longed to ask, *Stephen or Andreas*? Asking would leave Bernhard with greater knowledge than she herself would gain, and the imbalance kept her mum. Besides, how would Bernhard know which lupine it may be, and in fairness, it may not be a lupine at all. Plenty of natural wolves populated the woods of this region. And had he not said for the last few weeks? It could not be either Stephen or Andreas Baron then, could it?

"Forgive me for asking—I don't mean to imply you are not worthy of the task—but why your mother? A woman would be best suited to the last. After the death of your two sisters—"

She silenced her words when pain shut his eyes. Bernhard's mother, Maria Dreger, had sent word to her second cousin's court the summer before. A tragedy had befallen their family. Bernhard was the youngest of his clan, his two older sisters akin in age to Gerwalta's own siblings. One night, they'd gone out to run the standard set of patrols. Two days later, their pack's king alerted them to the discovery of the women's corpses.

"I'm sorry, Bernhard. I did not mean to—"

"At ease, cousin." He held up his hand. "I mourn, but I do not linger in my pain. But to answer your question..." Bernhard held his arms out wide. "I am here because I am a man. My mother or any other woman would track a wolf straight away but would be harassed out here in the open world. They'd defend themselves, of course. Draw blood and even kill, if needed, but that would draw attention, make complications. Mother believed a man could be trusted to hunt down and deal with one vagrant lupine. Luckily, and though she is loath to admit it, I am a man."

"Are you? I hadn't noticed."

He made a great show of sucking the juices of the meat off his fingertips. "Yes, you have."

Heat flared in her cheeks, spreading down her neck. Suddenly, looking at Bernhard became as impossible as looking at the sun. "I don't know what you—"

He cut her off. "Why aren't you married yet, Walta?"

At least that question she could answer without revealing any of her heart. "Because the Matron has not yet decided upon my husband."

"That's a lie. Oh, don't look at me that way. I'm not saying it's *your* lie. She's more than decided your fate, she simply isn't certain you're ready yet. What is holding her up?"

The questions danced on her tongue, but Gerwalta knew how music could mislead. "I wouldn't dare assume. I do not know my mother's private thoughts. If what you say is true, and she believes me still unfit, then it is so. Perhaps that is why I have been dispatched for this task, one that, as luck would have it, I believe is the same as yours."

"You chase the rogue?" Bernhard blinked three times. "There would not have been time for word to carry so deeply into the Schwartzwald and for you to come as far as Ulm."

"I set out from Schloss Wolfsretter a week ago to accompany the konigswolf at my mother's command. We were sent to chase a rogue from the Triberg pack."

Her kin across the table looked about, as though the konigswolf she'd mentioned were just over her shoulder. "I have sensed no wolves in Ulm."

"We were… forced to adhere to our natural inclinations and travel separately. We almost had his brother trapped in a village two days from here, but he managed to slip away. Andreas is not in Ulm. Truth be told, I have no idea where he is."

The use of the familiar name raised her kin's eyebrow and the pitch of his voice. "Andreas?"

"Baron," she quickly amended, as though the invocation of his family name would clear the accusation building in Bernhard's mind. "I use his given name to distinguish him from the rogue in question, who is his own brother, Stephen. Andreas as konigswolf petitioned the Matron to try and recover his brother before he became a danger. My mother granted that request on the condition that I accompany him."

"So, what you're saying is…" Bernhard ran a finger lazily through the air. "…the terror this wolf is causing is *your* fault—"

She choked on the implication, a hacking, guttural noise escaping her throat. "I do not think that—"

"—and that, in a fit of rage due to a conflict with the konigswolf—and I know that the fault *is* his, for he is a wolf and you are *my Walta*—you deserted your mission and left him to his own devices; a most grievous act which will draw your mother's ire should she learn of it."

"How would she possibly learn—"

"And that *now*," Bernhard pushed on, "in order to complete your mission, and gain your mother's favor so that she will agree to our marriage, we will demonstrate our superb partnership in tracking down not only this rogue, but also the konigswolf, and assure they cause no more problems for the laity or for us."

"By saying assure no problems, do you—" Gerwalta cut off, finally taking in the full measure of what Bernhard had just said. "Did… you just… *propose* marriage?"

Suddenly, he wanted to play innocent. "Certainly not. I am a righteous wolfsretter, and loyal to both my mother as well as yours, our beloved Gunda Faust, the fearless Red Matron." He rose, extending a hand in her direction. "Come, Walta. Let's set about finding those wolves. Perhaps you'll be wed come spring if we are successful. Perhaps I will be too."

"You are far too certain of yourself for a man."

"You are far too uncertain of me for a woman."

Gerwalta took some relief when her eyes closed before midday. Sunlight drained her, just as it did any of the dark ones. The sun shone for the laity; the night was for lupines, wolfsretter, slayers, and, yes, even vampires.

After such a bold display by her kinsman, she wondered if Bernhard might not suggest they bed down together. Luckily, he took pity on her weary and beleaguered state, procuring another room at the inn where he himself stayed. He even managed to arrange a bath for her, a luxury indeed. When they reconvened an hour after sunset, the respite had renewed her spirit.

Better yet, for the first time in a week, the scent of lupine did not cling to her person.

"You're traveling like you're a merchant."

Bernhard negotiated a sack of foodstuffs and supplies from one of the last vendors to close down his booth in the market, throwing it onto a cart to which a single horse was hitched.

He grinned at her jibe. "A necessity this trip, I'm afraid. In fact, that is in part why I arranged for the strongmen you met, so they could watch it while I slept in the day. I had not planned to share my true nature with them, but such plans had to be negotiated once they began to question why I'd hired them to guard an empty cart."

The horse's mane felt like silk against her hand, reminding her of a wolf's fur—what little she knew of the feel of it. "A good question. Why not simply wait until you were in Ansbach to see if it was even necessary? I'm certain the markets there are just as able to provide such goods."

"I thought hiring the men near our own Schloss would help ensure they'd be encouraged to return. If I'm unable to get the body of the wolf back to Ravensburg before full moon, it could reveal too much to the wrong people."

Meaning, people who didn't have families within grasp of Bernhard's mother. Wolfsretter rarely looked outside their own communities for assistance, and when they did, they made certain to be discreet.

Bernhard continued. "Mother asked me to return with the body, should the wolf of Ansbach turn out to be a lupine, so it could then be returned to his family for burial."

"And so that no men would discover the creature was actually a lupine come next full moon, you mean."

A wolf would hold his beastly form if he died in it. Until the next full moon, that was, when even his corpse would assume the semblance of a man come sunrise. If skinned, the pelt would remain unchanged. Such furs were prized possessions of Matrons.

Of course, most dead—dark ones and laity alike—did not remain above ground long after passing, but wolfsretter had learned better than to assume a quick burial. The expectation when hunting a rogue, then, was for his body to be brought back to his pack. Once with them, wolfsretter cared little what happened to the remains.

Then, what he said struck her. "Bernhard, what do you mean, 'returned to his family for burial?' The rogue we're after is from the Schwarzwald. Surely, his body would need to be returned there? Or is there a wolf missing from the Ravensburg pack as well?"

His face blanked momentarily, before the corners of his mouth lifted into a grin. "We haven't confirmed he's gone rogue, or simply came to dire ends. Of course, if this turns out to be your Stephen Baron, you're welcome to the corpse. I'll even lend you use of the cart, though you will have to get your own horse." He stroked the sumpter horse's black mane. "Terese and I are old friends."

So a second wolf *could* be involved. Only, if the reports coming prior to that of livestock deaths, neither Stephen Baron nor the Ravensburg rogue would have time to commit those offenses with time for the news to travel back. She also recalled the rumors that had been filtering into the Schwartzwald in the weeks before. What was going on?

For the moment, Gerwalta didn't feel it prudent to share such ruminations with her cousin. It could simply be the consequence of a surge in the natural wolf pack populations. It had been known to happen before.

"If it is Stephen and he winds up dead, I'll force his king-wolf-of-a-brother to draw the cart. Look at this trouble he's caused! Imagine what would happen to us in these days of religious fervor if the Church became aware of our existence."

Gerwalta shuddered, recalling Stephen's words in the forest a week prior. Since, all she had done was to imagine just that.

ELEVEN

Once he'd calmed down, Andreas realized his folly. The Schwartzwald lay far behind him, and with it, the sanctuary the Black Forest provided. He would have to make his way from this point forward not as a wolf, but as a man, and a man would need funds, shoes, a hat...

Pants.

More than anything, however, he needed patience. In hunting his brother, he had an equal in both cunning and determination. A superior, perhaps. The only advantage Andreas could truly boast was his unparalleled size. Two years lay between Stephen's whelping and his own, but they'd been like twins as children. Even then, both knew they were strong candidates to claim the role of king. Unlike the laity royal houses, the leadership of the pack wasn't necessarily hereditary. Coming from a prestigious bloodline that, if their mother was to be believed, stretched all the way back to Asena, the pack saw both as viable prospects when Ugo Kroner passed.

It was up to Stephen and Andreas to take fitting mates, to father strong pups, and to carry their family's legacy into the future. Being king would aid either of them in reaching those goals, but it was in part the pack who determined the wolf that could claim rule in the case of the former king's death. It was only when some of the females turned to questions of the heart that Andreas prevailed. When asked how they would choose their mates, Stephen asserted himself, saying he would take of the pack she who he thought was strongest, and for the good of them all, impel her to be his mate ere his kingship was won, and whelp as soon as possible. Andreas, on the other hand, would seek in his mate a meeting of both heart and mind, and that the shewolf he selected would ask for his paw, for he would win her over with merit, not might.

Andreas won the day, but lost the admiration of his younger brother. Spite at the perceived disregard wove the threads of Stephen's discontent into a loose net. As he dragged weary feet into yet another town on the road to Ansbach, lost in echoes of thought,

Andreas realized he'd always known it would come to this. Well, mayhap not this specifically, trying to chase down his brother before the fourth daughter of the Red Matron found him and did God knew what, but a duel, in which only one could emerge alive. After all, both could not be konigswolf, could they?

Stephen possessed an unbreakable spirit, one which did not thrive under another's rule. He demurred when ordered but grumbled about the consequences sure to ensue. Always pushing, always prodding, always trying to tempt Andreas into an argument. He'd finally done it by declaring his intention to wed one of the laity, and a royal at that. Only, instead of allowing their argument to escalate to a king's challenge, Andreas had preemptively disowned his brother and told him to leave.

It was a moment of cowardice and passion, but what was he to do? Kill his only brother? Allow himself to be defeated? Neither fate was acceptable, and now, no other option remained. Either Andreas would return to the Schwarzwald with a reticent rogue tamed and reclaimed, or with a body to bury.

With Andreas's next step came the awareness; the time for fate to determine which outcome would come to pass had arrived. Their gift was also now his curse. The moment he was within a few thousand paces of where his brother would be found, Andreas sensed him. Each footfall weighed heavier than the last. The king closed his eyes. Scented the air. Changed direction. Took three steps. Changed again. Every bit of ground gained increased the pressure he felt just beneath his sternum, an inherent sense that his brother was near.

As Andreas rounded a corner, finding himself in view of the village's only places of business, he found himself fretting. By now, his brother would sense him too. Even though he was downwind, they were close enough now that Stephen could also detect Andreas's essence in the air. Trepidation grew as the distance narrowed, and the instinct of each other's presence increased. Stephen wasn't running anymore. Perhaps he was tired of the chase. Perhaps he'd hired thugs and this was a trap. Perhaps he simply wanted to face down his konigswolf and beg forgiveness. Andreas knew not what lay before him. Hopefully, answers from his kin.

Outside a pub, Stephen sat at a table alone, his hands curled around the handle of a stein. "Abandon this quest, Andreas, before it is too late."

"I cannot." Andreas shook his nerves away, even as he honed

his power, sharpening his words as imbuing them with obligation. "As konigswolf, I demand your obeisance. You will return with me. If we leave tomorrow and make haste, we can be back in the Schwarzwald before full moon."

Stephen's rolled his head in a lazy arc. "I have no intention of going with you, not now or ever again."

An invisible fist punched Andreas's heart. He'd given a direct order, invoking king's prerogative, and his brother had brushed it off like an annoying gnat. A tick in Stephen's smile signaled that they had both come to the same conclusion: the younger wolf had truly gone rogue. Or, at the very least, given his allegiance to another king, though that seemed unlikely. With that knowledge, all matters of pack dynamics washed down the river; Andreas had lost not only a packling, but the last living relative he had.

"Why are you doing this?" the konigswolf asked. "Trust me, Stephen, I do not wish you nor your bride intended malice. I cannot demean her character, for if she were ill natured, you would not have loved her. If it were my decision, I would release your bounds and wish you joy. But we both know that cannot happen."

Stephen scoffed. "Do you really still believe that 'last of our bloodline' hodgepodge? It was all fallacy, a way for our father to manipulate our loyalties to a dying pack."

"I don't care about the bloodline!" Not entirely true, but that wasn't the point right now. "If you don't come back home and submit to me before the pack, you'll go moonmad."

"You mean lunacity? I don't believe in *that* either. An old wife's tale, something shewolves tell their pups to keep them obeying king, father, and wolfsretter. And, ah, yes, the wolfsretter... now there's something a proper king would rally against, and something you're doing nothing about."

The change in direction left Andreas dizzy. "I don't understand what you mean."

"Of course, you don't. You've fallen under their blanket of lies. You think you're actually *konig,* but how can you be a king when you can't even decide the fate of your subjects? Wolfsretter are really the ones in charge, and your leadership? An illusion."

"The wolfsretter are a necessary balance to us, a demand of nature. We can live in the world of men because they are there to push us back if our animal natures overtake us."

"Funny that they don't seem to care if a natural wolf attacks men."

Heat began to gather under Andreas's neck. "If you hadn't gone rogue, I'd show you just how much of an illusion my kingship is by ordering your hindquarters back to Triberg."

Stephen persisted. "What you are, Andreas, is a convenient tool for *them*. They allow a konigswolf to keep the pack managed, but the moment something goes awry—say, your only brother decides to walk away—they send one of their accursed lot to clean up the mess. Then again, maybe that's what you were after all along." He tilted his head and softened his tone. "The Faust girl may have attacked me first, for all you know, but you didn't take the time to search for the truth. You simply rallied to her side and saved her. *From me.* How… curious."

It boiled over now: the rage, the frustration, the refusal to hear another word. Andreas shot to his feet as his arm lashed across the table, taking his brother by the collar and hoisting him into the air.

"Damn it, Stephen! This is not you. You are a good man, not a rebel! Don't make me end you. It will destroy me. Come. Home."

No sooner had his canine teeth grown long then flashes of red and blue caught in the corner of his eye. Guards. *Imperial* guards. And they were pointing their weapons at him.

Andreas read the situation, and knew he'd have no chance. Stephen fell back in his chair wearing a cocky grin that could anger saints.

The konigswolf put together the unspoken truth with ease. "Made new friends, brother?"

Stephen waved his fingers through the air, and the two guards lowered their swords, though stayed near, poised to strike. "Let's just say, the Queen is *very* concerned that I should arrive at court unharmed. She and Ferdinand will be very eager to meet me once he understands the service I can perform on his behalf."

The queen? Surely the lady love of whom Stephen had spoken was not the emperor's wife. But that issue was irrelevant. What was of concern now was the threat that had been made.

With two laymen within earshot and focused on his every word and deed, Andreas knew he must paint his thoughts in tepid colors. "If you reveal too much, I will be forced to disown you and repossess your properties. If the Triberg sheriffs need help to enforce my rights as your paterfamilias, so be it."

"One day, brother, you will understand the greater good that I have done for all of us." Stephen nodded, and the guard on his right stepped forward. "Knock him out, but don't kill him. I have a use for him, one that requires his being alive."

As one of the guard's arms twitched, beginning to carry out the order, Andreas's animal mind took over, weighing his options: Fight or flee? Surrender or shift? The consequences of both options played out in the time it took an eye to blink.

A moment of pain as the hilt of the soldier's sword grazed his temple, and then all became black.

TWELVE

Gerwalta paced by the fire, spinning a web of damnation over the ways of the laity. No argument she could make, however, moved Bernhard.

"But I am a red Matron's daughter!"

"*And* I am three years your senior, and *second* born to your mother's eldest cousin," he countered. "Not to mention, if a member of the laity sees you and I stalking around the edges of the woods, they'll suspect my intentions with you."

The jest had still been partially sincere; the townspeople's eyes would follow a couple of outsiders closer than one passing transient, milling about.

"I sometimes suspect your intentions with me."

"When we are wed, I shall make those abundantly clear. For now, be reasonable. Even though you and I both know you outrank me, there are practical matters which make my going alone best, not the least of which is the storm brewing. I'll not have your mother coming for my skin if you are struck down by lightning. You're not coming along, and that's final."

"But…"

Bernhard managed to press a finger to her lips before she could utter another sound. That simple act, the feel of his flesh against hers, was enough to cut off any utterance Gerwalta may have been contemplating.

He turned at the door long enough to say, "It is fortunate to have found something that renders you speechless. It's a bit of knowledge that may come in use in the future."

That had been hours ago, before the sun had even arisen. How had this maneuver been pulled twice on her? Gerwalta concluded that she'd never again accompany dark one males away from the Schloss or the packlands. Out here in the world of laymen, they got too many ideas.

Finally, as the town clock struck two, the door opened and Bernhard's scent, a mix of worn leather and wine, floated in on the breeze along with him.

"Finally!" The warm bubbles she'd felt from his touch had long since burst, leaving only irritation. "You've been gone for hours. You said you were only going to have a quick look... about... and..."

Gerwalta's ire shriveled in the shadow of Bernhard's engrossing unease.

"What is it?"

His hand went to his head, pulling the hood down. With a sigh, the red cloak faded into nothingness.

"I caught a lupine scent right before sunrise," he started. "I gave chase, but he was fast. So much faster than any werewolf I've ever chased. In the end, by the time I caught up with him... The wolf had already managed to kill again. A young boy, just outside town."

Her hand went to her mouth. "God save his immortal soul." Suddenly, the ramifications of the truth fell upon her. "There is no option now: Stephen must die; that is our law. A wolf may defend himself if attacked by a layman, insofar as he does not reveal his true form, but he may never take human life elsewise. A little boy against a lupine? There is no defense. When day fades, we will pick up his trail and do what needs be done."

And what needed to be done was allowing Stephen to continue towards his goal of reaching his beloved. Gerwalta still had an imperial court to get to. Stephen was her excuse to get to it. The delay in follow through would allow her time to plot a way for his escape to happen.

"There is no need to track the wolf." Bernhard loosened his collar, pulling his shirt off over his head. Only then did Gerwalta notice the red patches on the front of him. Dark crimson stains where blood had soaked and dried.

"You've already killed the wolf," Gerwalta concluded.

The sympathy in Bernhard's stare faltered. He grimaced. "Would that upset you?"

Not exactly, though her mother would be disappointed.

No matter; Gunda Faust did not require a spark to set ablaze, and Gerwalta knew she could withstand the fire such news would light. Though as she contemplated the ramifications, the wolfsretter realized there was more to it. Sorrow nipped at her soul. Surely, the boy's death had upset her. But as Gerwalta searched the miasma of her feelings for clarity, she found her concerns turning not to the fate of the rogue wolf, but the brother who would mourn his loss.

Not that she could say that to Bernhard. To show empathy for a wolf—what kind of a huntress would that make her? Not the kind he or any righteous wolfsretter would want to wed. Not that she was overly eager to meet that fate, either, but of all the choices her mother would have, Bernhard was the only one she could envision herself growing to care for.

"Not upset. It's only... I was charged with the task of exterminating the rogue, if the need came about. I worry that my mother will use the fact that a man bested me in that task as a mark against my character," she proffered. Only, that made her think about Stephen's character, and what little she knew about it. Bernhard had never met the wolf; he would know even less. "How do you know the lupine's identity? Did it take its layform and have words with you?"

Her cousin's forehead furrowed. "No, but it is not the possible rogue from the Ravensburg pack. A process of elimination would then suggest it must have been Stephen Baron."

"But what if it wasn't?"

No doubt word has reached you, as it has my pack, of the recent attacks on livestock in this valley? Natural wolves, of course; all my pack are accounted for.

"You're quite certain it was a lupine that killed the boy, not a natural wolf?"

"Are you suggesting I could not tell the difference between the two when face-to-maw? The smell alone would prove it if my eyes did not."

True, Bernhard would make no such mistake. That didn't mean, however, that the lupine he'd chased had killed the boy. Nor that that lupine was, in fact, Stephen Baron.

"I need to witness his body with my own eyes ere I sleep. My mind will not be at ease until then."

The disappointment etched into Bernhard's features ebbed. "I did not slay the demon."

"He got away, then?" Ah, hope. She turned, pulling the silver she'd deposited as candlesticks on the nightstand of the shelf and setting it on the table. "I will pick up his trail immediately. There is a storm in the air, and neither of us wants to be in the open when it hits."

A chill ran down her back as Bernhard's hand grasped her arm. He spoke into the back of her neck. "No need. The townspeople caught him."

"Laymen caught... a lupine?" Tension pulled the skin on her forehead taut. Gerwalta turned, finding herself chest-to-chest with her potential spouse—a fact she would have lingered on if not for the confusion stealing her thoughts. "How is that possible?"

"I, too, doubted it. But somehow, through some cunning, they did. They've tossed him down a well, where I was able to catch a glimpse of him. It *is* a lupine, not a natural wolf."

"Put him in a well?" Something about this didn't make sense. "Did he not drown then?"

Bernhard shook his head. "It is dry as yet and plenty deep enough that he cannot escape. They plan to set him ablaze once the coming storm passes and the sun rises."

"Why is there a dry well?"

Bernhard busied himself removing his silver, creating from it a dish that he positioned between Gerwalta's candlesticks. "It's only recently dug. The walls have not even yet been walled by stone."

"Where is it?"

"Outside town, to the west."

Thunder rolled outside, a promise of a torrent creeping its way across the sky toward them.

Gerwalta made for the door. "I will find it, then."

"Whoa, there, Little Red."

Bernhard managed to pull her back before she'd gotten two steps. Gerwalta's eyes went wide as she discovered that, while her thoughts had raced to see that which seemed present but hidden, Bernhard had rid himself of all clothing above the waist. His chest... so solid, so sculptured. Sinew and strength rippled under his skin as he wrapped his arms around her.

"That storm is barreling in. If the lightning finds you, you're dead. Trust me, the well is deep and its walls, clay and mud. The rain will make it too slick to scale. He will be there ere the weather clears."

Despite a voice inside her telling her that the last thing she should do is pull away from his embrace, a twist in Gerwalta's stomach would not ease unless she saw Stephen at the bottom of the well with her own eyes.

"I *must* be certain."

"Gerwalta, I cannot allow you to—"

When she pressed her blade to the exposed skin at his throat, the man before her drained of color. "Why is it you feel you have the right to command me?"

"I will be your husband." He ran a tongue over trembling lips. "Surely my wishes must carry some weight?"

"That does not mean obligation. For now, you must settle with my vow to return before the rain."

She was out the door ere Bernhard opened his eyes.

THIRTEEN

"Oh, no. Oh, no!"

"It couldn't be. You couldn't have... Could you?"

"For the love of... WAKE UP."

Fire flared on the tip of Andreas's snout, jolting him awake. He leaped to his feet, determined to flee. One pounce later, he fell backward. The burn blazed again, this time on the underside of his front right paw. The konigswolf pulled back his leg, finding a gleaming, metal disk pressed into soft, barren ground.

"Up here, you infuriating...*argh,* just look up!"

His eyes followed the rotation of his ears, taking both toward the cloud-filled sky.

A sky which seemed to be at the end of a long chute, of which he was at the bottom, and against which Gerwalta Faust's red hair fanned around her head, her silver eyes like stars above.

"Change so we can talk, and hurry! There's not much time."

Given the fact that the wolfsretter had just silvered him, reluctance lingered in heeding her demand. As he couldn't make fur nor fang of his current predicament, however, Andreas supposed it was the only option. His bones broke and altered, hindquarters becoming just hind and legs to arms. His laymen form was no favor to him now; as Andreas was rendered a man once more, a driving, terrible pulse pounded between his eyes. A knot on the back of his head rose up to meet his hand.

"Ow!" Closing his eyes dulled the pain. "Where am I?"

"Other than at the bottom of a well, not important." Gerwalta disappeared from view. "Put your back against the wall. I'm coming down and there's not much room."

"You're what?" Was she insane? Into a pit with him? How would she get out? How would *he*? "No, stay!"

She was not one of his wolves; his command meant nothing to her. How she managed to negotiate such a tight space was beyond him. Within moments of the wolfsretter's boots touching soil, she bent over, fetching a metal object from the ground, all without touching him.

Gerwalta shot up, pointing the silver medallion that was the gift bestowed to her people upon their induction into service at his chest. The lip of the disk seared the konigswolf's skin. "The truth or I end you: did you kill the boy?"

"What boy?"

"Was there more than one, then?"

Thunder rolled overhead, but not a muscle in the woman's face moved.

"I have killed no one!" Enough with her inane question. He needed his own query addressed. "Now I demand you tell me where I am and why you're keeping me here."

"You think I put you here, at the bottom of a well to be dealt with later by a bunch of townspeople?" Gerwalta's empty hand flailed to the side. "Since when do the wolfsretter leave justice to laymen? We had nothing to do with this."

A patchwork of memories struggled to weave together through the milky darkness of his recollection. Swimming near the top: a face which brought both love and anger to the surface.

"Stephen!" Andreas growled his name. "He had soldiers with him. *Royal* soldiers. He did this."

Her medallion dropped to the side. "Stephen? You saw him?"

"I did. I..." Her words caught up to him. "Did you say *we*?"

"Gerwalta!"

Both of their heads lashed up just in time to see a handsome face framed by blonde locks and a red hood. Distant storm light flickered, lending further illumination to the silver of his eyes.

Andreas felt every one of his defensive impulses fire. The growl erupted from his throat from behind bared teeth, rumbling its way up the walls of the earthen well, complimenting nature's drums. If his threat made any impression, the blond wolfsretter showed no evidence of it. Gerwalta, however, did not hesitate to display her thoughts, pushing Andreas back against the wall again.

"Your concerns now lie with me, not him. Stephen... Are you telling me he's confirmed rogue, and on top of that, he's under guard by the empire?" Her bottom jaw worked, and Andreas envied the restraint she showed so uncommon to her kind. "And now, he's killed a child."

But the konigswolf still believed in his brother. "If there is a dead boy, it does not mean Stephen killed him. That *any wolf* killed him."

"Are you suggesting two lupines so close to full moon and in a heated debate with each other might not slay an innocent who drew too close to their struggle?"

"I cannot deny the possibility and you know that. But I also know that the world of man faces many more dangers than werewolves." Why had his anger risen, when he himself had just admitted it might be true? "If I can see the boy's body, *smell* it, I will know if his death was from my brother's maw."

"How would I know you'd be telling the truth?"

Something in her gaze, a certain softness or, perhaps, desperation, struck him, setting Andreas on a strange precipice. A sympathetic wolfsretter? One who wanted to believe in *his* better nature? If he allowed himself to look over the edge, he'd fall and suffer the rocks below.

And he was *so close* to falling where Gerwalta Faust was concerned.

"You wouldn't *know*, Fraulein." Without understanding why *he* suddenly felt a need to comfort *her*, Andreas stroked her cheek with his muddy hand. "You would have to *trust* it."

He didn't need his flesh on hers to know of the uptick in her pulse. His ears picked up the sound, reflected in his own, as their eyes met. Gerwalta's lips parted, perhaps intending to rebuke his forward actions, or perhaps because she had meant to, but reconsidered.

Of all the times for animal instinct to kick in, it would be now, wouldn't it? The way her bottom lip quivered, how the swirls of wind that tunneled down the shaft swirled the loose red hairs, the way she inhaled so deftly, he wouldn't have picked it up had he not be staring at her... The touch of Gerwalta's cheek suddenly seemed insufficient. Andreas wanted...

Irrational things. Impossible things.

Dangerous things.

A male wolfsretter's bellow from above broke the spell. "Gerwalta, we *must* go!"

As quickly as the temptation arose, Gerwalta's sudden fear subdued it, diverted it, redirected it.

"What frightens you?"

Her eyes shot up. "The storm."

Were her kind such frightened children concerning weather? "It's only a little thunder and lightning."

"Precisely, *lightning*. It's attracted to silver, and silver is attracted to us. Hence, lightning seeks us. Unto death, as it were."

Fear quickened his pulse. "You must get inside."

"I know, only, first we must—Herr Baron, what are you—Herr Baron? Herr—Baron!"

In the space of a thought, the konigswolf wore fur once more, the bottom of the well just wide enough for his paws to anchor. Gerwalta, thrown against the wall by the power of his turning, gawked. When he sunk down, sinking low, it took her a moment to understand what he'd implied. Then, knowing his intent, it took her a moment more to believe it. A lupine was no beast of burden, and one's pride and independence, thorns upon which many a casual gardener had pricked a finger. For a king wolf not only to offer a mount, but to do so for a wolfsretter, was a heretofore inconceivable occasion.

Another demon finger poked across the sky, chased by thunder with such ferocity, both the woman next to him and the man peering down from above called out. Gerwalta trembled, even as she crawled on to his back and pulled on his fur so tightly, he winced. The rain which decided to fall upon them from above just at that moment weighed heavier upon him than her lithe frame. He could not delay; within moments the earthen walls rising above them would grow slick.

Andreas coiled, and then he leaped.

"What are you—" Her comrade's words died, before he bellowed out, "Walta! Take my hand."

Great was the strength of the king, but it had not quite been enough to make the surface. Andreas's claw craved dirt, clung to it for dear life. Under paw, soil shifted, just like the muscles in his back, burning, trying to hoist himself and his rider the last few feet to safety. Gerwalta managed to take the offered hand, and with a tug from the male wolfsretter, she fell forward unto the flat earth. He wasted no time in gathering the woman to her feet and whisking her in the direction of a scattering of buildings just a short distance away. Andreas lost sight as he slipped a little, his maw back beneath the level of the ground.

It should have freed his strength enough to pull himself up, but his body refused to comply. The blow made by the guard and a day of sitting in his wolf must have drained him more than he'd realized. Adrenaline had pushed him to save the wolfsretter, but would he be able to save himself? Andreas looked back over his shoulder, mentally preparing himself for the fall and the impact that would assault his body below.

"Walta, leave him!"

Suddenly, his world turned red.

The cloak he'd been raised to fear? The crimson veil he'd been forced to respect as king? The thing he'd always known was the only enemy capable of destroying him...

Saved him.

"Andreas, quickly!"

He obeyed, taking Gerwalta's magically-apparated riding hood in his maw, as the wee mortal form struggled to pull his massive body free of the well.

"Please, Bernhard, help!"

"But he's a—"

"Bernhard, I'm giving you an order!"

Did *she* have command over *him*? Even though he'd known the Matron ran the roost in wolfsretter society, did that authority trickle down to subsequent generations? It must have, for as quickly as Gerwalta demanded it, *Bernhard* complied.

They all ran for salvation the moment their feet hit the ground. Andreas tailed them as soon as he'd managed to get his bearings. Thank god for the dark and tumult, for it masked the light of the moon and any chance a villager could peer out a window and watch a man and woman run full speed into the nearest barn, with the wolf who may have killed one of their precious children seemingly on their heels.

She should run faster. *Run faster!* If a man, he'd have yelled it at her. But Gerwalta suffered the consequences of looking back over her shoulders. It was slowing her. Damn it, could she not feel the sting of the lightning gathering strength in the cloud above? He could, and if it was such a danger to her, she must.

Bernhard lashed open the door, turning on his heel, cycling his hand to urge them on. "Walta, do not worry about him. Just—"

The sizzle. The shift. The crackle.

The bolt.

He had to.

Andreas crouched, pounced, attacked.

And barely got her inside before the lightning found him.

FOURTEEN

All night and well past dawn, Herr Baron had not awoken.

The smell of charred wolf flesh still permeated the air. At the crack of dawn, Bernhard had preempted any awkward discoveries by accosting the landholder, intending to claim that he and two of his kinsmen had taken shelter from the storm in his barn, and offer silver coins for the inconvenience.

For the moment, their secret was safe. But the cows in the corner of the barn were growing restless, their utters bulging with milk. Soon, the farmer would have no choice but to come, and when he did, he'd see the bulky wolf who'd been in the well the night before, the fur singed off his hindquarters and his flesh charred on the surface.

How could konigswolf sleep so deeply? He deserved it, of course. If Andreas had not leaped at her when he did, the lightning would have claimed Gerwalta herself. Unlike the lupine, she would not have survived. Few mortal things could kill a wolfsretter: a stab through the heart, beheading, disembowelment... These things would destroy any of the dark ones. But lightning? Vampires, slayers, and wolves would smart after a strike, but the wolfsretter alone would perish.

Yes, if she could, she'd have given him a feathery down bed, fresh sausages, and asked if she might draw him a perfumed bath in appreciation. For the moment, however, she needed him to wake the hell up and take his lay form before the villagers discovered their demon wolf harbored in the barn.

A bucket of frigid water finally slapped him into consciousness. Herr Baron's eyes and mouth shot open as he shifted in an instant from animal to man. The konigswolf cursed the sun and all the saints as his head lashed around, trying to find reason in his surroundings. All too soon, the memory of the previous night dawned on his face. Baron spun, examining the injury that had followed him from one iteration to the other. Black and blue blistered skin made up his backside. A shame, truly, for she remembered from her brief glimpse his *backside* had been rather fetching for a wolf. His hands curled around his body, making him wince as he pushed at the cooked flesh. A moment later, his hands circled forward. Gerwalta half hid her eyes as the konigswolf took inventory of his manly endowments, grinning when he found them without flaw. She couldn't help but let out a tempered laugh.

The sound drew his eyes, to where Gerwalta stood in the barn rafters. Gerwalta wondered if he was busy comparing her to the disembodied head of the ox mounted for luck to the main beam, thinking he'd like to make her serve the same fate. The emotion he wore was one she could not decipher.

"Are you unharmed?"

Which was why his words took her so aback.

Her mouth fell open. "How can you ask me that?" In a slight shift, Gerwalta walked off the end of the beam, falling with perfected grace beside the konigswolf. The distance would be enough to injure most laymen, but Gerwalta scarcely made a noise in the effort. She only hoped she had not slowed her descent so very much that he noticed the unnatural leisure with which she landed. "After what you endured, how can that be your first question?"

"Fraulein, it is the very reason I endured what I did." He looked like a statue, a creature of stone which would not move lest she breathed life into him. "Were you injured?"

"No, you... You *saved* me." Something foreign invaded her senses, a pull toward a wolf, a longing to set his mind at ease. But all too soon, Gerwalta's sense of self returned. She squared her shoulders. "But there is still some matter to attend to, Herr Baron. The boy... My cousin has gone to inquire about his whereabouts. You *will* still hold to your word; you will inspect to see if Stephen was responsible for his death."

"Right, then." The chill of her formal tone drove the tenderness from his gaze. Herr Baron coughed once, planting balled fists on his hips and casting his eyes to the floor. "You are certain, then, that I am not responsible?"

"Methinks a wolf who would put himself in the way of such harm to save his enemy is unlikely to have attacked an innocent child who could offer him no threat."

"Is that what we are, Gerwalta?" Boldness in using her given name brought his eyes to hers. "Enemies?"

Why the questions should strike her dumb, she knew not. Before she could muster an answer, however, the barn door swung open and a red-cloaked figure entered.

Bernhard's arms were full, a heaping assortment of cloth, victuals, and something oily and pungent inside an animal skin. Seeing the two of them facing off, he let everything fall to the ground just as soon as he cleared the door.

"Bread and cheese. A paltry meal, but the butcher is part of the hunting party and will not open his shop today. The clothing may not fit you, wolf, but it will have to do. And here—" Bernhard nudged the animal skin toward Herr Baron. "A salve the farmer in whose barn we are standing passed along. I thought it a rather odd gesture, when I mentioned nothing of your injuries, but he bade me make use of it."

Had she really been in such mortal danger that Bernhard would show the lupine kindness in appreciation? Gerwalta grinned, still unclear why that pleased her.

Baron took up the skin and dabbed his finger into the paste, pulling a small sample to his nose for inspection. Gerwalta assumed he'd apply it to his burns once he was assured of its content. *Not... that...* her interest would be piqued by watching him contort his body again, making the muscles under his skin pull and stretch. Instead, the naked lupine grabbed the empty bucket and the stack of clothes and made his way to the cows in the corner.

"Modesty now, Herr Baron?" Bernhard asked. "I assure you, we are both well-seasoned wolfsretter and are unaffected by your natural condition."

For her part, Gerwalta was not so sure that was true.

"Even so..." He pulled on a set of britches that proved to be far too short, even if they did fit him around the waist. "This salve is one used in the milking of cows. Keeps the udders from drying and cracking. This is the use the farmer intended."

Bernhard didn't raise a word of protest, instead turning to her as the lupine found a short stool and set to work on one of the heifer's teats. "I have both good news and bad news."

"Out with both in whatever order you like," Gerwalta said. "It will change the net to rearrange the gross."

The male wolfsretter nodded. "The villagers are laying this attack at the feet of a werewolf."

She clutched her chest. "We've separated from the world of man for nearly three hundred years, and still, they know of us."

"Ah, but that is the good news," Bernhard continued. "Their conception of werewolves and the truth of lupines seems divorced. Nevertheless, it will mean we must be even more cautious as we go about our business here, for the slightest thread could unweave the tapestry."

"What will they do, throw me in a pit *again*?" Andreas grumbled in the background.

Gerwalta chose to ignore him. "Luckily, it seems laymen no longer recall the existence of wolfsretter, and Herr Baron has demonstrated mastery of his animal spirit, so I do not fear any error on his part. Still, we should not linger."

"My men will be ready to leave just as soon as we've had a chance to stop and see the boy's body, under the auspices of our making condolences to his kin. But we have another problem."

She blinked twice. "Yes?"

"When the villagers discovered the wolf escaped, they were incensed. They've formed a hunting party and are preparing to search the woods. I cannot blame them. A child is dead, and they need to take from nature what, in their view, it has taken from them."

"Surely you are not suggesting that we give the konigswolf—"

"No," Bernhard said. "But they will need *some* wolf to sate their fury. Since the other lupine is likely long gone by now, that means taking from whatever stock the local forest holds."

The squirt of milk stopped midstream.

Gerwalta had no time for the sentimentality of a lupine for his natural cousin. She nodded once. "I understand."

FIFTEEN

A mother's sorrow is sharper than any knife and twice as lethal as any poison.

Even before the door opened, wails rent the air. Andreas felt his knees buckle, the force of memories past washing over the present, leaving his footing pulled in a riptide of emotion.

The rail-thin, gray ghost of a man looked out at them, sneering his words. "What is it?"

Bernhard Dreger snatched off his cap, holding it before him in his hands. "Apologies for the intrusion. Sir, my wife and I were passing through town last night and this morn heard the terrible news. We've come to offer our respects and our prayers."

Andreas couldn't explain why the vein in his temple throbbed at the assumed identity the male wolfsretter assigned Gerwalta. Inwardly, he lectured himself. *Stay focused. Stay silent. Stay in control.* Outwardly, he became aware of the old man lifting his eyes to appraise the wolf in disguise standing behind them.

"And him?"

Bernhard looked back over his shoulder for a moment, a proper acknowledgment that passed quickly. "My wife's brother, sir. He's a simpleton, but a good man, and devout in prayer. Of course, we understand if you'd prefer we left you…"

Bernhard leaned forward a slight bit, and the way the old man's eyes lit up suggested that the young wolfsretter had deliberately let his sacred silver medallion slip into view. A family might turn away others in a time of grief, but a poor village home would not be so quick to let a wealthy merchant's attention go unheeded, no matter the circumstance. The senior member of the household stood aside, inviting them in with a sweep of his arm. Inside, women embraced the grieving mother. The father, nowhere in sight, must have been with those canvassing the woods in search of the culprit.

Bernhard and Gerwalta made a show of giving respects to

those in the room, all while Andreas made his way to the tiny echo of a human laid out on the cottage's only table. Someone had covered his body in linen. He'd been washed then—likely to clear the blood away—but it didn't matter. As soon as Andreas dropped to his knees in prayer beside the body, a panel of aromas gave away the truth. The konigswolf's posture was no ruse; he prayed in earnest for the poor victim's soul, adding benedictions for the suffering family, the village, even the wolfsretter behind him.

Before he rose, his whispers besought heaven for one more who hadn't suffered yet, but would. "An eye for an eye. A tooth for a tooth."

A life for a life.

The boy reeked of his brother's scent.

That was not a surprise, however. What *did* take him aback was the marker of a second lupine, one not of his pack.

And female.

Andreas crossed himself as he rose and turned to Bernhard and Gerwalta, both offering what comfort they could to those in mourning.

Bernhard cut off a man similar in age to himself. "Herr Seidel, I understand a hunting party is after the wolf which escaped last night."

The villager blinked his surprise. "You seemed to have learned a great deal in short order."

"It is because of my wish to be of service." Bernhard gave a respectful nod before continuing. "I would consider it an honor to assist. I am a marksman of some renown in Bavaria. An excellent tracker as well. I can fetch my bow from my men at the inn and join the others at once."

None within earshot raised any objection, and several voiced their gratitude. Soon enough, the three of them were heading toward the door, and Andreas found himself locked against his better nature in debate.

Stephen was his packling, his brother, his responsibility. Now that he'd confirmed the rogue wolf's involvement in the boy's slaying, Andreas was dutybound to rectify the situation. But this second wolf?

He knew not her situation, her pack allegiance. He knew only that she'd taken several bites into the boy. To disclose another wolf's involvement to the wolfsretter, however, would be to doom a stranger to the...

Gerwalta had said it herself, hadn't she? To the *enemy*.

They paused some twenty paces from the cottage, Bernhard pointing toward the collection of timbered houses just off in the distance. "My men are there. Tell them to ready the horse and the cart. We'll be about our way ere I return."

Gerwalta caught her cousin's shoulder as he turned to go. "Absolutely not! I am not being set aside for a third time to appease laymen expectations! And do not think I'm letting you wander off alone when there is a rogue wolf unaccounted for."

"Stephen will have fled by now," Andreas supplemented. "I have had no sense of him since I awoke in the well last night. If he was concerned with the outcome of what he wrought here, he would have lingered long enough to make sure I was good and framed for his misdeed. He considers me as good as dead."

"Be that as it may, Herr Baron, my cousin is right. The villagers need an offering to account for the life lost. We'll need to reap a natural wolf."

His fists tightened at his sides. "An innocent animal."

"To make amends for the life of an innocent boy!" she snapped back before turning to Bernhard. "I'm coming on this hunt. The sooner we find a scapegoat and offer it up, the quicker we can be. I overheard talk that the hunting party is heading west; I suspect that will drive the animals east. You tend the villagers and keep them hunting toward the river, and I'll skirt the hills and find a sacrifice."

Bernhard shook his head. "And I'm supposed to be any more at ease with *your* going off by yourself under the same circumstances, merely because you are a woman? No, I refuse to allow this."

"Every moment we debate and haver, Stephen gains. This is not a discussion. I have determined our course of action."

The male wolfsretter crossed his arms over his chest, examining his kin at some length. "Woman or no, I do expect a little more deference when we are wed."

"Wed?" The word was out of Andreas' mouth before he could think.

The wolfsretter turned on Andreas with dueling expressions. Bernhard wore smugness in his features, a bold pride that boasted a snagged doe. Gerwalta, on the other hand, radiated embarrassment, as though her deepest, darkest secret had just been laid bare for the world.

"All is assured except the formalities," Bernhard said. Then, turning, back to Gerwalta, he continued, taking her feminine yet fatal hands in his. "Dear heart, I'll remind you once more that here among the lay, ladies do not head off to the forest to hunt dangerous predators alone."

He couldn't believe what he was saying. Andreas couldn't believe what he was about to *do*.

"She will not be alone." Andreas stepped between them. "I will accompany her. If confronted, she can feign a lady's delicate nature, and I can maintain my act of being a simpleton. But Fraulein Faust is right; we need to be diligent about resuming the road, and I assure you, no matter how good the two of you are at tracking prey, *I* am better."

SIXTEEN

They waited for Bernhard and a few men who were late to the day due to their chores to gather. Her cousin passed her one more pleading glance, but Gerwalta would not be moved. She responded with a barely perceptible shake of her head. He grimaced, then left.

One man deterred, one more to go...

She spun on the konigswolf as soon as the forest gave sufficient coverage. "I do not require minding, Herr Baron. Stay here. I will circle back after a short while, regardless of whether or not I find a target."

"You will find a target," he assured her. "Your instincts hold with mine. If there is a pack in this forest, the leader will guide them away from the angry footfalls of men. But you are wrong to go in alone."

"I am trained to fight lupines. You seriously think the less intelligent and smaller natural wolf will present any problem?"

He took two steps toward her. "I do, and for the very reason you just cited. You have been *trained,* but you have not had sufficient *experience*, nor enough failures to correct your misconceptions."

The wolfsretter tried to remain focused, driven. She'd need to render a weapon. Turning, she found a fell tree, offering up its limbs. Two branches, thick enough to provide a base to her creation and small enough to be easily swung, each segment about the length of her forearm, would do the trick. Gerwalta summoned the silver woven in threads under her tunic, graphing blades onto the length of wood clenched in her hand.

She pulled the double-headed axes to eye level, examining her workmanship. "Are you suggesting I would be a better huntress if I were a bad one?"

"At first, yes." His footsteps fell soundless as they veered away from the well-worn path made by the villagers into the underbrush. Above, September's autumnal kiss had already brought a blush to the foliage. The floor of the forest, still damp from the previous night's rain, had begun to resemble one of Zelda's many calico cats. "Experience, not imagination, teaches us where our fallacies lie."

"I've also been trained to be a proper wolfsretter wife and mother. Are you saying I should set about obtaining a practice husband to make me a better bride?"

"I'm not certain one would need to go to such extremes to earn some knowledge in that area." He paused. "But have you even ever kissed a man?'

Struck dumb by the question, her feet stilled. When she slowly turned to study his features, she found an earnest man asking an earnest question. "Have you?" Then, realizing the folly of her retort, Gerwalta closed her eyes and huffed. "Kissed *a woman,* I mean. I thought your kind only mated once and for life."

"Fraulein, there is quite a bit of ground one can walk before *mating.*"

Really? "So you have, then?"

"Kissed a woman?" His tone held no shame. "Of course, I have. When I am blessed to find my mate, I endeavor to provide her a lifetime of not only companionship, but pleasure. It is my duty to her happiness, to make sure I am equal to the task." He leaned forward, his voice conspiratorial. "Is there some concern that Herr Dreger would be unable to... *fill* the role of your spouse?"

The insinuation and overly familiar nature of his question shot fire up her spine.

Yes, that was the reason. The *insinuation.*

"That is none of your concern."

"It should be yours. At least I know my mate will always be true to me; wolves cannot commit adultery once bonded. At least, not without extreme pain. A wolfsretter, on the other hand..." Andreas crossed his arms and shrugged. "Not that I would be interested, but he is a rather handsome lad, and you would need him to conduct your house's business in the layworld."

How infuriating. How impossible, insulting, improper, and infuriating! "Not that it matters, for the purpose of a mating... a *marriage,*" she corrected as she set her improvised weapons down on a fallen tree, "is security and procreation, not *pleasure.* I am quite certain my... *skills* will be deemed appropriate when the time comes."

Herr Baron leaned against an oak tree, looking smug, despite his too-short pants and the pull of the undersized shirt against his chest. "For Bernhard's sake, I hope so. I've been the recipient of an inexperienced kisser's attempts before. It is an awkward experience. You ought to practice. Get the feel of the cloth before it is cut, so to speak."

"Fine." She crossed this distance to him without thinking. "Kiss me, then."

The wolf went stark white, his eyes falling with a red leaf from above and landing on the ground. "Fraulein, I wasn't implying that—"

"Come now, wolf!" He was at least a hand and a half taller than her. Gerwalta found a rock just a few steps away that would solve that and leaped atop it. "Show me what I supposedly have to gain, if you're so great at it." Gerwalta opened her arms out wide. "For Bernhard's sake," she mocked, "kiss me."

When Herr Baron lifted his gaze again, Gerwalta was convinced the rock beneath her had melted, leaving her struggling to stand.

She'd never known the feeling of being hunted before. Of being the sole object of a predator's intent. Now, she couldn't escape it. The man was gone, leaving the wolf in his place. Baron intended to eat her, consume her, to lick every morsel of meat from her frame and leave her a pile of bones on the ground.

He licked his lips, slowly, methodically.

Sensually.

"Very well, for Bernhard's sake."

Six languid, long, lumbering steps from where he had been leaning against the tree, brought him to a place where he could lean into *her.* Only when his breath brushed her lips did she truly grasp that she'd been caught, that she was as good as a doe pinned to the ground, despite her two feet planted firmly beneath her. His arms stayed at his side, even as hers rested upon his shoulders. His eyes drifted closed as his head angled. Despite the leverage of the stone, she was still slightly shorter.

All the anticipation? All the heat that had suddenly welled within her? It died with the first press of his lips to hers. Nothing. No desire, no shudder, no effect. Other than having a wolf's spittle on her mouth, which hardly seemed a good payoff.

"Fraulein?"

"Yes?"

Her eyes fluttered open, just as he pulled back just enough to look at her. "You have to open your mouth."

"I—Oh! I didn't know. I—"

But he didn't wait for her to stop. Instead, Baron pressed his lips to hers again, and the last thing Gerwalta was, was unaffected.

It was like the heat of her awakening fire, fed by a thousand suns and stoked by five thousand logs. Andreas was the animal, but she was the one driven by a primal nature. Her arms embraced the lupine's head, her fingers running through his hair. Even as his mouth worked hers into rapture, it took a moment for Gerwalta to realize the moan she heard was her own. Then again, his mouth was muting it. And his mouth! What delightful things it could do when not speaking.

Then, just as suddenly as it had begun, it ended. Andreas pulled back, creating a buffer of air between them. Some part of her took delight in the fact that he was breathing just as hard as was she. Was she as flushed as he appeared to be? The wolf seemed to be positively stunned, as though he'd been knocked over the head with a club. Another step back, and the chill that pressed in on Gerwalta was actual as well as emotional.

He lifted a hand, as though telling her not approach. Only with that gesture did she realize she had been attempting to do so.

"Jesu, woman, are you certain you've never..." Andreas let out a hoot. "That was your *first* time?"

"Of course, it was!" Then, worrying about what he implied, she ran her fingers through a pool of self-consciousness. "Why, was I so bad at it?"

"Bad at it?" The wolf ran and through his hair and grinned. "I assure you, Herr Dreger will find you *more* than sufficient. You nearly *undid* me. You—"

His words cut off at the same moment they both turned.

The rapid *lub-dub* of their hearts was no longer about what had just happened, but what was about to transpire.

Gerwalta scented the air. "Lupine or natural wolf?"

"Natural wolf, of course."

He rounded on her just as he began to pull the rope which had been improvised for a belt from around his waist. Gerwalta had barely reached him to keep the trousers from falling in time.

He blinked at her, confused and visibly amused. "What are you doing, Gerwalta?"

She bristled, fixing her ire on him. "Do not presume such familiarity with me, wolf."

"I know your taste now, *Fraulein*. I think that entitles me to address you by your given name privately, if not publicly. My name isn't wolf, incidentally. In case you forgot, it's Andreas." His eyes darted meaningfully to his lower portions. "I'll agree that they do not suit me, but the pants would look worse on me as a wolf."

"But if you remove them, you'll be nude."

"As I was this morning in the barn, and you made nothing of it then."

That was before I kissed you, she thought, but conditioned herself to remain stoic. "Give me a moment's start." When he conceded and held his pants aloft, she turned to grab her weapons. "You can catch up."

"You don't mean to harm them, do you?"

His words caught her dead in her tracks. What did he suppose she'd intended when she crafted her blades? "I don't mean to invite them to supper."

"But they are innocent animals."

"As are you, but there is still a dead boy and the villagers must have blood." Her cloak would help contain her scent and her sound as they tracked, and so, Gerwalta summoned it, welcoming the familiar feel of red fabric against her arms and neck. You knew that was why we were out here. Do not act surprised that I'm following through."

He held up his hands, examining them. "Perhaps I should

have stayed in the well. Ultimately, Stephen was able to kill the boy because I was not a strong enough king to dissuade his rebellion. And now, one of my cousin wolves will die in my stead, for my sin."

"Andreas, even if you could have stopped Stephen, what he does now he does of his own free will. You *cannot* hold yourself responsible for this."

The king of wolves stared into the distance. "I don't even understand. My brother may be rebellious and proud, but he is not a killer. He is not a—"

His words stopped suddenly.

"Andreas?" Bearing her axes in her grip, Gerwalta turned back to him. "He is not a *what*?"

Suddenly, her companion shook his head, as though waking from a reverie. "It does not matter. I will take the wolf, Gerwalta, for it is my sins for which he bleeds. I will not put this on you. I will not condemn you in my people's eyes in that way."

"Your people would think less of me for killing a natural wolf?"

She left unspoken the obvious question: why should the king wolf care so much why his packlings thought of her anyway?

He nodded.

"Why? They are beasts, not rational creatures."

"The lupines say the same thing of you."

Without deference to her modesty, the konigswolf shifted then, and dashed off in the direction of the pack racing towards its doom.

The pack of seven moved along a stream. Compared to a lupine, the natural wolf looked tiny. Barely the size of Maximillian's hounds, the creatures would come up only to a hand above her knee if they stood beside Gerwalta. What they lacked in height, however, was accommodated by sheer mass. Even through the fur, their muscles rippled, with haunches as thick as tree trunks.

Unlike lupines, the pack moved with an odd sense of

connectedness, as though they were different fingers of a hand reaching in the same direction instead of individual creatures. Two wolves at the center stood out by virtue of the deference the rest of the pack gave them. *The king and queen,* Gerwalta concluded, *or at least, whatever way they are known by the rest of the pack.* They would not be her target, for the effect that would render on the pack as a whole did not serve her purpose. Instead, her eyes focused on the smallest of the wolves, a brawny-colored male with yellow eyes and a ripped ear.

She looked at the base of the tree she'd climbed, catching Andreas's green eyes. Eyes that stayed human despite the canine features that surrounded them. Her finger sliced the air, pointing to the intended target. Andreas looked to the pack, observed for a moment, then hunched down. The patches of brown and flaxen fur blended against the forest floor, like patches of sunlight dappling the earth. His movements defined stealth, each step calculated and placed in such a way as to cause no sound. Even as Andreas approached, a gentle breeze blowing his scent away, the pack remained unaware.

Until Gerwalta herself, vying for a better view, leaped one tree closer. The act itself did not rouse them to her presence, but her losing her grip on her ax handle did.

Phhwehhh... flmp.

The pack lifted their collective heads form the stream, one of them yipped, and they were off.

"Damn it!"

The wolfsretter fell. No time for grace, she must keep up. Andreas had a head start, and it was his tail, not theirs, she tagged to follow. Her cloak flew out behind her as feet pelted ground, buying up the distance between them. Soon, she found herself beside Andreas's hindquarters, then his maw, and a moment later, she had surpassed him.

"Woohlph!"

If he thought she'd understand, he was mistaken. As it was, there was no time to stop and wonder what he was trying to say. The wolves were in sight, just a little ahead. The smallest one took up the rear, and ahead of him, three... no, four more.

Which left three unaccounted for. Had they split off?

It was a question she would not have to engage much though in, for in the next step she took, it was upon her.

It had to be the king wolf. None other of the pack were this size.

It will go for your throat. The lessons of her training resurfaced in a heartbeat. She curled inward, trying to reposition herself completely underneath the beast – not a place she particularly wanted to be, but then again, the underside of a wolf didn't have teeth. Only, able to look up now, she realized the animal atop her was not one of the natural wolves at all. It was Andreas.

The pack wasted no time in surrounding them, the missing three completing a circle. Gerwalta took to her feet, preparing herself for the moment the first would strike.

"Damn lupine!" she bellowed, keeping her eyes busy surveying the pack. "What in the hell were you thinking? Was this all a trick to get me out here to kill me?"

She wished he would shift back into his layform, if for no other reason than having the satisfaction of yelling at and with him, but he stayed in fur. If he heard her words, he gave no indication, instead keeping up the rumble in his chest. The natural wolves began to circle, slow deliberate paces, Andreas turning in time with them, his teeth always bared in the king wolf's direction.

She would get dizzy if this kept up, and while that in itself wasn't a threat, a wolfsretter unable to keep on her own two feet did not live long in battle.

"Enough of this!" she bellowed. "Forward!"

But the moment she lifted her foot, she was pulled back. She looked down to find Andreas's hand, his laymen hand, on her wrist.

"We cannot do this!" His voice approximated the growl of his wolf. "They have done nothing wrong."

Were they just going to pretend they weren't surrounded by wild animals baring white, gleaming fangs. "You came to help me! Don't turn on me now."

"It's not about them. It's about us. I won't let you take one of them, Gerwalta. Hasn't enough innocence been destroyed?"

"Yes, and I will not allow for more." She jerked her hand back.

"A boy is dead, and we owe the aggrieved a life. A wolf's blood must soak the ground, and I refuse to let it be yours, Andreas."

She turned, summoning the little bit of silver left concealed on her person. A moment later, a silver knife no longer than her finger appeared in her hand. She pulled it back, aiming for the ripped-eared wolf.

"Gerwalta, no!"

And let it fly.

The victim yelped. The pack scattered. The blade was too small to kill the wolf, but it landed in his chest front leg such that running would not be possible.

Gerwalta seized the moment, pulling the wolf's feet from beneath him before flipping him over on his back and setting about binding his feet with a bit of wire kept always in her pocket.

"Gerwalta, they're going to kill him."

She closed her eyes, lecturing her heart not to reveal the turmoil within. "I know, and I'm sorry, but there's nothing else we can do. I wish there were. I wish I could change..."

She cut herself off before apostasy beset her.

"This is just the way things are."

SEVENTEEN

He wasn't sure what was the greatest tragedy he could attribute to this day, when there were so many from which to choose. Was it that he'd confirmed his brother had killed an innocent child and attempted to frame Andreas himself for the murder? Or perhaps the fact that another lupine from outside his pack had been involved, bringing an unknown third party into what should have only been family business?

Could he point to the fact that, having caught an innocent natural wolf to serve judgment for Stephen's heinous actions, it was Andreas himself who, forced by the need to keep their cover, carried the creature's bound body back to the village? That would have been a grievous deed, but none of these things weighed as heavily on him as the most transformative event this day... Lo, any of his days.

For one brief moment, he'd wanted the wolfsretter as his mate.

The howls of a hundred generations of his forebears couldn't recall the desire that welled up within him hearing her simple plea: *kiss me*. Andreas tried to rationalize his longing. Lupines had been bullied and coerced by their kind for centuries; how could he not feel a rush of vengeance overtake him when the auburn-haired and ivory-skinned Gerwalta Faust presented a golden opportunity to take advantage of her innocence? Or was it *she* who took advantage of *him*? Surely Fraulein Faust would know his loyalties would be tested by uncovering Stephen's misdeeds. Did she believe he could be swayed by the promise of her affections? It would be just like her type, to use a lupine's reliance on physical sensation for the base of action.

But the moment he'd watched her tackle the wolf he now bore on his shoulders, tying its limbs together the way he tied a calf or a pig to take it to market...

The forlorn faces of the somber village hunting party blinked and brightened when they came into sight, driving deeper his guilt. Before he could spoil their festivities, Gerwalta rounded on them and dappled lies with the ease of a child blowing on a frosted dandelion.

Artifice came so naturally for her. He'd have to remember that.

"Bernhard! Oh, Bernhard, you won't believe it! Andreas here was very sad he couldn't assist you, and he got the notion in his head that he was just as capable of hunting as you all were. Well, I tried to talk him out of it, but you know how he gets. He ran off into the forest, and nary a weapon on him at all! By the time I tracked him down, there he was, holding the wolf and stroking it like he was holding a puppy! Luckily, I'd managed to take of a spool of wire I saw in that barn we stayed in last night, so we were able to bind the wolf and bring him here. Isn't that marvelous?"

But in her eagerness to cover their truth, Gerwalta's lies had been spread too thin. A man wearing a sneer and incredulity in his features stepped forward.

"Spool of wire from the barn, you say?"

Gerwalta flinched for only a moment. "Yes, I hope that was all right."

The poor girl, rarely found outside her family's luxurious castle and who had probably never been in a barn before the previous night, couldn't have known how precious such a commodity was. That a village farmer without a noble patron would have little if any wire, let alone a spool of it, could never have occurred to her. She just assumed.

Luckily, Bernhard Dreger picked up on his kin's misfortune. He rushed forward, rubbing her arm as though petting a dog. "That is great news, dear, but I'm afraid that was *our* wire. I took it from our cart last night to keep it from rusting in the rain or being stolen."

Right on cue, Gerwalta manufactured a pout. "Oh, dear... I didn't know, darling. Well, in any case, we *can* remove it once we return the cursed creature to the pit, could we not? It will still be usable?"

He took her tiny, dangerous hands in his. "Of course." Then turning to Andreas, Bernhard kept up the act. "Well, then, Andreas, what are you waiting for? Put it in the well. It's just over there."

Andreas sighed and shut his eyes. Every tear-stained mourner's eye in the proximity fell upon him, and the weight of their expectations almost buried him. As though reminding Andreas that they were not so different, the wolf atop his shoulders whined. Cried. Called on a brethren for mercy. The konigswolf commanded his feet to move, but his body protested what his soul knew to be wrong.

His eyes flew open when Gerwalta's arm hooked his, and began to pull him and the wolf toward their ruin. "What are you doing? Walk!" she whispered so silently only a dark one would be able to hear her.

Andreas shook his head. "His blood... His blood will be on my hands."

"His blood is on Stephen's hands. As is the child's." Then, leaning up, her tones turned acidic. "You or the natural wolf, Herr Baron. One of you will be at the bottom of the well when we leave this village."

He swallowed hard and wondered how he ever could have put his mouth on such a vile creature.

But in the end, she was right. *Lord, as you commanded Abraham, so now Gerwalta Faust commands me. Put in my arms a lamb in the place of this sacrifice, if thou art merciful.*

God may grant grace, but men knew no such beauty. They killed the wolf. They hacked off its maw. They dressed him in clothes and placed a wig atop his head and cursed out his name.

And, yes, Andreas did believe that in the end, that creature looked somewhat like him.

EIGHTEEN

Stephen had learned to cover his tracks. Or more precisely, how not to leave any.

The female wolf who was traveling with him wasn't as careful. Which meant, either she was foolish, or she was arrogant.

Two days had passed since the village, and other than the occasional utterings necessary when people traveled together, the lupine and the wolfsretter kept their own counsel. Not that Andreas would have been able to get a word in edgewise had he wished to speak; Bernhard's attempts to woo Gerwalta would have been visible to a blind man. It was a curious thing to observe, given how the decision on Gerwalta's husband would be dictated by the Matron. Why was Herr Dreger so fastidious in his campaign for her heart, if the object of his amour did not hold the reigns of her marital fate?

And why was Gerwalta falling for it, knowing that her mother with a snap of her fingers could choose another, rending the daughter's heart in two?

Bernhard insisted that Gerwalta ride in the empty cart as he rode the horse. The male wolfsretter made convincing excuses; even though they arrived in the Bavarian forest, they were still apt to meet laity on the path. A lady would not walk; she'd be given use of any form of comfort they had.

He dwells too much on the customs of men, Andreas thought, seeing in retrospect the error of his own abuses against Gerwalta's nature. The woman was a warrior, proud and true, even if green in her practice. It had not been right for him to force her to obey his decree, as though she were one of his packlings. Not that he subscribed to wolfsretter's being superior, but that did not mean he could not give her respect.

How was it that a lupine could understand this, and Dreger, one of her own kind, could not?

Nico and Hans, Herr Dreger's two hired hometown goons,

also rode mount, two mares presented to Andreas as thanks for finding the wolf. They were amazed at his willingness to give up such gifts, but what use did a lupine have for a horse? Unlike cows, sheep, and pigs, the animals were too sensitive to his nature to allow him to mount.

When at last they had some cover of trees, Andreas took his wolf and kept pace in parallel with the others, still traveling by day and stopping at night to maintain the fallacy of their mission. On the third night, he sensed her away from the others and found Gerwalta sitting on the lowest branch of a tree, contemplating the stars.

When their eyes met and Gerwalta conjured her red cloak from nowhere, he thought it may be a sign to keep his distance. When the wolfsretter pulled the garment from her shoulders and tossed it his way, however, he understood her intentions for his modesty.

He suffered through the passing pain, moving from four legs to two in a matter of seconds. Andreas felt like a baby, swaddling himself in her garment, but it was obvious she had something to say to him, being here beyond the earshot of their traveling companions, staring at a moon which grew more pregnant with each night of the journey, swelling his anxiety about the inevitable.

Wolf though he was, Andreas was still a man, and knew to let her come to her words at her own pace.

"I owe you an apology."

"Oh? I didn't know your kind did that."

Gerwalta took the jab in stride, which gave Andreas his second surprise in as many minutes. He ought to just listen to her without rebuke, for how often were occasions when a wolfsretter would lower herself to humility?

Luckily, she picked back up without prompting. "A lupine and a natural wolf are two very different creatures, but you must have felt conflicted nonetheless. I should not have made you do that. It needed to be done, but I should not have made you be the one to bear it to its death. Especially when..." A long inhale, followed by a longer exhale. "Especially when it was my fault that the boy died."

He blinked his confusion. "Fraulein Faust—"

"*Gerwalta*, Andreas." Her bright eyes, their natural blue instead of the inhuman silver they became whenever her pulse picked up, glistened in the moonlight. "I thought we agreed we could allow each other that privilege in private."

"Very well, then, *Gerwalta*." He pulled the cloak around him more tightly and settled next to her on the low-lying branch. "There is some truth to what you say. I am a wolf, and as a wolf, I would want nothing more than to blame a *wolfsretter* for every evil conceivable. But I'm also a man, one who aims to be forthright and moral, and I can in all good conscious assure you that you are not to blame in any fashion for the tragic events in Ansbach. I scented Stephen all over that boy's body."

"But if I had taken Stephen prisoner when we encountered him before…"

"Stop." He put a finger to her mouth, stilling her words. "Do not tread down the path of undone deeds, for it is a never-ending road of fallacy and self-destruction." He dropped his hand just in time to reposition the cloak before it fell to the ground. "What if I had never quarreled with him about wanting to mate a member of the laity? What if I had run just a little faster, no matter how weary I was, and managed to catch him after we separated? What if I had never tried to appeal to him when I got to Ansbach and just fought him there and then?"

"What?" Gerwalta's gaze swung from the sky above to the wolf beside her. "You said you saw him, but you actually *spoke* to him?"

He hadn't meant to keep it secret, though he likewise had not been eager to share. Still questioned why he had. Was it an inclination to slight a wolfsretter, or the guilt at letting the opportunity to stop his brother go to waste? "Yes, briefly. I begged him to give up this foolishness and return with me, but it seems there are bigger games afoot than some eloping lovers."

"Meaning?"

"My brother is planning to reveal our kind to the Emperor, to offer us as soldiers in his armies."

Was it the arch of silver light across the sky above, or the words that made Gerwalta look so pale? "We exist in parallel. Wolfsretter will fall under the royal eye and the holy see as well. It will be the tale of Jataka all over again."

"Jataka?"

She nodded. "A wolfsretter in the House of Amber, long ago in the distant east. One day the lay prince of her land discovered her in the midst of a hunt. He saw her wield silver. To keep her silence, he demanded she provide him an egg made of silver as a wedding gift, when he wed. She agreed, thinking it a small cost to keep her secret. But the prince tricked her, and married a new girl picked randomly from the villagers each day. Soon, the prince had many silver eggs, but he always wanted more. He thought Jakata *made* the silver, wouldn't believe she could only *reshape* the metal. In anger, he killed her and cut her into pieces, thinking he could find the silver she hoarded inside her. He found nothing, of course."

"It sounds like a nursery story."

"It may be," she conceded. "But that doesn't make it any less possible, or detract from the lesson it teaches. If laymen know of our abilities, they will exploit it until we have nothing more to give. And then they will have our blood. The wolfsretter will perish."

Part of him wanted to say it was about time her kind had a fear of domination by others; lupines certainly had suffered oppression long enough. But some curious quirk in him fretted when he thought of Gerwalta subjugated to the human qualms of god and country. As little sense as that made, it hardly mattered now. There were bigger threats at hand.

"Gerwalta, as much as it pains me to say this, I understand what must be done. I left the Schwarzwald hoping to bring Stephen home, but now my mission must be to stop him at any price. I take some comfort that we have been brought back together, for while I am konigswolf, my palace is a forest, and my subjects, lupines. The castles and court of the laity are something of which I know little, but in which you, reared in matters of diplomacy by your mother, are well versed. If I can get close to Stephen, I will ensure he either submits, or yields. But I cannot do this alone."

He reached for her by instinct, but delighted when she did not pull away. Her hand... It was so lithe, so soft, so velvety. How could this be the hand of so demonstrable a foe? How could so tiny a hand, which fit so naturally into his, be of a creature born to tyrannize his pack?

"Gerwalta, please. Help me do this. Not for me, but for all wolves and—"

"It was my mother's wish that I allow Stephen to get to court."

Shock blew back his touch. "What?"

"She..." Internal strife played across her features. "The Matron saw an opportunity to allow me to spy at court. She commanded that I allow Stephen to flee long enough so that I could have an excuse to visit."

"But why would..." Reasons permeated his thoughts and searched for words, but found them lacking. "What cause would Frau Faust have in that?"

"My family has been the supplier of silver and craftsman of its implementation to the imperial court for a century, but recently, they've turned favor from us. It is hurting my mother's purse."

He sucked on his bottom lip. "Your lot commands silver. How could you possibly be hurting in the purse?"

"Not all debts can be paid in silver, Herr Baron. We require the same things you do: foodstuffs, linens, taxes. Silver pays taxes and buys influence, but it is not accepted by a cheesemaker or a carpenter without talk. And as Jakata's prince learned, we do not *create* it. Its supply is not inexhaustive, for if was, it would not have nearly as much value as it does."

He nodded as the truth sunk further down. "So your mother was using my brother's betrayal to her advantage? How dare she... How dare any of you—"

Before Andreas understood what was happening, his words died as Gerwalta threw her arms around him and buried her head into his chest.

"I never would have agreed." Hot tears fell down her face and soaked the downy, sparse fur that followed him into a layman. "If I thought it was going to mean an innocent boy would die, and that I'd have to force you to sacrifice a natural wolf for my oversight, and that you'd have to hunt and kill your own kin, I never... But to think it almost led to your death... Andreas, I... I..."

"Shh..." Her auburn hair, laced in braids that ran down her back, still managed to be soft under his palm despite its binding. "Hush, now. I never would have sought her help if I had thought it would lead to you and me—"

Big blue eyes found him in the darkness when she looked up, and it didn't take long for her lips to follow.

On the occasion of their previous kiss, Andreas had complied to her request more as a dare than a desire. This time, when his mouth began to move against hers and his hands rose to thread through her hair, pushing lose her auburn braids, it was for no other reason than he wanted to partake of her.

Because *he* wanted *her.*

Gerwalta moaned into his mouth, the tiniest vibration that sent his animal urges soaring. He couldn't remember when he'd let go of the red cloak that hid his modesty, or when the two of them had moved from sitting on the branch to lying on the ground, her body beneath his and her thighs pressing into his hips, holding him in place.

He pulled back only when breathing demanded it. Gerwalta's eyes shone in the darkness, two gleaming silver discs which blinked into existence when she realized he'd stopped.

"Why are you doing this?" he demanded. Only, was he asking her, or himself?

"I shouldn't. It's forbidden. If my mother ever discovered I'd kissed you... There is no greater crime for a wolfsretter than to give herself to a wolf."

"Crime?" Andreas pushed himself up on his arms, hovering over her. "What is the punishment?"

"Death for the wolf, exile for the wolfsretter." She blinked up at him. "Is this not forbidden for lupines?"

"Of course not, though I can't imagine a konigswolf would take well one of his packlings mating a wolfsretter. Death seems a bit of an overreaction, though." He lowered himself again, pulling towards her lips. "But it may be worth it."

And as though she'd awoken from a dream, Gerwalta lashed her eyes closed and began to slide out from under him.

"The moon!" She grumbled as she rose to his feet, pointing skyward and laying all blame on the celestial bodies overhead. "We're two nights from the full moon, and it's... *doing* things to us."

Andreas doubted it. Otherwise, the scenes that would ensue each month between lupines and patrolling wolfsretter of the Schwarzwald would make a cow blush. Nonetheless, Gerwalta had been right to note the precarious tilt of the lunar cycle. In two nights, Stephen would fall victim to the moon's pull, powerless to stop the shift. If he were in the hands of the laity when that happened, what would become of him?

And what would that mean for them all?

Andreas was pulled from his reverie by Gerwalta's perturbed voice. "I am so sorry, Herr Baron. I am young, and unwed, and I... I..."

"You desire a man in your bed."

His bold assertion turned her apologies to shock. "You must think me wicked for thinking of such low acts in times such as these."

"It is never wicked to want what is natural." He couldn't help the errant thoughts running like rabbits through a meadow in the garden of his mind. "You do have... options, Gerwalta." His eyes turned meaningfully back to the direction of the fire where the others lay fast asleep as he too gathered his feet beneath him. "Bernhard seems quite taken with you, and you do not shun his attention. Your kind does not have the lifelong consequences we wolves do from... such informal dalliances."

She crossed one arm over her stomach to grab the opposite elbow, rubbing the back of her neck with her free hand. "There are other consequences than a mating bond to consider. And there's...."

Her eyes burned even brighter, if it was possible. Wide gazed and looking like she'd been struck by lightning, Gerwalta turned to him. "Was it only one wolf who killed the boy?"

Andreas felt sweat dapple his brow, heard his own heartbeat pounding in his ears. His mouth dried. His pulse spiked. "How did you know that?"

The wolfsretter's mouth transformed into a scowl. "All the reports of livestock attacks... Both Bernhard and I being sent at the same time to chase down rogue wolves... The imperial court shifting its silver supplies from our stocks..."

She reached for him, pulling Andreas by the hand, deeper into the forest. "Your brother is walking into a trap."

"What?" With a forceful tug, he managed to both stop their forward advance and spin Gerwalta his direction. "Gerwalta, what are you talking about? How did you know about the second wolf?

What does it have to do with anything?"

"Don't you think it funny, Andreas? We set out from Triberg at almost the same time Bernhard is sent by his mother, one of the vicematrons under my mother's command, from Ravensburg, both of us pursuing a lone wolf? When he said he was following the report of a wolf, those may have been his mother's words. I assumed it was Stephen, but no, there *is* a second wolf, one I am willing to bet defected from the Ravensburg pack, lured away by some lady love to the imperial court. And probably, far more than that, all coming together on a full moon. Think about it, Andreas. Your brother told you this woman and he were going to reveal lupines to the king, did he not?"

"Yes, but..."

"Stephen is your brother, and I do not doubt he is such a different man than you are. He would not leave his pack to be with some laywomen, knowing that he'd go mad in a few months. I know the saying goes love drives one to madness, but I do not think one preempts the journey for the sake of love."

He could argue strongly with her on that. Another time, perhaps. For the moment, the outlines of what the wolfsretter was presenting began to take shape in his understanding. "Someone's creating a new pack, a feat that takes a female and male wolf. That's why the other wolf I detected in Ansbach was a woman."

She looked into the distance. "You can learn that from the scent left on a victim?"

"Of course." He bit his tongue before telling her how he could smell something very female and very enticing about her even at this moment. "I'm sorry I didn't tell you, but the other wolf is not my pack. She is not my problem to solve."

Gerwalta's hand tightened into a fist. "No, but she's mine. Someone's trying to form a pack loyal to the crown. Your brother has been hoodwinked. Come, we must make it to Nuremberg by full moon."

"Wait!" He arrested her hand and pulled her back around. "What about Herr Dreger?"

"You mean my well-intentioned cousin who keeps insisting that I, a woeful woman, should not do my duty merely because I am the fairer sex?" Gerwalta rolled her eyes. "Do not misconstrue my meaning. Bernhard is a righteous wolfsretter and a brave warrior, but I've grown weary of his attempts to preserve my honor by locking me away."

He swelled with pride at hearing her put the boorish brute in his rightful place. "Then we depart without him. Though I must point out, it will be difficult for me to get into the imperial court without clothing."

Her eyes cast down as her cheeks reddened, as though Gerwalta had just remembered that a nude man stood before her. Or perhaps recalling that same said nude man had been atop her and kissing her breathless just a few moments before.

"Not to mention, all our provisions are with the others," he continued. "We'll be trying to accomplish two days of travel in half that time, all without any funds or food."

"Surely between the two of us we can make do with what the forest and our wits provide."

"And do you have silver enough to purchase appropriate attire for me when we get to the city?"

"I hope so." Her hand when to her chest, rubbing her rib cage. "Though I will owe apologies to all the gentlewomen of Nuremberg for denying them the view."

All the breath escaped him, but before he could say anything to follow, Gerwalta retrieved her cloak and took to the trees.

He took to his fur and followed.

NINETEEN

Gerwalta ran.

Not for the sake of reaching Nuremberg, though that was, of course, the goal. She ran forward, ever forward, because if she paused for a moment, she'd have to face Andreas, and the truth of what had happened – *was happening* – between them.

Though, she promised herself, nothing *further* would happen. Not so much had transpired, if she thought about it. She'd merely kissed Andreas. Twice. And pulled him atop of her, but that, only once. If anyone found out, could she merely claim that she'd been teasing the wolf, playing into his fantasies to earn his cooperation and get her to court? It would be believable, as long as nothing further happened between them.

And it wouldn't. It *couldn't.*

She paused on a branch, pushing her fingers to her lips and whistling. The wolf on the forest floor beneath her bayed before coming into sight. In two clicks, he grew into a man.

"What is it?"

Gerwalta pointed to the horizon, to where a hill rose in the distance, veins of stone streets, timbered houses, and the tower of a castle on its highest peak. A bright red banner flapped against the pale blue sky.

"The emperor is in residence."

Andreas's hand went to his brow as he squinted, the sun framed just over her shoulder. Already at midday, the beams of light served as a clock ticking down the hours until sunset. "If you're close enough to see the flag, you're close enough to be seen by them. Come out of the trees."

He had a good point. Probably best to do away with the red cloak as well. In a sigh, its existence ceased. Gerwalta stepped off the branch and proceeded to fall at a very slow, and very leisurely, speed.

By the time she'd come to ground, Andreas's jaw had come to rest atop the leaves as well. "You can fly."

"No, I cannot."

"Well, you certainly didn't *fall* out of the tree. I could have run to the river and back in the time you took to reach the ground."

"It's rude to criticize." Gerwalta fished out the clothing she'd bought off a peddler on the side of the road earlier that morning. They'd be too loose below and too tight above, but Andreas would be clothed. "Only Matrons fly. It's considered a divine sign of one's propensity towards leadership. Now, put these on. We should be to the city walls in an hour or two, and we'll purchase you something better fitted there. Speaking of the river, I'm going to go refill our skins. We'll head back to the road and—"

He grabbed her hand and twirled her as she attempted to walk away. "I bet that's how you jump so high, so easily, isn't it?"

"*All* wolfsretter can jump high."

"Not like you. You were up in the top of that barn in Ansbach. That had to be the height of three men, and there wasn't a ladder anywhere! And why you jumped into that pit without fear of how you would get out." He let go her hand and twirled. "It was amazing. *You're* amazing. Just when I think I've come to understand you, you have another secret. But, wait." His words died in the air along with any trace of joy in her features. "If it is considered a sign of one meant to be Matron, does that mean you—"

"It means nothing," she interjected. "It is ancient foolishness, old superstitions."

Understanding failed him. "But to lead a pack—a *clan,* is a great honor. Why would you not want that?"

"Because the last thing I want to be like is my mother," she said stoically. "Severe, withdrawn, always keeping my children at a distance and only seeing them as pawns in securing my power. I *want* to be married off, Andreas. Perhaps it will mean leaving the Schwartzwald and rearing young in one of our lesser territories, but it will remove me from that horrid home where I am always another thread for others to spin."

"But as Matron, you'd have the ability to change all that," he argued.

"No, Helga will be Matron," she insisted. "It has been expected since we were young. This last fortnight, seeing the torment you're going through having to oppose your own sibling, makes me realize how much I'd never want to be on the other side of mine."

Gerwalta shook her head, and shooed away the subject. "We don't have time to dwell on this. We must press on. Come, we're running out of time."

Two things could kill a wolf: silver inside the head, or silver to the heart. Gerwalta was his silver, and she was burning a hole both above and below.

It was foolish to let himself fall for the wolfsretter. No good could come of it. They'd never be together, they certainly *could* never be together. Oh, he was fairly certain he could seduce her, if that's all he was after. Some part of him took devious glee at the prospect of ruining one of her kind for all others. But it would ruin him too, for to lay with Gerwalta would trigger his mating bond. His heart would forever be hers, and no doubt she'd stomp on it. Away from Schloss Wolfsretter, on her life's first grand adventure, she'd indulge a thrill, embraced him in passing. But as soon as she saw how he'd grovel at her feet once bonded, she'd lose all respect for him. Her heart would have no such restrictions, and how would he cope when she inevitably moved on to another?

They arrived at the city walls as the sun turned down from its zenith. A crowd milled about, waiting to pass through the gates into the safety of the city before nightfall. Andreas tried to arrest the overdrive of his senses. Villages were taxing enough, but this... There were too many scents, too many noises, too much to see. The konigswolf closed his eyes, breathed in, tasted the air. Bread, meats, rot, urine, flowers, mud, perfume... It all swirled together in a miasma of experiences not his own. He felt dizzy, overwhelmed, clingy. He reached for Gerwalta's hand as his body swayed.

"I know." Her body became the foundation which lifted him. "It's hard for me, too."

"People. Everywhere." He leaned on her. "So many people."

"It will be easier once we're inside the palace walls," she assured him. "Come."

A ripping of cloth hit his ears, followed a moment later by

pressure against his eyes.

"My father does this with the horses when he fears there's too much to worry them. I know you're not a horse, but perhaps it will help."

"It does." And it did. Simplistic though it was, it did. "Thank you."

She pulled him like the blind man he'd become through the gates and streets of Nuremberg. "My medallion bears my family crest. It should get us into the castle if I claim to be representing my father on business to the court."

"Don't you mean your mother?"

"No, we're in the heart of the lay world now. My mother, as a woman, has little standing here. It is my father, or sometimes my brother, who must always conduct our business with men."

Foolish laity. Unlike the matriarchal wolfsretter, wolves were always ruled by a male member of the pack, but a king wolf would never dare insinuate his mate was his inferior or not due respect and deference merely because she was female. "Are either your father or your brother known at the imperial court?"

"No. All our affairs are conducted through the Duke of Württemberg or by correspondence."

Andreas turned, forcing Gerwalta to the end of his arms. He took off the cloth covering his eyes and pulled at the leather cord which hung around her neck. "I'll have to pretend to be your brother, then. I'm far too young to stand place for your father. His name is Maximilian, is it not?"

"Andreas!" She clasped his hands. "Don't be foolish. If the silver touches your skin..."

"Then I'll be careful it doesn't," he insisted, very delicately pulling it off her neck. "If a woman from a wealthy family comes seeking business without a proper letter of introduction or chaperone, it could raise suspicions. We must be quick. Sunset is hours away. I feel its weight in my soul."

And as he delicately leaned forward and slipped the cord around his neck, he felt the weight of the silver as well. It settled on his chest, two layers of clothing the only thing keeping it from burning another scar into his flesh. Andreas delicately teased the metal disc under his jacket but above his undershirt, feeling like a man as he was being shoved into to a torture chamber, moments before the door closed. The object of his death was so close, it had merely to move into place to kill him.

Luckily, the wolfsretter protested no more. There was logic in his actions, and she knew it. "Can you sense Stephen? Would you be able to sense the other wolf?"

He shook his head. "I'd be able to smell her if I crossed her trail, but I can't perceive wolves not of my pack like that. What about you? I thought wolfsretter could sense any wolf if they were close enough."

She closed her eyes, breathed deep, exhaled.

When she kept silence, he prodded her. "What is it? Do you sense them? Which direction?"

"Every direction. I..."

But she never got to finish what she was saying, for a moment later, Andreas felt the sword at his back and his hands went into the air.

TWENTY

In a heartbeat, Gerwalta overrode the anxiety of her senses and assessed the surroundings.

An imperial guard, distinctive by his red and black stripped pantaloons, held a weapon to Andreas's back which she couldn't see. Short sword? Perhaps, but from the angle of his shoulder, more than likely a dagger. The guard behind him, however, had three blades within command, including the one whose hilt was in hand. They'd angled themselves away from the street where common folk went about their business. They didn't want to bring attention, but why not could be anyone's guess.

"Fraulein." It had been so long since Andreas had addressed her formally, it sounded foreign from his lips. "I'm sure these guards only wish to detain us and bring us inside for further questioning by their superiors. No need for dramatics."

"This smithy speaks true." The larger of the two guards jerked his head toward the gateway. "Make no fuss, and we'll make no holes into you."

Heart racing, she somehow managed to calm her nerves, ease her hands, relax her posture. "Very well. Gentlemen, please…"

Nuremberg Castle, one of the jewels of the Holy Roman Emperor's crown, didn't impress her nearly as much as she'd supposed it would. Perhaps because she'd been raised in a castle, if one much smaller. Its luxuries didn't surpass Schloss Wolfsretter; there were merely more of them for the eye to behold. Its walls would be easily scaled by a dark one, and to her quick observation, only its central tower which she'd observed even from far outside the city, appeared to be truly secure.

Immediately past the first bailey, the guards took them left, then right, and then they began to descend a winding stairway, all the while the tingle in Gerwalta's fingers growing stronger. That she had more silver to craft a weapon like her hand ached to hold! She dare not speak; just because the guards had obviously known they were wanted didn't mean they knew why, nor what they were.

When they entered a corridor lit dimly by torches, Andreas's hand found hers, clutching so tightly he threatened to drive all the blood from her fingers. A moment later, she knew why.

Their scent saturated the senses.

"Go to the end of the hall, then knock once," the guard said, giving them both a push forward. "We'll be here just long enough to make sure you don't turn and run."

Andreas hissed, and Gerwalta suddenly remembered the injury caused when he saved her from the lightning. It would heal with the passing of a full moon, he'd said, but that event had not yet had a chance to pass.

"Do you scent Stephen on the air?"

The konigswolf stopped, taking in a long draw of air through his nose, closing his eyes in concentration. A moment later, they opened again, reading of sadness. "No."

Gerwalta paced on. "No matter, we must see this through."

"Gerwalta, wait." He pulled her back. "I should go first. They will expect that."

"Wouldn't lupines be more cordial to a lupine leading a wolfsretter?"

"Or find it suspicious. But then again, I am supposed to be a *male* wolfsretter, so would I lead a *female* wolf?"

"Of course, you would! You'd lead *any* wolf, because as a wolfsretter, *any* wolf is your inferior and beneath you."

"So you're saying you should be beneath me? Mayhap being a wolfsretter is not so bad."

"Are you sincerely making a jest at a time like this?"

Having reached the door, and with the guards still poised at the far end of the hall, Andreas made to raise a balled fist. Gerwalta managed to knock it away just as he tapped. She tried then, getting just treatment from him. In the end, neither would know who knocked, but they would both remember they'd entered the room together.

It seemed a veritable children's story, one filled with genies and shahs and silver chalices. How had such a room, in which opulent lounging couches covered in fine oriental fabrics encircled a wooden table atop which a golden plate the size of a shield held the last fruits of summer exist in this castle? More than that, how did its occupants come to be? On every surface, a lupine. A dozen total, each in the distinct dress and manner of his origins. Gerwalta knew something of regional variations of fashion. On occasions when other wolfsretter visited her mother's court, she had learned their manner. That one was Prussian, the red-haired wolf Flemish, and one wore a hat she thought similar to that of a distant cousin from Budapest.

As Andreas had concluded, none proved to be Stephen. The one at the center of all their attention, however, *was* female.

Radiance did not suit to describe her. Tall, shapely, with blonde hair peeking out from under an elaborate headdress of gold and red. The fabric twisted around her waist in a golden and purple thread must be silk. Gerwalta had seen it on each of her sister's bridal gowns, and remembered its reflective sheen. Around the lady's bodice, feathers dyed in colors like those of her red-yellow dress and cape gave her a plumaged appearance.

The woman was a noble, no doubt of that. But given the tingles in Gerwalta's chest when she concentrated on her, she was also a wolf.

She stepped forward, taking the eyes of the dozen wolves seated on sofas and propped up with pillows around the room. "You've come a long way to be here, haven't you?" she said in Andreas's direction. "And to do that and give yourself away at the last minute by flashing your medallion in public, it really was quite..." She rolled her fingers. "Amateur."

Gerwalta instinctively clutched at her chest, her heart leaping. Only then did she recall that it now hung from Andreas's neck. They'd bought the ruse so easily, it almost concerned her. But, if Andreas could only sense his own pack, surely the same was true of other wolves. They could smell wolf, of course, but there were so many other scents from those assembled, not to mention the underlying aroma of mildew that hung in the air, for despite the pretty dressing they were still in a dungeon. It may be too difficult for the female to discern that it was *Andreas* and not *she* who was the wolf.

"I am Aldhild, and I am the queen of this pack." The beautiful shewolf turned on heel to Gerwalta. "What is your name, and how did you come to be here? My invitation was only to *male* wolves."

"Queen?" Andreas asked. "Who is king?"

"There is no king, measly wolfsretter," Aldhild hissed. "Your kind probably thinks you are the only dark creature who can be ruled by a woman, don't you? I cannot blame you; most of my kind thinks the same. The members of my pack, however, have learned better."

A low rumble of laughter came with the queen's flicked finger inviting the reaction. When she turned on Gerwalta, the distraction had allowed sufficient time to conceive a cover story.

"My name is Rohese." Where it had come from, she knew not, but there was no time to hesitate, and no opportunity to offer alternatives. "I followed my cousin, unbeknownst to him, to see where he was going."

"Your cousin?" She looked in turn to each of the wolves on the perimeter. "And which of my strapping beasts is he?"

"I do not see him here," Gerwalta admitted. "His name is Stephen."

"Ah, *him*." The shewolf's eyes brightened with understanding. "Stephen unfortunately failed to prove his worth to me when given the chance."

Beside her, Andreas stiffened.

But Gerwalta had dealt with enough powerful women to know the truth usually remained in the shadow of the spoken. "Do you mean killing the child outside Ansbach?"

Aldhild nodded. "There's no place in my pack for a wolf who refuses *any* order I issue. Once he refused to kill the boy, I knew he never would be capable of seeing out our vision. Stephen even fought me when I gave him a second chance, telling him to stand aside as *I* killed the boy. Me! He even tried to save him. But Ansbach was some time ago, and I left Stephen in no condition to follow me. How is it, then, that you were still able to track us all the way here to Nuremberg?"

Gerwalta laced her hands behind her back. "When I could not find Stephen's trail out of the village, I picked up yours."

From the corner of her eye, she saw Andreas flinch. Something about that wouldn't add up.

"I am very careful not to leave a trail," Aldhild insisted, suspicion narrowing her gaze.

"True, *you* did not," Gerwalta admitted. "And most wolves—pardon, most *male* wolves," she let the dispersion settle around to the affronted parties before continuing, "would have abandoned the quest there. But after the villagers told me about an imperial coach that had passed through town the day before, an auspicious event for someplace as insignificant as Ansbach, I assumed there was a connection. His majesty owns very many fine stallions, but none of them as yet bred without the ability to stink. *Their* trail was all too simple to follow."

Aldhild's arm lashed in Gerwalta's direction. "There, boys!" she said, grinning. "There is why a female is your natural superior. She sees not just the prey, but it's environment. Tell me, Rohese, what news of your cousin? I left him alive. Barely, but still."

Gerwalta hid the smile when she noticed Andreas's frame ease with relief.

"Stephen is no longer my concern." She folded her arms over her chest. "He was always a bit of an embarrassment anyhow."

"And the wolfsretter?" Aldhild asked. "How is it that he came to be in your company?"

To his credit, Andreas did not miss a beat, though his spirit must have been shaking upon learning the news about Stephen. "I am with her because I am a fool," he said. "She manipulated me, seduced me while not whetting my thirst. My heart burns with desire, and she mocks it."

Gerwalta affected her best seductress, turning to Andreas and running a fingertip down his chin, over his chest, tracing his ribs. She didn't know if Andreas was acting or not when his eyes fluttered closed and he took on the expression of the love-drunk.

"Easy, darling. I only said I could not mate you yet, not with the permission of my king. Or perhaps, my queen."

Aldhild blinked. "And you think I would invite you to my pack?"

"I'm saying I would be interested in exploring that opportunity." She lifted herself to Andreas, praying he wouldn't do anything to give away their lie, and pressed a kiss to his lips. Then, turning a bold brow to Aldhild, added, "It comes with a very obedient wolfsretter who has told me all their secrets. Oh, yes, over the last week or so, Maximillian has been *quite* the songbird. For example—" Gerwalta stepped forward, her hands very suggestively tugging at the brocade cord tied around Aldhild's waist. "Did you know that a wolfsretter is powerless to break a silken restraint?"

The queen's eyebrow arched. "Surely one of us would have known that if it were true."

"Perhaps, but then again—" Gerwalta set about untying the simple knot that kept Aldhild's corded belt from falling, then eased it over her hips, into her hands. "Have you ever seen a wolfsretter *wearing* silk?"

The queen shook her head. "Bind him then, and let us talk more. Frederick!"

At her bellow, one of the larger wolves leaped forward. "Yes, my queen."

"Put Maximillian in a cell. Rohese and I are going to have a little chat, shewolf to shewolf."

TWENTY-ONE

Frederick, along with a rather dullard of a wolf whose name turned out to be Wilhelm, led Andreas to his "cell" — a side room without windows and with a heavy iron door. Even for a wolf, Andreas struggled to see in through the blanket of black. Luckily, his ears worked fine, and his captors were either too foolish or too confident to observe silence within earshot of where they kept guard.

"Think she'll join us, that Rohese one?"

That from Wilhelm, whose accent suggested German was not his first tongue.

"Hope so," Frederick responded, the lilt in his voice signifying he was very, very Saxon. "If the queen's plan succeeds, we'll need to start mating immediately to grow our pack. Strength in numbers, as they say. And that Rohese… Let's just say it wouldn't disappoint me if she ended up in my sheets."

Andreas fought the urge to use the strength he knew he possessed as a konigswolf to push open the door and force both the insolent curs into submission.

"Yeah, but you heard what that wolfsretter said." Here Andreas could picture the two wolves motioning to the closed door behind them. "'Seduced me.' *Seduced.* You don't think she's already given her bond to *him*, do you?"

Frederick chuckled. "What would ever possess a wolf to turn his back on his kind and mate with the enemy?"

Love would, you fools. Love would possess him!

The errant thought flashed through his mind too quickly to recall… and there it was. The truth, undeniable and resilient, that had laid hidden behind a wall of history and tradition his heart had been pulling down, brick by brick, since they'd left Triberg. All Andreas's biases, all his kind's past, all his notions of proper and possible… they surrendered to the immutable reality. He *loved* Gerwalta. He wanted her, as his bride, as his mate, as the mother of his pups.

It was treason.

It was salvation.

It would be the death of him, quite literally, if it ever became known to her clan.

This love was *deadly.*

Bogged down by the enormity of his heart's revelation, Andreas lost track of what the two wolves prattled on about, or how much time passed. Other than the growing pull in his innards, the sensation present whenever full moon was nigh, he became unaware of his physical connection to the world, drifting away on flights of fancy of ways he might be able to woo the wolfsretter.

She slipped into his cell between his vision of her on their wedding day, and his dreams of their wedding night. So distracted was he, that Andreas took a moment to realize the form of his beloved was asking him a question.

"What?"

"Did they hurt you?" she said in a whisper, though with such annoyance in her tone he knew that she must have said it more than once.

"No, I'm…" Andreas clicked his tongue against a dry palate. "You are a brilliant creature, Gerwalta."

"It will all come to naught if you don't listen to me and do exactly as I—"

Wolfsretter may play politics, but wolves wore their hearts on their hides. Now that he knew, she must too. "I love you."

Her suddenly silver eyes blinked bright in the darkness. "Come again?"

Had he not been bound, he would have taken her into his arms and kissed her proper. At least those peculiar glowing orbs of hers gave him an approximate target. Andreas leaned in, pressing his lips to hers, waiting for her to understand his intentions. None came, though the mere fact that he touched her sent a wave of lust, driven by the moon, spiking through him.

The silk cord only tightened as he pulled on his restraint, but his ardor cooled when he felt the sting of silver press against his chest

"I said, I love y—"

"I heard what you said! Are you moonmad already? We haven't time for your soggy emotions! We are in terrible peril, and I only have a moment or two to explain to you how we're to survive. I need you to be the konigswolf right now, *not* some confessor of puppy love."

"Do you doubt the virility of my feelings?"

"I do not doubt the virility of your *anything*," she confessed. "As my mother would say, shove it down! There is work to be done."

"But we must—"

"*Zzst!*" Gerwalta hissed as she pushed the palm of her hand to his mouth and tried to press on as if he hadn't just laid bare his heart to her. "Now, listen. Aldhild has lured away a wolf from each of the packs within a ten-day journey of Nuremberg, each of them the brother of a king. Stephen was just one of those whose allegiance she stole."

"A female lupine running a pack," he grumbled. "Such an unnatural abomination."

"As a woman descended from a long line of female leaders, I'm going to pretend I didn't hear that. Anyhow, she says there is something called *lupus regina* in legend, a female wolf as a sort of empress of kings. She plans to ally herself with the laity crown, royal to royal, as it were."

"I have... heard tell of this," Andreas admitted, schooling his animal mind to ignore how close she remained. "They say the mother of Romulus and Remus was such a creature, but I thought it was always a myth."

"Are *we* not myth, Andreas?" Gerwalta asked. "Aldhild intends to remake our world. She thinks the time has come for the emperor to become the master of the church, not the other way around, and she intends to be the power behind the crown."

"And she told you all this openly, willingly? How is it that she even believes *you* are a wolf?"

"Because I am a woman. And because the pull of the moon has disabled her rationality as it does with your kind. *And* because I've spent so much time with you, I *smell* like you."

He felt a hedonic pull in his groin at the thought that he'd marked her, but pushed it down. Gerwalta was right; he'd seduce her later, when they were both certain they would survive.

"She has offered me a place in her pack, but as she's done with each of the other wolves, I must prove my loyalty."

"By agreeing to return to the Schwartzwald and killing the king wolf off? Good of you to agree; it will give us the opportunity to escape and think of…"

"No, Andreas. She thinks you're the wolfsretter, remember?" Through the darkness, Andreas heard Gerwalta's movements as her hands wrapped around his body, taking up the slack of the silk cord which still bound him. "And because I was so able to convince them that I have you smitten and eating out of the palm of my hand…"

"As I just told you, I *am* smitten, and I'll eat out of whatever you tell me to."

She continued as though he had not spoken, "She has asked me to bid you create silver manacles, in which I am to be led into to the emperor's presence just before sunset. When I shift into my wolf, and made calm by her command, you are to release my restraints. Then, to demonstrate the might of a lupine, she will order me to kill you."

There was so much wrong with that, he didn't even know where to begin. "This cannot possibly work."

"Why not? You are a konigswolf. You, like Aldhild, can keep your lay form during a full moon, can you not?"

"So the theory goes, though I have never had a cause as yet to attempt it." He shook his head, even though he knew she could not see it. "Regardless, what goes against us is the fact that you will *not* become a wolf. What will Aldhild do when you prove at sunset not to be a lupine?"

"It doesn't matter!" Gerwalta exclaimed. "I will be bound by silver. I carry my weapon before me as I walk. I know Ferdinand by reputation. He does not abide fools. Once Aldhild is shown to be a fraud, he will order her—and by proxy, us—removed."

"And if she herself takes her wolf and attacks?"

"Did you not hear the part where I said I will be going in with *silver directly at my behest?"*

"And so you will, what? Slay a werewolf before the emperor? Without revealing what you really are?" he asked. "If the emperor learns you can wield silver, I think he'll have more interest in your kind than mine."

"I won't let anyone see. I'm good at hiding my weapons."

"And how, then, shall I go about forming silver manacles? I can't even touch the stuff, let alone craft it into restraints."

"We'll... find a way. We must. There's no..." A hiccup in the air betrayed her. "I will not let her exploit wolves like this. It will either end with your kind being forced into military service, or slaughtered at the order of the church. I will save you. I must save you. I—"

Just then, the door behind them swung open. Though the lantern's light was not bright, it pierced a hole into the darkness that had them both squinting. Their interloper turned out to be Frederick, and the way he molested Gerwalta with his eyes threatened to draw Andreas's wolf to the surface.

"Come now, love, and bring your pet," he said. "Sunset is nigh."

TWENTY-TWO

Two packlings shepherded them across the courtyard, the inner bailey, and then, the climb started. Up, up, and up, ascending the tower they'd seen even while outside the city, until even a dark one had to pause to catch his breath. Near the top, Aldhild stood outside a heavy oaken door.

"Go below and wait for the others," she told her two wolves. "I will escort them from here."

She slipped an iron key from a hidden pocket of her dress. The shewolf extended a welcoming arm as she opened the door. Even with the setting rays of the sun blasting through a westward arrow slit, the room veritably gleamed.

"Take only what you need, Herr Faust. Quickly, though. Time is running out."

It took a moment for Andreas to remember that, under current circumstances, *he* was the wolfsretter. The werewolf wandered into the room and found himself entombed in silver. He managed to tamp down the screaming voice inside of him that told him to run, that this place was dangerous. And it was, though not just for the obvious reason. The truth remained that he had not gained a magical ability to transform the metal in the last hour. Not for the first time, the konigswolf whispered a silent prayer that Gerwalta had a plan to pull off this farce.

"How is it that you, a lupine, have access to the imperial treasury?" For the moment, he would stall. Within reason, for the sun dipped further down with each passing moment. Even if he, as a konigswolf, could maintain his laymen form, he did not expect it to be easy.

Aldhild grinned her condescension, stepping towards him. "I was able to pull thirteen wolves away from their much-beloved brother kings, and you question my ability to twist the whims of a layman?"

What would a wolfsretter say? What would a wolfsretter say? "A wolf who can be either man and beast might be a danger to us as well. It would behove me not to at least ask."

"But it would be foolish of you to expect me to answer." Aldhild flicked an oversized serving bowl setting on a table, drawing a ding with a fingernail and making Andreas flinch in fear of her welfare. "Now, claim your silver and let us be on our way."

Andreas threw his hands up into the air. "What do you propose I do, make my way through the castle clutching tea sets and dining platters to my chest?"

"Or you could just take this cache of silver coins, heartstrings." Gerwalta made both wolves turn at once, kicking a bag formed out of suspiciously red cloth. Its contents clinked. "Dozens of coins, conveniently collected into a sack. Even if they do bear Ottoman markings, silver *is* silver."

The shewolf's head cocked to the side, saying "I do not recall seeing that before," as Andreas made the same motion and, his grin delirious, mouthed to Gerwalta, "heartstrings?"

Gerwalta made work of pulling up the bag from the ground. Even with the protection of the cloth sack, Andreas struggled to overcome his trepidation as she handed it to him. Should one coin fall out as he jostled the surprisingly heavy cache up the stairs and managed to sear his flesh, the game would be up.

He made a show of inspecting the contents. "I suppose this will work well enough, assuming we need only *one* set of manacles and chain."

As Aldhild peered into the bag, he chanced a look at Gerwalta, who gave him an acknowledging nod.

"Fine, then, bring it along."

The shewolf led them from the treasure room. Andreas expected them to head back down at that point, but much to his surprise, they started up, until at last, they came to the end of the stairs and, he'd presume, the top of the tower.

Andreas leaned over to Gerwalta as Aldhild passed until a room behind another door. "A wolf would say 'my pet,' or even 'lambkins,' but never heartstrings."

"Forgive my ignorance, *Herr Faust,* but I am not well acquainted in the language of lovers – lupine or otherwise."

"You will be. Once I've managed to convince you to love me, you'll be able to write poems and compose melodies in thirteen tongues."

Gerwalta strained to keep her voice at a whisper, though the flush in her cheeks was speaking volumes of truth. "Andreas, this is *not* the time for love-making!"

"I agree. Reluctantly." When it was, they would be alone. And undisturbed. And needing provisions for several days. "How were you able to make your cloak into a small sack like this? Can you alter its shape the way you do silver?"

"I didn't alter anything." Her face screwed up. "It was sitting there, with all the coins already in it. Seemed the quickest solution to our query."

"Yes, but what gets us out of the next challenge?" He swallowed down the crawl of his skin, the ache of his bones, forcing his body under his command. "What is taking her so long? Sunset is minutes away."

"We feel it too, you know." Gerwalta turned big blue eyes up to him. "The sunset. It's tugging at my senses."

"Good, then you'll know when to howl. A wolf always does when pulled by the light of the moon. It hurts more than when we take our fur willingly. If your ploy is to make *her* seem she's lost her wits, you seeming to do the same should also reflect back. And remember, you must act as though the silver causes you great pain."

"And you must remain a man. I see the sunset torturing your body already. Fight the draw to change. I cannot do this alone. Not in a way that would not spill blood."

"I will do what needs be done." He sighed. "All this relies on Aldhild herself playing along. What if she just decided to take her own fur instead?"

Gerwalta swallowed, her eyes peeling away. "Then *I* will do what needs be done."

"You don't mean…"

"Andreas Baron!" she whispered with aggression. "No matter

what has happened between us, I am still a *wolfsretter*. It is my duty to ensure she does not pose a danger."

"But she is a *queen!*" Andreas argued. "Her pack is too new for her to have formed a strong bond with her second. You destroy Aldhild, you leave her pack not only without command, but naturally inclined to avenge her. And on full moon!"

"What choice do I have?" Gerwalta's wide eyes flashed not anger, but fear. "I can flee an attack, but you cannot. What if she sets her pack on you? What if... I can't lose you, Andreas! I won't. I refuse to."

Gerwalta crashed into him. When her lips met his, the konigswolf felt it wash over him: love. Pure, utterly determined love. Even if Gerwalta never became his mate—and how could she, given the obvious—he would never love another. Even knowing his constitution could wash out his heart and paint it in the color of any other shewolf—he'd never allow himself to betray her.

And he would keep his laymen form, even under the pull of the full moon. For it was what she needed of him. Andreas would change the laws of god to do what Gerwalta required, or die trying.

The door of the chambers opened. They flew apart as though ricocheting off each other, creating distance where there had been none. Without hesitation, and despite having been both on the edge of tears and driven by passion just moments before, Gerwalta snapped into her assumed persona as though it were merely a scarf she need throw about her shoulders.

"Is it time, my queen?" she asked. "Shall the wolfsretter shackle me now?"

"Yes, only..." Aldhild strolled out, holding up a pair of *iron* manacles on a chain in her hand. "Use these, which you should have no difficulty in handling, Herr Baron, or I fear our little red riding hood will slip her silver bonds and go scampering back, over the river and through the woods."

His confusion stood mere moments of reflection as a man garbed in a red cloak rounded the shewolf.

"Well, if it isn't my dear cousin," Bernhard said. "And her little puppy."

TWENTY-THREE

The glint of silver flew from Bernhard's hand too fast for Gerwalta to stop it. For one brief moment, she called out, only to find relief the next when the metallic disc warbled, losing shape, transforming moments before landing square against Andreas's hands and wrists. The sack of silver coins crashed and spilled out over the stone-cobbled floor, as did Andreas a moment later.

The konigswolf wanted to bellow; that much Gerwalta could see. But what drew her concern more were the pulsations beneath his flesh, the ripples of bone and muscles contorting, converting, his inner wolf fighting to get free.

"Andreas, stay with me!" she begged. "I need your voice."

Tortured grunts came from his throat. "The... silver..." he croaked. "Take it off!"

Gerwalta fell to her knees, working her will against the poison grafting into his skin. She reached out again with her power, willing the metal to obey. "I cannot. It's... It's..."

Her distraction left the betrayer an advantage. Bernhard swooped, slapping the iron manacles over Gerwalta's wrists, using the chain that linked the set to yank her to her feet.

"Blood-claimed silver, cousin," he said. "I believe that's the term you're searching for. The coins are as well, by the way. I knew your training would draw you to that cache."

"Blood-claimed silver?" Impossible. "That power is only to be used for the claiming of a fire medallion and in the forging of a wedding band!"

"A quaint, old tradition I've chosen to ignore, for obvious reasons."

"You cannot seriously mean that you..." Gerwalta looked off into the distance, her face contorting. "How could you run so much silver through your own heart? The pain you must have endured..."

"Will all have been worth it, once I set our world right." Bernhard yanked the chain, forcing his cousin to his side, her face to his mouth. His vicious tongue licked up her jawline, even as Gerwalta struggled to pull away. "Now, listen to every word I say, or your wolf will die."

Somehow, Andreas managed his feet, even as Aldhild took him by the arm to guide him toward the room that lay just beyond the door.

"Did you really think I wouldn't recognize a wolfsretter when she stood before me?" the shewolf asked. "Or a wolf who bears such a close resemblance to the brother who tried to kill me?"

As was the tower, so was the room: wide, round, with only one way in or out. Or so she thought, until Gerwalta looked across the space, through the flicker of candlelight, and saw another door opposite them. The tower had no external stairs she'd observed from the ground, so it must lead to the wooden parapets she'd noticed when first they'd crossed into the bailey. That could be her escape, if she could break free of her captor's hold. Only, how could she leave Andreas behind?

Begging was the desperate act of the defeated, but it was the only road left for her to tread. "Please, Bernhard. Think about this! If you expose us to the laity, every woman, man, and child wolfsretter will become their servant. We'll be exploited and persecuted. Wolves will be enslaved and sent forth as cannon fodder!"

To her dismay, her cousin only laughed. "Is not our highest calling to protect the laity from the lupine? And yet, how many laymen walk into the fields of death, while wolves stay hidden away in their forests and ravines? Our fault is not in exposing them, Gerwalta, it's in helping them keep hidden. I've done only what every Matron has been too much of a coward to do."

"What you've *done*?" As they were dragged forward, the truth dawned over Gerwalta's face. "The emperor already knows about us."

"Yes, we do."

Neither of their captors needed to speak, for in the midst of the sparse room was a single man who represented the multitude. Surrounded by six soldiers with silver swords, and with regal bearing, attire, and demeanor he fully laid claim to the title "emperor."

Though she'd had encounters with nobles, Gerwalta knew Ferdinand only from rumor and reputation. He looked every bit the caricature drawn in her head, from his oily, ebony hair which twisted at the ends, to his wiry mustache, to the armament of his prominent proboscis which ruled, in addition to half of Europe, a goodly portion of his face.

She called out as someone took a staff to the back of her legs, forcing her knees to buckle and hit the floor.

"Don't you touch her!" Andreas's gravelly voice evidenced his animal nature rearing its head. "I'll kill anyone who lays a hand on her. I'll— *Argh!*"

His cries overpowered the hiss of searing flesh. Gerwalta bucked, kicked, bit at the air. Anything to get to him. Anything to free him.

"Andreas!" she called out, wishing she had her medallion still. "Don't worry about me. Concentrate. Stay a man. Stay with me now, as a man."

"Is this the fierce warrior I was promised?" A finger hooked under Gerwalta's chin, pulling her eyes up. Ferdinand stood just inches away. "I do not see how *this* creature—this meek, crying woman, could possibly be stronger than you, Herr Faust."

Bernhard's voice came from behind her. "It is the way of my kind. The women are stronger. At least, physically. As to the gifts of the intellect, each man and woman is doled out a share as seen fit by our mighty creator."

The regent sneered as he drew back his hand and stood. A few flicks of his hand, and two guards rushed from their posts, hooked her under her arms, and pulled Gerwalta to her feet.

"And you're certain *this* is the one who you wish for your bride?" he asked. "You've brought such riches into our coffers, I'm certain a noble match could be made for you. The Duke of Saxony's third daughter, perhaps?"

"His Majesty is very kind, but I'm afraid that to take a laywoman as my wife would defeat the purpose of our agreement. If you wish for Fraulein Barvat and me to assure in a new age of lupine-led assaults against your enemies, it will be necessary for us to draw from our own in matters of family." He rounded on her at last, that vile snakeskin kin of hers, and continued. "Gerwalta is the only unwed daughter of our High Matron in the clan of Red, who will fall before me when I bring her the royal decree proclaiming my command over all wolfsretter. She, in turn, will command Gerwalta's acquiesce to me, and a wolfsretter *always* obeys the Matron. Bloodlines are quite critical for our ability to dominate lupines. I am certain *you* of all people can appreciate that."

"Yes, bloodlines are the fabric which keeps the monarchy strong." The emperor then turned to Aldhild. "Fraulein Barvat, this is the—what did you call him? I remember I found it quite amusing. Oh, yes!—the *king wolf* you've selected from your new pack? I can see he, even in his layman form, is a strapping specimen, but will you be able to woo him away from this—" Ferdinand tossed a dismissive wave Gerwalta's way, "*lady?*"

Gerwalta felt like she'd been punched in the stomach. Whatever happened, her fate had ultimately remained unchanged. Bernhard was the most likely contender for her hand when she'd left Triberg, and that would be no different if his scheme succeeded. Andreas, on the other hand... She couldn't stomach it. Couldn't accept that he'd be given to mating by force. That the konigswolf would be bonded to anyone. He deserved to be happy, to love and be loved.

Like she loved...

The wolfsretter cut off her own apostasy before it could grow roots.

Aldhild bowed her head before speaking. "He is the brother of the one I wished, your majesty, but that is little concern. In fact, Andreas is an even better prospect, and once I claim his mating bond, he will be helpless to reject me. It is imperative for the mated wolves to be dedicated to one another. He will be loyal to me and me only. He will kill if I ask him to, and for you, by proxy of my dedication to the crown. He comes from a noble lupine bloodline, one whose renown will help me to bring the other packs under my authority."

"And by mating, you mean..." Ferdinand acted out a crude gesture with his wiry hands.

How had Aldhild learned to act so demure? She even blushed. "Yes, my liege. We are ancient beasts, and ancient rites still bind us."

"Lucky bastard." A momentary, lustful curl perked in

Ferdinand's expression before vanishing in a wink. "Do what needs to be done, and be cautious that the truth of these events never reaches the church. Both of you will report to me in the morning so we can start to plan our assault east. Finally, I'll have soldiers who can stand against that cursed Wallachian convert! Serve me well, and you will be rewarded handsomely."

Bernhard and Aldhild knelt as two soldiers followed the Emperor from the round room, their footfalls diminishing with every step down the circular tower stairs. At Aldhild's command, the doors were closed, and the four remaining soldiers, two of them still holding Gerwalta on her feet, remained.

"How could you do this?" Anger dipped her words in red as she faced her cousin. "To your mother? To your Matron? To your people? To *me*?"

"To you was the simplest part, heartstrings." Bernhard grinned, balled fists on his hips. "If I hadn't done this, your mother would have married you to me, if for no other reason than to assume my mother's Matronship once she passes. A man could never be trusted to rule a wolfsretter homestead, could he?"

"Seeing what you've done with such a little taste of power, can you find fault in such thoughts?" She leaned toward him, her voice becoming deadly soft. "Do not fret, cousin. If you try to touch me now, you'll be woman enough, when I'm done with you."

Bernhard bore his teeth, pulling back his hand, readying the strike. Gerwalta refused to flinch.

"Bernhard!" Aldhild called out. "Do not be distracted. If I do not claim Andreas tonight, our plans may come to ruin."

Forced to turn his attention, the blow remained unthrown. "I have bound him in silver for you. If he takes fur now the way I've wrapped him up, it won't be without losing a foot. He will remain a layman. What more do you require of me?"

A growl lumbered in Aldhild's chest, ripping out in frustration. "Fool! The mating of a pack leader is an auspicious event, requiring the witness of the pack on full moon. That is why everything we have orchestrated has been for this night. Either my pack must be brought here to the tower, or Andreas and I must be guided below."

"It seems that this is something for which plans should have been made before."

"If you will recall, *I* wished to have the audience with Ferdinand in the dungeons, but *he* insisted on the tower."

Bernhard crossed his arms and examined the space. "Here feels more secure than the dungeons. Though I will not savor having to witness such animalistic rituals."

Aldhild coughed a laugh. "You'll see who the animal is come your wedding night. I will return shortly. Once I claim Andreas, we will move on to the next part of the plan."

With that, the queen of the Nuremberg pack took her wolf, her fine clothing ripping into shreds, and then took her leave.

TWENTY-FOUR

His cries had dulled, but whimpers remained.

Gerwalta wished she knew what to say, what to do. If he could take his wolf, at least Andreas could fight his way out and be safe. She *could* save herself, if only she could make it to the parapet door. The soldiers may give chase, but she'd outrun them. Only, she'd never outrun the guilt of knowing she'd left Andreas behind. Besides, how far would she get? Aldhild would order her pack to chase her down. Maybe she'd get out of the castle, perhaps even the city. But exhausted after pushing so hard for two days to make it this far, she wondered if she had the ability to go two more hours without collapsing.

"Was the plan always to take me as your bride, or was it just convenient that I came along when I did?"

Bernhard looked up from the ball of silver he bounced in hand, indifferent to her now where before he'd been so tender. "Convenient is the last word I would use. There was a moment in Ulm, when my thugs cornered you in the church, that I debated letting them kill you. Or at least, letting them try. It would have given me a chance to escape without my plot being revealed. But, yes, I have known for some time that when this plan came to fruition, you were the one I wanted. Fourth daughter to a powerful Matron, trained in diplomacy and just the right age to carry my seed... In the end, I rather enjoy doing away with the artifice of formally seeking your hand through your mother."

"I could still refuse." Gerwalta put as much iron into her voice as it would hold. "It is not customary for a daughter to reject the husband her mother selects, but it is not unprecedented."

Bernhard pushed himself away from the wall he'd been leaning against and came to face her. "Refuse me, and I'll inform your mother of your..." His eyes flashed quickly to Andreas's shivering form on the ground. "...disgrace. Aldhild said she smelled you two all over each other, and I've noticed the way your eyes light up when they linger on him."

"My mother would never believe me capable of that."

Even as she said it, guilt pulled within her. How it hurt to imply Andreas was so undesirable, so loathsome.

"But she'd believe it of the wolf. Gunda was probably testing his trustworthiness as much as yours, sending you on this mission. If you survive her judgment, it would only be in exile, and Andreas would be killed, mate of the Nuremberg Queen Wolf or no. Face it, Gerwalta, you are beaten. Besides, the Red Matron has been eyeing me for some time as a proper spouse. Assured, of course, by my status as the only surviving child in a region where dominance is critical."

"And was that a convenient coincidence as well?"

Her cousin sneered. "Oh, no, heartstrings, I killed both of my sisters. This plot did not rise into existence with the dawn."

"Monster!" She pulled taut her restraints, feeling the bite of the iron manacles into her flesh. "Cur! What makes you think I would ever marry you? That I would ever love you?"

"Love?" Bernhard threw back his head and crowed. "When has love ever mattered to one of our kind? No, heartstrings, let me make this quite plain: your role as my wife will be to *grow my seed*, both in mind and in body. The wolfsretter will be remade, starting with our children. We will dominate the wolves, and be ruled as Lord God intended, by the will of men, not women. The wolves got that much right."

"But Aldhild—"

"Aldhild is an abomination!" He growled back. "An anathema, turned away by her own kind. She was on the edge of madness when I found her and found a pack to take her. She owes me her life, and I've used every bit of my influence over her to twist her to my whim. The shewolf *serves me*, just as you will *serve* me."

Her anger had heated the kettle of her eyes. Even as Gerwalta struggled to hold back the tears, Andreas's whimpers broke her. "Please, Bernhard. Let us go. Let *Andreas* go. She has a whole pack from which to choose a mate."

"Why, so he can be yours instead? You would lower yourself to be a wolf's bitch?" Bernhard spit in her face. "You're lucky I'm saving you from the folly of your feminine heart. This is why a woman should never rule."

"I would never—"

But if he heard her say that now, it would look as though she were appealing to Bernhard's philosophies. It would crush Gerwalta to have Andreas think she thought any less of him because he was a wolf.

"You would," Bernhard insisted. "His fate is really your fault, you know. Aldhild's mate was supposed to be the brother. Of all the wolves she recruited to form her pack, she desired him most, probably because he was the hardest to break. Andreas Baron was the only king to come after his lost packling. When Stephen saw his brother had debased himself, from a wolf's perspective, to accept the help of a wolfsretter, he felt the depth of his brother's love and his loyalties divided. Even after Aldhild got his eyes back to her, and I threw Andreas down the well to frame him for killing the boy, *you* had to rescue the konigswolf, didn't you?"

The events of those two days flashed in her mind's eye. It couldn't have been, could it? Gerwalta inspected the fabric of her memory like a sack that had grown a hole that refused to be found. When would Bernhard have even had the opportunity to confront Andreas? But then she recalled the way he'd insisted he needed to be the one to canvas the village, for it was the layman's world, and there a woman had no power.

The hindsight of her stupidity crushed her spirit. It was her fault, all of it. But how could she have known that by saving Andreas, she'd be dooming him at the same time?

Gerwalta drew some comfort from the sensation of the pack's approach from the tower stairs below. Now that there seemed no way to change the outcome of this horrendous series of events, she was eager to have them be done with. This battle was lost, but the war could not continue unless she lived to the next confrontation.

The doors opened at the back of the chamber, bringing with it a cacophony of snarls, growls, and clashing metal.

Bernhard turned, even as he crafted the silver blob back into a dagger. "About time, Aldhild! Take your bloody mate, then. I'm tired of minding your—Who are... Who are you? You're not Aldhild!"

Gerwalta's head shot up, seeing the balances tip despite not understanding how. Bernhard and the four laymen guards assumed a formation, squaring off against a dozen wolves, teeth bared and claws long, led not by Aldhild, but by a silver wolf with a patch of brown behind his right ear.

As the parties faced each other, all forgot about the two prisoners. She used the chaos to her advantage, falling to Andreas's side, pulling at his restraints.

"No!" He called out as she attempted to wrench the links apart. The act only drove the lip of the cuffs deeper into his wrists. "You must flee!"

"I am *not* leaving you."

"Listen to them!"

Gerwalta looked up long enough to see the guards fending against a wolf each, while her cousin had spun some of blood-claimed silver into a shield and sword, and was using it to fend off the advances of not one, but three wolves.

Andreas grasped her hand. "It's full moon, and a wolf lusts for blood. They will destroy you."

"Leaving you will destroy me, and I—"

Her words died as the flickering shadow cut across them.

The maw was more teeth then flesh, the wolf's lips pulled back so that his long, sharp, fatal fangs filled her vision. Only inches away from her face, she knew she was done for. No silver in this room would obey her command, and attacking from below she'd never be able to overpower the beast before her.

The joy in Andreas's voice sieved through the crackle of the pain. "You're alive!"

Gerwalta's head cocked to the side as the lupine settled back on its haunches and yipped. She knew this wolf. She'd faced him once before.

"Stephen?"

If the wolf's teeth weren't to kill her, his reaction might. Stephen leaned forward and pulled his tongue across her chin, the closest thing to a hug a lupine in his wolf could do. How was it possible? And how was he rationale enough not to simply rip her to shreds at this very moment, under the light of a full moon?

"We'll have to explain the details to her later, brother." Through his suffering, the konigswolf managed to sit up. "After we've had the chance to survive. Go, do what you must."

Gerwalta wasted no time in helping Andreas to his feet. Were she a man and larger, she'd not have been able to needle under his arm and hoist him with her shoulder. "What must he do? How is he here? Who are these other lupines?"

"Later, love. We need to run. Stephen says there's a troop of imperial guards on their..."

No sooner had they taken two steps toward the door than dark-clad soldiers began to file in. A quick sweep of the room brought the count of wolves, including Stephen, to ten. The imperial fighters might outnumber the lupines two-to-one, but unless they brought silver blades or managed to remove limbs or heads, they had stepped into a battle they were destined to lose.

Stephen set himself on all fours, a barrier between wolf, wolfsretter, and the violence.

Gerwalta looked about, and caught sight of the small, wooden door on the far side of the room. "Come, this way," she said, dragging Andreas along.

"But that goes to the parapet. We'll be trapped at the top of the tower with no way to get down."

She pushed on, throwing the door open, taking in the full moon's glow like a salve. "That room is filled with moon-crazed lupines and soldiers who likely have orders to see to our retention. We'll wait until they kill each other off or move on to other grounds, and make our escape. There is still the question of what to do about Aldhild."

"We need to do nothing. For better or worse, she is dead."

"What?" She turned on the konigswolf as she lowered him down. "How do you know that?"

"Because Stephen killed her," Andreas said, unable to hide a prideful smile. "He snuck into the castle just before sunset, following our scents. He encountered Aldhild as she returned to claim her pack, and challenged her. He victoried."

So Stephen was king. Was that a good thing? Everything

they'd experienced until now led her to believe not, but then again, Andreas's brother had just stood between her and danger *and* licked her face. "And now suddenly, your brother likes me instead of wanting me dead? How did that come about?"

"He does not lack intelligence, Gerwalta. He read the situation and saw that you're on our side. Also, there's the fact that you're my mate." Andreas held up his hands, wincing, blood trickling down the insides of his arms. "Can you remove these, please, love?"

She slapped down his injured paws. "What did you just say?"

"The manacles: take them off. They are silver, you know, and I am still a lupine. They *do* sting a bit."

"Not about the bloody manacles!" she shouted. "What do you mean I'm your mate? Did I pass out? Does it…" She swallowed her awkwardness. "Does *mating* not engage one's body as much as I've been led to believe? Did we *consummate* and I was not aware?"

His face screwed up. "Darling, when we *consummate*, you will be aware, in every inch of your body, intimately. *Feverishly.* But no, to the best of *my* knowledge, your maidenhead is intact." He shifted, taking her hands between his blood-streaked fingers. "You are my mate, and I yours, not because of any meeting of our bodies, but because of the joining of our hearts."

Things went from sweet to peculiar in the beat of a bird's wing, as Andreas chirped out some very wolfish sounds through his very glorious laymen face. When Gerwalta met that with only confusion, he explained.

"It's something wolves say to each other. It means, *'my heart beats in your chest.'*"

To his disappointment, she scoffed. "You're injured and you're delirious," Gerwalta declared. "No more foolishness. If we don't find a way out of here, neither of our hearts will be beating regardless in whose chest they reside."

He lifted his hands once more. "Manacles?"

Disappointment reclaimed her features. "I can do nothing, I'm sorry. Bernhard blood-claimed the silver. Only he commands it."

"Then how do we get these off?" The konigswolf shook his arm, making the chain connecting the two cuffs rattle.

"Blood-claimed or no, it is still silver. We need only find a smithy."

"Or I could remove them willingly."

They turned. Bernhard's sword dripped with blood. Lupine or laymen? Did it matter? Neither would make his blade any less sharp.

He raised a shield, though the arrogance in his face served as well, making Gerwalta want to keep a goodly distance from him.

"*If* properly motivated, that is," he continued. "Agree to my terms, Walta, and I'll let him live."

Gerwalta spun, seating herself on Andrea's lap, determined to take any blow her errant cousin may throw the konigswolf's way. "Enough. Aldhild is dead, and her pack's allegiance has been claimed by another. You have no grounds for holding on to Andreas now. Let him go."

"No grounds?" His toothy smile irked her. "So I was imagining him kissing my bride-to-be, then?"

She faltered. "He... *I* kissed *him*. You cannot hold him at fault for my—"

"Exile for a fourth daughter would be particularly cruel, wouldn't it?" Bernhard pressed on. "You do not have the combat training of your sisters, nor the ability your brother might have to succeed in the world of laymen. You'd be turned out from home, without a clan, fated by birth to be an enemy of all wolves who could then kill you without ramification."

"No!" Andreas shifted his weight beneath her, forcing Gerwalta to rise along with him. Though he still feigned when she placed herself between the two men, he did not demure in sight of Bernhard's silver. "Do not threaten me, Betrayer. I kissed her, and by God, I love her. And I will never, *never* let you or any of your kind touch her."

Gerwalta let out a hiss as her eyes closed. "Every word you speak signs your execution papers, Andreas. Please, stop. Do not hand him the very weapon he will use to strike you."

"As far as he's strayed from honor, do you think he was waiting for legal justification to kill me? I was dead the moment he knew I loved you." The width of the parapet proved just enough for

Andreas to circle the wolfsretter before him. He held up his hands, displayed the bubbling, bleeding flesh warped by silver. "I ask only that you remove these chains and give me a fair chance to defend myself. I am weary from the silver, weakened from travel and turmoil. You will finish me in short order, but at least let me die as the king I am, and not the groveling inhuman creature you think I am."

Before she could interject, Bernhard grinned, saying, "So be it."

The silver fled Andreas's wrists, and within moments, where the battered man-king had stood, the lord of the lupines remained.

"Andreas!" Gerwalta lunged forward, but too late.

The wolf charged, snarling, barking, teeth-bared and dripping. Bernhard leaped, grabbing one of the timbers of the tower roof which extended off the parapet with his free hand and hoisting himself out of the striking path. The energy behind his pounce had sent the konigswolf flying, and Gerwalta cried out, fearing he'd fallen. He hadn't, but his top half hung precariously over the railing, the bottom half of the massive wolf trying to find purchase on the stones beneath his feet.

"The reason we keep to the trees, is because they so fear heights. Or didn't you know?" Bernhard dropped down, pacing. "Not all daggers are made of silver, heartstrings."

The dark, brooding look of his eye struck her deep in her gut. Bernhard was hunting, and she was the prey. Her cousin was a fearsome predator; she knew by reputation and, to some extent, observation. But every warrior had a weakness. Both cousins had been trained to listen. For a snap, for a pant, for the rustle of leaves.

They'd never been taught to listen for the silence.

Unlike the wolfsretter, Andreas learned from his mistakes. To charge? That had been a mistake. As was to attack from the front. The konigswolf moved with such determined, deliberate, delicate movements, claws retracted and maw closed, he made nary a sound.

All Gerwalta need do is keep her cousin distracted long enough...

"I would rather die than let you touch me, traitor!"

He feigned insult, splaying his hand over his chest in overly dramatic fashion. "Oh, love, such cruel words for your intended. But I remind you, I'm not the one who debased herself to tarry with a beast. Do as I say, or I *will* see you ruined! I can always find other wolves and scare them enough to do as I say. I will make good on my promise to train an army of lupines for the emperor, and I will flood his coffers with so much silver, your Gunda Faust will have no choice but to bow down before me."

His arrogance is also a weakness. Exploit it. "So you're saying that if I agree to be your wife, to foster your plots and serve your agenda, you will let Andreas live and allow my clan to continue to prosper?"

"Prosper may be an overstatement, but I will assure that Schloss Wolfsretter has sufficient resources and contacts to maintain its Matron. What's more, I will assure they continue to live, and that your… *indulgences* remain unknown."

With that, the man before her reached a hand to his sword, and pulled from it a generous pinch of the metal. The remaining blade immediately liquified, filling in the gap, healing. Within moments, Bernhard had wielded the small amount of silver into a hoop crowned with the emblem of a rose.

"Take this ring, and my hand, and help me lead the dark ones out of the shadows, with our kind ruling them all."

Even as Andreas tested his balance, a prelude to his strike, Gerwalta kept up the act.

She started to reach for the ring, and took it at the very moment the werewolf leaped.

TWENTY-FIVE

Andreas had heard stories of the odd sensation one has when he realizes he's to die. As though time slows down. As though thoughts speed up. As though life comes to an end in an instant, and the totality of it stretches on forever. It had not occurred to him that saving Gerwalta would result in his death, but he could not find it in himself to be sorry for saving her life at the cost of his own. What would a worthy wolf not give for the woman he loved?

Bernhard, that cursed snake, turned only in time to catch a wolf streaming through the air, moments from contact. By the time he'd pivoted in an attempt to get his sword between them, they were both sailing over the wooden rail of the parapet.

And then, all that was left, was to fall.

Andreas settled into an expected wave of contentment, accepting the inevitable. His only regret, that he'd never heard Gerwalta say she loved him. She must, he could see the truth covered by the thinnest veiled expression, but to have heard the words from her mouth... That would have made his life truly complete.

As Bernhard's visage plummeted towards the ground, he noticed that the wolfsretter became smaller in his sight, instead of constant as he'd expect when falling with him. How odd the experiences of death.

"Didn't... you... hear me?"

It was Gerwalta's voice. Or at least, it sounded very much her, only harsher, straining, almost guttural.

It was at that moment that Andreas realized he was in tremendous, terrible pain. On his rump. A wolf's tail had not been designed by the creator with the purpose of being used as a handle, but such was their situation, for his beloved had literally caught him by it. From the pull he felt, Andreas wondered if it may actually separate from his body, leaving only a nub.

"Change! I... need... your hand... to pull... you up!" Gerwalta demanded, straining to tug him up to the parapet where she had somehow managed to remain.

Until he realized, she wasn't on the parapet at all.

The konigswolf pushed down every instinct in his body telling him to run, despite the fact that he was hanging in midair, held up by nothing but Gerwalta's grip, and she held up by nothing but the grace of the Lord Almighty and an ability to do the impossible.

"Change... back!"

But if I do, where does my tail go, love? What will you be holding on the other side?

The answer to that did not encourage him to comply in the least.

There was a choice to be made, and made very quickly. On the one paw, he could refuse to change, likely fall to his death or at the very least, to his great detriment, and in doing so, allow Gerwalta to appear to have been his downfall. It may cover their romantic tracks enough for her to return to her family with her reputation unscathed. Or, he could comply, be saved, and in turn, strive to be the death of them both.

He'd rather spend a lifetime fighting for her than a moment dying without her.

Andreas would have called it a leap of faith, but the use of any description including "leap" didn't appeal. Mustering all his strength, the wolf pulled his body in, curling his spine and bending up at the waist, even as he raged a war against the pull of the full moon above beckoning him to remain in fur. Gerwalta seemed to understand his attention; better to grab on to something frankly more grabbable on the top half of his body than to try and hold him by the... *leg.* In one consuming expenditure of her strength, she heaved him skyward, as though attempting to toss him back onto the parapet.

A brief moment of paw, and a split second of skin. Andreas reached.

"I've got you!"

Gerwalta's two hands gripped vicelike around his wrists just as the ground below tried to claim him as a victim, sending another ripple of pain as his shoulder popped out of its socket.

"Andreas!" She pulled even harder, and likely would have lifted him too, if not for the fact that, lingering in midair like a cloud, Gerwalta had no solid service against which to gain leverage. "I'm going to float us down. Don't let go."

"I thought…" *Breathe*. "…you said you…" *Whimper*. "…couldn't fly."

"I am *not* flying. I am falling very slowly."

"So you have fallen for me at last? It did take long enough."

"Keep at that, and I will slay you myself ere we reach ground."

"You will require no weapon. I am in love with you. You need only tell me that you do not feel the same, and I will fall down dead."

If he was expecting some sort of passionate embrace or at the very least, kind words, when again they stood on solid earth at a safe distance from where Bernard sat, broken and breathing fast, the konigswolf was sorely mistaken. In this case, literally. Gerwalta reached up, not for his embrace, but for his shoulder, where his arm hung at an odd angle at his side. With an upward jab, the dislocated appendage cut daggers into his sense of manhood. Like a wolf, a forest animal, Andreas knew better than to call out when could be helped. This couldn't be. At least his cry was brief and the pain equally as transient.

"Matters other than your heart require attention, Herr Baron."

"You wish to give attention to other parts of me?" He grinned, despite the truth of her words. "Your grip on my tail was amazingly firm."

The wolfsretter was rendered Janus-faced. Outwardly, she wore a scowl, but he did not believe the blush in her cheeks was from anger. Gerwalta spun on her heel, conjuring her cloak as she did. Intrigued by the development, he proceeded to follow her as she crossed ground to her errant cousin.

Bernhard did not rise, though he did lift his head to observe them. The blood would have turned the stomach of any fair maiden. Gerwalta, however, was made of tougher materials.

Andreas stated the obvious. "He landed on his own sword."

"It's silver," Gerwalta stated flatly. "It won't kill him,

unfortunately."

"A fourth daughter? Who'd have thought?" The gurgle in Bernhard's voice likely meant he'd sustained internal injuries. Either that, or he'd bitten off part of his tongue when he'd landed. Possibly both. "Does Mommy know you can fly?"

"Why does everyone keep accusing me of flying?" the other wolfsretter huffed, crossing her arms over her chest. "If I could, why do you suppose I have not escaped before now?"

Andreas looked at her askance. "Why didn't you?"

Gerwalta ignored the konigswolf, leaning at her cousin's side. "Let us speak of a new agreement, Bernhard. One where you are allowed to live in exile, but live nonetheless, and you never speak a word of my betrayal to anyone."

"And, what, simply tell the Emperor that we have had a change of mind and no longer intend to serve him? Too many know for us to pull back the truth now, regardless of whether I live or you die."

"You heard Ferdinand. He's keen that the church not learn of his associations with us. There are many, many ecclesiastical ears and eyes in the court of the Holy Roman Emperor. I'm quite certain everyone who knew was in that room. Only his closest guards would have been trusted to accompany him, and they're sworn to secrecy."

"But Ferdinand knows." Bernhard's bloody smile spread wide across his face. "Or are you contemplating regicide, cousin?"

Before Gerwalta could offer her return, a blanket of growls fell over them.

Both wolf and wolfsretter turned, Bernhard for his part swiveling his head, to where a very bloody, very fearsome, very threatening pack of lupines was stalking slowly towards them.

"Andreas?"

The instinct to protect overrode extant realities. Gerwalta stepped in front of the konigswolf, arms wide, hands itching for silver.

Behind her, a rumble of low laughter emanated from Andreas's chest. "You are a darling, lambkin, but no need to fear me. No wolf in Stephen's pack would harm me without his order, even on full moon."

"Stephen's pack?" Her arms dropped as she spun to him. "Your brother is a—"

Without letting her finish the question, the konigswolf leaned in and kissed the tip of her nose. "We're not getting the resolution to this we would have expected, are we?"

No, in so many ways.

Gently pushing her aside—she suspected in a show of dominance, for the sake of maintaining their audience's respect—Andreas approached the pack just as the wolf at its center, whom she recognized as Stephen, emerged. Being that they were kin, and as they all had just been through a heated, deadly confrontation with both traitors to their kind and imperial guards, she supposed she shouldn't judge them for their sentimental reunion, full of whimpering and, in Stephen's case, excessive licking. She hadn't the proper time to do it anyhow, for soon enough Gerwalta found herself observing the most peculiar thing with stark fascination.

Andreas, as a man, and Stephen, as a wolf, began to carry on a conversation.

"No, I agree, you couldn't possibly come back to the Schwartzwald now."

Yip, yap, whine. Pointed staring while breathing heavily with ears pulled back.

"We could seek the wolfsretter's aid with—"

Teeth bared. Snarl.

"Peace, brother, it was merely a thought. My suggestion, at the very least, would be to leave the Holy Roman Empire. If Ferdinand wants retribution, he'll come after you first."

Whimper. Yip.

"Yes, England *might* be a good idea. A bit of water between you and here would offer some security. You might even consider Scotland."

Growl.

"*Not* Scotland, then..."

"Gentlemen!" Gerwalta wondered if it were wise to express

her frustration so openly, given a group of moon-crazed packlings restrained only by Stephen's good nature were within striking distance and she was without any weapon. "May I remind you that we are *still* in the courtyard of Ferdinand's most prized castle, having just slaughtered his most trusted guards and several of his valuable conspirators? Perhaps the pleasantries can be exchanged once we have *escaped*?"

Bark. Yip. Cocked head.

A grin spread over Andreas's face as he turned to look at her for the briefest moment, then returned his gaze to his brother. "Yes, as soon as she realizes it." Before Gerwalta could inquire the meaning behind that cryptic statement, he turned on her. "What of him?"

The konigswolf jerked his head in Bernhard's direction.

Gerwalta pivoted and observed with some amazement how her cousin managed to still be so smug despite laying on the ground, impaled on his own sword. "The sliver cannot kill you, Bernhard, but the bleeding will unless I take you to a physician. If I draw the sword from your body, will you swear to leave the Red Clan regions forever, and renounce this foolish pride of yours?"

"You could accompany my brother's pack to England," Andreas added. "They would be more easily settled in a new region if accompanied by a wolfsretter for balance."

"I would rather die in battle than live exiled and ashamed."

He pushed himself up slowly, even as the pain warped his features and the blood trickled down the outside of his attire. His silver sword had entered his back, on the right side of his body and angled upward such that its tip jutted out just below his rib cage. Bernhard wrapped his hands around the bloody point, bringing on a new trickle from his fingers and accompanying that which flowed from his abdomen. With a deep inhale and shaky exhale, both of which seemed to cause him great agony, the form of the sword melted, pooling liquid for a shimmering moment before it reformed, blade out and handle in hand, in the wolfsretter's grip.

"A pack animal should respect that wish." Bernhard turned his head and spit red, before dragging his tattered sleeve over the corner of his mouth. He lifted the sword. "And that's all you are, a pack animal."

Stephen took two steps forward, growling.

Andreas waved his brother back. "At ease, brother. If we kill him, even in battle, it will only work against us. Let him stay, if he wished, and sew back together his cloak of deceit. I think he'll find it more difficult without our help. Gerwalta—" He held out his hand to her. "Come, love. It's over."

The fact that her head spun hearing his endearments meant their story was anything but.

"If Stephen is to leave, take this night and the final moon to run together as brothers. I will meet you come dawn, on the Ulm road, so we can make the journey together."

The konigswolf looked at her with narrowed eyes. "And Bernhard?"

She shrugged. "He is still my kin. You raced across the land for yours. Surely I can take a few more steps for mine."

If there was one thing the wolf understood, it was family. Andreas smiled and gave her a nod. Then, for no reason she could fathom, he pulled her into his embrace, his naked flesh against her regrettably clothed figure, and kissed her to distraction.

He bit her bottom lip before pulling away. "Tomorrow, we need to speak of my intentions. They are honorable, I assure you."

A half smile ticked up on her face as she dared a looked down the planes of his stomach. "Evidence suggests otherwise."

Andreas said no more, but the look of lust that filled his eyes was enough to make the wolfsretter swoon. Two blinks later, he had shifted, and the pack made their escape.

Bernhard turned his head and spit. "You cannot truly be in love with one of them."

"Who said I was?"

"Your eyes, even if your red, rosy lips still deny it." The sword dropped down somewhat. "You know the consequences from such a union, do you not? Or was it a lie all along? His supposed errand to retrieve his brother an excuse for the two of you to get out from under the press of your mother's thumb, and under his... well, I don't suppose it would be his *thumb* he'd be pressing against you, is it?"

She ignored his barb. "How long have you been conspiring with vampires, Bernhard?"

The sudden pivot made him blink thrice in rapid succession. "What are you talking about?"

"The only lupine pack which spawns female kings is in Constantinople, and the coins in the red bag were marked with Ottoman words. I can't read it of course, but I recognize it from correspondence my mother receives from the Clan of Black." She took two steps forward, despite her lack of weapon. "Aldhild—or whatever her name truly was for I suspect that is an alias—must have come from there, along with enough trinkets to buy an audience with the Emperor himself. Silver tributes are not what a lupine would choose, though. Vampires wanting to seed dissension in enemy territory, however? If I were them, that would be my move."

"You see ripe fields where only fallow ones lie." He raised his sword again. "Will you end me or no? I grow weary."

"That's why you have the cart, and your two hired thugs, isn't it?" she continued. "Because a portion of it was promised to you if you cooperated. You *sold* your people's honor and secrets for what? Silver? Silver you did not even *earn?*"

"Spare me your lectures of honor. A leader *takes* what is desired, but force and by fury. Only a slave accepts whatever pittance his master sees worthy to give him, expecting nothing more."

The footfalls came from the corners of the courtyard. Soldiers, ones who would finally been roused and readied, pulled away from dinner and dormitories, approached with haste. Time was running out.

"Is that what you believe you are, a slave?" She pointed to the tower above. "Every man save the Messiah is a slave to something or someone. All you did was find a new master, but I don't believe it was Ferdinand. Who is it, then? Who corrupted a righteous wolfsretter?"

They fell in now, the soldiers, coming to stand in a circle about them. She did not know if the imperial men knew of her cousin, or would offer Bernhard any deference. All she knew was that they all had swords drawn, and she did not.

"You, you there!" A half-dressed man with a bushy mustache and rosy, plump cheeks called out. *He must be the captain,* Gerwalta thought. "Drop your weapon. We have you surrounded. Let the lady go, and we shall spare you."

Bernhard spat blood. "*She* could kill every one of you before you could blink. As could I." His gaze sharpened. "You know that to be true, don't you, Walta? Even injured as I am."

"You could." There was no point in denying what was true.

"You want to know who corrupted me? To whom I am truly indentured?" Bernhard pulled back his sword, as though to strike her. "I fear you shall meet him anon, when I am gone. A monster, Wall. That's who. And I'd rather face Lucifer than him with my failure. Goodbye, cousin."

He spun, darted, swung. Mortal men were no match, but Bernhard would have them justify his own death. As ten swords simultaneously sliced into Bernhard, severing limbs, opening his stomach and letting his guts spill forth, Gerwalta took advantage of the distraction, turned, and ran as fast as she possibly could.

TWENTY-SIX

The child who found him on the road and delivered Gerwalta's message couldn't have been more than eight. Old enough to heed direction without the intellect to ask too many questions. Young enough to repeat meaningless things like "not coming" and "go back without her" without understanding the pain such words inflicted.

Heartache weighed down his steps, Andreas's sorrows sinking into his boots. The journey back to the Schwartzwald took so much longer without her, the road harder on his feet. At least when he reached the place where fields gave way to elms and oaks, he could take to the woods instead. Five days in, the konigswolf reclaimed the natural rhythm of his kind, sleeping in the day, traversing the woodlands by night. When hungry, he did as animals would: hunt down small prey and partake of it. When he tired, he rested.

When he longed for her touch, the wolf threw back his head and bayed.

Had he read her wrong? Andreas didn't think so. Gerwalta's kiss lit fires within him, consumed him. She'd never tipped her heart fully to him, yet he felt the truth of her sentiments instinctively. He couldn't explain to any rational creature how their affections had grown, and in so short a time, but it was what it was. He *loved* her, and it had come about without a mating bond and despite their conflicting natures.

He wanted her to be his wife.

There could never be another.

The waning moon looked impaled on the edge of Schloss Wolfsretter's fortress tower, the dim light enough to illuminate the forested valley that stretched out below.

Gerwalta knew Andreas had made it back; Helga had reported that she'd learned as much when she'd returned from her patrols two nights before.

Gunda Faust grumbled. "Despite your lack of follow-through."

The youngest Faust ate the insult without objection. "My mission was only to accompany the konigswolf and to keep my eyes open at court. Making my way home with him was not a responsibility you laid at my feet."

It didn't surprise her that he'd gotten back faster than she did. No doubt Andreas gained some ground the very night they'd fled Nuremberg, running with his brother one last time before Stephen fled for England. After that, the konigswolf could have taken to four feet as soon as the forest allowed. Meanwhile, Gerwalta labored on two, using the distance and time to construct both a cover for their exploits, and to lecture her heart on what its priorities must be.

Her mother let out a guttural chuff. She did so hate cheekiness, even more so when the cheeky one was also stating the truth.

Then, seeing an opportunity to impress upon her Matron the utter disgust she would have felt doing so, added, "Besides, what cause would I have to be a travel companion to a lupine of my own free will?"

"Yes, I see how that would have been..." Gunda's unnatural youthful face screwed up. "...undesirable. But you did do as I asked, did you not?"

Gerwalta dared a direct look at Helga, all while schooling her features and her voice, desperate not to reveal her worry. "Did Herr Baron not share with you the details of the journey?"

Her eldest sister liked to adopt an air of authority, practicing for the time when she would become Matron. Or so Helga assumed she would, as the eldest righteous sibling, with the others having demonstrated no other traits which would suggest an exception to the chronological selection.

Then again, no one knew that Gerwalta could fly.

Helga crossed her leather-clad hands over her chest and clicked her tongue. "Refused to say anything more than his brother is dead, then asked me to leave him and his pack alone for a while to mourn in private."

"Stephen is dead?" Gunda raised a precarious eyebrow. "Is that true?"

She swallowed her relief. Thank goodness that the story she concocted would mesh with what Andreas had said. "Yes, Stephen was killed after reaching the imperial court. But not by me."

Helga's arms dropped to her side. "By who, then?"

"By Bernhard Dreger."

Even the Matron flinched at that. "Maria's son? What cause would Bernhard have to be in Nuremberg?"

"One of his own making, I believe," Gerwalta said. The key to selling a lie was to blanket it in just enough truth to keep the deceit warm. "It was Bernhard who has been undermining our silver contracts."

"That's impossible!" Gunda protested. "I provide Maria's clan with plenty enough silver to serve our sacred duty. It would not be enough to undersell me. And even if it were, to undersell me with *my own silver!*"

Suddenly, Helga laughed, throwing back her head and cackling. "Oh, don't you see, Mother? This is just another of Gerwalta's attempts to avoid marriage. She knows you've chosen him as her intended."

Gunda was anything but amused. One slashing look cut Helga down to silence. Apparently, Gerwalta was not to have known about the arrangements. Curious, why? It wasn't as if she would have objected to Bernhard, back when she was ignorant of his scheming. It was something else, then, wasn't it?

"It will be quite impossible to marry him now," she interrupted. "Bernhard Dreger is dead."

"But you said..." Gunda pressed fingers to her temples. "Enough of this piecemeal explanation. Tell me the whole of it, Gerwalta. What happened in Nuremberg?"

"Bernhard was conspiring with a female lupine queen to reveal our kind to the emperor, and in so doing, to enlist all the dark ones in the war with the east."

She left out "under the command of the Imperial Court." Better to handle one catastrophe at a time, and only as needed.

Both her mother and her older sister blanched, but it was Helga who recovered first. "A lupine *queen*?"

"An anathema," Gerwalta confirmed. "A shewolf king. Don't worry, sister. She has also been slain."

"Good." Gunda rose from her throne. "While the number of corpses you left in your wake is more than I would have preferred, you did what needed to be done to resolve the issues before you. I will write to Maria and demand she appear at court immediately to answer for Bernhard's betrayal. But where was she getting so much silver?"

Here, Gerwalta resumed the lie, even if just by omitting the truth as she knew it. Then again, what did she really know? Nothing about what she learned in Nuremberg either indicted or absolved Maria Breger of involvement, but nothing Maria could know would be able to implicate Gerwalta's own wrongdoings. And if Maria wasn't involved, her testimony in the Matron's court would release her from any punishment.

Her mother descended the dais and raised a gloved hand to stroke her daughter's cheek. "I know you had some softness towards Bernhard. It was one of the reasons I sought to match you with him. Do not linger on his memory too long. A traitor is worthy only of disdain."

She swallowed back the lurch in her stomach. *Would she disdain me if she knew my heart?* "I shan't, Matron."

Gunda's hand dropped away. "When Maria comes, we will have our answers. You have done well, Gerwalta, inflicting your will on a king wolf in the lay world. Your father worried that keeping you from patrols would make you soft, but I assured him, you were the toughest of all my daughters."

Beside the Matron, Helga flinched for a brief moment, but she dare not speak.

Their mother continued. "You will begin patrolling the packlands with your sisters henceforth, tomorrow, after you've had a chance to rest."

"If it would please the Matron, I would start now, tonight."

Even Gunda quirked an eyebrow at that. "Zelda and Gretchen will have nearly completed their rotation now, and the sun will rise in an hour or so."

Could she sell the lie? She'd never know unless she tried.

"I managed to keep the konigswolf under my control for nearly a fortnight. I do not want Andreas Baron thinking merely because we are back in the Schwarzwald, that I am any less of a threat to him."

The Matron grinned. "Very good, indeed. Go then, and bring him to heel. The nerve of him, telling *us* to keep our distance so he can mourn. What does he suppose we are, fools?"

TWENTY-SEVEN

In the back pasture, little Jacob and Jelena Kosner crawled over a fallen tree nearly as tall off the ground as were they. Minding pups at play was not a usual task taken on by the konigswolf, but since returning from his sojourn, Andreas sought anything to distract him from his own thoughts. It also gave Wilhelm and Lisi, the pups' parents, a rare opportunity for intimacy. Perchance it would result in another Kosner pup, and blessing from the Lord if it did. The pack needed its legacy secured.

The next king would not be his child, after all.

So what if his bloodline would die out here in the Schwarzwald? Who could say if his heritage was truly so special to begin? Only the word of ancestors long dead, and an agreement among peers to consider it truth.

Jacob Kosner had come into his fur just this past summer, a strapping lad at six, and sharp as a blade. The boy's brown curls bounced on his head as he ran in circles, chasing his sister. The girl, a year younger, was lithe, but her older sibling had a keen advantage. Where a boy was one moment, a small, juvenile pup bounced about the next. Lisi Kosner would foam when she saw. Jacob's britches would be ruined—again—but such was the woe of raising a lupine child.

The wolfling nipped the little girl's ankle, making her call out.

"No fair!" Jelena stopped on the spot and pushed balled fists into her hips. "Andreas, tell him no fair. I can't take fur yet!"

He reached for the child, pulling her up to rest on his knee. "He ought to be glad about it too, ey? The moment you can, I think it's Jacob who will be on the run."

Jelena held up her two index fingers to her mouth, feigning fangs and making a yipping sound. "I will bite his butt."

Andreas threw back his head and surprised even himself with the laugh. *Bless a child to shed light in the dark recesses of the broken heart.* He planted a kiss atop Jelena's amber crown. "Yes, you will, darling. You—"

His senses alerted almost too late. No sooner had he perceived the presence of a wolfsretter then he looked across the field and saw one standing there, out where the fences bordered the forest.

The child shook in place, but her little brother placed himself between her and the interloper, ready to do everything in his power to defend his sister.

"Jacob, take your sister back to the house. I will deal with the wolfsretter."

The little girl's voice shook. "Is she going to kill us?"

Jelena's words nearly broke his heart. The children were the most vulnerable, and the least able to understand the nuances of the dynamic the two species maintained.

"No, my pet, but that does not mean you should not run. Go now, and ready yourselves for bed. I will come to help you shortly. Fraulein Faust only wants to talk."

He hoped.

His young packlings did not wait for further encouragements; they sped off with haste, leaving Andreas to make his way across the field.

He trudged his way across the distance, all the while scanning the treeline, looking for the second flank. The Matron's children always patrolled in twos. Much to his surprise, he could detect no second party.

"You are in violation of our agreement, Fraulein Helga," Andreas called. "You are permitted to patrol around the boundaries of our farm, but you are supposed to write an official request to enter the grounds unless in cases of utter need."

The wolfsretter did not speak. Instead, her lithe hands drew to her head, whereupon she pulled down the hood of her cloak, revealing herself not to be the Matron's eldest daughter at all, but the youngest.

The konigswolf lectured his body to stay upright. "Gerwalta?"

Her words were soft, timid. "We must speak. Quickly. Are you amenable?"

Andreas nodded. She turned then, also surveying the trees for company, before motioning him to follow her into them. The konigswolf checked on his young packlings once more. In the distance, Jelena and Jacob had nearly reached the home in the center of their cleared lands. They'd be inside in a moment, and none other of his pack were close enough to observe them.

The twenty-three steps that took them away from the pasture, over the fence, and into the privacy of the trees were the heaviest he'd ever trod, weighed down by contemplation.

"Gerwalta, please. Tell me what happened. I was so fearful—"

She gave no chance to finish his query. In the time it took her to turn, Gerwalta was on him, lips to lips, mouth to mouth, and heart to heart.

Gerwalta's kiss robbed him of a man's reason, left nothing but the wolf and its hunger. Blood raced through his veins, an animal urge to quell his questions and satisfy his longing. Andreas's hands skirted down her backside, fixing a grip that allowed him leverage. He pulled her up, her legs encircling him at the hips, all as she continued to devour his kiss. Only when he took his own mouth back and used it to nip at her neck did she have a chance to speak.

"Bernhard is dead."

"Good." Then their secret was safe.

"My mother thinks Stephen is dead."

He pushed her back into a thick oak, pinning her there, using the freedom it allowed his hands to pull at the buckle securing her cloak just under her throat. "I told Helga as much."

Her hands pressed into the sides of his face. "Tell me you love me."

"You have my heart, my fealty, my..." The konigswolf threw back his head and chuckled. "Whatever you want that I have, it is yours. I surrender all to you."

Gerwalta pressed a kiss to his lips. "Do I have your will?"

"I serve you, my lamb." He pulled back her collar, revealing a tempting morsel of collarbone, which he immediately felt obliged to suckle. "I am your slave."

Her fingers threaded through his hair, pushing him harder into his labors. "Then mate."

He laughed against her flesh. "I am attempting to, dear heart."

"No, not... Not me."

The konigswolf stilled. "But I love *you*."

"Irrelevant." Gerwalta let her legs fall, reclaiming her own two feet. "Andreas, you must."

He didn't feel like kissing her all of a sudden. No, that was a lie. He very much desired it, but that same mouth which fed his heart was now saying things to break it. The space that grew between them was so much more than physical; it sank into his skin.

His voice sounded foreign to his own ears. "Knowing how I feel for you, you would have me take another as wife?"

How could she smile and cry at the same time? The wolfsretter: duplicitous even in emotions.

"I would have you be happy." She placed a gloved hand on his chest. "Is it not true that your heart will fall to whomever you first bed?"

"It's the defect of my kind, making traitors of heartstrings. But Gerwalta, how could I bed another when it is *your* body I want beneath me?"

That made her gasp a little. *Good,* he thought. *I grow weary of being the one always to burn while she can stay so cool.*

"Andreas... You must have realized this could never be. You are a wolf. I, your sworn enemy and overseer. If any of my kin learn that I've so much as kissed you, it means your death."

Was that truly her concern. "And your exile?"

Her hands caught him just below his sternum, pushing him away. "Fie, my exile! What life could I have knowing my childish desires had ended you?"

But a konigswolf in love was no easy thing to eschew. He reclaimed her hand, pulling it to his lips, kissing the back of her knuckles. "Then we'll run away."

"No! Your pack needs you, especially on the heels of losing your brother."

"They'll come with us then."

"Force them to give up their homes, their livelihoods, just to satisfy your own heart? What kind of king would force his people to do such a thing?"

The solidity of his determination turned to sand flowing through his fingers. "Perhaps if we kept to the shadows..."

"And how would I hide such a thing from my husband?"

"Husband?" Andreas blinked fiercely, as though blinded in the moment. "But Bernhard is dead."

"He is, but I believe my mother now feels this mission of ours has somehow proven my mettle. She will marry me off soon enough. Andreas..." Gerwalta crossed to him, putting a hand to the huffing wolf's cheek. "Take a mate. Give me the comfort of knowing there is someone here able to love you in my stead."

"Would that you say it once, Gerwalta. Then, maybe you could not so easily deny what your heart—" He leaned into her touch, closing his eyes, savoring the moment. "Please, Gerwalta. I would hear it from you."

"Andreas, I... I *Iah*... I... I cannot."

A snap of branch, a rush of wind, and the konigswolf opened his eyes to find himself alone.

A lesser man would grieve. In fact, Andreas had been grieving since the morning after Nuremberg. But as he walked back across the field toward the farmhouse, he had to lecture himself not to skip, lest he give himself away. His wolves would want to know why his demeanor had turned about with such force and so fast. He'd have to tell his pack eventually, of course. Even the dullest lupine would notice his king take a wolfsretter as mate. First he'd have to win her hand, however. Then, he could go about changing their hearts.

Gerwalta Faust had said many things just now, but one thing she had not said was that she did not love him. Even if she had, it would be a lie. He tasted her love in their kiss. Scented her desire in the air when they embraced. Heard the spike of her pulse when he spoke of his hunger for her body. The matron's fourth daughter was just as gone on him as he was on her. They *were* mates already, in every way but the deed. He wouldn't discount Gerwalta's hesitance to submit to her own heart; he was not so blinded by his feelings to discard reality. When they succeeded in being together, their union would fly in the face of centuries of tradition.

But as he'd told Gerwalta, he sensed a change in the winds.

A new world was coming, one in which a wolfsretter and a lupine could be together.

One in which he would wed himself to a wolfsretter, and where Gerwalta Faust would be his bride.

THE WOLF
AND THE
WATCHER

RED ORIGINS

BOOK TWO

ONE

Andreas Baron, konigswolf of the Schwarzwald pack, could split logs from Michaelmas until Christmas and still, the angst would remain.

Wilhem should not have been surprised, therefore, to find half of the fuel they'd need to make it through winter chopped and piled. What *did* surprise him was how his king achieved the work of three lupines in one night.

"Good health, *mein konig*?"

Andreas paused, the axe raised high, to glare at his packling. "Do you question my constitution?"

Wilhelm's eyes cast to the ground as his body curled in on itself. "No, Andreas, of course not."

Andreas let his tool fall to the ground and rounded. "Then what business?"

The packling dared a glance upward. "Lisi is asking you to come sup before she puts the pups to bed. It is nearly dawn."

"Give your mate my thanks, but I am not hungry."

"But, *mein konig*, you haven't eaten a proper meal in two days. Or did you sneak off to the forest to take down a few coneys again?"

The kingwolf huffed. "And if I did? Am I not a predator? Should I not eat of the land as a predator is wont to do?"

Lord forbid the konigswolf should think his prerogatives were being questioned twice in so many winks. "It is justified to draw from the world that which it gives willingly. But you are also a man, and a man needs rest. Even the Almighty allowed himself his due on the seventh day."

The Almighty had never had to fight off the urges of a full

moon growing near while living in the shadow of the woman he loved. How long had it been since they'd spoken? A year? At least that long.

"It has been a long night. But there's still much wood left to split."

Wilhelm patted Andreas's shoulder. "We'll do it together tomorrow. Come along now, my king, or Lisi will have both of our paws in the trap."

Snap.

Wilhelm fell in behind his king as the sensation gripped them both: a lurch in the stomach, a buzz in the head. They were no longer alone, even though neither could spot their interloper through the nearby trees.

The wind shifted, carrying the scent of freshly cut pine and silver.

"Curse the devil! What do they want?" Wilhelm asked. "And just when we're about to bed down for the day!"

Andreas wondered as well, but knew no matter how much he hoped, it wouldn't be her. Gerwalta patrolled these woods now, as she'd done since they returned from Nurenmberg, but the one he loved could slide through the trees without being spotted. More likely it was Helga, the Matron's first-born daughter and heir apparent, dropping by for a weekly shake down.

"Go, Wilhem." Andreas pushed his packling toward the direction of the farm as he himself turned deeper into the forest. "I'll be along shortly. Tell Lisi I'll help square away the pups for bed."

"Just as long as you tell whatever red-hooded ninny this turns out to be that she ought come at a more decent hour." Wilhelm moved along, but called back over his shoulder. "Next time you're hunting about the forest, you ought to find one of them to eat. Do us all a favor."

Andreas cringed at the thought. Animal though he was, hunter though God had made him, he'd never partake of dark one flesh. As he made his way to the forest's edge, however, he did consider other things that he could do involving his mouth and one particular wolfsretter's skin.

The image in his mind knocked the wind from his lungs and

put his heart into his manhood. He found himself arrested, struggling to forgo a much more pleasant projection of what lay before him than humiliation.

And then suddenly, he caught the sight of red hair blowing in the breeze.

"Resplendent."

The word leapt from his heart unto his lips before he could stop himself. His love stood before him in her warrior's cloak, a deep scarlet fabric that stood out against the snow-kissed monochromatic backdrop of the winter forest. A berry ripe for eating. A rose blooming among ruin, waiting to be picked.

She was not the same untried flower he'd journeyed across the land beside a year before. His love had passed from a young protégé barely come into her powers to hardened warrior of a wolfblood-hungry heritage. Her stoic resolve proved that the fantasies he'd entertained of their next encounter, one that began with her running into his arms and out of her clothing, were simply that—make believe.

"Herr Baron." Gerwalta's arm jerked into view from under the folds of her red cloak, bearing a scroll in her outreached hand. "I come on behalf of the Matron."

Formality was a cruelty for those who loved. It frosted the heart, chilled desires. Andreas found himself playing the role she'd forced him into.

Smile absconded, the wolf seized the paper, breaking the Matron's red wax seal. "It is an invitation to a ball."

Gerwalta met his raised eyebrow with silence.

"At Schloss Wolfsretter," he continued. Other details were brief, but that didn't make them any less curious. He pushed the scroll into a pocket in his coat. "Why is the Matron inviting me, a lupine, to a wolfsretter ball?"

"I do not question my mother's decisions. I cannot say." The first crack in her resolve emerged, and much to his dismay, it was to huff in frustration. "I was charged with delivering the invitation to you, Herr Konigswolf, and I have done so. If you wish to discuss that matter further, you may send word to my mother to…"

He caught her by the arm as she spun to leave. He'd have thought he'd kissed her, the way her body lit up at his touch, her cheeks blushing, her heart pounding.

All signs of attraction. But were not these also the signs of an oncoming attack?

Gerwalta fixed him with a poisonous glare. "You *will* unhand me, for your sake."

If she wished to hurt him, she could. Gerwalta wore no silver in plain sight, but a wolfsretter rarely did. Andreas had no doubt that with a flick of her fingers, the metal would leech from the hidden confines of her attire and burn rivers into his skin. Her touch was worth the pain.

Instead of moving away, Andreas stepped closer, bringing her back flush to his chest, his hand still clasped on her arm. "I would rather *hand* you, Walta. Excessively."

"I thought we settled this matter the last we met." Her words made the chill in the air feel warm by comparison.

"Only if by settling you mean that you asked me to do something abhorrent, and I refused." His mouth danced over the skin beneath her ear, and still, she did not move. "I will never mate another."

"Then you'll die alone and without an heir."

As soon as his lips closed over the juicy lobe of her ear, it was over. Andreas did not know when Gerwalta had moved, for every moment and every movement had taken on such a dreamy state, his being was liquid without fine borders. Only when her warmth was filled in by pockets of cold did he look up to find his hooded love peering down at him from the tree limbs above.

"Why torture yourself like this?"

"Tis you who tortures me, love." He opened his arms, beckoning her. "Your denial is the mace that strikes my flesh. Your absence, the chains that bind me to hope."

"Hope? To what end?" she spat back, stepping off the branch, drifting gracefully down with inhuman leisure. "Every word you utter of this love lunacy dips the quill to the inkwell from which your death warrant is written. For a whole year, I have left you be so that you may squelch this idiocy. Did you waste your time on fantastical dreams of reunion? Why are you so intent to die?"

"It is death for me *not* to love you. Walta, please…"

She didn't allow herself to touch ground, remaining in a hover, bobbing like a feather on the rippling stream. Nevertheless, when he stepped forward and took her gloved hands in his, though the conflict warred in her eyes, she gave no retreat.

"…I will have but one love and one mate, and it will be you."

"Please, stop." Her head lashed to the side. "I beg of you, forget me. Find another. Have a dozen pups and teach them well to fear my kind, as even I fear my own."

All his tenderness took flame. "Who do you fear? Has someone hurt you? Name her and I'll have her throat."

"Killing the Matron would only lead to the destruction of your whole pack."

Tentative words belied the fervor of injustice he felt. "Your own mother causes you injury? By what measure and with what purpose?"

"For the desire to see me wed, Herr Baron, and by whatever measure she deems necessary." Her hand fished into the hidden pocket on his chest, pulling out the very missive that had brought her back to the packlands. "Invitations are going out to houses from Eire to Anatolia. A call for the Matrons of each territory to send any eligible son who wishes to vie for my hand. From those, she will choose whomever she deems worthy, and my consort that man shall be."

"But…" Andreas's mouth went dry. In what terms could he object to such a disgrace? If the tongues of man had such words, he did not know them. "You love *me*."

"I am the daughter of the Red Matron. I love whomever she commands." Gerwalta elevated herself a little more. "Please, forget me. Come to the ball and let your silence be my favor. Do not give my mother any opportunity to question her dominance, and especially do not look at me the way you are now, or all will know your love for me. It is bad enough that I feel it even still."

Before she'd allow another moment of protest, Gerwalta

disappeared into the virgin light of morn.

TWO

She made sure to put her feet back to solid ground the moment she'd gained a goodly distance. Then, she struggled to keep those feet pointing toward home. What a lamentable fool she'd been. She'd avoided Andreas Baron for a year *because* she feared seeing him would spark her feelings once more. When her mother had given her the invite to the ball, and the explicit instruction that *she* would be the one to deliver it to the konigswolf, she'd retaliated for the first time in her life.

"Why should I tolerate a werewolf at the ball? Do we mean to sicken my suitors?"

Gunda rubbed the crumbs from a bit of fruited bread from her fingers. "I agree, it's loathsome. But this is an occasion when many a bloodline's envoys will be watching for what kind of a family and daughter I'm offering in marriage. Having the konigswolf there, and assuring he demonstrates obedience, gives an opportunity for me to observe your suitors' reactions. I will choose a husband who delights in Baron's pain."

Even now, the thought turned her stomach. She hated to speculate on how her mother had planned for Andreas to "demonstrate obedience." The ball was still two months away; perhaps that would be enough time for her to wage a passive campaign? Her mother, however, was no fool. Would Gunda suspect the truth?

For the moment, Gerwalta resolved to pass the day in bed, entertaining happier imaginations. One of the few good things that came out of her experiences with Andreas Baron was the understanding that she liked kissing perfectly well.

Gerwalta was also willing to bet she'd find the other acts of lovemaking even more agreeable. As Gerwalta passed into the keep and overheard two of her siblings talking, her ear caught on her name, arresting her.

"... and I want to know why she gets to have a ball," Helga, her eldest sister, said. "Mother didn't feel the need to undertake such an elaborate affair for either of us."

Zelda, third-born daughter, clicked her tongue. "You know that Mother always intended Bernhard for Gerwalta, so that she could send them off to live in Bavaria and strengthen her eastern flank. But now, with Bernhard and Maria dead—"

Gerwalta winced at that, still wondering if she were somehow responsible for her great aunt's death. No one knew what was revealed by Maria when she'd been summoned to court. Gerwalta had been the one, however, to bring light to the plots of Maria's son, Bernhard, as well as the one to see to his death. Could have sparing Bernhard and dragging him back to the Schwarzwald had somehow exonerated her aunt? Or was Maria part of some grander conspiracy?

She'd never know. Maria had been relinquished of her powers by the Matron, and at some point shortly thereafter, was found dead in the castle. Had it been suicide or something more sinister? A plot devised and executed in the shadows so that Gunda could have plausible deniability? No one within the confines of Schloss Wolfsretter dared fret over the justice a relinquished should receive.

"Well, she needs to marry Gerwalta off to someone, doesn't she?" Zelda finished. "Now that Gretchen and Pierre have taken control of Maria's region, Mother can spread the influence of the House of Red beyond our little corner of the forest with the right match."

Helga hummed her agreement. "She still fears what has come from the east with the Ottoman advance. My silver says Gerwalta finds herself in the Balkans or even Anatolia come spring."

Zelda laughed. "Ah, just picture that! Our little sister, riding bareback and living in a yurt."

"Do they really live in yurts?" Helga's voice suggested both amazement and disgust. "Well, then, the House of Night is hardly better off than Andreas Baron, are they? At least the lupines here have a solid roof overhead."

"And cattle and sheep sleeping under their floorboards." Zelda gagged. "Can you imagine, the smell of their dung tickling your nose morning, noon, and night? It's bad enough when we have to get close enough to the lupines to smell *them*."

"Imagine what's like to be mated to one." The women fell silent for a moment. "Do you think they mate, you know, mixed?"

"Mixed?" Helga asked. "What do you mean? Man and woman? I should say so. They certainly have enough pups running around all the time, don't they?"

"No, I mean *mixed*. You know, whilst one of them is a beast and the other, laity. Animal upon man. Or perhaps, woman."

"Is it not bad enough they mate at all?" Helga returned. "In any case, I'm delighted mother agreed to my plan to invite the konigswolf to the ball. His farmer stupidity should make for entertaining times. Imagine *him* trying to dance the Volta!"

Gerwalta struggled to contain herself. She wanted to dart around the corner and lay into the pair of gossiping goats. Andreas Baron was *not* stupid. He was engaging, complex, compassionate... and a thousand other kinds of wonderful that they should wish of their own husbands.

Still, there was some truth to his being ignorant, though what shame there was in not knowing a thing because there wasn't a need, Gerwalta couldn't say. What use did Andreas have for court dances and wolfsretter etiquette? She herself had been drilled on such matter since infanthood and sometimes forgot protocol. But surely he could gain some elementary knowledge before the ball to avoid embarrassment if he were advised. *She* could even teach him the basics, a dance or two...

Though it would mean spending time with him, and *that* was where she'd be stupid. She'd barely avoided the temptation of his proximity as it was. She'd have thought a year spent afar would douse her passions. Or, at least, his, which burned hotter. No such luck. The only thing time had bought was tinder, and if allowed a single spark between them, they'd both combust.

Someone tapped the wolfsretter's shoulder from behind. "Fraulein?"

Gerwalta's pulse exploded. Not because of the castellan's presence, though she immediately chastised herself for being so wrapped up in her own thoughts she had not heard the laywoman's approach. Rather, because the chattering in the antechamber beyond had abruptly cut off, making her older sisters aware of an interloper handing on their every word.

"Therese." Gerwalta said as flatly as possible, pulling her cloak out of being. "What is it?"

Helga and Zelda by this time had gathered themselves and joined their youngest sibling in the hall, eyes narrowed, questioning without words what might have been overheard.

The castellan's eyes weighed down with annoyance. Half of Therese's gray hair came about from the bickering of the four daughters. The other half, from Helga's abuse.

"You mother is asking you to join her in the tower."

Helga cackled as Zelda gasped and Gerwalta blinked in confusion.

"What possible business could mother have with *Gerwalta* that would be worthy of visiting the tower?" the eldest asked.

Normally, Gerwalta would snap at such condescension. Respect her elder siblings though she must before their mother, when left to their own devices, every instigation was met with retaliation. *As though she considers me some sort of threat.* Gerwalta couldn't understand what had possessed the heir apparent. Perhaps if Helga knew Gerwalta could fly, there'd be cause, but she didn't. No one did.

Except Andreas.

Therese continued. "I am merely a servant to this house, Frau Helga. It is not my place to infer any of the Matron's business, nor is it *yours*."

Few in the castle could hope to talk down at one of the Faust women and get away with it, but Therese was castellan, her sole duty was to ensure the sanctity and security of Schloss Wolfsretter itself. If that meant keeping Helga's ego in check, so be it. She had the scars to prove she was willing to assume the risks.

Helga turned her eyes to the ground. "Apologies, Frau Sainte-Maire."

"Accepted. Now, Fraulein Gerwalta?" Theresa jerked her head to the left. "If you would, please follow me."

Schloss Wolfsretter, having been built on a cliff that rose high above the valley, had no need for a wider view than that afforded its locale. The purpose of its tower was not to keep watch over the outside world, but to draw the gazes of those within its walls. There were no stairs leading to its top, per se. Rather, there was only a corridor where stairs should be. Only the righteous could ascend, and only by the working of silver to create a walkway that pooled into existence before each step and disappeared in her wake. The effort to climb to the top took excessive amounts of concentration and no little amount of silver. Though in Gerwalta's case, that needn't be so. She could fly if she wanted, if she were fool enough to expose her secret.

She hoped what her sisters said was true, that her mother would choose a suitor for her who would take her far from the Schwarzwald. If she remained too close to Andreas, too many secrets could come to the light of day.

Finally etching out the last step, then reclaiming the silver and shaping it into a block she left at the landing, it was some shock that she found her mother's dining table set for dinner, and seated at it, a man with pale skin, eyes of coal, and cropped, ebony hair. Handsome? Perhaps, but in a subdued way. The looks were a ruse, she understood on some unconscious level. A beautiful trap. He smelled of threat, despite his humble musculature and lack of any visible weapon. No one mentioned a visitor. Would not her gossip-loving sisters have been clucking if they knew? How had he gotten into the tower without any of the wolfsretter below the wiser?

He rose when their eyes met, and Gerwalta pulled herself from distraction to bow her head in due diligence.

"My apologies for the interruption, Matron. I was told you wished to see me." She raised her head, moving concern from the stranger's presence to his purpose. "I did not know you were in audience."

"No need for apologies, Gerwalta. I meant for you to meet." The Matron deposited her stein on the table as she gathered to her feet. "Spatar Goran Karahan, I present my fourth-born daughter, the Righteous Gerwalta Faust of Red."

Her official title? So rare were the occasions, she'd forgotten the proper decorum. Should she, like the laity, curtsey? She didn't wear a dress, unless one counted the bottom edge of a tunic as skirting. Opting for wolfsretter etiquette, Gerwalta crisscrossed her arms tight into her chest and stepped one foot behind the other. No sooner had she endeavored to undertake the gesture, however, then she was stopped by Karahan's sudden appearance right before her.

Gerwalta leapt back, instinctively drawing a weapon into being.

Karahan's hands went out wide, showing empty palms. "Peace, Fraulein. I thought you perceived my nature and would know of my manner. I did not attend to frighten you."

"You…" She swallowed, hoping to wet a mouth that had suddenly gone dry. "You were just across the room."

Annoyance iced Gunda's tone. "He is a vampire, Gerwalta. Did you not understand that?"

The revelation should have made her more alert, but curiosity and amusement brought a smile to her face. "A vampire? In the Schwarzwald?" Then she recalled that she held a spear in her hand, its blade aimed for his heart, and allowed it to lower. "Apologies, but you are the first of your kind I have encountered in person… Spatar, was it?"

He grinned, taking her fingers in his hand and brushing a kiss against the back of her knuckles in the style of the laity courts. "The title is Romanian," he dropped her hand, "akin to your *Fürst*, I believe."

A prince? A prince of what? What kind of dark one held political office, and what would he be doing dining with the Red Matron?

"The Spatar comes all the way from Wallachia to extend a hand of friendship," the Matron said, refocusing their attention. With a wave of her hand, they sat. "He is an honored guest."

Gerwalta settled herself at the table, to the right of her mother, as the Spatar resumed his seat. "A friend is a most welcome thing indeed, Herr Spatar, though I do not think it required so long a journey."

The vampire's mouth cracked into an open smile. *No fangs.* Did not vampires have long canine teeth like the lupines? That's what she'd always heard. Did they shift into some other form as the wolves did?

"You were right about your daughter, Frau Matron," Karahan said. "Very observant. In truth, Fraulein," he turned back to her, "I have come via Ravensburg."

"Oh?" A stone dropped down Gerwalta's throat and settled into her stomach. "What business had you in Ravensburg, then?"

"I wished to hire a wolfsretter. One who could... eliminate the threat of a band of vampires causing some measure of disruption in the east."

At least he's not coming chasing the stories of what Andreas and I did in Nuremberg, then. The young wolfsretter lectured her manner, daparate not to show relief.

Gerwalta wove her fingers together and leaned over the table. "Is not this something a slayer would address? I was given to believe they balance your kind the way we do the lupines."

The vampire buried his frown behind a downward glance. "Verily, Fraulein, if I wished to kill the lot of them, that would be a wiser course of action. You are not a slayer; I cannot blame you for being unaware of the idiosyncrasies of vampires. You see, our natures prevent us from inducing the death of our own blooded-born. I do not know for certain if my asking a slayer to terminate my clutchson would, in fact, trigger my own death, but with seven involved, I need to be certain all are contained. Unfortunately, I do not have seven lives to give for the effort."

Gunda lowered her goblet. "Would not another bloodline would perform the deed for the right price?"

He clicked his tongue. "To do so would sow the seeds of a blood feud. No, Frau Matron, I am the author of this legacy, and I will write its final chapter the way I see best."

Her mother bobbed her head. "And we are somehow the quill you will use."

"As I cannot terminate my seven sons, I would have them contained. I wish for a wolfsretter to seal them in silver. I would then commit their care to you and your descendants."

"My descendants?" The wolfsretters exchanged furtive glances before Gunda continued. "How would you compensate my progeny?"

The vampire patted the corners of his mouth with a bit of cloth, though to the best of Gerwalta's recollection, he hadn't sampled a single thing on his plate. "What is it you wish, Frau Matron? Gold? Jewels? Land? I have all this and more and will give it gladly to see this task accomplished. I have a particularly fine estate just over the mountains to the south, on the edge of your dominion. If you wish it, it is yours."

Hunger narrowed Gunda's eyes. A Matron's power was drawn in part from the size of the region over which she reigned, and the amount of silver found therein. No doubt the Matron was considering now that the rich veins running through the southern regions of the Schwarzwald might also be found beyond the mountains. Not to mention, with four daughters at her disposal, having a new Vicematron to rule over an expanded territory would help secure its loyalty.

"That is fair payment," Gunda agreed, sitting back and drawing her goblet to her lips. "For the capture, that is. For the continued custodianship, I would ask something more."

Karahan dipped his head and opened his hands, palms up, on the table.

Gunda drank leisurely, set the goblet down, centered herself, and grinned. "You will owe me a blood debt."

For a creature who couldn't blush, the vampire's countenance boiled. Most mortal creatures would crumble under the fury of a vampire enraged. Gunda Faust was not *most* mortal creatures.

"How dare you!"

The Red Matron siphoned a bit of silver from a candlestick. The globule swam about her fingers, a tiny fish darting about on her whim. "You're asking me to send one of my warriors into harm's way and risk her life. To capture a single vampire? Perhaps that would merit the estate alone. But seven? I should ask for *seven* blood debts in kind, but I will settle for one. I believe the offer quite generous."

Karahan grew small in his chair. "Fine, it is agreed, though..." His hand shot forward, one long finger extended. "...do not fool yourself for a moment that this is a good thing. You marry the fate of my bloodline and yours, there's no telling what the consequences may be."

If there was one fault for which Gunda Faust could be tacked, it was her inability to see fate beyond her own grave. "As it will be, let it be so. We have a deal, then. You have disposal of Gerwalta." The Matron raised her hand in indication. "She recently proved herself a credit to my bloodline in a matter outside the Schwarzwald."

Karahan dipped his head in Gerwalta's direction. "Fraulein Faust, I will see to your provisions. What is it you will require?"

It was the Matron, however, who answered. "She needs only be pointed a direction, and to have silver at her side. To contain seven undead, some significant portion of it. Can you arrange its safe transport?"

"Of course." The vampire looked insulted by the very instigation it could be otherwise.

Gerwalta roused herself, bowing to both mother and guest. "I will see to my affairs, then. Mother, the ball?"

"Shall be delayed until such time as your return," Gunda said. "Though do make haste. I will tolerate the House of Night in my dominion, but no longer than is necessary."

She wanted to ask her mother why she'd invite the only bloodline that rivaled their own to compete for her hand if she found them so distasteful, but how could she with an outsider amongst them?

The young warrior bowed to acknowledge the order before turning on Karahan. "If I can ask, Herr Spatar, where is it we are traveling to? I may have need of different attire depending."

"Of course, Fraulein. We are bound for Venice. I will bid you good evening and prepare my own for departure. Meet me in the village at sundown."

There truly was a god. Such a trip would take weeks, months perhaps. Even dark ones could not cover such a large distance in less than a fortnight. Another month, at least, of remaining unbound to a husband. If only it could be forever.

"Very well. Until tomorrow, then."

A pink and amber sky served as backdrop as Gerwalta walked through the south gates, carrying only her cloak, the clothing she wore, a measure of concealed silver, and a smidgen of gold with her. Food could be bartered or hunted. Weapons forged with her power. Water was all about on the ground in the form of snow. Her boots were wearing thin, but there was no time to have a new pair made.

Besides, no other could equal the comfort. The peasant boy Andreas hired to break them in last year had been truly inspired to place them on a cow for a day. Not all laymen ideas were poor ones.

Half way down the mountain, the world turned upside down.

A flash of red, a swish of flaxen hair, and suddenly, a silver-studded staff pressed into Gerwalta's sternum, pinning her to the ground.

"Do not think I do not see what you are after, little sister."

"Helga?" Gerwalta gasped. "I... do not..."

"Silence!"

Bright lights flooded her vision as the butt of Helga's weapon met her temple. As the weight lifted, her body instinctively curled into a ball, fearing further onslaught. Slowly at first, then suddenly, her eyes regained focus, the fleeting light of day a salve to the pain.

"Do you not think I understand what you're about," her sister said. "First *exposing* the Dregers, now convincing mother to let you play party to some rich and powerful vampire's ploys. I'll credit you with this sister: your professed disinterest in leadership blinded me to how well you were plotting to obtain it."

"I *am* disinterested." Gerwalta rolled over on all fours, lecturing herself not to evidence her torment. "Everyone knows that you'll be next Matron, and that includes me. I am only carrying out the task our mother has set before me as a dutiful daughter."

"Did the Matron command you to *execute* Bernhard?" A few feet away, Helga held her bostaff at the ready, prepared to strike if Gerwalta counterattacked. "Surely you must have known how impressed our mother would be by your ability to slay the very man you were to wed."

Summoning every ounce of determination, Gerwalta pushed herself to her feet without wincing. "You misunderstand, sister. Bernhard's death was self-defense; I am owed no glory for that kill. Nor should you envy my assignment to this task. I am being sent to capture seven vampires. *Seven!* Even you must know how dangerous such a deed is. I was selected not because it is an opportunity to prove my worth, but because I am as I ever was: an expendable asset."

She'd only meant to present a rationalization, but it amazed

Gerwalta how the words hung heavy with truth.

Helga retracted first her weapon, then her person, making no attempt at amends or reconciliation. Instead, she turned, pausing to add over her shoulder, "When I am Matron, little sister, that will be no less true," before she disappeared back into the forest.

THREE

This time when he sensed one of their kind approaching the hamlet, Andreas did not wonder over which came. He scented her on the wind.

Only, why was she here?

"Herr Konigswolf?" She drew to a stop when she caught his eyes in the square. "What are you doing here?"

"I am here because..." he said sheepishly before regaining his confidence. Was he not a king? Why did he cower before her? "Well, because, I am leaving Triberg, of course."

Her face went white. "What?"

"Temporarily," Andreas quickly amended. The smile she tried to hide warmed him. Not so different after all, was she? "Walta, how do you—"

"Ah, Herr Baron!"

They both turned to find Spatar Karahan, his arms filled with three casks, walking their direction.

"And Fraulein Faust." He gave both a friendly nod as he passed. "Good to see you both. We're all here then and ready to go, I presume?"

Her jaw dropped. Ah, so she was not aware of his involvement. Curious, as hers was the only reason he'd agreed to the journey. But if not for him, *why* was she here?

Gerwalta turned on him. "Explain."

"You first."

"I am under contract to Spatar Karahan on behalf of the House of Red."

"A contract to what?"

"*That* is none of your concern."

He stepped closer. "A marriage contract?"

"What?" Her face screwed up. "Of course not. Why would I wed a... *foreigner*?"

Her quick substitution protected the truth from a passing layman who looked at them both with utter confusion. It was not that wolfsretter and lupines never came into the village, it was that it was never together. She did not resist when he took her by the arm and dragged her to a space between two buildings, hidden from public view.

"What are you doing? Get your hands off me. I *will* silver you."

"No, you won't." He spun her about. "The truth now, Walta, what is the nature of this contract?"

"To use silver to trap a few renegade vampires, if you insist to know." Her hand flattened against his chest, shoving him. "Which does not require the aid of a lupine, so go home."

"I will not. I *cannot*."

"And why is that, precisely?"

"Because I volunteered myself to be your bodyguard."

Her eyes went wide. "Why would *I* need a bodyguard?"

"I assumed it was some sort of trickery, a means to disguise my purpose at your instruction. The moment when Karahan said he needed a wolf to help protect Fraulein Gerwalta Faust, I volunteered."

She huffed and tried to walk past him. "I will speak to Karahan to resolve this. Leave, Andreas. I do not want you here."

He took her by the arm, pulling her flush to him. The heat between them? It kindled without need for flame. "Where do you want me, Walta?"

Gerwalta turned her eyes away. "Please, do not distract me with attempts at lovemaking."

"You think I merely *attempt*, good woman? Mark my words, when I am successful, you will not mind so being *distracted*. And nothing you can say will stop me from coming. If you think I'm going to let you wander off without my protection, whether you will it or no, you clearly don't understand my commitment to your good fortune."

From blushed to blanched in a moment, she conjured her cloak, a reminder that the piece of cloth he'd have to go through to find her heart was more than merely physical. It wrapped about her soul with the same tenacity with which it fell upon her shoulders.

The wolf's head cocked to the side. "It marvels me each time you do that. Is it always red? Why a riding cloak? You don't even ride."

"Yes, it's always red. That is my dominant bloodline and all I can conjure. And a riding cloak? I don't know. I suppose because that's what my family does. Other bloodlines manifest their cloaks in different…" She cut herself off. "Why are we discussing this?"

"Because that's what two people in love do, they endeavor to learn about each other."

The wolfsretter rolled her eyes. "Why do you endure with this fantasy? Do you think this is some tale of old, and we are two destined lovers brought together by fate?"

His brow furrowed. "Of course, not. There's no such thing as fate."

Gerwalta threw her hands up in the air. "Fine, come then, but if you think you're going to make love to me all the way to Venice, you have another thing coming."

The weight of what was being asked took on the form of a lodestone in his stomach. "Venice? But it's…"

Thronged by people. Barren of forest. Surrounded by water.

Ruled by vampires.

She grinned. "Did you not know that part?"

"Our discussions never progressed that far."

She finally managed to skirt around him. "I know how much you hate crowded places, Andreas. Nuremberg is nothing compared to Venice. Travelers have brought us tales: they say the city folds in on itself like a cake. People, buildings, and more people."

He cleared his throat, regaining his resolution. "More the reason for me to accompany you. I will brave all to protect you. It is my duty as your future mate."

Gerwalta's eyes rolled in full measure as she turned away. "Lord protect me from delusional wolves and besotted men, and most of all, from those who are both."

"And the silver?"

Gerwalta looked up from the manifest Spatar Karahan had provided upon her arrival for examination. *In case she wished to add to it before leaving,* he said. These vampires and their preoccupation with material things. Why did he not understand that her kind needed little? The only thing she did need, however, she did not see listed.

The vampire demurred. "No need to be concerned; I have made arrangements. Venice will be ready for us when we arrive. In the meantime, I trust you have enough for the journey?"

Her hands instinctively went to her abdomen, rubbing the plates concealed on her person. Until they arrived at Venice, there wasn't need to mount any defense; they had no enemy on the road save the occasional, itinerant highway men. Surely between a vampire lord, a fourth-daughter wolfsretter, and a konigswolf, they could muster enough force to deter such efforts.

She bobbed her head as Karahan's footman, an enlightened layman by the name of Francisco, brushed passed, buckets of water for each of the horses swinging from his stubby arms. "Indeed."

The Spatar scanned the moonlit village roads. "We should depart to make as good a measure before sunrise. Where is Herr Baron? He has not changed his mind, has he?"

If only. "No, he is there," she vaguely motioned to the very alcove in which they'd had their tete-a-tete. "Waiting. Observing."

Annoying.

The vampire drew in a deep breath and then, leaning forward, squinted his eyes. "Are you certain? I can make out no sign of him."

"Spatar Karahan, Andreas Baron is a konigswolf. Do not assume that you have any hope of seeing him when he does not wish to be seen. He could stalk a rabbit in the desert without detection. He will make himself known when the need arises."

And it must have arisen now, for as soon as the words slipped out, Andreas rounded the corner and strode into the square. Now that the anger had subsided, and she could take him in at large instead of a hand's length from her face, she observed him at leisure. Thus, the surprise.

Andreas's garb may still be that of a farmer, but it was by far the finest frock a farmer could have. The deep blue waistcoat boasted brocade, even if a simple loop. It fit him tightly from shoulder to waist, though tapered somewhat after that over a pair of brown breeches that did not have a single remade stich or bit of fray. The baggy coat over and white shirt under appeared freshly laundered, or perhaps, never worn. The only bit of his person she did recognize from previous interactions were Andreas's boots: well-worn animal hide, easily pulled off in case the need for taking one's fur arose.

He made a slight bow of his head when he reached them. "My apologies for keeping you waiting."

For this vision, she'd have waited for the saints to rise from their graves. Gerwalta motioned to the vampire standing to the right.

Karahan clapped his hands. "Good. I shall ride inside—" The vampire pointed to the coach behind them. "—there. I would suppose that both of you prefer to go on, ped-a-ped?"

Andreas looked to Gerwalta for guidance. The wolf nodded. "Yes, I believe that is best."

"Wonderful." Karahan proceeded to open the passenger compartment door. "If we keep good pace and are graced with good weather, we should be able to make Venice just in time, three weeks from now. It would be quicker in summer, if we should be able to cross the Alps, but it is winter now and the roads over the mountains are closed."

A chill ran down her spine. Two weeks with Andreas. Two more back. Their previous endeavor had barely been more than a fortnight, and it still proved enough time for them to fall in love. Where would a month and then some leave them?

"Fraulein Faust, I trust you have a proper gown to appear at the court of the Doge when we arrive to Venice?"

Her eyes went wide. "You said nothing about visiting vampire royalty."

Karahan sneered. "An assumption on my part that you would expect it. No mind. If you have nothing, Messer Mazzi can provide."

Mazzi? Who was Mazzi?

She looked at herself, then to the wolf grinning sheepishly beside her. "What about him?"

The Spatar gave the konigswolf an assessing look. "If you're able to keep your present wear in such condition, Herr Baron, I believe it would be wholly suitable. By the by, if I can say, it is a fetching waistcoat."

"Thank you, Spatar." Andreas bent at the waist to acknowledge the compliment as Karahan moved to open the coach door.

Flabbergasted, Gerwalta turned a flack jaw on the wolf who offered her hand of assistance. Then, squaring herself, she drew up and away from the wolf with haste, landing on the front bench in a brew of annoyance.

FOUR

Three days out of Triberg, they passed into lands outside Gunda Faust's control.

Gerwalta circled her shoulders as though trying to work away the anxiety of leaving her clan's region for the first time. "I need to run."

Andreas, walking on wordlessly for some time, began to take off his overcoat. "I will accompany you."

"I would prefer to be alone."

"Did not we discuss this last time we traveled? In the land of the laity, proper young women do not strut unaccompanied through forest in the middle of the night. It is unlikely you'd encounter anyone at this hour, but this is still a laymen road. Perhaps ahead there are travelers who've stopped to make camp for the night."

"I have no intention of adapting the feigning nature of lay women simple to avoid judgment by those whose opinion means less than nothing."

Andreas bristled. "And what of my opinion?"

Gerwalta gave him a fleeting burn of her eyes before they silvered over the moment she pulled her cloak into being. With that, she was off, leaving Andreas's questions unanswered.

The werewolf heard a chuckle to his left and turned to find the vampire watching from an open window of his coach, amusement barely concealed.

"And you?" Andreas asked. "Do you think it proper, her being about all alone?"

"Oh, dear Herr Baron. If a layman meets *her* on the path and assumes any liberties, I fear he'd not live to see the sunrise."

Andreas grimaced. "I see you will be no help."

"Not in the way you're hoping, no. But do carry on. I find your behavior around each other highly entertaining. When one grows so old in years as I have, such amusements are fewer and far between."

Gerwalta had not gotten too far down the road when his scent carried upon the breeze. *Damned, persistent wolf.* She spun, manifesting silver claws over the tips of her leather riding gloves.

Andreas paused, smirking. "Are you a cat now, Walta?"

He used her silence to close the distance between them, taking one of her hands in his, gingerly rubbing the back of her gloves while avoiding contact with the metal. "It is a bad ploy. Recall that dogs chase cats."

Before he succeeded at drawing her hand to his lips, she pulled back, rounded, and continued her way up the road. "Cease! You know your efforts can come to naught."

"What do you mean, to naught?" He kept apace, though with his relaxed manner, his hands laced behind his back, she'd have thought him strolling an avenue instead of shuffling at a wolfsretter's speed. "By my reckoning, we will be away from the trappings of our familial duties for at least a month. We should make use of the time."

"But we will go home again, will we not?" she said. "And all the issues that kept us apart before will be waiting, with interest. Dismiss this lackadaisical fantasy you've concocted that there is a path for us to be together. I assure you, there is not one that does not end with your death."

"I know this. I *understand* it, even."

She stopped, spun. "And yet you endure?"

He stepped into her space, bringing them chest to chest. "I cannot stop. I have fallen in love with you, and not to honor the desire of my heart is its own kind of death. If I am to choose between the two, I will fight for the one wherein you call out your pleasure beneath me."

She would *not* give him the benefit of knowing how those words sent a pulse of anticipation through her body.

Though the way the corner of his mouth twitched, she suspected he knew.

Damn wolves!

She turned, increasing her pace. "Consign yourself to a lifetime of unrequited love should you wish. I, however, am getting married."

Sweeping feet, he circled on her, walking backward. "Tell yourself that, my lamb. Oh, your mother may march you out like livestock in the market. You may even become betrothed, but you'll never find a lover in your bed."

Her face boiled. "Stop discussing anything in the area of my bed! We will never be together, least of all in bed."

"It may be the floor. Or the ground, even. We are both dark ones; there is no need for us to carry on as the laity do."

The silver kissed his throat as she struck, drawing a droplet of blood to the dagger's edge. His eyes showed no fear, but his tongue finally stilled.

"You are determined to forget your own nature, Andreas, do *not* presume I will do the same. I am a wolfsretter, I am your superior, your dominant. If you insist on taking advantage of a momentary weakness on my part a year ago—"

"It was hardly momentary, pet."

Her fingernail bit deeper, drawing a gasp from the king. "*If* you insist, then I am well within my rights to end you."

Their eyes became the bridge of their tensions. The skin beneath her silver smoked, hissed, poisoned him, but Andreas's stare had the same effect on Gerwalta.

Karahan emerged from the coach which had come to rest on the road behind them. "Why have we stopped?"

Francisco coughed, his German true but heavily-accented with foreign flavor. "I believe the woman's about to kill the man, sir. Didn't want to miss it, I'm not likely to see a fair thing like her get the best of something his size again."

Karahan's brow furrowed before his form dissolved, becoming smoke. The cloud of his being funneled through the air, before assuming a corporeal form just a few feet from standoff. He snatched up Gerwalta's hand with the speed of lightning.

"With all respects to you and your prerogatives, I must insist that until the terms of our contract are fulfilled, you not set about destroying each other," the vampire lectured, snapping each from the showdown. He lowered Gerwalta's hand to her side by force. "Put aside this transgression, whatever its cause, until you are on your own time and ground again."

The vampire, seemingly satisfied that the storm had passed, meandered away. "You may resume passive-aggressively charming each other at will."

Her disgust took the physical form of a curled lip as she turned on Andreas. "You *are* insane."

"No, Fraulein." The Spatar squeezed the konigwolf's shoulder. "He is in love. Men in love do crazy things, but that does not make him crazy."

Andreas blinked. "But you will pay me then?"

"Yes, Herr Baron. I may have taken advantage of your zeal, but I will not exploit your time."

"All men are fools." She spun on heel, huffing. "Venice grows no closer by the flapping of lips in lieu of the actions of our feet. Hurry, so that we can be all the faster to leave it."

FIVE

The German tongue found no friend where they stopped to rest or resupply. Gerwalta's French gave her three more nights of utility, but beyond that, even it became scarce.

Dawn tickled the horizon of the twelfth dawn, their camp made as usual on the side of the road, when Gerwalta awoke to the feeling of fur on her fingers. The wolf licked her gloveless hands. In between sleep and waking, she pushed away the nudging snout before closing her eyes again. She let the lazy web of sleep pull her back down, entirely at ease.

"Gerwalta, wake up."

Her body shook. She opened her eyes again, this time to see the man, not the wolf. Dead leaves clung to the curls of his chestnut hair, the unkempt mass of it wet with dew.

And he was, as wolves had the aggravating habit of being, completely nude.

She closed her eyes again, though this time from propriety instead of fatigue. "Do put on something before you rouse me from sleep."

"I'll not indulge your attempts at modesty. You know full well what my naked form looks like, and I have no shame wearing it. Even if I were not in love with you, I am a lupine and this is our way."

"And what of Francisco? He is a layman and a devout Catholic. Seeing a naked man might send him into hysterics, or worse, confession."

The wolf grimaced. "It matters not. They are both gone."

That succeeded in bringing her to her feet, her cloak-turned-coverlet falling to the ground.

Gerwalta worked her boots on to her feet. "The coach?"

"Also gone. And that's not all." The king-wolf's head turned toward the nearby road. "There is a scent of lupine on the wind."

Gerwalta reached to her belting, pulling the two custom-carved wooden hilts she'd commissioned after her last trip with Andreas. She'd learned not to assume appropriate bases for her weapons would always be found just lying about the forest floor. In a wink, her silver reserves obeyed, pulling long and filling into thin, eager blades the length of her forearm.

"To the best of my knowledge, there are no packs in this area. Why would there be a lupine here?"

"Just because I am one does not mean I can explain the actions of all. Each lupine is his own man, driven by his own needs and desires."

"Save me the philosophy lessons, Andreas." She pointed to the deeper forest. "Lead us. You are a better tracker than me."

"That must have cost you some pride to admit."

"Pride is too high a cost for denying the truth, and often turns deadly if done with haste."

"Who is philosophizing now?"

"Andreas!"

Without further retort, the konigswolf took his fur. Gerwalta took to the trees, though winter had left the branches bare and her red cloak made for easy placement against the brown and black of sleeping oaks. To her surprise, he led her not into the thicket where a lupine was more likely to be found, but directly up the road. A quarter hour had passed when Andreas came to a sudden holt, his body tense. His massive head swung right, swung left, swung right again, before his deep brown eyes searched for her in the canopy.

"What is it?"

A high whine lifted on the air. Gerwalta used each of her senses, trying to discern what had Andreas in such a quandary. Neither sight nor sound nor scent informed.

Until the arrow so narrowly missed her and caused her to shift that its proximity threw off her balance.

The earth would hit her hard, but that wasn't what concerned her as she fell. What did was a wolf of golden pelt who'd just emerged from behind a row of boulders, looking intent on causing the injury the fall would not.

She landed with a thud but knew her survival depended upon ignoring the pain. Andreas howled, tickling her defenses, rousing her instincts. The golden wolf leapt, attempting to clamp his massive jaws, but the wolfsretter managed to arrest her descent and throw herself backward and out of the way. By the time she was on two feet, she had her blade in hand.

The golden wolf rounded, teeth exposed, a growl in his throat.

Gerwalta readied herself, leaning back on her stronger foot, preparing to lunge. "Come along, then, wolfie. Taste my silver."

But no sooner had it sprung than a blur of red and brown fur whisked across her vision. Andreas bit, the golden howled, growled, countered. Fur flew, as did blood, all the time the pain on Gerwalta's shoulder peaking with each move she made. What to do? Her strength, her precision? Her injury compromised both. If she dove in between them, attempting to strike, she'd be just as likely to hit Andreas as the attacking golden.

And then she spotted it: the coach, sitting just off the road, somewhat obscured behind a bank of stout firs. Even the Spatar's two horses were reigned properly, waiting to proceed if only given the command. Was the vampire still secured inside? What of his human?

The tide of the battle of wolves had begun to shift, Andreas's victory all but assured once the smaller lupine he was fighting accepted he'd been beaten. Gerwalta, then, crossed to the trussed-up kit and knocked on the door.

"Spatar Karahan. Are you in there?"

Would he hear her? *Could* he hear her? It suddenly occurred to Gerwalta that she knew very little of the nature of vampires, something she best remedy if she was expected to face one down, let alone seven.

She pressed her ear to the door. They weren't in direct sunlight here amidst the trees, but did that matter?

Finally, when she'd just about convinced herself that she *needed* to open the door to be certain, a voice called out.

"Yes, I am fine."

Gerwalta let out a halted breath. "And Francisco?"

The voice was softer this time. "He is... in *here* with me."

Gerwalta's face screwed up. "Why would he be in..."

Abruptly, she cut off her own words instead of laying down evidence of her ignorance.

"Very well," she amended, spinning around as sounds of conflict rose anew. "Stay in there safe, the both of you, until I retrieve you. There is trouble afoot, but nothing Andreas and I cannot handle."

Back in the fray, she found the wolves engaged. Andreas could defeat him; she knew he could. But for some reason he showed restraint. He wasn't going to allow their attacker to walk away, was he? Though a lupine, he must know the fallacy of disengaging with honor in a conflict which had none.

Nothing else to be done except what must be. She withdrew the silver, gathering it in her hands, forcing it to spin out long and thin. The cord did not need to be extensive; a single loop would do. She made it so, then used the distraction of their continued battle to gain distance. Andreas caught sight of her only as he leapt, throwing herself on the back of the beast trying to kill him.

The silver loop tightened, finding skin beneath fur. In an instant, the lupine howled in pain.

They were far from the Schwarzwald where German was the tongue of kings, but what else could she do? "Who are you? Why are you trying to kill us?"

"Don't bother asking. I know who he is." Andreas followed suit, shedding fur and standing on two feet beside her. "His name is Gerhart Hessian, and he is of the Wehr Pack."

"The Wehr Pack? But we passed through their territory days ago. What would he be doing this far from his packlands?"

"What, indeed." The konigswolf nodded. "Remove his binding so he may lose his fur. Give him a chance to tell us."

Furtive eyes looked to the wolf to get his visual assurance that the situation was well in paw. Andreas caught her eyes, the unspoken promise palpable in the air. *I won't let him hurt you.*

The wolfsretter turned back to the captive lupine who,

despite the pain evident in his eyes, kept his teeth bared. One deep breath of moist, winter air, and with her exhale, the silver liquified, flowing in rivulets back up her arms.

Andreas descended, his massive biceps and thick thighs working under taut skin. The konigswolf was fearsome as an animal, but even as a man, he fell upon the beast before them, forcing him to submission.

"Take your skin, rapscallion!" Andreas demanded, pushing the creature's maw into the mud. "I will have the truth from your tongue, or I swear, I will send you home to your king without it."

The gray wolf flexed, trying with one desperate huff to break free, until the fight fled from his eyes. His body eased with a whimper, his chest cycling a breath as he began to shift under Andreas's hold.

"There you are." The king-wolf scowled. "Now, out with it. Why are you after the vampire?"

"Vampire?" Gerhart asked, wincing as Andreas shifted atop him, pressing down on the pressure points most effective for a man. "Why would I be after a vampire?"

Gerwalta blinked. "But you were trying to make off with coach."

"The coach?" The lupine became partner to her confusion. "I didn't touch the coach. It was that layman who's with you who did. I watched him."

Andreas and she exchanged a look.

"Why would Francisco move the coach away from us?"

"I do not know." Gerwalta scanned the nearby forest. "Possibly, to assure privacy."

"Privacy?" The konigswolf repeated. "Privacy for what purpose?"

She didn't know how to properly convey meaning without implication, so instead, she just made some vague gesticulations with her hands, adding after, "As I understand it."

"Oh?" The lines in Andrea's forehead flattened as his brow lifted, his eyes going wide. "Oh, I see." He cleared his throat. "Well then, Gerhart. If you weren't after Karahan, you were after us. Why?"

"Because my king commanded it."

Andrea's brow furrowed. "What cause would Michael have to bare fang against me? He and I have no quarrel."

"I cannot, nor would I, presume to know the workings of my king's mind."

The way Gerhart's king conducted the leadership must be different from how Andreas went about it, Gerwalta thought. Whatever bias her siblings held against lupines inherently, not even Helga would disagree that Andreas governed through diplomacy and open dialog, not brute force or unclear ultimatums. There seemed to be some wager among her older sisters about when such a strategy would fall under the weight of its own fantasy.

Gerwalta wracked what she knew of the Wehr pack from her brain. It was a collection of about two dozen lupines whose packlands lay on the southern reaches of Red territory. She herself had never interacted with any of them, but her mother had, and very recently.

Helga.

"Gerwalta?"

The concern in Andreas's voice anchored into her thoughts and pulled them back to the present. Gerwalta blinked away her confusion, wondering if it had been moments or minutes that she'd been lost to world. It was funny how a stark realization could do that, create a wake of time that distorted understanding.

"It was my sister."

"Which one?"

"Helga. She... She thinks I am threatening her claim on the matronship. How convenient would it be if I met a tragic death outside the jurisdiction of the House of Red. Helga ordered the Wehr konigswolf to see to me murdered."

Andreas turned his attention back on Gerhart, forcing his hand behind his back, twisting his wrist to induce a bite of pain. "Is that the way of it?"

Gerhart squealed. "How do I know? But if you were any kind of self-respecting konigswolf, you'd kill her yourself rather than curl up to her when you sleep each day."

A wave of nerves ran through her. Curl up to her? Andreas slept some distance from her each morning. Did he not?

Even if that wasn't the case, the larger issue was plain: Gerhart had been ordered to kill her by his king, and she knew nothing but death or the revocation of the order would keep him from carrying out the command. Without further word, Gerwalta drew the silver cord in, collapsing it into a broad-edged dagger. She readied a lethal blow before Andreas caught her arm from the air.

"Gerwalta, wait!"

Frustration fueled her anger. "For what? You heard what he said!"

"Precisely. He is acting of compulsion, not his own conscious. *He* is innocent."

"Do you suppose his disdain for me would be lessened if he was acting of his own regard?"

On that stark truth, the konigswolf's eyes twitched, before his face became somber. "Even so, it would not be deserving of death. If all wolfsretters and lupines slaughtered each other based on emotions alone, we'd all be dead."

She softened around the edges. "I have no desire for his blood, Andreas, but only his own end will keep him from carrying out the deed. His king has commanded it, and it is obligation."

"I agree."

That stopped her quicker than did his grip. "You agree, then, that I need kill him?"

Andreas pushed her weapon hand to her side, "No. I mean that I agree that under his king's command, he will not stray. However, there is another way."

"Another way?" Her knowledge did not suggest anything but that one of them must die. "What?"

"If he pledges his fealty to me now and becomes of my pack, I can divert that command."

What the devil? "You'd invite an enemy to harbor under your maw?"

"He is *not* an enemy. Why can you not understand that?"

"Because I don't understand wanting to show mercy to my would-be killer."

"Love her?" Gerhart piped up. His rusty gaze turned on the king. "You... You... betrayer!"

Andreas huffed his frustration. "And now the mirror shows its reflection."

As Gerhart struggled, trying one last time to wriggle out from Andreas's hold, the wolf king picked up the captive's hands before smashing both back over his head. Gerwalta heard the bones crack.

Andreas did not stall. "Just because I make you pack does not mean I have to like you, Gerhart. And I don't. But I'd rather hate your hide than see it made into a wolfsretter's rug. Submit to me, and I will remove this burden to your soul."

"And serve my days as pup to a king whose betrayed his kind? No, thank you."

Gerwalta drew her blade high in the air. "My way, then."

"No!" Terror pulled the color from Gerhart's face. "Fine. I submit! I accept you as my king, I pledge my fealty. I pledge my life!"

Gerwalta panicked as both wolves grew still, moments before Andreas threw his head back. Despite his layman form, the konigswolf managed a howl, a deep, crisp wail, joined a moment later by this lupine struggling beneath him. A quickening. She'd heard stories of it, read accounts, but the sacred act was rarely witnessed by one of her kind.

Andreas had barely stood when his balance faltered. Gerwalta maneuvered beneath him, keeping him from the ground. A moment passed that way before he began to find his footing again. She'd credit him this time with not taking advantage of circumstance, making no crude implication or suggestive quip. What he did do, however, was much worse. With aching tenderness, the konigswolf reached a hand to her chin and pulled her eyes to his, smiling.

And then, he was back on his feet and walking away, leaving her insides wobbling.

Damn wolf.

"Go to Triberg," Andreas ordered his new packling. "Find Wilhelm and ask him to assign you a place to bed down and a share of work. You are now forbidden to kill any wolfsretter."

"And do not tell anyone that Andreas loves me," Gerwalta rushed to add.

Andreas's face cycled from annoyance to understanding. "And tell no one of our relationship," he acquiesced before turning to Gerwalta and adding, "But at some point, it will become known, and as soon as you admit it, we will need to discuss how to handle that discovery."

She let him fall to the ground. "You really are quite frustrating."

Gerhart grinned when he and his new king sat eye-to-eye on the ground. "Is this the pack I've agreed to join to save my life, one where the king moons over a matron's bitch? I might be tempted to reconsider my pledge of fealty."

"Gerwalta will be happy to separate your head from your body, if you like."

His new packling shuddered. "At least this one loves you, though a nose full of snot that will do for you."

The Wehr pack could benefit from a lesson in manners. Andreas swept his hand across the air. "Off now. When I return, we will become better-acquainted."

"And her?" Gerhart nodded at Gerwalta.

Andreas bobbed his head. "If she lasts the week without admitting her feelings, then I'll be a pup's first fang."

SIX

Andreas's head rested on her lap as his body rose and fell with the gentle waves of slumber. Given that he'd saved her life, she couldn't find the will to push him away when he'd rolled near her by the fire, finishing out their day sleep stretched atop her red cloak.

The konigswolf had been so overtaxed by the quickening, he'd not bothered to pull back on his breeches. Gerwalta would like to say that her eyes had not taken advantage of the unobstructed view. It wasn't as if she'd never seen a naked lupine before. Not even as if she'd never seen *Andreas* nude. But that did not mean she'd had opportunity to examine at length... well, his *length*.

Truth be told, she found the actual *implement* rather unimpressive. It was a funny looking thing, like a toadstool that had barely managed to peek out from a patch of loose soil. She couldn't understand, therefore, why her sisters seemed so enamored of their encounters with their husbands. Perhaps a lupine's asset was different? For all she knew, perhaps the whole procedure with them was different. They were half-animal, after all. Surely that must have consequences in the realm of intimacy.

She knew the basics of the marital bed, at least the mechanics of it, to say. Would that tiny thing even be big enough to go inside? Gerwalta closed her eyes and tried to imagine it, but the vision was more comical than tempting. But the moment she imagined herself straddled over him, bending down to taste his kiss, and his hands rising to cup her breasts, the last thing it was, was comical.

It wasn't until Andreas's lips pursed against her fingertips that she realized she'd been tracking the contours of his mouth.

His grin broadened into a smile. "What are you thinking of, love, that has caused such a change in your scent?"

It had taken several moments for Andreas to realize the tickle on his lips was not part of the dream in which he'd been enveloped. It was better, for it was truly happening.

Only a king's ransom of self-restraint kept him still for so long. He knew Gerwalta would not undertake such affections whilst he was awake. Not yet, anyhow. But he'd seen her feigned annoyance and indifference begin to fade these last few days. She had stopped calling him *Herr Baron* or *Herr Konigswolf,* regressing to Andreas. When he deftly neared her while sleeping in the day, she no longer unconsciously pulled in on herself. After the previous excitement, it had been *she* who offered *him* a share of her cloak-turned-bed to stay off the frosted forest floor.

He let her fingertips indulge in their exploration for as long as he could, wondering if she would make further endeavors to explore boldly. Her movement slowed, the pressure amplified, her heartbeat ticked up and her breathing deepened. And then came the change in her scent. He remembered it from one of their previous encounters, the distinct mix of pine and cold air and feminine hue that signaled her arousal.

After that, how could he possibly stay still?

"What are you thinking of, love, that has caused your eyes to silver over?"

Like the children's tales of old, the waking moment spoiled the spell.

Gerwalta's hand retracted. "I have no idea what you mean."

No, she would not dismiss it with such a casual denial.

The wolfsretter yelped as he turned over and hefted himself on all fours, crawling over her with such speed, it made her dizzy. "Your mouth is too pretty for lies, my pet."

She fell on to her back, for there was no where else to go. His weight settled atop her in the most delicious way, and finally, she did not fight him. In fact, one of her legs hitched up, buckling his hip, bringing them into better alignment. It may the preamble to a defensive move, but if so, she was delaying its execution for some reason.

"Fine," Gerwalta huffed. "Allow me to rephrase: it *means* nothing."

"What doesn't?"

"That I find you attractive. You are handsome, and you are nude. And I am… of an age to appreciate such things for their own merit without the complication."

"So, all you desire is my body, not the heart within it?" His mouth descended to her neck. He could dig the well before collecting the water if she wished. "You do not think that dissuades me, do you? There is a reason it's called 'making love,' Gerwalta. The physical act kindles the emotions beneath it."

"There are no emotions beneath it. I respect you, perhaps I still even like you, but that is all. I am quite sure what you're implying requires marriage."

"You don't need a husband." Another roll, and her body did the most amazing thing: it rolled back. His hands traipsed down her sides, anchoring around her lower back. This time, her other leg rose, and she folded her ankles behind his back. Sweet mercy, if not for the cloth of her breeches, he'd be inside her. His body recognized the proximity, drove him to mimic the act as though they were nude. Gerwalta's hands embraced him, pulled him closer. Her nails raked into his back.

The heat where they were nearly joined… he could feel it. Feel her tensions building. Feel her desires pooling.

"It will be…" She swallowed hard; a guttural noise that made him increase his pace. "…difficult to wed without one."

"You're not going to be wed." Roll. Counterroll. Dear Lord, she was undoing him. Was she, too, as close to the edge as he? He did hope, for he wasn't sure how much longer his restraint or her passion would at last.

"You're going to be…"

Push. Pull. He lifted one arm as his other reached under her hip, pulling her hard into him as he gave another roll.

"…*mine.*"

"I will n—nah—*ahh.*"

Gerwalta's head lolled back, her chest heaving with breath. Her nails pierced his skin. Andreas didn't care. She was climaxing from his touch, riding pleasure from his actions. She could have half the blood in his body if she wanted it.

She could have his *anything*.

Which pushed him to say the worst possible thing. "Gerwalta, I love you. Let me mate you now, here. Let me make love to—"

In a heartbeat, it was over.

Gerwalta flipped him with ease, reversing their positions. Andreas grinned as the wolfsretter straddled him, her arms pinning his back over his head. Until he saw the look on her face, that was.

Anger flared in her cheeks. "Do you really think you'll just mate me and be damned with my needs? My wants? My expectations?"

Had she just tacitly acknowledged the prospect? *Stay focused*. "You want me. Do not deny it: I can taste your desire in the air."

"Just because you will be bonded to me when we make love does not mean I will be to you."

His smile lit the forest. "*When*?"

"If!" she rushed to amend. "I am not a lupine. A wolfsretter expects to be courted. There are formalities, customs..."

Why was she telling him this? Did she want him better educated on how to woo her? He was eager for the instruction.

Andreas tried to lift his lips to hers, but her dominance prevented it. He found himself a hand's breadth from her mouth, his gaze lingering on her lips. "Name it and it shall be done."

"You must learn to dance."

He blinked thrice. "Sorry, what?"

"Court dances," Gerwalta said. "And I fear the motions are a little more complex than *this*."

She rolled her hips only meaning it as mockery but cursed the beautiful friction the movement induced.

Andreas threw back his head and bit his lips. "Mercy, Gerwalta. If you wish for me not to make love to you, mercy. I am already on the edge of arrival."

Now she blinked. "Arrival?"

"Yes, love, what just happened to you… *almost* happened to you, it will happen to me too."

"Do you think me a fool, Herr Konigswolf? I am not some little shewolf unwise to the ways of men and women. Just because I have not done the deed myself does it mean I am ignorant of the process. Remember that I have three older sisters, and Lord help me, an older brother who does not think our corridor of the castle has an echo."

It had not been his intent to insult her, but he'd managed the feat, nonetheless. *Curses.* He had to be cautious. Gerwalta's walls were beginning to fall, but if he pulled too fast, he'd be crushed under the wreckage. He could see that now. He'd gone after her like she was a wolf, but as she herself had reminded him, that was hardly true. If he wanted her as a mate, he'd need to also pursue her on her terms.

He doused his desire and fell back, pushing his laced hands behind his head. "Do you propose to teach me these dances? These courting rituals of your kind?"

"Yes, though not so that you may court me, but because my sisters and mother are all anticipating your ignorance of such things at the ball. They mean to make a mockery of you. I only desire to keep you from making a fool of yourself."

"Then I shall learn to dance." *Tell yourself that's all it is, sweet.* "In turn, you will learn from me the ways of lupine courtship."

"Courtship?" She laughed. "As I said, I am aware of what *courtship* entails. I take off my breeches and you shove your manhood into my maidenhead until you shudder to a close."

"It sounds rather unseemly when you put it that way."

She pointed at the part of him that remained hidden beneath her. "I looked at it while you slept. It hardly seemed the thing of poems and ballads. Besides, I am *not* mating you. Do not think you will trick me into your bed by disguising such acts as mere education."

"You misunderstand, Gerwalta. You wish to teach me a form for court dancing. I wish to show you a form of dancing to court."

"Then it is different for lupines."

He jerked his head up. "What is?"

"Nothing, no matter." Gerwalta rose, smoothing out the skirting of her tunic. "Do not joke, Andreas. Court dances are another form of diplomacy. They are not a child's game."

The werewolf licked his lips. "Neither is seduction."

Further discussion ceased as they both detected footfalls in the nearby brush. A string of expletives fled Francisco's tongue as he emerged from a patch of trees. He got one look at Andreas and threw his hands over his eyes.

"Pardon the gander, sir. I didn't expect to come back and find you... *occupied*."

Gerwalta and Andreas exchanged a look before the latter said, "No need for embarrassment, Francisco. Nudity is a common among lupines. But I can see it makes you uncomfortable. I'll dress."

"I thought I told you to wait until I returned?" Gerwalta accosted the layman as Andreas began to hunt for his clothing. "So, you left us behind on purpose? Why?"

"Begging your pardon, Fraulein, but it was the Spatar's command. He said I should check to make sure you hadn't torn each other up in the process of doing..." The stout man's cheeks blushed. "...whatever it was you two were about. Also, the Spatar thought, if there was danger, it may wish to trek out early today, unless, and I quote, 'they need more time to work out their differences.'"

Gerwalta's hands balled into fists. As Andreas pulled out his clothing from where he stored it in the undercarriage of the coach, he watched a narrative play out in the wolfsretter's expression. Frustration, confusion, realization and finally, determination.

He strolled over to her, put his hands on her shoulder. "I'm not going to ask what you're thinking, love. I just want to know that it doesn't end with my death or at the very least, castration."

"You are quite arrogant to suppose all my thoughts are of you," she spat back, pulling herself from his touch.

"Good, so I am safe." He turned to collect his shirt.

Gerwalta cackled. "Hardly."

SEVEN

Suggestions to make camp for the day went unheeded, and soon Gerwalta deduced why. It was a break in routine, giving her a chance to engage Karahan.

"I would ask to ride with the Spatar for a space, if you have no objection."

Andreas trudged along beside her, his eyes constantly scanning the forest. "What cause could I possibly have to object? Go, consign yourself to a confined space with a blood-thirsty dark one."

"Vampires are not known to feast on lupines or wolfsretters."

"My fields in Triberg are not often burdened by elephants either, but I wouldn't trust one to be released there."

She cackled. "Are you saying it is merely lack of opportunity, and that I may not go?"

"I do not nor would I ever tell you what you may or may not do. You're not my pack."

She couldn't resist an opportunity to tease. "And if I were your mate?"

He laughed into his shoulder. "I know what you *assume*. You think lupine husbands—*any* husband not a wolfsretter, is a domineering brute."

"You're saying you wouldn't be?"

"I told you before my mate shall be my equal. I would no more command you than you me, though I will strive always to stay in your good graces." He jerked his head to the coach rocking along the road behind him. "Go. If I hear anything concerning, I will not hesitate to rip his throat out."

A nod, and then Gerwalta turned and flagged Francisco to slow the horses. The door swung open after the first knock.

"Fraulein?"

Gerwalta pulled herself up on the riser. "May I pass some time with you, Spatar?"

The vampire looked up from a book spread on his lap, giving her a gracious smile. "You may, of course."

As soon as the door was closed, she eased into her inquisition. "I spotted a clocktower to the south. We are approaching another town."

The vampire resumed his study. "What of it?"

"Will you hunt there?"

The book stayed stationed, though his eyes rose to meet hers. "Why do you ask?"

She feigned loose interest. "A wolfsretter does not have much opportunity to learn of vampires and their habits, and I am cursed with curiosity. So far in our journey, when we've been in the proximity of a clocktower, you've gone off alone and come back looking much flusher. What is this city we are approaching, and why is it our destination? It cannot be Venice; it is not an island."

Though, given the time they'd been on the road, they *must* be getting closer.

"Venice is actually several islands." The book lowered. "This is Padua. We will stay with Messer Mazzi until it is time to advance into Venice."

"Padua? I have not heard of it." Her finger traced the bench beside her. "Still, it is good to have such friends. Do you have many, in many cities?"

Karahan's eyes narrowed. "Are you asking specifically, Fraulein Faust, about my friends in Nuremburg?"

She sat back, as though the distance would protect her. "I see the rumors are true; vampires can read thoughts."

The corners of his mouth rose along with a twinkle in his eye, and it amazed Gerwalta how this man—this dark one—could be so charmingly young and old at the same time.

"There is no reason for me to mislead you on this. Vampires

cannot read thoughts, though that is a common misconception. We can *plant* them, even ask one to reveal what he knows. Some minds are stronger than others, and some do not bend at all. Dark ones, for example, are immune from our skills."

"If you could not read my thoughts, then how did you know I intended to ask you of Nuremberg?"

"Your kind are not known as wanderers. When your mother mentioned you'd successfully completed a mission in Nuremberg, the imperial city, I suspected there may be unusual circumstances involved."

Gerwalta pondered a moment, playing out the consequences of withholding, or pursuing an adversarial tit-for-tat. Something about his revelation brought her to confess her own.

"There would be no reason for a vampire to journey to Ravensburg," she said. "It is a small town, barely more than a village, with no strategic importance to dark ones or the laymen. Something brought you there, and then to Triberg."

"Indeed." Karahan grinned and leaned in toward her. "Your theory?"

"While you were in Nuremberg, you spoke with the Emperor."

"I never said I was in Nuremberg."

"You did," she insisted. "You did not say 'if I have a friend in Nuremberg.' You said, 'are you asking about my friend in Nuremberg.' The statement tells me there are such friends to inquire about and citing it when I gave no pretense means it was the first place to come to *your* mind."

"What an intriguing intellect." The vampire's head seesawed as he pursed his lips. "Yes, I saw the Emperor, but I spoke not so much *with* him as *to* him."

"To what end?"

"Let's just agree that neither of us benefitted from his knowledge of our world. Now, he hasn't any."

A great knot in her stomach unwound for only a moment until she remembered what had driven her to speak with Karahan to begin with. "But you, I deduce, learned something from him about *me*."

His eyebrows arched. "Did I?"

She nodded. "You told Francisco to give Andreas and I some time alone to work out our differences."

"Is that what the youth call it these days? Differences?"

And there it was. "Despite what you may think, Spatar Karahan, there is nothing going on between Herr Baron and myself."

"He was awfully quick to volunteer himself for this mission when he learned you were the wolfsretter needing protection."

"I *do not* need protection." Nevermind that without Andreas's help, the surprise wolf attack may have worked. "I'll admit that the man is smitten with me, but that does not mean I reciprocate his feelings."

"You're either lying to me, Fraulein, or you're lying to yourself. Both, I'd venture." The vampire's eyes narrowed. "I have daughters too. I know the tricks a maiden plays to encourage her lover's attentions."

"Be that as it may, it does not mean I am such a maiden."

Any humor passed away from the vampire's face. "Your pulse ticks up every time he looks at you. Not only that, but it also ticks up when *you* look at *him*, even if he is unaware. There is also an inordinate amount of consideration and respect between you for two species so frequently opposed. I only joined fact with fancy."

His eyes turned to the window. "Also, a wolf I happened upon in Ravensburg told me a very curious story, of a hooded dark one who had saved him and others, lured away by an anathema wolf-queen, and who had amazingly admitted her love for a one of his kind in Nuremberg."

"I never admitted my love. I—"

Her words died on the air, even as her heart raced to explode. What had she done? *What had she done*?

"I mean that—What I *meant* to say is—"

The Spatar held up a hand. "I am not your Matron, Fraulein. You owe me no explanation, for I make no judgements on the aspirations of the heart."

"*You* may not, but every lupine and wolfsretter of good standing would." Fear emboldened her. Gerwalta reached out, setting her gloved hand on the vampire's knee. "Please, Spatar Karahan, I beg of you, tell no one what I've said, nor what you've seen. Within months I will be wed, and this situation will be consigned to the regrets of youthful indiscretion. But if it ever becomes known that anything happened between Andreas—*Herr Baron*—and I, he will be executed."

"That would be a terrifically poor use of a perfectly good alpha."

She blinked and retreated to her side of the cabin. "What did you call him?"

"An alpha. It is the common term for a konigswolf in the region from which I come. A bit gentler on the palate, I think." He rolled his tongue around in his mouth. "For all its linguistic tenacity, German is quite a severe language at the end of the day."

"I'm afraid I don't understand."

"I have no reason to disclose anything about your relationship to anyone," he continued undeterred. "You have my word, and I extend Francisco's by proxy of my powers. Neither of us will reveal your feelings for the wolf. But I must wonder, Fraulein, what are his intentions if he knows such a romance has deadly consequences?"

"The moment I understand the thoughts of the lovestruck, then I shall be the wisest woman who ever lived."

The vampire laughed. "Just a thought, Fraulein. If it truly is your intention to wed another and be a 'proper wolfretter' when you return, why not use this time away from judging eyes and loose tongues to indulge in that 'youthful indiscretion' rather than pull away from it? If you were immortal like me, I'd understand forbearance. But you are not; you will age and die. You have so very little time, when things come down to it. Do not waste it, and do not squander it for the sake of what anyone else thinks is proper. You will lie alone in your grave when you die regardless of with whom you share your bed whilst you live."

EIGHT

World weary, they entered town just after sunrise, as soon as the gates were thrown open. Whatever Nuremberg had been, Padua was just the same, minus an imperial palace. Covered in stone, crowded by smells and the people and animals responsible for them, even at an early hour, both lupine and wolfsretter felt it close in on them. At least it was not market day. That would have brought in a greater menagerie and clogged the passages of town.

Francisco pulled the coach to a stop and climbed down from his bench. "Are you at all ill, Herr Baron? You've gone quite white in the face."

Gerwalta stepped out of the coach at the same time, the first Andreas had seen of her in an hour. She'd dispelled her mystical red cloak, perhaps because the air here was not quite so cool as before, or perhaps because Karahan, familiar with the region and its customs, thought it ill-suited.

"Andreas?"

She rushed to his side at Francisco's words, hooking her arm through his and bringing him up to a proper stand. His beloved's attentions delivered magic, a primal refocus that reminded him they were far from home in a place surrounded by strangers. Instinct, roused by her touch, brought his attention to her well-being and moreover, her defense. Immediately, he straightened, scanning their surroundings, looking for a threat.

Francisco laughed. "Heavens be praised, Fraulein, you have a saint's touch. Look at how you called him back to himself." The coachman lifted a hand, adding from behind a smile, "Maybe you can cure me of my soreness from the ride?"

Rationality divorced itself from Andreas's actions, and he growled at the poor layman, whose arms immediately dropped to his side.

"Then again, maybe not."

Within a moment, Andreas recalled himself. Holy Mother, if a well-intentioned layman triggered this sort of defensiveness in him now, what was it going to be like once they were mated? Then again, she *was* drawing attention. Every man within sight of them pointed, speaking behind hands with each other.

"Herr Baron!" Gerwalta's light touch became a stinging grasp, her grip so tight around his forearm she threatened to break bone. "Do control yourself. Saints preserve, it isn't even near full moon! What the devil has gotten into you? It is only Francisco."

"I must concur with the lady, Herr Baron." Karahan stepped out of the coach and down into the street, despite the bright morn. "He is quite good at his job, and loyal to a fault. You can be assured, he has no intentions with her, despite what those lupine instincts suggest."

"Spatar Karahan?" Gerwalta looked to the coach, then to the vampire, repeated the process. "How are you not—"

"Bursting into flames?" Karahan completed for her. "I'm afraid, despite the stories, my kind doesn't do much bursting. We char after a while, eventually becoming stone, but the process takes time. The older the vampire, the shorter. Luckily, I'm only about three hundred."

Andreas demurred, looking to the footman who'd begun unloading boxes from atop the coach. "Apologies, Herr Francisco, the road was long and weariness dulls my civility."

Luckily the layman proved good-natured. "I dare say it does that to all God's creatures."

Karahan waved them up the street. "This way, now, children. I can be out in the sun a spell, but I do not enjoy it. Best to get off the streets before I crisp. It does tend to draw attention. Francisco, wait here with the horses and my goods. I will tell Messer Mazzi to send along his staff promptly to collect it and you."

"Yes, sir."

Moving swiftly towards one of the nearby residences, a stately rowhome built of stone and four stories tall, Karahan barked a laugh. "Come along now, Fraulein. I daresay Angelo will have a whole wardrobe of things you can wear that are less... let's say, suggestive."

Gerwalta examined herself. "My attire is overly modest if

nothing else. What am I meant to believe it suggests?"

"It is well-suited to your nature and your calling, but I'm afraid in Padua, women to do not wear breeches in public. Only men do."

"So, they believe I'm a..." She stumbled with the words. "A crossdresser?"

"Yes, madame. Or worse, an actress."

Her hand landed on her chest. "I'm not sure which is worse. Very well, if I must wear a dress, then I shall. Only, I do not like how they are so open about the bottom."

As she pressed past, Andreas watched her backside, the rounded shape shifting with her legs, he hoped that whatever this Angelo Mazzi had, included many layers of undergarments and a generous number of peticoats, or he'd be thinking about that *opening* far too much.

As konigswolf, Andreas had never needed great wealth of knowledge of vampires or slayers. Still, he found himself questioning what little he did know. Seeing a vampire lord greet a slayer in the way of old friends, he wondered how foes managed to demonstrate such warmth. Wherein, aside from Gerwalta, every wolfsretter he'd ever known had considered him a pest worthy of loathing.

Wolfsretters and lupines could learn from their city cousins.

After embracing their host with genuine amenity, Karahan extended an arm and swept the air back to where he and Gerwalta stood in wait, moving his tongue away from Italian.

"Messer Angelo Mazzi of the Solari Padua, may I present my companions on this quest: King Andreas Baron of the Triberg Pack, and the Righteous Fraulein Gerwalta Faust, Fourth Daughter of Gunda Faust, Matron of the House of Red."

Andreas had expected to find a man with light skin and a round countenance for some reason. That's how he thought of the sun, and shouldn't a creature which harnessed its power be of like appearance? A silly thought, he realized, taking in the high cheek bones, silky ebony locks, and olive skin of a man even his packling shewolves would go crimson over.

Mazzi's blue eyes grew wide as he hastened to bend at the

waist. "Your highnesses, welcome. It is a great honor to host you."

Gerwalta let out a little grasp. "You speak German."

"I do, Fraulein. I speak many languages," he concurred, righting himself. "Slayers often study many tongues, as vampires tend to move about. You'll find very few vampires in the Doge's palace are native to this region. Most travel the Mediterranean's great cities. Athens, Istanbul, Cairo..."

"The Doge of Venice entertains vampires?"

The slayer shook his head. "Oh, not *that* Doge. No, the layman Doge, Nicolo Sagredo may host the occasional pirate or Medici, but he minds the laity and is, as far as I know, unaware of the ebb and flow of the undead in his city. Luciana Martelli, the vampire doge, on the other hand...."

Andreas's mouth dropped. "The vampire doge is a... woman?"

He didn't have to look at Gerwalta to feel the burn of her glare, as though questioning a female in a position of power was an insult meant for her. He couldn't help it though; lupines were patriarchal, and the last exception he'd seen to that had nearly cost him his life.

"Oh, yes, and quite a woman at that." A blush rose in the slayer's cheeks, one that spread to Gerwalta's as she met his eyes.

Do not growl. Do not growl.

"But that is neither here nor there. You must be quite tired after being on the road so long. Knowing my old friend, I'm willing to bet Igor kept pushing you on, not letting you stop in a real place with a real bed for.... How long did the journey take from the Schwarzwald, a fortnight?"

"Igor?" Andreas turned on the vampire. "I thought your name was Goran Karahan?"

It was the slayer who answered in the bluster of an explosive hack. "Is *that* what he's calling himself? Saints preserve us, Igor, where did you come up with that one?"

Karahan blanched, demurring his head. "I do wish you'd respect my privacy, my friend. A persona is no easy thing to cultivate, and I would not have mine thrown out with the ease of turned milk."

"Ah, bash with that!" The Italian stepped forward, draping an arm over Gerwalta and Andreas, taking them underwing. "Welcome to my home, my new friends. Rest, relax, and this evening at dinner, I will tell you all the dark little secrets Igor wishes would wash away with time. Then, I will pull out my finest spirits, and we will taunt sobriety until morning. Yes, it will be a grand evening indeed."

NINE

There was a great deal of difference between wearing a *dress*, which Gerwalta did with little complaint, and wearing whatever contrived device this was, the application of which required assistance from two of Mazzi's female servants and a saint's patience. Wool stockings, drawers, petticoats, a corset, stays, an odd kind of bustle that came in a pair and were worn off the hips instead of the rear... and that was just all the things that went underneath the preposterous silk coverlet on the outside!

"Do female slayers wear such things?" Gerwalta asked the girl who spoke French.

Bernice translated the question to her fellow lady's maid, which prompted the other to say something back that set both giggling.

"What are you laughing about?"

The smile on the servant's face fizzled. "Apologies, mademoiselle, but it's only... Well, Portia said that they do, but they don't wear it for very long."

Suddenly, her garments felt tighter and looser at the same time.

The fire on the hearth flickered as the air in the room shifted. Both servants leapt to their feet as the door opened and a huffing Andreas plowed into the room.

"This is a bone too far!"

The servants fled, making for the door as Andreas planted himself before Gerwalta, holding his arms akimbo. "Look at me. *Look at me*! A wig? I am expected to wear *a wig*. And that's just the start of what is wrong. Have you ever heard of a lupine donning silk stockings? And what kind of breeches only come down to the knee? Don't even get me started about this coat! It looks like I'm wearing a skirt, like I'm some sort of shewolf in heat. And..."

"Andreas!"

It was at that precise moment that his eyes finally fell upon her, and with that, his tongue stilled.

"Look at *me*." She attempted to walk forward and found the task impossible without a great deal of swooshing. "Do you think I am without complaint? I don't know if I'm going to dinner or blowing out to sea."

His eyes traced the outlines of her bodice which, unlike the lower half of her body buried in a veritable mound of pink silk, fitted tight, enhancing the feminine flip of her hips.

And, because the dress was Italian, pressed her breasts into a cruel form of submission, both constricting and framing them.

The beast in him salivated.

Gerwalta snapped her fingers, breaking the lupine's concentration to her womanly assets. "Herr Baron!"

He sparked to attention, regaining her eyes. "Sorry, did you say something?"

Wolves were such men.

Or was it the other way around?

"I quite understand your issue, but no doubt we are not to be subjected to Italian clothing as a mere means of torture. Remember, vampires are city creatures, and they like to put on airs. It will be much easier to corner our prey if we blend in with its environment. I daresay if I wore my red cloak, and you your farmer's frock, these vampires we are to trap would see us coming from some distance away. Consider this practice."

The lust dissolved in the wake of the practical. "But how are we to move in this attire? If I were to take my fur whilst dressed up in this ninny-wear, I'm as likely to find myself trapped as not. Silk is not unlike a wolfsretter: soft to the touch, thin to the eye, but tough as iron when tested by force."

"That almost sounded like a compliment. Was it intentional?"

He grimaced. "I have never disrespected your kind's capacity or strengths. It is a fool of a konigswolf who would do so."

Every time she wanted to be surprised by what he'd said, she found herself more astounded still by *why* he'd said it.

"Be that as it may, I believe we are obligated for the moment to, as the saying goes, do as the Romans do. Let's make the best of it we can."

Her arms went out, falling gently on the air, as she prepared her opening pose.

The werewolf huffed. "Now? You wish to teach me dances *now*? You add insult to injury, Walta."

"Our sojourn is nearly half-over already. How many more opportunities will we have? Mazzi's maids said dinner isn't for another hour; it is a sufficient time to practice."

He crossed his arms over his chest. "I take no issue with playing a court jester before the wolfsretter. It is no insult to my person to be thought of as ignorant of courtly ways. I am."

"But you agreed to this! I will not have you made to look the fool, even if you would not feel it."

"Why would *you* care how they perceive me?"

Implication weighed heavy in his word. Fine, if that's what it took to bring the wolf into submission, she'd give a little in his direction.

"Just because I refuse to indulge your unrealistic fantasy of our union does not mean I do not care for you at all. You may be willing to endure the slings and arrows of my family's insults, but it won't be on my watch."

She assumed a position before the fireplace. "First, the bow. Left foot forward, then back, then bend slightly at the knees."

The demonstration came in time with the instruction, and though he allowed one more look of concern, he soon gave in. To her delight, he proved an apt pupil, quick to learn and ready to please. In short order, Andreas had become the master of La Volta and passed reasonably well on the Allemande, though all her instruction suffered from the fact that they were just one couple and without music. Though Gerwalta attempted to explain different rotations, she knew from experience nothing replaced reenactment.

"And we end, as we began, with a bow." She demonstrated

proper form, but when she raised her eyes, she found Andreas standing straight, gawking.

She looked down at her attire, wondering if in all their swishing and swaying, one of her stays had come undone.

"What is it?"

Andreas reached out, taking her hand. "If I wasn't a lupine, I'd never know you were not a laywoman. You can look and act just like one of them. How did you learn all this anyhow?"

"My family's trade takes us into laymen circles from time to time. Though occasions have been few for me, I was still given the proper education if need ever arose for me to entertain guests."

"Wearing something like—" Andreas motioned broadly at her. "—this tent?"

She laughed. "No, we don't fancy ourselves capable of Venetian fashion in the Schwarzwald."

"Thank the Lord Almighty. How do these Italians manage to reproduce in such quantities with such troublesome clothing?"

"Andreas!" She tried to hide her smile behind her hands, but her laugh eked out all the same.

The wolf had no shame. "Do not tell me the thought did not occur to you."

"It most certainly did not."

"Liar!" He pulled her hands away, drinking in the humor of her eyes. When they met, the laughter dissolved, and looking anywhere else would have taken herculean effort.

He stepped closer, dropping her hands and placing his on the crown of the bustles hiding her hips. "It was the first thing I thought when I walked in and saw you in this. I said to myself, 'Andreas, you want to ravish this creature, that much is plain, but how would you go about it?'"

"With a great deal of effort, I would suppose."

He stepped closer. "Do you suppose they would bounce if you wore them while making love?"

"I do."

His hands slid up her sides, the silk tickling her under his fingers. "We should endeavor to learn."

She withdrew moments before his lips reached hers, parading across the room in a huff.

"*Enough!* Why must you constantly tempt my resolve? I am a strong woman, but I am not unbreakable. Please stop encouraging my affections."

"Perhaps, love, you are unaware that the point of seduction *is* to encourage affections."

"But seduction to what end?" She threw up her arms. "Why are you so determined to sacrifice yourself to win me, when you'd lose me and your life *by* winning?"

"Dearest Walta, do you not realize that your love is worth dying for?" He stepped forward, taking her right hand between his own and raising it to his mouth. Andreas's lips caressed the bare knuckles. "You left me alone for a year in hopes that my love for you would fade. It has not. It *cannot*. I am here on this earth to love you. If that means my death, I am already dead. You are not saving me by denying me; you're subjecting me to purgatory."

"There is no future in which we can be together."

"Love, we are together *now*."

It ended there: her ill wishes, her spite, her arguments, her resistance. The wolfsretter crashed into him, pressing her lips to his, her arms thrown around his neck. The force of her person and her wardrobe were more than the lupine was expecting, but he saved himself from toppling over in time to catch her legs as she jumped up to encircle him at the hip.

And then, without warning, she was gone.

His eyes flew open, prepared to see Gerwalta performing the type of emotional acrobatics that was becoming her calling card, but what he discovered was much worse:

His love was pressed against the wall, her arms high overhead and held by a pair of ghostly white hands.

And a vampire was feeding at her throat.

TEN

Andreas let loose the beast, the pain wracking his every limb, anguish tormenting his bones and breaking his body into pieces until another creature took its place. The feat was achieved in the flap of a gnat's wing. Andreas leapt forward, instinctively set to devour that which threatened what was his.

Kill him.

All wolves knew the legend: that there had once been a time before slayers and wolfsretter, when vampires and werewolves stood on opposite sides of the battle, enemies to the last. He felt that truth now beat as his own heart, driving him to murder, to rend, to destroy.

But wolves were meant to fight in packs, not solitarily and inside a lady's chamber.

The vampire's head flew back as Andreas's maw wrapped around his leg, rending muscle and hitting bone. It was the oddest duality: the taste of something dead, the sweetness of fresh meat. It danced in glory upon his tongue as none other had. The evisceration ended abruptly as the vampire moved with speed lightning would envy. The creature streaked across the room, pulling along the complicated set of dresses, bustles, and underthings that entombed Gerwalta Faust.

He still tasted her, followed the scent as it streaked through the house, the growl rumbling in his chest. Despite the power and agility of this body, wolves were not meant to be graceful in doors. A side table in a hall toppled over as he rounded a corner, shattering whatever dish or vase had rested upon it. Andreas hit the stairs just in time to see Gerwalta's feet disappear.

"What is going on?"

"Vampire, and a hostile one."

The konigswolf did not slow when he heard voices behind him. Mazzi and Karahan bit his heels as he reached the top step, both the vampire and the slayer quicker on two feet somehow then he managed on four.

"Which way, Herr Baron?"

The Spatar looked to him for direction, and Andreas was happy to provide.

A hall, a chamber, a balcony.

A jump. The roof of the neighboring home.

Red tiles cracked and slipped under his feet as Andreas tried to shore up his footing. No use; as his limbs explored every cardinal direction, they displaced more tiles in each one. Finally, the only direction his legs could go was down. Andreas barked, then yelped as his body filled the hole. He had not fallen through, but he also had nothing beneath him against which to gain leverage and rise out. He wondered if the occupant of the home in whose roof he was now pegged could see his paws dangling from their ceiling, and what they may think of that.

Mazzi rounded him with ease, holding up a hand. *Much good that will do,* Andreas thought. *Slapping cannot be a very successful defense against vampires.*

Only, the Italian *didn't* slap Gerwalta's captor. He didn't even touch him. What he did do was so much more amazing.

Mazzi *made* sunlight appear in the dark of night.

The vampire's grip went slack as he threw his hands over his face, releasing Gerwalta in the process. The wolfsretter, despite her excessive wardrobe, gained a solid stance. As she moved, however, Andreas understood she hovered more than stood. Not a single tile slipped beneath her, and the ridiculous dress had enough slack to help her pull off the deception. The vampire, however, could not hover and had been rendered blind. Consquently, he fell to all fours to keep from toppling backward off the roof. The act told Andreas two things: one, he was not the only dark one challenged by heights. And two, this vampire still feared falling. He was fresh from his creche and unfamiliar with the resilience of his immortal body.

Mazzi's steps fell like dew. "You're not from the Vicenze creche. Who sent you and why are you here?"

The vampire only shook his head.

The ball of light dancing on the Italian's hand increased the slightest increment. "I take it you've never met one of my kind, then. You do know at this range, I need merely to flick this your direction and you will die, do you not? But I can see you are new to your fangs. I have some sympathy for your ignorance. Tell me what I want to know, and I'll let you live."

Was he insane? Gerwalta wasn't some innocent girl snatched from the shadowy street; she was attacked inside the home of a slayer. What possible goal could the vampire have but to kill her, and quite on purpose? Did Helga's influence extend all the way here? If so, how would she know where to find them?

The vampire buried his head between his hands. "I was sent to kill her. She is my first blood."

The slayer looked back over his shoulder at Karahan, who kept a safe distance, lingering in the window of Mazzi's home.

"My friend, any chance he is born of your line?"

Karahan shook his head. "But that does not mean he has not fallen under the Ravens' influence."

"Then you'd have no objection to my killing him?"

"I wouldn't even if he were a Dracule." A sinister hue Andreas had not noticed before gleamed in the Spatar's eyes. "I disavowed any of my son's progeny, just as I disavowed him."

Without removing his proxy hold of the assailant, Mazzi chuckled. "If only that let you kill the whelp yourself."

Gerwalta had grown tired of prattle. In a blink, she summoned silver—in which of her many bolts of fabric had that been hiding, he'd like to know—and had created a blade. She crossed the vampire, anchored her hands on his scalp, and pulled him to his feet. His back leaned into her shoulder.

"Who sent you?" she demanded, pushing her blade to the base of his throat. "Who wants me dead?"

"You're wasting your time," Karahan called from the window. "He's a sapling of a vamp executing the order of his creche, not so unlike your wolves obeying the orders of a king. This vampire is too new to the fang to have a mind of his own. He's obviously been ordered to stay silent, and silent he will stay."

Andreas would not believe it himself if he didn't see it, but

Gerwalta growled her frustration. No sooner had it registered—the sound stirring a desire that was bordering more by the day on need—than she pressed the dagger into the vampire's flesh, drawing a slow, molasses-like drop of undead blood.

"Fine, then. Tell me who gave you the order."

"I'd do it, son," Mazzi patronized. "Fraulein Faust here is a daughter of the infamous House of Red. You'll be no less dead if she cuts off your head then if I hit you with my solarium."

"I'll die anyway if I come back without her life beating in my veins."

What did that mean, "her life beating in my veins"? Surely nothing pleasant. Not for the first time, Andreas worked his legs, hoping to at least rock himself backward enough to free a limb. If he could just get one paw on the roof proper, pushing himself backward with the aid of the angles would assure his freedom. Just as he felt the tiniest leverage, something grabbed him at the paw.

Everything that followed happened instantaneously. Gerwalta let go her captive, diving in Andreas's direction. The vampire in turn pursued her. Mazzi's sun-ball flew, attempting to keep the latter from reaching the former. Something yanked at his leg, pulling him through the hole he'd created and filled.

A shudder of black cloth, and then, blackness itself as he fell into the dark of the void beneath his feet.

ELEVEN

As a dark one, sunlight and Gerwalta had never been kindreds. When she dove in the direction of Andreas's disappearing body and the ball of energy Messer Mazzi had conjured whizzed by her en route to the vampire, she too felt its burn. The crackle of the flame and the hum of the energy blistered her arm, despite missing her completely. It must be strong enough to kill the vampire who'd attacked her. Only, when she landed on the roof near the hole that had swallowed the konigswolf and turned back to make sure the enemy was vanquished, she found her expectations spoiled.

Where the vampire had been, a silver shield as tall as a grown man stood, the billow of a black cloak fanning out behind it.

"Impossible."

But it wasn't. In fact, given time to reason, she'd have found it quite logical. Why should the interloper not be here? Because he was a wolfsretter? That had not prevented *her*, had it? Venice—as far as she was aware, the entire peninsula—fell under the control of the purview of the Yellow bloodline. What was a wolfsretter from the House of Night doing in Italy? Their region was that of the Safavid and Ottoman empires, not the West.

Little time was afforded her to absorb the shock of another of her kind having deflected the blow. Fingers of gray smoke funneled through the air with much too much deliberation. In a few blinks, the mass condensed and took shape. Behind the opposing wolfsretter, her assailant, found himself braced by two vampires of unnatural muscular endowment. Each held his arms in a manner that made the attacker grimace.

Good, at least he'd gotten some unpleasantness.

"Messer Mazzi," the one on the left said, he of flaxen hair and a noble countenance.

"Messer Brunelli," the slayer returned, adding on further words in Italian that made no sense to her. But as Gerwalta relaxed her ear, she found certain ones stood out due to their similarities to French. Slowly, meaning began to take shape.

Disobeyed... Confusion... Apologies...

Andreas was a konigswolf; she knew the fall into the house did not harm him, and now that their enemy seemed neutralized, she meant to get to the bottom of what had happened.

"Are you attempting to say," she cut into Mazzi and Brunelli's conversation in her most formal German, unsure if she'd be understood by the vampire, "that what has happened here was some kind of misunderstanding?"

The handsome man's violet eyes shifted her way. "*Non parla la nostra lingua?*"

"I do not believe she does," Mazzi answered in German. "Fraulein Faust comes from the Schwarzwald."

His German dripped with Italian seasonings, but all the same... "*Scuzi,* Fraulein, but as I was telling Messer Mazzi, this young one misunderstood his directions. On behalf of our master, I offer you my humblest apologies for the inconvenience."

"Having fangs sunk into my neck is not what I would call an *inconvenience*." She straightened. "Who is your master? I am owed restitution for this *misunderstanding*."

Mazzi skirted to Gerwalta's side, speaking into her shoulder. "Fraulein, please. Brunelli is the Doge's second in command, as well as her consort of two decades. His apology is her apology." He cleared his throat before continuing in amplified tones so that all may hear. "We accept in anticipation."

Brunelli bowed. "We are delighted this could be resolved without further conflict." He didn't look delighted, particularly as he scowled in Gerwalta's direction. "We hope that we can still expect you tomorrow evening for *la Carnivale*?"

"Messer Brunelli, it is the highlight of my year."

The Doge's second turned back to her. "I will send a new dress, Fraulein, to replace the one this fool so shamelessly stained with blood. I look forward to dancing with you tomorrow night."

"To dancing with...." Her voice sputtered as formality loosened itself from her grip. Gerwalta was not unskilled in the art of diplomacy, but she was not its most ardent fan. The wolfsretter plastered a dulcet smile upon her face and recalled the silver in her grip from its service. The metal licked back up her arms and plated itself in ringlets around her forearm. "Messer Brunelli…"

"Please, call me Massimo."

Gerwalta tried not to gag. If this rogue thought he could deter her with flattery… "Very well, then. *Massimo,* I have been a member of my own court long enough to know misunderstandings do, on occasion, occur. But mark my words, there can be no confusion. This vampire attacked me and clearly told us he had been sent to dispatch of me. What part of that was the result of misinterpretation?"

Massimo did not waver for a moment, letting a cocky grin cover his face. "I intend to find out come sunrise. I suspect, however, that he errantly believed he was meant to subdue and capture *you.*"

But if not her, then who? The respect, if only ceremonial, that Massimo showed for Messer Mazzi suggested they were on agreeable turns.

Like a clock striking twelve, everything sank into place, and just who the assailant had been dispatched to collect became all too clear.

Andreas! She ran for the last place he'd been…and stopped. A queer sensation tickled her insides, and its identification drove her to double her speed when she resumed.

A sliver of moonlight from the half-disk in the sky peeked down, sending a searchlight into the darkness below. Gerwalta's eyes lingered beyond the hole through which the wolf had fallen only long enough to let her adjust and her heart shatter.

He was not there. The werewolf who not two minutes ago had plummeted from view, had disappeared completely.

She regained her feet and spun on her heel, even as the unwelcome undead dissolved into clouds of smoke and the wolfsretter jumped from the roof, disappearing against the dark of night.

"What have you done with him!" Gerwalta's feet cracked slate with each step she bolted, chasing the pillars as they snaked through the air.

"Fraulein, stop! You'll fall."

The slayer's arms caged her from behind just as her foot reached the edge of the roof.

"I will not. I will…"

"Fall to your death is what you'll do," Messer Mazzi said as he yanked her back. "Unless you can fly."

But she *could* fly….

But who knew who could be watching? The wolfsretter from the House of Night may still be lingering within view. True to their legend, he may be hidden in plain sight, invisible to any but those by whom he wished to be seen. And if anyone found out, her hopes for getting away from Triberg would be gone. She'd do anything to protect her secret, even let Andreas be taken.

And that proved why she didn't deserve him.

But she'd be damned if she wasn't going after him, because *he* didn't deserve *that.*

Gerwalta ceased her flailing and allowed herself to be pulled back. "This is the second time Andreas has allowed himself to be captured away from me, and by god, it's going to be the last."

"Whatever they want him for, Fraulein, it is not death. At least, not immediately, or else that black hood would have run him through with his silver instead of shielding the sapling."

She couldn't disagree, but if they weren't after killing Andreas, what did they want him for?

TWELVE

"Drink this. It will help with the nerves."

Red liquid swirled inside of a green-tinted glass pressed to her palm.

"I am not nervous, Messer Mazzi." Gerwalta looked up from the offering. "I am furious."

The blond-haired Italian sputtered. "Surely, Fraulein, you do not think *I* had anything to do with this."

"No, I do not." She turned to Karahan sitting by the fireplace, his eyes chasing flames. "But I believe *you* did."

Even the reasoning had seemed off to her at the beginning. Why would *she* need a bodyguard? Gerwalta had dismissed Karahan's patronizing; all men thought women weak. Except the wolfsretter, where females bested their male counterparts in strength and cunning. So why have a wolf along to protect her?

Because that wasn't why he was there.

Gerwalta stood and paced toward the fire. "Was it true, what you told my mother? What you told me?"

"Everything was true." He sipped at his own wine before adding under his breath, "I simply did not tell you the *whole* truth."

She set the unsampled drink down on a nearby table and settled into a comfortable position. "I will have it, then."

"Have what?"

"The *whole* truth, Spatar." She leaned forward. "Now."

Karahan passed her an amused smirk. "How old are you, Fraulein?"

"I hardly see what *that* has to do with any—"

In a flash, he was upon her, his fangs bared, the gruesome

creature he kept hidden within unleashed and a breath from her throat.

"Watch yourself, Igor," the slayer said from behind. "We are old friends, but I'll not hesitate to kill you if you attack this young woman."

"It is exactly because she is young that I do this." His tongue flicked out, licked the hollow of her throat. "You taste as if you've barely come into your womanhood. Now, how old are—"

"Twenty-two!" The words came of their own volition, the fear palpable on her lips. "I was twenty-two last December. I am no child."

"You are to me!" the vampire spat, before spinning on his heel and going to stand again by the fire. "I have walked this earth for over three hundred years. I have lauded saints and I have fostered sinners. I have overthrown the men of God, and I have fought under the banner of gods of men. I *know* what evil is, Fraulein. I birthed it that cursed night in Istanbul when, young in my fangs, I birthed *him*."

"Birthed him?" she gasped. "Birthed who?"

Karahan spit his name out like a curse. "Vlad Tepes."

She knew the name. Curse her, but she knew the name. "The Prince of Blood? But he's dead!"

"Do you think I'd risk your life and mine if he was?" A gristly laugh rattled in the vampire's chest. "No, Vlad is very much alive."

She grabbed the glass and downed the contents in one tremendous gulp. "But what does this have to do with Andreas?"

Here, Messer Mazzi picked up the thread. "All invitees are expected to pay tribute," he said. "The Doge demands that each vampire paterfamilias supply."

"And this year, she asked for wolves." Gerwalta put together the rest for herself. She turned to Mazzi. "Then you did know of this."

He turned away in shame. "I *suspected*. The friendship Igor and I have been able to share is only possible because we've learned when to be curious and when to mind our own business. It is a necessary balance, as our natures are so inherently opposed to each other."

She looked at Mazzi, at Karahan, back at Mazzi.... "Tell me

this then: why come all the way to the Schwarzwald to collect a lupine? Why travel all the way to Triberg when you yourself admitted to encountering the pack in Ravensburg? It would have made for a shorter trip."

"Of course, I could have snatched one from anywhere. I came to the Schwarzwald not for Herr Baron," Karahan admitted, "I came for you."

Her innards lurched. "Why am I so special?"

"Because I am not a cruel man," he said. "I could have contracted any wolfsretter to bond my sons in silver, but how to save all the wolves brought in chains to the Doge's Palace?"

The wolfsretter's heart threatened to burst. "You mean the wolves are in danger?"

"I believe so, yes." An open gaze bespoke wonderment, respect, hope. It was such an odd look, one that she rarely saw on anyone's face, let alone a dark one's. "While chasing down one of Vlad's plots, I found myself in Nuremberg and heard the story of a young wolfsretter with blazing red hair and an explementary heart, who rescued wolves from a corrupted alpha female, and I knew... I knew!... that *that* woman would be the one who could deliver both the dark ones and the laity from my mistakes."

The weight of expectation settled heavy on her shoulders, collapsing her lungs. Gerwalta struggled to breathe. "I should have killed the laymen who witnessed my misdeeds."

"There is no need, Fraulein. I remade their memories. One did get away, but often the rants of a single man carry the weight of the air he exhales in making them." He crossed from the fire, lifted her chin. "But please know, what you did in Nuremberg was no misdeed. It was an act of compassion rarely seen in your kind, and I need you to have that level of conviction again."

She swallowed down her emotions, making mincemeat of his flattery. "You hired me to trap vampires, Spatar, not lose the man I love."

"Save him, then, and the others who've fallen victim to Vlad's plots."

"And in turn, will you save me?"

"Save you?" His hand pulled away, as though she'd suddenly lit on fire. "From what?"

She leaned to the side, locking the silent slayer in her gaze. "Messer Mazzi, would you say that the Doge's court is highly politicized?"

"Is it not the underpinnings of a royal court to be so?" he laughed.

Ah, Italians and their humor. "Did you take *Massimo's* explanation as Bible truth?"

"Ah, yes, I see what you're getting at." Mazzi stood. "I believe that the vampire who attacked you was acting on someone's order, though I trust Massimo did not know of it."

For the first time in their acquaintance, Karahan was thrown for a loop. "What does that mean? What is she getting at?"

"This is the second time that someone has attempted to kill me since we left Triberg," Gerwalta said. "My would-be assassin wants me dead, but only by a means in which their touch would not be felt."

Karahan shook his head. "It is merely coincidence."

"Coincidence is never coincidence." Her tattered dress wreaked of vampire. Torn to threads as parts were, beyond the repair of even the most talented of seamstresses, what shame was there in removing the outside layer and throwing it to the flames? "I don't believe your finding me was an act of your own doing, Herr Spatar, though I'm quite sure the plots were engineered for you to think so. Vampires were behind the plot to expose lupines to the Holy Roman Empire, but a vampire would have no need for confiscation in targeting me, nor would a wolf know the truth of my acts. No, it is one of my own who wants me dead, and as you're using me to solve your problems, they're using you to solve theirs."

"But what problem could another wolfsretter have with you?" Karahan asked. "And how would they learn all this anyhow?"

She had no idea on the first part, but the second made perfect sense. "Spatar Karahan, what led you to Nuremberg?"

He hesitated. There must be such a measure of light he'd bring to matters he'd prefer left in the dark. Only when her gaze burrowed into him did Karahan relent.

"I don't know how familiar you are with the House of Night, Fraulein. Before Vlad decided to engineer the genocide of lupines himself, he first tried to get them to do it. They refused, and in retaliation, Vlad raided their silver mines in the Degirmencik province. I simply followed the path of that silver as it came north, and into the coffers of the Holy Roman Emperor."

"Through my cousin Bernhardt's effort," she said when he'd finished. "The Vicematron of Ravensburg was a woman named Maria Dreger, Bernhardt's mother. After my mission to Nuremberg, she was called in for questioning. My mother relinquished her of her position and vanquished her, but Maria was found dead the next day. Someone in the House of Red did it, though no one has owned it."

"And then you were attacked soon after we left the Schwarzwald. Karahan's mouth fell open. "Someone in your mother's court wants you dead, too. Do you know who?"

"I have suspicions, yes, but knowing she is behind the plot does not tell me who will execute it here."

Mazzi puckered his lips, then nodded. "Massimo Brunelli might know."

Gerwalta turned on the slayer. "Why?"

"Massimo wants you there in the open. His invitation in front of others meant as much. He had meant for you to be sneaked in."

"He meant for me to be concealed?" A student of conspiracy and intrigue, she did so hate that she hadn't anticipated this. "The Doge's second in command is one of your conspirators?"

Mazzi nodded. "Who better to cut off the head than the very hand which bears the weapon?"

A cannonball exploded in Gerwalta's ribs as she realized just how true a statement that was.

She continued, "Even if I carry out this act and trap the Ravens, I will arrive home a corpse if those communicating with Triberg are not exposed. Part of your plan involves the capture of Tepes and his men. The other, overseeing their imprisonment. I cannot assure that if I am dead."

Karahan, it seemed, was not the type to renegotiate terms. His temple wrinkled as he turned on her. "Then I suggest that you not die. Your internal court politics is none of my concern. I have already agreed to a blood debt to your mother. If she wished it paid, that is for her to decide. For now, I expect you to save yourself."

And with that, he smoked from the room.

THIRTEEN

Andreas bit in the direction of whatever had him by the ankle, but that only made things worse. Silver thread looped around his maw, drawing it closed. A moment later, the binding roped his paws as well. The lupine was bound and tied like a pig being readied for market.

The animal within recognized its predictament, and Andreas gave into instinct. Thrashing, he tried to loosen his restraints; the act drove the bindings deeper, nesting into his fur, the silver blistering flesh upon contact.

"If you want your love to live, calm yourself!"

The words were German, but the speaker was not—nor, given the slant of the foreign tongue, was he Italian.

Andreas finally overrode his wolf hearing the words. He'd vie for his own freedom, even if that meant drawing blood, but he would not do so if it meant bringing any harm to Gerwalta. He stilled, turning to search the darkness for his captor. A form took shape against the darkness, more a silhouette than a person. Only when his eyes refused to focus further did he understand the truth of what he was seeing, though clarity did not partner with belief. After all, being from the Schwarzwald, the konigswolf had never seen a wolfsretter not born of the House or Red, let alone one of the House of Night.

The man removed his black hood, showing that the coloration did not end with his attire. His sable hair fell in gentle curls that kissed his shoulders. Inkwell eyes stared at him, peering out from a face clouded by a thick beard and patches of skin the color of parched earth.

A shiver went down the length of the wolf's ridge. He let his body go lax. There was no point in fighting.

"Good." The corner of the dark man's mouth rose. "I'm going to remove your restraints and you will come with me with haste and without sound. Do as I say, and I swear to you, the red hood will not be harmed."

Without the ability to fly unto the roof and protect Gerwalta himself, what could he do? As soon as he was free of the bonds, despite the sting left where silver had touched his skin, Andreas rose to all fours and followed.

Wolves were not intended to ride in coaches. That much became clear as they whisked through Padua and rode toward the sea.

"Are you certain you would not take your lay form?" the wolfsretter asked as he stepped into a boat that was thrice the length of its width. "I do have clothing here in the boat for you. If modesty is your concern...."

Andreas shifted into his skin without another thought, drawing wide eyes from the oarmen who began to recite the rosary.

The lupine pointed at the terrified laymen. "Your oarsman is not in the fold?"

"He is an employee of the Doge, but there are few lupines in Venice. It's likely the first time he's ever witnessed a transformation. That or...." The wolfsretter's eyes raked down the plains of Andreas's hard stomach, coming to rest on the rise of hips. "Are all wolves in your pack so liberal with your nudity? This is Venice, Herr Baron, not Florence." He grabbed a drape of clothing from behind him and threw it up to Andreas on the quay. "Cover yourself."

The distance between the island—or *islands* as he discovered when they neared—did not last much, but by the measure of its culture, it was like a new world. With rare exception, stone and masonry covered all land. Houses, churches, and cobblestone streets collapsed in on each other. The oarsman guided them first from the shore to open waters, then into a great channel which divided the sectors of town into three primary masses, and into a series of smaller and smaller canals.

Their boat slipped through in the night, lit only by the long torch affixed to a post rising from the prow, passing under an occasional bridge that joined pathways overhead. No matter how he attempted, Andreas's eye could catch little of these pedestrian lanes, for their byways in turn twisted, as though the city had been planned and laid down by the roots of a mighty tree and not the whims of men.

"Everything is packed together so tightly."

"Yes, it reminds one of Istanbul."

Andreas turned upon the wolfsretter to find a like look of growing apprehension. "Is that where you are from?"

"If only."

"If not there, then where?"

The dark man laughed. "It is... not for me to discuss."

"And what is?" Andreas said. "Where are you taking me, and to what end?"

"That is also not for me to discuss." The wolfsretter leaned over the side of the boat, dipping his gloved finger in the water. "My tongue knows a thousand tales, and in each of them, a dagger."

With one more bend behind them, the boat pulled alongside one of the buildings. Between two poles which stuck out of the water and served as breakers, a small dock extended. The man who assisted them unto land beared fangs as both passed; Andreas ignored him. He was here only long enough to discover what threat a wolfsretter of the House of Night represented and disarm any who may threaten Gerwalta. Tossing fur with a fanged parasite may be necessary, but he'd not engage in it unless forced.

"What is this place?"

The wolfsretters led the way through an opulent courtyard decorated by marble statues and roses. "The Doge's Palace. It does not matter; you are not here to see her."

A new voice spoke. "No, you are not."

Regal. Terrible. Powerful. Deadly.

The man who descended from the grand central staircase was dressed in black finery and wearing his family's coat of arms molded in gold on his chest. The vampire took each step with deliberate precision, as though prowling. His pale skin contrasted with the black hair which ran in streams over his shoulders. Andreas's inner wolf rumbled, fight or flight instincts difficult to subdue. The animal within recognized a predator—the man, an advisory.

The new arrival continued. "There are many faults with the ways of my kind, in my opinion, but some demented conception that only men are capable to rule is not one. Once in a blue moon, an odd female *can* be worthy. Nor do we, like the wolfsretter, automatically declare the so-called fairer sex superior. Every vampire lives and dies on the merits of his or her own abilities, be it strength, cunning, or an acumen to reign. Luciana Morelli, third vampire Doge of Venice, excels in all three."

"And you?" Andreas squared his shoulders, turned toward the vampire. "What do you excel in?"

"Dominating Luciana." He extended his arm, surprising Andreas with a gesture of neutrality. "Welcome to Venice. I am Vlad Tepes of the Dracule bloodline."

"Andreas Baron, Konigswolf of Triberg." Not knowing how else to respond, Andreas met the gesture in kind. "Why am I here, Herr Tepes?"

The vampire grinned, even as he turned and invited by a sweep of his hand for Andreas to follow, the German-speaking black wolfsretter trailing as the other drifted away. "You have been traveling in the company of a vampire calling himself Spatar Goran Karahan."

"I cannot deny it."

"Have you some allegiance to him? Owe him some favor?"

"No, and I owe allegiances to no one but my pack and my mate."

Tepes drew to a stop. "But you have no mate."

A keen piece of knowledge for someone he'd just met. Of course, if the wolfsretter could speak to his feelings for Gerwalta, at the very least rumors to that effect might be swirling at court. Only, who would want to speak on such matters, and to what end? They'd only just arrived in Venice. How could the court of the Doge know what Gerwalta's mother did not?

The comment could not have possibly been meant as an offense, but it stunned all the same. "I am courting my intended. It is just a matter of formality."

As in, Gerwalta's eschewing hers.

"My wishes for your joyous mating, then." A few more steps

found them in the lushness of a courtyard, its garden still green in the crisp of the Venetian winter. The craftmenship of the stonework beneath their feet spoke of wealth, and the smoking pots of smoldering incense on the edges perfumed the space with the scent of roses that might have been present had it been summer.

"Why you are here is simple. I wish to employ your services."

"They are not available."

"Ah but wait until you hear my offer." Tepes drew to a stop in the middle of the courtyard. "Tomorrow night is *Carnivale*. A silly tradition, in my opinion, but one observed with some relish here in Venice. The Doge will play host to every vampire who calls this island home, as well as several coming from further ports."

No doubt then the timing of their quest. Whomever these errant blooded sons of Karahan were, they would be at such a celebration.

"Karahan has come a long way to attend." Laughter rumbled in the vampire's chest. "I can see from the raised angle of your brow that you were unaware of this."

"There is no reason for the Spatar to burden me with his affairs."

"No, of course not, but he should have let you know that in the tradition of my kind, he has brought a gift to offer the Doge. Further, he should have told you that *you* are that gift."

Andreas flinched. "I beg your pardon?"

"This year, every bloodline was expected to present the Doge with a lupine. *My father* selected you."

They came from nowhere, but suddenly they were everywhere. Vampires, six in total besides Tepes, flanking his every side. Instinct said to shift, but a silver collar suddenly forced around his throat held him in flesh. His strength betrayed him, and reason fled. Andreas fell to his knees, crying through the pain as the sextet drug him to the side of the courtyard, through a door, past several rooms, and finally into a windowless cell in which sat a silver cage.

Correction: cages. As they tossed him in, the sizzle at his throat eased. Andreas peered out through watering eyes as the last drops of silver returned to their master.

The black hood.

Tepes leaned in. "Are you ready to hear my offer now, Herr Baron?"

The konigswolf glared.

"Good. Tomorrow night, when my father approaches your cage, Mehmet," he motioned to the wolfsretter behind him, "will be watching. He will revoke the silver so that you may escape, at which juncture, you will kill Karahan. When this task is done, I will guarantee your safety out of the city. I will pay you with your still-beating heart."

It took more than the pain of silver to make the kongiswolf turn his back on his principles. "I will not harm someone who has given me no offense."

"Ah, so you're one of those rare lupines with the ability for higher thought—and by virtue of it, like to negotiate."

Tepes leaned in, clutching the bars. "Counteroffer: kill Karahan, and we will let both you *and* your beauitful traveling companion live."

Andreas's blood ran cold. "You will not lay a finger on her."

"Do as I say, and I will not."

With a quick sweep of his head, Andreas took in the sight of the other cages. "And them? Are they under your employ too?"

"No, Herr Baron. They are here as food. You could join them on the menu, if you wish."

A wolf would escape a trap no matter the cost, even if it meant chewing off its own foot. A werewolf was no different. "You promise that Gerwalta will be unharmed?"

"Of course."

"Fine, then." His head hung low. "Agreed."

FOURTEEN

Sleep refused to share her bed, no matter how the wolfsretter lectured herself that she needed the rest. She visualized forms and tactics, remembrances of training she'd done as a girl. Strategy dictated control of the konigswolf, and by proxy, the pack. Divide, isolate, conquer: those were the rules when facing more than one adversary. Surely taking on multiple vampires would be no different. Only, once she knew who they were, she need only divide, isolate, and *capture*. Thank god they were all men and Venetian fashions favored her figure. Only, could she still walk, concealing so much silver under the petticoats she wore?

A knock on her door at sunset roused her from what little sleep she'd managed.

Mazzi's lady's maids were punctual if not brave.

"Come in."

Who entered was no maid. He wasn't a lady.

Violet eyes found her through the darkness. Crimson lips pulled a sinister smile, framing pearlescent fangs. "Fraulein."

Gerwalta sprang from bed, summoning a blade forged in the moment, ready to attack the vampire if he took another step. "I will strike if you attack. I will not be used as a fountain."

If he had any sense of inappropriateness, given that she wore only bedclothes, Massimo did not evidence it. "Dress and join us downstairs immediately." He dropped a swath of clothing on a table near the door.

"You have some nerve, Messer, to barge into my room and make commands of me when last night, your minion had me by the vein." She turned the blade in her hand. "What are you doing here and where is Andreas Baron?"

"They told me you may prove difficult." The vampire grimaced, his rough jaw working. "I have no time to flatter the curiosities of some… some… little red riding hood. Dress with haste and meet us in the dining room. Our time is limited and our mission, critical, if you want to save your wolf."

She shuddered when the door slammed in his wake, though not from the sound or the action. *If you want to save your wolf….* She knew Andreas was in danger, but she refused to acknowledge that he may be in mortal danger. Hadn't Karahan promised it wasn't so? Andreas, dead? Oh, certainly she threatened that it would be the outcome if he didn't cease attempting to make love to her, but *actually* die?

Her heart couldn't take it. If Andreas died then, and she hadn't told him that she loved him….

Gerwalta couldn't let that happen.

Karahan looked up from the flames dancing on the hearth when Massimo entered the dining room, burning twice as hot.

"You insolent, watcher cur!" the Venetian spat. "Is it not bad enough that you involved other dark one lines to clean up your mistake, but you didn't even tell her who you were?"

"She knows who Vlad is now, and that I am his blooded father." Karahan held up his hands. "I admit that I've restricted details on a need-to-know basis. Gerwalta has been hired to accomplish a task, nothing more. She is the means to an end."

"Then her life means nothing to you?" Massimo spat, fetching a tumbler of brandy from the table and pulling it to his lips. "For all your idealism, you're just as selfish as your accursed sons, selectively sharing truths and not caring who your deeds cut down in the process."

Karahan leaned forward in his chair, the definition of serenity. "Where is this spite coming from, Massimo? Where the concern? Could it be that she reminds you of Catalina?"

Rage suffused a voice which grew monstrous in its restraint. "Do not speak her name if you wish to live through this night, Goran or Igor or whatever fallacy you've created yourself as."

Just as the veiled threat was uttered, the wolfsretter entered the dining room, tailed by their host.

"Speak whose name?" Mazzi asked. "If it is Gerwalta Faust, worry no more, for she is here."

Angelo Mazzi was a fool of a slayer. More concerned about warming his bed with new conquests—male or female—than undertaking his sacred duties. If he had, then the rotten branch of the Dracule family tree would have been obliterated when they'd shown up in Venice six months before. Instead, they lingered, corrupting the vampires of a city much too small for so many laity deaths to go unnoticed. Every vampire community dealt with outliers, grifters on the edge of society who risked everyone's discovery with selfish, indecent action. The Ravens brought such behavior into the Doge's Palace, normalizing the irrational.

Massimo was about to bite into the slayer when he turned...

"Fraulein Faust—"

...and found himself dumbstruck.

Yes, she did bare some resemblance to Catalina.

Dedicated as he was to the memory of his deceased wife, the vampire's desires stirred, both for Gerwalta's blood and for her bed. Crimson cloth wrapped around a striking feminine frame. Black skirting in the center of the dress drew the eyes and begged a man of interest to wonder what lie beneath. Golden embellisments suggested buttons, and what did a button long for but to be undone? The Venetian court favored tight bodices, and this dress conformed. A sampling of cleavage where Gerwalta's womanly assets had been wrestled into submission teased the imagination.

And her neck.... Her beautiful, long neck which had already healed from the attack the night before, appeared now as untapped flesh, begging to be breached.

Mazzi grimaced. "Put away those fangs, my sanguineous friends," he said, switching the conversation from Italian to German for Gerwalta's sake. "She is not your breakfast."

Karahan turned to the wolfsretter, mumbling an apology, telling Massimo he had not been alone in his attraction. If even the old Dracule found temptation in this morsel, surely Vlad would want to eat her alive. Anyone who could hold the Bloody Prince's attention stood a chance at bettering.

Massimo retracted his fangs and pushed himself off the wall he'd been leaning against. "Fraulein Faust, I trust in dressing, you came to appreciate its design."

"Its design?" Karahan turned on Massimo. "Other than the fact that it's the precise color of rich blood as it flows from the veins?"

But it was Gerwalta who answered. "Silver has been sown into pockets under the skirt, and several of the elements in the... *supporting features* have also been constructed of it." She ran a hand over one of the bustles jutting from her hip. "Yes, the design is exquisite. It is also far too complex to have been put together since last night." She waited for a response that never came. "Fine, then. Keep your peace. Tell me again what the plan is."

Massimo gave him an admonishing glare before opening into explanations. "When you arrive, locate the seven men wearing raven-shaped masks. That would be Vlad and his generals. In turn, there are to be seven wolves who will be presented tonight at the Doge's palace."

Gerwalta blanched. "And by 'presented,' you mean?"

"As dinner," Karahan said. "We feed off the laity for sustence, but it is known among all vampires that the sweetest blood comes from other dark ones. Rare is it, however, that vampires and wolves find themselves in the same environs. The lupines harvested from each family will be served tonight as a holiday treat."

"But seven lupines together?" Gerwalta said. "Even if they are not a pack, they will function as one when under threat. I am certain a palace full of vampires would win such a confrontation, but no doubt several would be slain in the melee. That would hardly seem the desire of a gracious host."

Massimo clicked his tongue. "The wolves are being housed in silver cages."

The wolfsretter's jaw dropped. "The other wolfsretter. The one from the House of Night...."

"There are two actually," Mazzi said. "But never fear, Fraulein. They are allied with our cause."

"A cause, despite what's been made known to me thus far, that I am still unaware of. But I believe I am beginning to piece it together." She turned to Karahan. "Why do you wish to see the Doge deposed?"

Karahan kept his lips sealed and the truth, close to his heart. To expose it was to open himself to discovery.

Luckily, Massimo found a balance between confidentially and confidence and steered the conversation back unto secure ground. "Because Luciana, put in power in Venice twenty years ago to prevent Tepes's influence spreading, now fosters it. He's injected himself through her affections into the rule of Venice's dark ones. The Ravens already control Istanbul and all the regions which fall under the Ottoman flag. The Bloody Prince wants a war, one that will pit vampires against wolves, and—"

"Yes," Gerwalta cut in, emotions in her voice barely concealed. "That part I know. And since my activities in Nuremberg last year thwarted a plan that would have given rise to lupines among the Holy Roman Emperor's forces...."

"The gateway to the west for the Ottomans is Venice," Massimo said. "Our trade, influence, and location make Venice the perfect garden to plant a seed of discord that will lead straight to Rome, and through Rome, to its armies. Vlad learned the lesson about putting all eggs in one basket. This time, he will use all of the baskets. If all Christendom rises, it will favor his ambitions."

"Then he is a fool. This is no longer the age of Crusades. Europe is not the monolith he thinks it is." She shook her head. "It is not that I do not understand the danger, gentlemen. It's that I don't understand why the solution is merely to contain Tepes and his conspirators instead of kill them?"

Massimo rolled his eyes. "And they say *we* are the blood-thirsty ones?"

"The hoods simply have a different culture," Karahan countered, shooting daggers at the Italian. "She does not know that in our society, bloodlines are more than mere relations."

Mazzi handed the German woman a glass of brandy. "What he means to say, Fraulein, is that there are practical considerations... a system of checks and balances, if you will, that prevent the member of bloodline from destroying any of his or her own. The consequences can be lethal."

She chewed on that a moment before bobbing her head. "Understood. So, then, I have seven vampires to contain. That will call for signifigant amounts of silver. I suppose I am to use the cages then?"

"Indeed. Mehmet and Hasan, the black hoods, were critical to assuring the supply would be available on site."

This girl…. Her insights were impressive. She'd been trained in strategy. Well-trained.

"The seven wolves are each to their own containment, and as a precaution in case of any breakouts," Massimo continued. "During *Carnivale*, each of the Ravens will be assigned a cage to guard. The Doge will take first choice and first bite. When her fangs strike, all vampire eyes will be on her. That will be your cue to leach the silver from the cages and use it to contain Karahan's damned progeny."

The wolfsretter coughed, or so Massimo thought, until it became clear that she was laughing.

"Something amusing, wolf-killer?"

Her smile sank, her eyes sharpened. "Yes, that clearly none of you understand the nature of my talents," she spat. "Wolfsretters are not slayers. We do not put on grand light shows like that… *thing* that Messer Mazzi did."

"It's called a solarium, Fraulein," the slayer informed her. "It's actually a small flare of sunlight, and—"

Gerwalta waved her hand, cutting him off. "The point is, a wolfsretter's acts are swift, precise, and most importantly, covert. I cannot wield silver that I am either not in contact with or within my line of sight. In a room so crowded, and surrounded by hostile opposition? There is no possible way I can simultaneously warp seven wolf-sized silver cages, let alone use that silver to entrap seven deadly vampires."

The three men exchanged confused glances, as though they had just been informed the very air about them had been laced with poison and weren't certain if they should continue to breathe.

Finally, Massimo threw up his hands. "I told you, Goran, this plan is fantasy. Now thanks to you, I shall never have my revenge."

Karahan batted the air dismissively. "You are a young vampire, Massimo, but surely even your limited two decades of night have taught you that never happens."

"A child's saying, for someone who makes childish plans. This leaves me no choice. I will do what I intended before you filled my head with unicorn visions of a peaceful transfer. I will murder Luciana and send her to sleep in the sea, just like she did to my wife and child."

The old vampire's fangs slashed through his lips. "Do and die."

The Italian's chest backed Karahan into the wall. "I died with Catalina. It is only revenge that lives in me."

Both vampires threw hands over their eyes and hissed as the room blazed.

"Gentlemen, peace." Mazzi's solarium, a ball of death for the warring vampires that he used to regain their civility, cowed both dark ones, forcing them apart.

The wolfsretter stepped between them. "Listen to me, the both of you. Your politics are of concern to me only insofar as my love is now a prisoner because of it. I *will* go to this *Carnivale* to save Andreas, but I will leave you to your revenge and your intrigues."

Karahan slid in front of the retreating wolfsretter, who blinked her surprise. "Are you forgetting, Fraulein, that we have a contract?"

"Your contract is with my mother, not me. Take up your grievance with her."

"And you think your rescue mission will go that smoothly?" Massimo added. "Simply walk into the Doge's palace and walk away with a tribute wolf? As you yourself noted, there will be no end to the number of observers."

"I am amazingly inventive. I'll find a way to free him. And when I do, we will hasten to make our escape."

The slayer, his sympathetic eye falling on the innocent girl, clicked his tongue. "Oh, Fraulein, you forget that Venice is not the forests and fields you are accustomed to. It is an island. Where will you run when you reach the water's edge?"

"Yes, Gerwalta," Karahan said, daring to use her familial name. "Where *will* you run? Surely not back to Triberg. Even if you do manage to free Herr Baron, as you said yourself, you'll find no safe harbor under the dominion of the House of Red."

Her cheeks blazed the same deep crimson as the color of her gown. "Are you threatening me, *Igor*?"

"I do not mean to threaten, only to remind you that you are in a unique situation. One I could assist you to resolve."

She bit her lip, attempting to hide her fretting. "No, I will accrue no debt in this matter. Besides, where would we go, if not home? Forget the dangers to me, what will become of Andreas's pack if I do not return? No, we…. We will return. I, to wed. He, to lead."

"And your love for one another?" Karahan asked, lifting her chin. "Even if you survive, what of that?"

"What of it? It is impossible. I will convince my mother to force his paw, to arrange for his mating to another wolf, by force if necessary. And I will marry into a foreign line with haste. My would-be assassin only wishes to neutralize my ability to become Matron. I will leave the Schwarzwald by marrying into a foreign bloodline with haste, and Andreas will have a mate and a future."

"Or…."

His sing-songy interjection drew hope into her eyes.

"Or what?"

"Or we make a new contract, one between you and me, and not you and your mother." He pressed her cheeks between his hands. "I am a vampire of particular influence, Gerwalta. If you must marry, perhaps I can assure a *sympathetic* spouse, one that would allow you and Andreas to be mated, while maintaining the public illusion of a proper marriage. The laity royals do it all the time."

"No house would ever accept a wolfsretter being with a wolf."

Massimo, silent this long while, barked a laugh. "You'd be surprised."

"I would?" she asked him before turning back to Karahan.

He withdrew his hands. "Would Andreas stand ready to pass down his command to another wolf and risk moon madness to pursue you? The journey will be long and dangerous."

"I would do the same for him, if I knew it would mean we could be together."

Karahan clapped and rubbed his hands. "Then we will make it so. But you *must* aid in this task. I cannot do it without you. My son and his generals must be stopped, for the sake of all dark ones everywhere. Do this for me, *with me*, and I swear that no harm will come to Andreas, and that after, you will have an opportunity to live your lives together."

In an instant, the wolfsretter threw her hands around his neck and embraced Karahan.

With a firm jaw, she nodded. "If you can swear to this, then I shall find a way."

FIFTEEN

So many lights, so many voices, so many laymen and buildings and dogs running through alleys.

And so, so much water.

Messer Mazzi had been right to mock her plans to escape. How would she and Andreas succeed in fleeing across this? The long, slender boat that served as their coach-upon-the-water moved with enough grace, but she had never learned to swim. The sea between Venice and the mainland made any upon it an easy target for a properly-gifted marksman. Andreas, perhaps, could make it, if he was in any condition to do so when everything was said and done. But with her bustles and corset and petticoats? Her clothing would be her undoing.

And that was before considering the silver she had concealed.

A lick of a wave rocked their boat. Despite sitting, Gerwalta grabbed the edge of the prow for balance.

"Fraulein Faust?" Karahan's hand landed on her shoulder. "Are you all right?"

"I am fine." She righted herself. "Back to proper names, are we?"

The vampire laughed under his breath. "Yes, my apologies for presuming familiarity. I would advise not addressing me as Igor where we're heading."

She turned over her shoulder. "Why is it that you have two names, anyhow?"

"Oh, I have many more than two. A vampire lives a very long time, and by necessity, we must reinvent ourselves now and then. Especially if, like me, one finds himself highly engaged in the world of the laity. Names are like crops, Fraulein. You plant them, nurture them, grow them, reap, then cut them down to their roots until it's time to grow another."

"And just what fruit does Spatar Goran Karahan bear?"

"Goran is a perhaps the only thing preventing my son's efforts to seed the Ottoman forces. I have created the layman persona to use the Sultan's network of spies to my advantage."

"And Igor?"

The vampire's eyes cast out over the water. "Igor is the only thing that will keep it from happening in the future."

The oarsmen continued their labors, rowing them into the heart of Venice. This city.... It toppled on top of itself, a maze of stone and water. How were the captive wolves enduring it? She was more given to laity norms than Andreas, and even she felt the tightness in her chest pulling in.

"Fraulein?" This time it was Mazzi asking after her.

The slayer may be somewhat incorrigible, but he was kind.

"I am not accustomed to boat travel. It gives one a queer feeling of being ill."

"Perhaps you are ill, but it is not from the rocking of the boat." The brotherly Italian grinned. "You have had a tepid pallor about you since you excused yourself at my home to... what was it, pray?"

For a moment she shuddered. Did he somehow know? Could slayers sense silver whereas vampires could not? Even then, how would Messer Mazzi know the silver she concealed had been blood-claimed? Running so much through her heart in so little time almost killed Gerwalta, but she refused to head unprepared into enemy territory where wolfsretters of questionable allegiances dwelled. She would not have sole command of anything the conspirators had put to use in the cages, but she would have rights to what she herself wore.

"Ah, we are here." Karahan stood, the act so smooth, his balance so precise, the boat gave no evidence of motion. "Best to put your masks on then."

The vampire did so even as he suggested it. Gerwalta tried to memorize the features of the alabaster faux face crisscrossed by golden embellishments and capped with a black, triquarter hat. Turning to Mazzi, she realized she'd have a terrible time doing so, for his did not vary from the format in any significant way she'd recall after several moments.

"Fraulein, if you please?"

Gerwalta had no mask, but the trio of conspirators had planned it that way. After all, even though they'd smuggled in enough silver, why miss an opportunity to sneak in a little more?

The wolfsretter fetched a bag tied at her waist and loosed its drawstring. Inside, the silver coins toppled and clicked. In moments, they all obeyed her command, molding themselves into the image she pictured in her head. Irony was not an art in which she was well-rehearsed, but when the mask took the form of a wolf over her face, she earned Messer Mazzi's approval.

Even their arrival to the palace gates was by water. Footmen dressed in the most lavish servants attire she'd ever seen waited at the dock, aiding young maidens such as herself in gracefully sliding onto solid land, likely also assuring the guests that were disembarking were of the appropriate species, or at the very least, escorted appropriately. It only took a few steps into the entry courtyard for the whispers to die away and for fangs to show.

They wanted her, but which part of her? Her blood or her body? Both, likely. Perhaps the wolfsretter were animal enough to sense such things, for Gerwalta could not eschew the hungry glances coming her way. Nor could she dismiss the tingling in her fingertips and lurch in her stomach when she sensed the wolves. Seven distinct energies, just as she'd been advised there would be. Five were roughly the same to her, their taste feral and pure. One held a distinct ambiance of the familial. That would be Andreas, no doubt, and her heart lifted at the thought that he might sense her too and know his confinement was to end.

The seventh.... The seventh was something she'd never encountered before. Wolf, but a *different* kind of wolf. Temptation gripped her, but would she have opportunity to assuage it and do what she needed to?

"I feel like a cut of meat being dangled before dogs," she whispered into Karahan's ear. "Can they all tell so easily that I am potential food?"

"The heartbeat does give you away, I'm afraid." The elder vampire led her toward the entry to the house proper. "It is an advantage. Massimo knew what he was doing when he presented you that gown. Most vampires can be manipulated by good, old-fashioned lust."

She stopped, pivoting toward him. "Can you?"

He pulled her hand to his lips, his mask cut in such a fashion as to show his mouth. Most around were; no doubt a vampire would demand a way to display his ivory trophies.

"I have learned my lesson about indulging the flesh. The fang is a cruel master and an unforgiving a teacher. But you do tempt me to forget my learning."

"Well, if it isn't Papa Dracule himself."

They turned to find a stout man of perhaps fifty years wearing a mask molded to represent the face of the moon.

If irony is in fashion here, Gerwalta thought, *then no doubt this is a slayer.*

"Helsinger." Karahan dropped Gerwalta's hand and beared his fangs. Despite a terrible image, he kept his voice soft. "What are you doing here?"

Helsinger tipped the rim of a black hat ornamented with golden baubbles and bright blue feathers. "I would assume, the same as you."

A growl rumbled through Karahan's chest. Gerwalta blinked away her confusion. Who knew vampires growled?

"Harm anyone of my bloodline and the consequences would be dire."

"I assure you... Spatar Karahan, I'm told you're going by these days, is it? Is that the persona you keep in your Society of Watchers?"

It was bait that Karahan left unnibbled.

"In any event," Helsinger continued with a twirl of his hand, "do you really expect that I can allow your sons' tyranny to continue? Three laymen deaths this week alone, the bodies drained of all blood and left in the canals to feed the fishes. Either they will answer for it, or the Doge..."

"*None* of my bloodline!" Karahan hissed, stepping into the slayer. "I am resolving the situation tonight. All you need do is stay out of my way."

At this juncture, they were joined by Messer Mazzi. The Italian slayer didn't brandish a solarium—would that have any effect on another slayer, she wondered—but he did produce a rather intimidating dagger from under one sleeve which he took to Helsinger's side shield under his cape.

"Helsinger," Mazzi said. "I would hate to think you're here to encroach on my territory."

"Only insofar as pursuing hostiles from my own, Mazzi."

Karahan's lip curled. "Go back to Budapest, Frederick. I am already busy cleaning up this mess because of your foolish father. I do not want you here causing any more."

Helsinger lunged. Mazzi pulled. Suddenly, Gerwalta had her blade at the interloper's throat. The vampire mass thronged nearby stilled, partaking of the unexpected entertainment with undivided attention.

Helsinger signaled his surrender, hands at the level of his eyes. "Peace, then. I may fight vampires, but I will not fight one of my own. Nor would I dare to take up arms against a woman."

Gerwalta's upper lip curled. "It is good to find a man who recognizes his limits."

And with that, Helsinger withdrew, making for the docks as Karahan took the wolfsretter by the arm and lead her inside, beaming nearly as brightly as Mazzi's solarium.

The vampire took her arm, escorting her in, as she pulled her silver back from sight. "Very impressive."

"I didn't do it to impress you. We have a bargain, one you cannot uphold if you are dead." She shifted her massive dressings around a shrubbery in a stout ceramic pot. "He called you a watcher. A watcher of what?"

Karahan shrugged. "People, times, events. We are a loose network of vampires who attempt to chronicle the major shifts in dark one culture, to document and to preserve."

"To what end?"

"Why, to find a cure, of course."

She stopped, looked at him askew. "Are you ill?"

"We all are, in a manner of speaking. All dark ones are at least partially human. If we were not, we could not reproduce with the laity."

The very thought of such a coupling made her face screw up.

"I merely speak of *possibility*, not a preference," he said. He took her arm and encouraged her to continued. "Helsinger thinks we have sinister plans afoot, however, and that we are somehow looking for secrets and weaknesses with which to exploit all creatures. Given that the only Watcher he knows is me, and that my bloodline is guilty as charged, I cannot entirely fault his conclusion."

"Perhaps, but you certainly do not seem like you're trying to exploit anyone."

A cloud overcame his features. "If only you knew, Fraulein."

SIXTEEN

Andreas eyeballed the silver cage before him. He couldn't put it off any longer; he'd need to get in. The black-cloaked wolfsretter who'd brought him to Venice, Mehmet, had shaped it in such a way as to allow ample width for arms to be pulled through without touching, but that was only if the vampires who sought to drink from him were careful not to tug and pull.

"What do I do if they drink too much before Karahan approaches?" the lupine asked. "If I am too weak to attack...."

Tepes clicked his tongue. "I have told the Doge that I will guard the cage with the wolf who will kill Karahan. Only she will take your vein. That very act will draw Karahan forward. He'll attempt to talk her out of it. He still believes he can bend her ear."

The konigswolf raised an eyebrow. "Can he?"

The Bloody Prince's eyes wandered to the right. "Surely you don't believe yours is the only aid I've sought tonight."

Andreas saw the threads of the weave. "Another wolf will target the Doge if she refuses to act her part."

"But she does not know which one. No one does, except the wolf and I." The vampire clapped Andreas on the shoulder. "It is time, Herr Baron. Do as I say, and I will see to it that your beloved survives tonight. Fail, and.... Well, I've always been curious about the taste of red hood. I hear they are quite sweet, from the vein and... in *other* places."

Before the konigswolf could mount a proper retort— something in the way of ripping the vampire's throat out, Tepes was a cloud of smoke drifting over the floor. So stunned was he by the feat that when the Turkish wolfsretter approached him from behind, he did not notice.

"Do not give the bloodsucker the honor of your anger," Mehmet said. "He does not respect women. He either drinks them or beds them to the point of death, then tosses their bodies aside, used and forgotten. Such a man deserves neither time nor consideration."

Forcing loose his fists, Andreas turned. "That does not mean he does not pose a great threat."

Mehmet grimaced. "For now."

The konigswolf's head tilted like that of a curious pup. "Meaning?"

"It will become clear when it becomes clear."

Mehmet motioned toward the one cage that remained unfilled and flicked his fingers. Silver bars became liquid metal, pooling in waves left and right, until a door manifested.

Andreas stepped in, careful that none of his flesh contacted the corrosive structure. "Will the other wolves all be permitted to go free?"

"It is not my concern."

"So the House of Night is not so different from the House of Red."

A loose motion of Mehmet's hands, and the bars of the cage reformed. "I do not speak Italian, and that is all most of the wolves know. It is possible they have struck some deal with the vampires; they are not in the habit of making their plans known to me. The only agreement I am party to is for the release of the shewolf."

"The shewolf? Why? What is she to you?"

The wolfsretter clenched his jaw and turned away.

"Oh, come now," Andreas said. "If all goes as planned, you will head east and I will run north. We are never to see each other again."

"But you might carry the knowledge, and that could cost her her life. Do not ask for a dagger from my hand and say you have no mal intentions. It would not matter; the blade was made to rend."

At that, Andreas cut off his query. "Then let us turn to more practical matters. Karahan: Does he have allies in the crowd that will come to his aid?"

"Two of note, one being he in whose home you were being hosted."

Mazzi made sense, of course. No doubt a vampire with a slayer at his back would not be trifled with easily. But in a palace full of vampires?

"The other?"

"He will reveal himself if he deems it appropriate."

"And that is all? Two allies, one who may remain in the shadows, taking on seven who have the backing of the Doge of Venice?" Andreas's head shook. "Do you think me a fool, Mehmet?"

"No, Andreas, I do not." The corner of the wolfsretter's mouth lifted as he ran a hand over the silver bars. "The most dangerous weapon is that which is invisible to the eye while in plain view. The most powerful warrior, one who is underestimated."

Tepes has no respect for women.

Among the wolfsretter, women were the dominant sex. Stronger, faster, able to work silver with an ease that left their male counterparts dizzy. Mehmet had managed to construct cages with the materials he'd been provided.

Gerwalta could build a whole prison.

A wolf feared silver, but Andreas found a new-born respect for his trappings. "It must take a tremendous amount of silver to contain a wolf. I wonder if it would be enough to contain a vampire?"

"An interesting question." Mehmet nodded. "I am not a slayer. It is not my place to speculate on such topics."

Andreas grinned. "No, you'd need a vampire of some wisdom to determine that course of action, as well as a warrior capable of achieving such a feat."

"Indeed, Herr Baron. And where would one find such a warrior in Venice?"

"One wouldn't."

Mehmet gave Andreas a slow nod before leaving in the direction of the courtyard.

SEVENTEEN

They stood like garrisons protecting the castle. Only, instead of being placed on the towers facing out, each of the six raven-masked men she'd identified stood at one of the pillars that supported the floors of the palace.

Trying to keep people out or hold people in? she wondered as she wove through the crowd.

The pull of the wolves proved stronger on the west half of the courtyard, but she could do nothing about that now. Gerwalta tried to stay focused, reminding herself that when the opportunity came, she must endeavor to trap the vampires she'd been hired to stop, not strive solely to save Andreas. If she did the first, it would accomplish the latter. If Karahan was a man of his word, he would take them to a land where they could find refuge. To a land where they could be together.

Her body shivered. Not from the chill in the air, but from the thought that in a very short time, she'd find a wolf in her bed. Their last encounter had nearly undone her resolve. Gerwalta could no longer talk herself out of the truth; she loved him. Yes, she could do as expected, return to Triberg, become a chess piece for her mother to position with just the right mate, but the thought of being with a man besides Andreas sickened her.

She'd resisted because she knew giving in to her emotions would be the same as signing his execution papers. Now, if she managed to complete this task, there was a way for them to be together.

Even if it did mean she'd give up her family and their homeland in the process...

Once more, she scanned the courtyard, straining to find the seventh raven mask that had yet alluded her. The first six had been easy enough to find. But now, as she took in the visions of fish and fowl, jesters and dukes, lords and ladies, her quest was fruitless.

Suddenly, the hairs on the back of her neck stood to attention. Someone was behind her. No, he was veritably against her back, his words tickling her neck as he spoke lowly in the court language.

"I am afraid that I do not speak Italian. Do you, perchance, know

German?"

"Fraulein, my German, like my touch, is as smooth as silk." He laughed, his lips pressed against her ear. "And what I said was, 'Is your mask any implication of your preference for bed sport?'"

Where there had been fascination, fury burned. Gerwalta spun, ready to dig her heels into the throat of the brash vampire when she froze.

A beak.

The last raven presented fangs for her approval. No matter the inappropriateness of his speech, she knew she could not risk it. Gerwalta was an expert hunter; few laymen could compete. She knew an elusive animal when she saw one. If she let this vampire from her sight, he could fly away.

A sweep of the room confirmed the others' unchanged positions. Gerwalta wove her arm through his. Karahan himself had told her she'd been dressed to be a feast to the eyes. Now she needed to suggest to the vampire there may be other parts of her he could feed upon. How wondrous a thing that the male of all species could be so easily misled by vanities. *It can be a powerful tactic in some situations,* she remembered being told when younger and still training. *Arousal draws blood away from the head in men, slows their thinking.*

Though she did have to wonder: as vampires had no pulse, did their blood draw anywhere?

"If you mean, do I favor lupines over vampires, I must admit my ignorance. I have never partaken of either."

"Ah, only your kind, then."

Her movements jolted, even as they bowed before joining the other dancers already swirling about. "My own kind?"

"I hear your heartbeat, Fraulein. I know you are a layman."

Play up his misconception. "You have found me out, Herr...?"

The dance demanded that he take her hand at that point, but Gerwalta had a feeling he would have done so anyway.

"Tepes. *Vlad* Tepes."

Her blood turned to ice as she pulled her hand back.

"You know of me." Amusement pulled at the corners of his mouth.

She nodded. "The Bloody Prince."

"And here I thought the laity called me only The Impaler."

Gerwalta's heart pounded. Was that true? Did she just give away that she was not, in fact, of the laity?

"There is no call to fear me, Fraulein. Though, if you do not slow that heart of yours, others of my kind might be tempted to challenge me for your attention."

The wolfsretter inwardly lectured herself on the heels of such sage advice. Why was she fretting so? Was it because her body, though outwardly healed of the wound, still recalled the pierce of fangs just the night before? But then she'd been unprepared. Surely a wolfsretter could stand her ground against a single vampire, if not ambushed. They had the advantage of speed, no doubt, but her strength did not suffer compared to theirs.

The night air vibrated as the first strike of midnight carried from the tower dominating the islands. If what Massimo had said was true, the lupines would soon be revealed to the audience. Even in her peripheral vision, her targets began to shift position, collapsing in on a set of double doors on the east side of the courtyard, the same place she had sensed the wolves.

It had been her body that attracted him. Perhaps it could keep him there as well.

"Is it only my *heart* that would draw them?" Gerwalta eschewed her fear and bolstered her courage. With a lithe finger, she traced an invisible line down her neck, being certain to draw attention to the thick vein showing through her pale skin. "Is that all that interests vampires?"

Vlad followed that finger with alarming focus. The vampire licked his lips. "Are you asking about my kind as a whole, or me specifically?"

Her own words sickened her. "Perhaps I am asking if you could give me a demonstration of your *impaling* prowess."

His fangs gleamed, twin daggers hungering for flesh. A few

nearby vampires had slowed their dancing, watching.

Vlad stepped forward, embracing her head in both his hands. "Tell me your name, so I know what to scream when I pour myself inside you."

On the east side of the courtyard, there was movement. Seven large carts, covered over with curtains so the contents remained hidden from view, drew squeaks from the wheels beneath. One by one they were lined up on the edge where the revealers were gathered. Three to the north end, three to the south end, each flanked by one of Vlad's men. Purpose called to her when the wolfsretter who'd defended her attacker the night before pushed out the last cart without aid. If Massimo Brunelli could be believed, this man was one of Karahan's coconspirators. It was good to see his physical strength proved great.

Vlad turned back to her. "Stay, have fun. But if any other tries to claim you, tell them you belong to the prince. As soon as this concludes, you will join me in my apartment in the palace."

She feigned anticipation, licking her lips and rolling up on her toes. "Yes, your Highness."

He leaned in, grabbing her chin. "And be certain to eat well."

"I do not understand." All said and done, that was a curious request.

"You shall need a great deal of strength to last through what I have planned for you." He leaned in, raking a fang across her lips. *Nipped it.* No blood, the action was only meant to play.

Or promise.

Or threaten.

"As soon as I can return, I shall."

Gerwalta waited a few moments before following. What a fortunate encounter. She'd written herself an excuse to be at the front of the assembly when the wolves were revealed. None would question her trying to stay in the line of sight of her potential paramour.

She began to make her way across the room when, on the north end of the courtyard, there was a tremendous crash.

EIGHTEEN

The Doge loved being adored. She adored being loved. Almost as much as she loved being feared.

Both of her fathers had spoiled her. The human one raised a pampered princess, and her father-of-the-blood consigned her beauty to the shelter of immortality. Even the voluminous, Venetian fashions could not blanket her many curves, and her handsome face and ebony hair tied in elaborate knots and swells made her an adventure that must be taken to be believed.

Massimo hated to admit he *had* taken it, but never from a place of true desire. It had been a means to an end, a way to get close to power. He knew better than to expect that he could rid his glorious city and republic of its vampire menace. By becoming one of them, and then finding a way to rule them, he could, perhaps, keep what had happened to him from happening to anyone else.

Now, victory was within his grasp, and winning all depended on the abilities of a single woman from a foreign land with questionable intentions. A wolfsretter, nonetheless. But could she really accomplish the mission? If Tepes and his generals were again contained, the Doge would lose her base of power. If the Doge lost her base of power, Massimo could rise against her. If he rose against her, and if enough of the vampires of Venice backed his claim, he would control the city.

Massimo flinched at the sound of the cymbals crashing. Schooling his features, he turned and carried out his role, taking to the Doge's side as her second.

"I welcome the noble families," the Doge began, holding out her hands. "You have come from all over the countryside, even from foreign shores, to join my celebration tonight. Across town, the mortals drink their wine and sing their celebrations. We let them, untouched. Untouched, for tonight, we dine not on the Venetian people, but on the tributes presented to our great republic by the seven families themselves. Tonight, we dine on... the blood of the lupines!"

A flourish of the Doge's hand was the signal for the raven-masked vampires on the east side of the courtyard to pull the coverings from the cages. Massimo averted his eyes. He did not care for lupines as a species per se, but they were also men, and he did not care to see any subjugated simply because of the creature god had made him.

Even if one of the wolves was a woman.

The slide of the Doge's hand into his own pulled open his eyes.

Luciana gazed on him with tenderness in plain view. "Why do you hide your eyes, my love?"

A moment he allowed for the disgust to boil within before shoving it away. He took on his role: the dutiful lover, the supporting right-hand man.

Massimo pulled the Doge's hand to his lips, kissing her knuckles. "I do not hide my gaze, I save it for your beauty."

She beamed. "As it should be."

He spoiled her rotten, because *that's* what Luciana expected. And the moment her lovers grew tired of sating her every need, she had them executed.

Or she ran back to one of her fathers. They took turns placating her need for constant affirmation. He expected no less of Vlad Tepes—Luciana's weakness gave him power over her, and detest Luciana though Masimo did, he did not discredit her power. Of course, she was powerful. She was a Dracule. But Igor… or Goran, as he was going by now…. The paterfamilias of his bloodline seemed both mighty and kind, balancing horror and humanity the way few vampires could. How, then, had he come to father so many disappointing children?

"Come." Luciana pulled him from his reverie and insistently toward the courtyard. "I will have first blood, as is my right, but you shall have second, my gift for my beloved consort."

"I have no desire for the werewolf blood." Massimo detested his dependence on laymen blood; drinking that of another dark one, however, felt too much like cannabilism.

"It is not about the *blood*," Luciana said. "It is that you demand it, and by receiving it, you grow powerful in the eyes of the community. Or do you not wish that they should fear you as they do me?"

They do not fear you, he thought. *They fear your fathers.* If there was one pity he felt for his lover-of-convenience, it was that she authentically did not understand she was a puppet ruler. Through his own tyranny, the Wallachian Prince had seized the power of the east, and through proxy and via Venice, soon he would have power over the west as well.

Unless Karahan's plan worked, that was.

Massimo took a breath, summoned a faux face of reverence, and followed in Luciana's wake.

Hopefully, for the last time.

NINETEEN

Andreas's brown eyes held an odd mix of reverence and fear. The reverence, from his love for her. But the fear? Wherefore the fear? She was a wolfsretter surrounded by vast resources of her most agile weapon. Even if she were to be attacked, Gerwalta could draw the silver from the cages to cocoon herself. For a short time, anyhow. Eventually, she would need to breathe.

But when Andreas's gaze drifted, she knew something more than generalized anxiety weighed on him. Was it anxiety? Did he believe she would allow him to become some hellwhore's food?

A line broke through the crowd as the Doge promenaded through the courtyard, the menagerie of masks in the shape of every animal pivoted in her wake. Gerwalta turned when she sensed the movements behind her, and found, much to her surprise, the Doge's consort and his familiar face.

Massimo caught her eye for the briefest of moments as he and the Doge walked past, the warning as clear as though he'd spoken the words aloud. *Do not give me away. Stay with the plan. Be ready to move, the moment is coming.*

Gerwalta's hands tightened into fists, her nails embedding into the heel of her palm. She longed to call the silver; all seven ravens were within view.

"A hair's breadth of difference can keep the axeman's blade from hitting its target."

Beside her, Karahan appeared as if by magic. How could he move so soundlessly?

"Where did you—"

He cut her off with some urgency. "You met Vlad."

A statement, not a query. Had Karahan been spying on her the whole time? Because of concern for her, or the plan?

Gerwalta swallowed down her fear when she realized the Bloody Prince himself caught sight of them talking. Just like that, where Karahan had been, now only air. She met his scowl with haste, mouthing the words, *I am yours.* Her inner wolfsretter rebelled at the act. She was no man's property to claim, and none had rights over her except he whom she permitted to claim her.

And that would only be Andreas. Thoughts of the lupine drew her concern, and she looked up to discover a very curious thing: frustration being thrown her way. Because another stood beside her when he could not? Because he longed for her? No, Andreas's eyes were not, in fact, looking at *her*. They were looking at the space *beside* her, to where Karahan had just been. But why would Andreas be frustrated by Karahan's disappearance? If he was jealous, he'd be glad of it.

Something was very wrong with this whole picture.

The Doge, a misty-skinned beauty with a complex of black hair atop her head, let go Massimo's hand and addressed Vlad. The words, all in Italian, had little meaning to Gerwalta, who only recognized "who" from its likeness to French. It didn't matter; she'd been through enough formal ceremony and pomp to recognize it for what it was. The Doge posed a question, then looked out across the assemblage, as though confirming that her due diligence in the exchange had been executed.

The wolves in the cages, despite residing in their lay forms, began to pace. Predators sensed when they became prey. Vlad returned some equally-rehearsed words before reaching through the cage and taking Andreas by the hand.

She turned, taking one last furtive survey, hoping to find Karahan mixed in with the crowd but ready to back her up if anyone attacked. Her hopes sank as Messer Mazzi's eyes met hers and he shook his head lowly.

Only then did the crowd gasp.

The wolfsretter spun, discovering the Doge, Andreas's arm at her lips, but Karahan's hand on her chest, pushing her away.

"Enough, Inga."

Inga? The Doge of the Venetian court was named Inga?

But there was no time to pause and consider. Already,

Gerwalta had missed her cue. She swept her gaze right, then left, checking her line of sight and her targets. The Ravens had come out from their posts a step or two, but they maintained their positions. That wouldn't last, given the scowl erupting across Vlad Tepes's face. A confrontation was emerging, and she had only moments before it was too late.

The wolfsretter focused her mind, called on her power, and beckoned the silver cages up and down the courtyard to obey her will.

And obey they did, shifting shape, bending, melding, becoming liquid streams in the air. But as they began to coalesce into pools of metal, Gerwalta came to a startling realization.

The silver was obeying.

It just wasn't obeying *her*.

And that was when Andreas pounced, knocking Karahan to the ground.

TWENTY

A spark landed in a bed of kindling, the room erputed into flame.

Royal courts were inherently violent places. The only difference between normal discourse and the cacpohny of battle around her was that the weapons in the former were words and here, fangs and claw.

For once, being an outsider brought an advantage; none had issue with her, therefore no reason to seek out and attack when the opportunity presented itself. All around her, vampires squared off, wolves freed from their prisons took their fur, forming a de facto pack intent on making way through the throng to freedom. Except for Andreas, strewn atop Karahan, attempting to chomp at the vampire who'd hired them, and the sole shewolf, who was... being flanked by the two wolfsretters from the House of Night? Was that their role here? Who was this grey-eyed shewolf to demand such consideration?

But Gerwalta couldn't concern herself with contrary behavior. She had to get Andreas off Karahan before the konigswolf destroyed the one man who may be able to deliver them to freedom.

"Andreas!" Gerwalta threw her arms around the wolf from behind, attempting to drag him off. Strong though she was, the mere fact that he outweighed her by a hefty sum made the feat challenging. "He is going to help—"

Karahan, though pinned, held Andreas's drooling maw in his hands and turned toward the wolfsretter. "Don't worry about me!"

"But Andreas will kill you if—"

Karahan met her eyes. "Do it before the opportunity escapes. Get them. My promise remains."

The one he made not to hurt Andreas, to aid them in escaping to someplace where they could have a life together.

She turned back to find the Ravens scattered. Three of them were stalked toward the edge of the courtyard, where three of the wolves had come together to close in on the Doge. Three wolves might be able to take on one vampire, but four vampires against three wolves would be a lupine blood bath.

Gerwalta had to stop them. At the same time, she knew that if she took down only part of the Ravens' number, the others would flee. Then they would all come for her and, if he lived, Andreas. She and her wolf would be on the run until the end of their days.

Never settling….

Never having an opportunity to start a family….

Gerwalta pushed away the warmth that overcame her at the thought. Now was not the time to dream of domestic bliss. She had to stop the three vampires closing in on the Doge, find the four others in the crowd, and do so with a line of sight to the silver, a line of sight now cluttered by a throng of spatting vampires.

There was only one way to do all that, but the ramifications….

She passed one more longing glance at Andreas at the same moment a vicelike grip took her shoulder.

"So, you're part of this, then?" Tepes growled. "When I'm done with you, you'll wish you were…. Your…. Your eyes. You're a…"

She knew what he must see; the evidence of letting her powers embrace her in full, of calling upon every measure of strength she had. Her eyes would be pools of silver now.

His grip loosened as her feet left ground, but shock cemented him to the spot. The Bloody Prince became small in her eyes as she rose into the air, called upon the seven pillars of silver, and began to embalm the vampires who stood between her and whatever came next.

Until Tepes turned on Andreas, that was.

TWENTY-ONE

He wished Gerwalta could sense his emotions the way another wolf could have. Then she would know how much he loved her, and how sorry he was for what he was about to do.

The moment the cage melted into a pillar beneath his feet, Andreas took his fur, the transformation of his features rending every stitch of the decadent clothing forced upon him into shreds. Only the highly polished heeled shoes remained behind without injury as the lupine leapt. The konigswolf embraced the animal within, leaving his humanity by the wayside. Only then could he have a future with Gerwalta. Only by living up to his side of the bargain and destroying Karahan could she survive to be his bride.

But the vampire under his paws showed strength beyond measure, not to mention patience. Karahan showed no interest in turning the tide. His only intent seemed to be in drawing a stalemate, holding Andreas's open jaws just inches from his throat with such ease, the wolf knew the vampire could throw him off if he really wanted to.

"Whatever you've been told about me is a lie. I intend neither you nor Fraulein Faust any harm."

That might work to disengage the lupine, if that was the basis of his attack—a fact that Karahan seemed to grasp intrinsically when the assault only intensified.

The first crack in Karahan's strength came in the form of a strained expression. "I will not allow them to hurt her either, but I can only do that if you remove yourself from me. The plan remains; she will end them. She will—"

But just then, something changed in the vampire's expression. Karahan's grip slackened, and the sudden shift confused Andreas enough to forestall his taking advantage. The Spatar's eyes fixed over the konigswolf's back, up in the air. A lupine was no cat, but curiousity snatched at Andreas all the same. He took his eyes off the man he was meant to kill and turned, following his gaze.

The moment he saw it, he knew any benefit to killing Karahan was gone. Gerwalta's form floated aloft, as high as the balconies jutting out from the second floor. She was flying in plain view of vampires, slayers, lupines, and worst yet, her own kind. The fact that two wolfsretters from the House of Night played witness would be immaterial, however. An event such as this? It could not be covered as easily as it had been in Nuremberg. News would reach Triberg, and when it did, it would change Gerwalta's life forever. There was nowhere they could run now that the House of Red would not pursue. A wolfsretter's ability to fly was practically a divine sign that such a woman was destined to be Matron. They'd force Gerwalta into the role, under threat of death if needed.

Or if they discovered her love for him, threat of *Andreas's* death.

"Let me up and I can protect her."

Andreas snapped back to the moment. *Not from the real threat. No one can.*

His paws pulled back. The corded muscles of his canine frame relaxed. He was not giving in to Karahan's request; he was letting go the fight. The moment Gerwalta's feet had left the ground, he'd lost her. The will to fight for anything, even himself, deserted him... for what was the purpose of living, if he could not be with the woman he loved?

No sooner had one vampire crawled out from beneath him than another tackled him from behind, viciously strong hands wrapping around his throat.

"You were supposed to kill him!" Tepes growled. "You damned, dirty dog!"

His body fought to endure, even as his heart sank. *Let him kill me,* Andreas told himself. *Better die in battle than alone or having gone mad.*

But Fate had not finished mocking Fortune. Gerwalta's silver-plated eyes peered down, catching the calamity beneath her. Suddenly, she let go her ascent, landing in a lithe crouch just behind them.

The wolfsretter pulled at the store of metal that had been Andreas's cage and made of it a mace, a silver stick topped with spiked globe. In one mighty swing, she walloped the unprepared

Bloody Prince upside the head, throwing off his balance and allowing the air to come rushing back into Andreas's lungs.

Beside Andreas on the courtyard stones, Tepes rolled over just in time to find the wolfsretter and her fearsome weapon preparing another blow.

"If you wish to live," Gerwalta bellowed, "leave my mate alone!"

His heart seized, then pounded so hard it made his head spin. Mate? *Mate*? Had she just…. Did Gerwalta just declare that…?

No time to dwell. The moment Tepes got his bearings back, he was on her.

Locked in a struggle for power, neither warrior realized that all around quarreling had ceased to play witness to theirs. Even the wolves turned snouts in their direction. Except for Andreas, whose maw captured Tepes at the ankle, jerking him back. A vile essence coated the konigswolf's tongue, the taste of flesh and blood that had turned stale and rotting.

Tepes shrieked, his suffering feeding Andreas's animal nature. The lupine's jaw tightened, driving sharp fangs into the meat of the vampire's calf. Deeper, deeper, seeking bone, seeking destruction….

You will not take my mate from me. You will not claim what is mine. I will have her; I will destroy you to win.

Such thoughts…. He loved Gerwalta, this he'd understood for months. But what he felt now…. It was more than love, it was…

The beginning of the end. The process which would end in their union, *could only* end with their union, had begun.

Mottled voices flowed in the air around him, but saying what? Andreas did not know. He could focus only on destroying that which threatened to come between them. But to what end? They could not be together, not now.

Only when the silver licked his flesh, driving slices into his front legs, did the hold break. Andreas's mouth released the vampire as pain drove him away. He looked up, blinking away his confusion, to find the source of his torment.

Gerwalta's eyes held the sadness of the world as her hand curled, commanding the silver under her power, burning into his flesh.

She didn't need to say the words for him to know the truth. It was a reminder, one she was loath to give, but it was critical that he receive.

Yes, they loved each other, but that did not mean they ceased being enemies. The pain reminded him of the one fact that would never change between them.

We are each other's death.

TWENTY-TWO

Gerwalta felt his pain as though she had forced it upon her own person. More than the physical, she also suffered the betrayal, the shock in his eyes. *How could you love me and do this to me?* But what else could she do? She'd wrapped five of the Ravens in silver, forced their bodies to smoke by collapsing them into urns no larger in height or width than her arm. She'd been on the cusp of securing a sixth when she'd noticed Tepes attacking Andreas. *Cut off the head, and the limbs will falter.* It was a truism of warfare, and that was what this had become: warfare. It only made sense then, to shift her focus to the Bloody Prince, forcing number six to collapse with such haste, she couldn't be certain if he'd survive it.

But when Andreas had caught Tepes by the leg and refused to let go, her task proved impossible. Forcibly wrap him in silver, and she'd likely take out half of Andreas's snout in the process.

She'd still love him if he had no nose, of course, but would she ever forgive herself if she was the cause of his injury? A konigswolf must be strong, be able to wield power and demand respect. What did she care if he was not physically perfect as long as he was alive? But the pack might not look upon deformity the same way, and she would not assume his permission when death might be the easier risk to tempt.

The only solution was to use the silver under her command to shock Andreas and loosen his grip.

She hadn't anticipated the other wolves taking advantage of the confusion to attack. In going after one of their own kind, Gerwalta had given the de facto pack a common enemy. They fell in from all sides, teeth bared, maws bloodied from battle. And behind the shewolf, who approached from her left, stalked the two wolfsretters of the House of Night. What? They were siding with the wolves? They were allowing themselves to be led into battle by a shewolf?

What followed all unfolded too fast to comprehend clearly and took her thought elsewhere.

Andreas let go his grip as Karahan's arms encircled him. Crushing his ribs, perhaps? She'd have to worry about that later. First, he needed to live. Suddenly, Tepes was free of Andreas's hold. Gerwalta forced the only silver she could wield with the encircling pack into submission. The boosted features of her gown went limp as she leached away the blood-claimed silver and forced it to ink over the Bloody Prince's frame.

"I am not a wolf, Fraulein. This will do nothing to—"

His words cut off as the silver began to compress. Vlad held up his hands, the shiny coating making his eyes go wide, as Gerwalta pulled the water-thin layers tighter, tighter, pushing the vampire's form into submission.

From her right, a wolf leapt. Massimo solidified in a black cloud of smoke just in time to catch him midair, a hair's width from his teeth sinking into her arm.

"Hurry, Fraulein!" he shouted, wrestling the beast away. "Stop Vlad!"

Would the other wolves stay focused on her, or attempt to help their fallen comrade? Gerwalta could not wait to see, and if it was indeed her, she could waste no time. Not in trapping Tepes, not in tipping her heart to the man she loved.

"Andreas..."

Silver fingers crushed in on the vampire, running veins up his neck, through his hair.

"I..."

It encircled the prince's neck, slashing flesh.

"...love..."

Tepes, desperately realizing what was going on, thrashed. Left, right, left, right... but the silver refused to slacken.

"...you."

A wolf's maw caught her at the wrist just as her last flourish did the necessary, leaving in the place of the prince, a tall, silver urn. The raven-shaped mask fell to the floor at Gerwalta's feet, along with precious drops of her blood.

The wolf bit hard, likely an effort to sever her hand from her arm. Agony took Gerwalta to her knees, and pain diverted her from the pulses of instinct to fight back. Only a moment later, when hot crimson rivelets splashed to the stones below, did she seek to find some source of silver.

Only suddenly, the pressure lifted.

Gerwalta looked up and found the man she loved, taken again of flesh, holding the wolf who attacked her by the scruff so high in the air, the poor creature's feet scrambled to touch ground.

Gone was the fur, but the animal still colored his voice. "If you hurt my mate again, I will have your pelt for my bed clothes."

Did the captured wolf speak German? Perhaps. It did not seem to matter. The way it pulled in on itself, letting out a high-pitched keen and folding its ears back, signaled submission. With a gruff grunt, Andreas threw the creature to the ground. The wolf whimpered, coming back into his layman form, and promptly running from the courtyard. Thanks be to heaven, none pursued, though whether due to distraction or an actual lack of temptation to sample the blood of lupine, Gerwalta knew not.

As soon as it was from sight, the konigswolf collapsed on the ground beside her, running fingers through her hair, pulling her head to his shoulder. "They promised…. They promised me if I killed Karahan, they would keep you from harm."

The lover's reunion ended as the Doge fumed into their midst.

Andreas shielded Gerwalta with his body, though the dark-haired beauty's fury focused squarely on Karahan.

"How *dare* you?" she demanded, her slender, gloved finger prodding the other vampire's chest. "How *dare you*! This is not Wallachia! Here, I rule. Here, I decide who—"

The blade burst through her front, spackling blood across both Gerwalta and Andreas's faces.

Karahan growled, long, frightening fangs dropping into existence as he moved to the Doge with speeds so daunting, it hurt to turn one's head in time.

The Spatar had Massimo on the floor in a blink, the Italian's face to the ground, Karahan's fangs hovering over his spine.

"We agreed she would not be hurt!"

Despite his position, Massimo did not falter. "We agreed she would not die!" he said. "I have not killed her, even though it is my right."

"You cut through her gullet!" Karahan snapped, lifting, then slamming Massimo's head down. "It will take her a week to heal from such an injury!"

"Then let her heal far from Venice." The Italian turned his head, spit out a mouthful of blood. "Only take her far from me."

"And leave you Doge?"

"And leave me to *grieve*. Properly, without having to lick her boots and flatter her fallacies. Take her and go!"

Gerwalta, fighting the dizziness, looked to the Doge and found what she'd expected. Yes, she'd been run through with a sword, the end of which still peeked through her abdomen, thick dark blood oozing from the wound. But the look of devastation on her face wasn't from the physical injury. It came from discovering who had delivered it.

"Massimo?" Luciana stumbled, reaching for the man who a few minutes ago, had been gazing at her like he had found a star fallen from the heavens. "Massimo, you... did *this* to me?"

Karahan pulled the shattered woman to his side. He looked at her, looked to Massimo, then back at her.

The Italian rolled to his feet. "You know this was justice, Karahan. You know what she did to my family!"

The Spatar's lips curled back. Without word, Karahan pulled the sword from the injured vampire's frame. He gave one disappointed look to Andreas, one gracious glance to Gerwalta, then swooped up the Doge in his arms and whipped through the courtyard.

Massimo turned his attention to Gerwalta. "You're bleeding."

"I'm...." She licked lips that had gone dry. "You saved me."

"And you saved us all."

"I...." She fell into Andreas's chest, wishing for warmth, for his arms wrapped protectively around her, and not the chill caused by so much blood loss.

"Gerwalta?" Andreas's hands threaded through her hair. "Someone help her!"

But what could be done? She was a dark one; her injury would heal, but that was only if she didn't bleed out first.

Her voice took on an ethereal quality, as though someone whispered in her own ears. "I love you, Andreas."

"I'll accept no farewells, love." His head lashed to the side. "Anyone, please!"

A flitter of black cloth fell in on her as one of the other wolfsretter appeared in her periphery. He muttered something, the words indistinct, as something cold stung her hemorrhaging wrist.

She closed her eyes and could not find the strength again to open them.

TWENTY-FOUR

Andreas was jealous of the fine silken linens tickling her form out of view. He wished it was his body wrapped around her, that he was claiming her as his heart and the animal within him ached to do. The patience he'd practiced during the year she kept from him strengthened his restraint.

But as her eyes fluttered open, love compelled him to her side. "Walta, how do you feel?"

"As though I've been preyed upon." Gerwalta's arm snaked out from under the blanket, examining her injured wrist. The silver Mehmet had affixed still held, the arm plate stemming the flow of blood and protecting the wound from corruption.

"Marvelous!" Gerwalta whispered, turning her arm to inspect all sides. "He actually managed to stitch together the damage... with silver. I have never seen our talents used this way."

"Yes, Mehmet was quite pleased with his work."

She wrapped her hand around the silver. "Sorry, who?"

"Mehmet. He's one of the hoods... the *wolfsretters* from the House of Night. Last night, after you passed out, he did that to stop the bleeding. He'd said you'd need to leave it on for a couple weeks."

Wolfsretter healed quickly, except from lupine bites. A consequence of opposing anatomy, he supposed. Where would the balance be if wolves suffered long from the burn of silver but their maw could do no more than render a temporary scratch? The burns Gerwalta had given him still ached, blistered bits of flesh across large parts of his body.

"Oh? I suppose there's no harm in that." Gerwalta shifted, her face screwing up. "Andreas?"

"Yes, my lamb?"

"Where are my clothes?" she asked. "Not that I am loathe,

mind, to be without such ridiculous garb. Saints preserve me from the calamity of Venetian fashion."

Gerwalta put all her weight to her good side, pushing herself up in bed. "We are on a boat." Her eyes met his. "Whose?"

"It is an Ottoman trading ship."

Her eyes narrowed. "Are we here as guests or as prisoners?"

"Guests, though 'refugees' may be a more apt term. He let his mind wander for a moment before returning to the point. "Karahan has left the city, taking the deposed Doge with him, it seems. But this arrived just as we were pushing off port."

The wolf stood and drew a sheet of folded paper from his pocket. On its backside, a purple seal, one bearing a form of writing she did not recognize, but the image of a creature she did: an eight-legged dragon.

"Messer Mazzi received this," Andreas continued. "It was forwarded by one of his servants to us this morning, and in turn to them from Karahan.

Fraulein Faust,

Even as I recognize that you completed the task for which you were contracted, and at the result of injury, I know whatever payment or gratitude I have would not suffice. By ridding the world of the Ravens, you have done a service to vampires and wolves everywhere. As to the revelation of your ability to fly, however, there were simply too many witnesses for any amount of sway or collusion I could muster to contain such information. I am sorry, as I know this development will have a great number of consequences for you and Herr Baron. My offer stands: if ever you flee from the Schwarzwald and seek sanctuary, Inga (the deposed Doge and my blooded daughter) and I will welcome you in Navarre, where I am known as Ignacio Montana de Corazon. Sadly, it is time to let Spatar Goran Karahan fade into history. Such is the consequence of immortal existence; we must ever adapt to being someone new, and with each iteration, we become less ourselves. Who will you become now? I hope I may meet her and have a chance to thank her in person.

With deepest appreciations,

Igor Khamarov, Paterfamilias of the Dracule Bloodline.

Andreas let the paper fall to the side, his eyes searching a nothingness between them.

Gerwalta's head worked through a slow bob. "Then I succeeded in capturing them all. What of the urns, then? What has become of them?"

"They came aboard with us." He licked his lips. "Walta, I wish to ask you something, and I trust you will give me nothing but the truth. Last night, many things occurred which may have led you to do and say things you might not otherwise—"

"You are wondering if I meant it when I called you my mate." She cut him off with a smile.

The konigswolf, however, thought the matter far too serious to be playful on the subject. "What Karahan said *is* true. Gossip runs before truth can put on its boots. Word will reach Triberg, and once they know what you can do, you will be the next Matron. It is a thing done; your fate is sealed."

Her head tilted to the side. "I thought you did not believe in fate."

"I do not believe that the divine sets before us a path we are obliged to walk, for what, then, would be the purpose of free will? But I *do* believe that debts may be drawn through tradition for which payments can only be paid or defaulted upon."

"I thought I had fallen in love with a wolf, and now I find a scholar beside my bed?" She shifted such that, if so inclined, he might see her bosom under her shift. Gerwalta's bosoms were works of art, though he admitted that might be the love talking.

"I am prepared, Andreas, to give my vow, my faith, and my body to you," she said. "I do not care what my mother or any of the wolfsretter *expect* of me. I let go such concerns when I embraced your love. Unless...." She pulled back, bringing the coverlet up under her chin. "Unless you no longer desire me? I did burn you with silver, but it was only to attempt to—"

He pressed his fingers against her mouth, stilling her words. Would that it was his lips instead, but he did not trust himself to stop when the only thing standing between them and consummation was consequence.

"Of course, I still desire you. I love you. You are the mate of my heart, and I will always love you. Only I have finally learned that you were right."

"What are you saying, Andreas?"

"I'm saying that our love does not render us immune to reality. You are amenable to me—"

"I am quite more than amenable. I would have you beneath me now if I could."

Lust ran through his veins, seized his nerves with a veracity no burn of silver could equal, and threatened to hijack his purpose. The konigswolf stood, putting distance between them. He *must* remain resolute. "Gerwalta, please, hear me out. Nothing would make me happier than to have you as my mate. But claiming you as my bride and denying all the wolves living under the dominion the benefit of your rule would be the epitome of selfishness on my part. As Matron, you would have the power not just to make *my* life better, but to set free from tyranny all the lupines in your region."

The red blaze of her cheeks deepened, but Gerwalta's passions were no longer set to intimacy. Rather, given the narrowing of her eyes, she might want to kill Andreas as much as kiss him.

Given the fire within him he struggled to douse, she could do the former by attempting the latter.

"You truly think that a Matron could so radically shift the flow of culture as to restructure our societies?" she demanded. "You would let our love die on the altar of something with no chance of coming true."

Shame weighted down his brow. "I would die for you, but I

must live for my people. As must you."

She guffawed. "So, we're.... You're... I'm...."

"Lamb, please."

Suddenly, her words, her fretting, her tremoring hands... all ceased as her eyes fell upon him with steely determination. "My mother was right. Never trust a wolf."

Any silver she could wield his direction would never hurt as much as that statement.

"You know what is truly funny?" Gerwalta crossed her arms and lashed her gaze away. "After you were taken from Padua, I was going to rescue you. You and only you. But Karahan told me if I did as I'd been contracted to do, he would help us escape to somewhere where we could be together, man and wife. Everything I did last night was to win that for us. And I revealed my greatest secret, because I was fighting for *us*."

What had he done? She loved him, openly proclaimed it, called him her mate. He'd campaigned for her heart, won it, then let it rot. He'd forgone his own happiness in anticipation of her benevolence for his pack, and in the process, turned her against them all.

Before he could utter a word in defense of his kind, the door behind them opened, filled by billowing, black robes. Mehmet took turns sizing both up. No doubt he could read the tension. If he knew of their argument, he said nothing on it. Instead, the wolfsretter waved a hand, saying "We need to speak. On deck, now," before abruptly turning to leave.

Gerwalta, shoulders squared, rose from the bed.

Andreas searched the space for something she might wear. "Walta, wait. You have barely a scrap of clothing on. Let me gather something for you to—"

She pushed by him, sparing him not a single glance. "A Matron-to-be needs no servant. And recall, Herr Baron, that as a wolfsretter, I am capable of seeing to my own."

With an exhale, her own cloak of heavy, crimson fabric fell over her shoulders and unto the ground, covering her form from the cold of night, and blocking him from the warmth of his affections.

TWENTY-FIVE

The midday sun shone overhead, offsetting the brisk seabreeze lacing fingers over the deck and through her hair. In the near-distance sat Venice, a black-and-gray pearl off the coast, its pink-hued tower, a pin placed by God to secure it in place.

Mehmet led them across the middeck to the rear of the ship, where the other wolfsretter and a woman of exquisite and exotic beauty stood. *The shewolf.* Her relaxed demeanor and unfamiliar attire made placing her familiarity somewhat difficult, but her gray eyes gave her away. But there was something else tugging at Gerwalta's instinct as well. The sense that there was another wolf—besides Andreas—in their proximity. Another below decks? Perhaps, only the sensation was more immediate, and somehow, unlike that any other wolf had ever given her.

It was the same sensation she'd had that night on the roof of Messer Mazzi's neighbor and again in the Doge's palace.

And then, as though she'd been struck by lightning, Gerwalta understood. She turned eyes on Hasan. "He's an asenaic."

That had to be it. A wolf who was not a wolf, a wolfsretter who wasn't a wolfsretter. She'd never met one before, but what else would explain the inconsistent and abnormal sense she had around him. Hasan was the child of a lupine and one of her own kind and that fact alone made his existence a crime.

Mehmet, at ease but a moment before, tensed. The long, twisted dagger he drew into existence gleamed in the light of day. The action, coupled with words in a foreign tongue, triggered the others to raise their guard as well. Suddenly, the asenaic bore two crescent blades which started as his wrist, arched outward, and curved back just below his elbow. His own arm served as handle. The shewolf, through some trickery or strategy, managed to pull herself within her robes in the manner of a turtle, before jutting out from the collapsing cloth in fully-fledged fur.

Even with the tension and urgency of the moment, Gerwalta

knew she needed to inquire on this design. It appeared these Turks had something to teach their German kin.

Mehmet held it to her chest. "How do you…?"

Gerwalta stole a quick look at Andreas, ready to urge restraint, only to find his eyes distant, his skin pale. She'd deal with the consequence of his broken heart later. For the moment, his shock numbed him at a convenient moment.

"Peace." She threw her hands into the air. "I do not wish to invite trouble. I have no cause to harm."

Andreas, though, had snapped from his trance. He pulled around her. "This is allowed in the dominion of the House of Night?"

Could this be the land Karahan had been speaking of? A place where a lupine and wolfsretter could be together and not fear persecution?

The tiny bubble of hope burst with Mehmet's averted gaze, the dagger gaining distance from her throat. "Encouraged? No. Tolerated with disdain? Yes. Hasan is a member of my House, but he has been disowned by our clan. As a wolf, however, he was accepted into Yasmin's pack. Until, that was, our Matron threatened to kill them all for harboring the dishonored."

Gerwalta's sympathies got the better of her. She tilted her head in the couple's direction, speaking although she knew the couple could not understand her words. "You were fleeing, looking for refuge." Then, turning back to Mehmet, she added, "but that doesn't explain your involvement."

Hasan spoke his foreign tongue behind them, the tone obvious despite the linguistic divide. After a few sentences, Mehmet hushed them.

"What?" Gerwalta asked. "What is he saying?"

"He is cursing Karahan," Mehmet said.

Andreas took a step back. "What of him?"

The wolfsretter hacked a laugh. "We are all here because of him. The vampire found us in Istanbul two months ago, said that if we helped him in the plot to overthrow the Doge and trap the Ravens, he would find us a place where we all could find sanctuary."

"And so you ended up in Venice?" Gerwalta asked. "True, there are no pack politics or wolfsretter Matrons to interrogate you, but such a city is no place for our kind. I felt tight in the chest the whole time I was there."

"No, it was not to Venice that he was to deliver us."

The mystery just grew deeper with every word the Turk said. "Then where were you going?"

"Isn't it obvious?" Andreas huffed. "They were on their way to Triberg."

Gerwalta whipped around. "Triberg? But why would they be heading...?"

But before the question was out of her mouth, her mind blended the loose clues into a whole.

Karahan's plan hinged on the inclusion of a wolfsretter, but he'd *already had* two involved from the House of Night. Yet, he'd come all the way from a distant empire to recruit *her.* He'd admitted during their sojourn that he'd learned of the relationship she had with Andreas from one of the wolves she'd rescued in Nuremberg. Was it so surprising if he'd known she could fly as well? She hadn't thought then that any of the wolves had witnessed it, but could she be certain?

"Karahan brought me here *because* he wanted me to be Matron." Had all the blood drained from her face? It must have. "He assumed I would have sympathy for an asenaic and a shewolf in love, because I was in love with a wolf myself. And if he gave me a task that could only be accomplished if a melee forced me to take flight...."

But that still left one thing unanswered.

Gerwalta shook her head. "That explains *them,*" she pointed to Yasmin and Hasan, "but it doesn't explain *you,*" she added, singling out Mehmet.

Andreas paced. "Let me fill that in then for you. Why else would a German-speaking Turk be heading for Triberg?"

If the konigswolf thought his rhetorical aside would bring clarity, he was sorely mistaken. But when Mehmet reached into his robe and pulled from it a bit of scroll bearing her mother's seal, it became clear.

"You were coming to compete for my hand."

"No, Fraulein, I was coming to *win* it," Mehmet said. "There hasn't been a hood born to the House of Night in five generations with the ability to fly. We fear that our bloodline has corrupted. But the House of Red…. For a century, each generation or two has been blessed. We seek to reseed our garden, in hopes some new trees may bear fruit. It was my intention to wed you and take you back to our home high in the Tarsus Mountains. Karahan never told me of the plot to make you Matron. He used me to his own ends, just as he used you."

Her pulse thundered in her ears. Gerwalta ran her good hand over her bad wrist, admiring the innovative silversmithing. Perhaps *her* bloodline had lost a few talents as well. "But it does not need be in vain."

For the first time, it was she who left Mehmet confused. "How so?"

If Andreas wanted her to be the Matron she didn't want to be for the good of his pack, then she'd assure the spouse she'd be forced to marry could be of like mind. "Yes, Karahan played us all, and we are all paying for that deceit. But how we got here doesn't matter. We must go forward with the consequences all the same. No, as a future Matron of the House of Red, I cannot return with you to your homeland, but our children could."

Mehmet's brow furrowed. "What of the ball and your mother's right to choose your husband for you?"

"In my opinion, she has sacrificed it by sending me off to become a vampire's puppet." She stepped forward before getting down on her knees. "Herr Mehmet, Righteous Wolfsretter of the House of Night, walk in night and hunt by moon with me. Offer me your fealty, and I will offer you my fidelity. Do you accept me as your bride, and will you consummate these, our vows, with your body in kind?"

He lifted an eyebrow. "What are you doing?"

"I am proposing marriage." Gerwalta went slack. "Was that not clear?"

Before Mehmet could answer, Andreas pulled her to her feet. "Walta, you cannot."

"Why not?" she snapped. "You said you will not have me, that I am of more use to you as a Matron than a mate. So be it. I will wed Mehmet and become Matron, just as you wished. Can you doubt that your pack will be treated better under our combined rule than someone my mother would pick? Look how he fought to protect a shewolf and asenaic!"

"But when I said I would not marry you I did not mean that you should marry...."

His arguments snuffed under the collapse of his own logic. Gerwalta pushed the stunned konigswolf aside, making her way toward her suddenly betrothed.

"I have one request, though, Herr Mehmet." She took to her feet. "We must wed immediately."

Even the Ottoman wolfsretter seemed dumbfounded at the success of his own campaign. "You do not need more time than that to prepare?"

"Would time bring us another choice? If anything, it dissolves this one we are to make. Word of my ability to fly will reach Triberg well before I do. My mother will quickly align a new path for me, and considerations of what I desire will find no welcome in her hands. But you must swear to me that you will never speak a word to anyone what I said to Herr Baron last evening. I will have your oath that you will do everything within your power, if rumors fester, to deny, and to uphold his good standing and keep him from harm."

"It is to my advantage to do so. I would not live in a foreign land *and* be branded a cuckhold." Mehmet's eyes focused on the wolf beside her as he withdrew his silver at last. "But you must also agree that this romance of yours ends today. My compassion for the wolves does not extend to one sharing my wedding bed."

The black-cloaked man looked at her, then at Andreas, and back at her. He held out his weapon hand.

Gerwalta took a deep breath, swallowed her heart, and reached out in kind.

And that was when they heard the splash.

Four bodies rammed into the railing of the ship in unison, taking in the sight. Andreas did not look back as he paddled—had he taken his wolf because it made the swim easier?—back toward the mainland.

"Andreas, you fool!" Gerwalta cried. "The tides will sweep you out to sea. Come back! Come back this very minute."

The konigswolf stayed true to his path.

Which, it seemed, was far away from her.

TWENTY-SIX

Gerwalta stood dumbfounded in the slayer's foyer, holding out the pouch of refused silver.

"What do you mean you have no use for it?" she asked. "At the very least, take it on behalf of your neighbor whose roof Andreas crashed through. We owe them repairs."

"Massimo has already made arrangements to have the damage repaired." Mazzi waved off her concern. "I am sorry that Karahan left without upholding his end of your agreement; it feels inappropriate asking you for anything in return. Tell me, will it be difficult for you to return to the Schwarzwald?"

She looked away. "It was foolish of me to suppose I could hide something so immense forever. Now that my ability to fly is known, there is nothing for me to do. At least my increased influence will be a boon for the lupines."

Mazzi chuckled. "I'm not talking about your flight. I mean your love for Herr Baron. Not many may have been able to understand the German you spoke to each other, but your eyes spoke more loudly than your words. Everyone in that room could see the heat between you as you fought for each other."

Terror pulled at the tendrils of her heart. "It does not matter. I have offered my hand to one of the wolfsretters from the House of Night, and he has accepted."

"One of the.... Your hand...." Mazzi struggled to find meaning in her words. "Surely you jest."

"I do not. We will exchange vows tonight before departing for Triberg."

Though thank grace they had agreed to delay the consummation until they reached Schloss Wolfsretter. Gerwalta may be bold enough to make her own match, but even she wouldn't dare to close out the finalities without her mother's approval. Not if she wanted to become Matron and not be banished on the spot. To that end, she had agreed that she would arrive to Triberg first and alone to deliver the news of her betrothal. She did not know Mehmet well, but she did not wish him harm. If Gunda Faust wished to fume over her fourth daughter's bold acts, she'd take the brunt of the flames alone.

The Ottoman contingent would arrive the next day. Gerwalta could only hope that Andreas would have returned by then, and that he'd be willing to accept Hasan and Jasmine to his pack. She'd like to have said she had no doubt of it; his compassion, like that he'd shown to the wolf sent on his king orders to slay her, was one of the things she loved about him.

Mazzi, however, was Italian. "But you love Andreas," he persisted.

"It matters not," she said. "Please, Messer Mazzi, believe me. I am heartsick over the whole affair, but I am doing what I must to protect us all. Do not salt my wounds."

The old man relented. "Then I wish you happiness, Fraulein Faust. As much of it as you're able to grasp."

The Matron's scowl came as no surprise. "How could you not tell me?"

There was no need to ask what. "I am a fourth daughter, a fifth child. I did not reveal that I could fly because I did not think myself worthy of being Matron. It is rightfully Helga's—"

Her mother bore down on her, a hand encircling Gerwalta's throat. "Who succeeds me is my decision. Both you and Helga need to remember that."

Her voice cracked from the pressure on her larynx. "Yes, Matron."

"And withholding this knowledge was an attempt by you to usurp that right."

"Yes, Matron. I can only beg your forgiveness."

Her mother released her hold, sending Gerwalta to the floor. "No, you do not. A Matron never begs. Learn this and learn it now, Gerwalta. It is only the first lesson I must teach you. That I should have spent *years* teaching you. We have so much now to cover." She shook her head. "So many years wasted on Helga."

Gerwalta lifted her head, looking across the faces of her family, gathered to learn the news of her return. Helga's eyes blazed. It lasted only a moment, etching away by bitterness directed squarely at her little sister.

Any fear she'd felt before? It reverberated in that icy stare.

But the Matron wasn't done. "Not only have you spent years keeping secrets, but now you have gone and arranged your own marriage? Tell me truly, daughter, are there any more secrets waiting for my discovery?"

She bit her tongue. The only one remaining would go with her to the grave.

Gerwalta searched the dust on the floor for her next words, wondering what she should do to quell her mother's anger. "No, mother."

Gunda crossed her arms and pursed her lips. "Good. Then let us proceed. Helga!"

Stunned that her presence was even recalled, the Matron's first daughter snapped to attention. "Yes, Mother?"

Gunda's arm lashed to the side, her finger extending to the outer walls of the castle. "Order the fires built for tomorrow night and send word to those who've already arrived for the ball that it has instead become a wedding feast."

"The… fires, Matron?" Helga, perplexed, looked to Gerwalta for guidance. "But *fauernacht* is not for another two nights."

"Did I stumble in my speech? Or do you think I am unaware of when comes the full moon?" The Matron did not wait for her first born to answer. "Your sister has made a mockery of this family, and we need amend it immediately. Tonight, she and her wedded will make good on their oaths. Do you hear me, Gerwalta? You will consummate your union and go about making yourself into a worthy heir."

She swallowed her fear. "Yes, Matron."

TWENTY-SEVEN

Gerwalta stared at herself in the looking glass, wondering who stared back. Surely this woman who she saw could not become a matron? But then again, was this not the woman who'd broken the heart of the man she loved, not once, but twice? Wasn't it she who usurped her mother's place in selecting a husband? Was it not she who had trapped the seven deadly vampires whose silver urns now were shelved in the wine cellar below?

Was she not the woman who was about to make love to a man she barely even knew to solidify her ability to carry out her own agenda? Perhaps Mehmet also looked with dread upon the act they were about to undertake. After all, he'd readily agreed to delaying consummation instead of demanding it as his right. Maybe he found her disgusting, and they'd never have one mote of the passion she and Andreas had, that the act of creating children would be a necessary chore they'd both slog through out of duty, and that his company and consort would cease when she'd born enough children.

It was happening; she was becoming her mother.

In the bailey below, the wedding guests reveled. A few, perhaps, with somewhat less exuberance. After all, they'd come to the Schwarzwald believing they'd be competing for her hand, only to be informed it had already been awarded. Gerwalta was no expect in marital matters, but she did not believe starting out with so many slighted would-be suitors boded well for Mehmet and herself. Whatever, such cares would have to wait for later. For the moment, her only concern was that she needed to descend and claim her husband.

She let slip her shift and summoned her red cloak, making it somewhat longer than usual so it draped about her feet and touched the ground. This was tradition: the bride wore only her colors into the tent. Her husband would remove it and place it on his own shoulders, signifying his acceptance into her clan. Then he would summon *his* cloak to wrap around her before they both removed them and... well, the rest was simply fornication, wasn't it?

Gerwalta took each step down from her room with deliberation, focusing on what need be done. A shift in her periphery stopped her, and she turned just in time to duck, sending Helga flying over her and landing at the bottom of the stairs.

Her sister was a gifted warrior; only a fool would deny that. She landed rough but in a skilled manner, quickly recovering, summoning a blade and awaiting.

"Helga, do not blame me for this," her sister begged. "I hid it as long as I could. I never wanted to usurp your claim to the throne."

"Oh, do not worry little sister, you haven't," Helga spat back, her blond tresses shaking with each word spit out. "Our sainted mother is in good health, with many years left in her body. That gives me plenty of time."

Gerwalta held her arms out, brandishing her chest. "Run me through now, then. I have no silver. Even my medallion has been left upstairs. I am defenseless."

"Do you think me a fool?" Helga spit back. "Everyone would know it was me. I would never be so stupid as to kill you myself."

"What will you do then? Conscript another konigswolf within our region to send one of his wolves to kill me? It must have so upset you when you learned your hopeful assassin failed to carry out his orders."

A half-cocked grin pulled up Helga's sinister lips. "As much as it would upset you, I'd wager, to learn that that wolf never made it back to the Schwarzwald."

Gerwalta blanched. "How...?"

"Do you really think I put all my eggs in one basket, little one? Remember that mother has spent years training me for the position I am due: I have networks of spies all over our region, and even far beyond it. In fact..." Helga drew her sword to her open palm, examining its edge. "You may be surprised what I know. Great Aunt Maria was."

So Gerwalta's suspicions had been well founded. Helga *had* killed Maria Dreger. But that wasn't what struck fear into the heart of the young wolfsretter as much as the greater implication of what her sister had just professed.

"What do you know?"

Helga lowered her sword. "You should run along now, Gerwalta. Your betrothed will be pulsing with anticipation. I don't know if anyone's ever told you. Although we women are the superior sex, our men are so much more... *licentious* than we are. They love coupling, need it even. You'll learn, when you go now and let your bridegroom partake of you, how the act of making love means so much to them." She balanced her chin on an index finger. "Oh, dear, I bet Herr Baron is in shambles tonight, knowing the wolfsretter he loves is in the arms of another. Of course, I know you never *consummated* your relationship with him. If you had, he'd be here tonight, trying to kill Mehmet. I wonder, if I were to wander down to the packlands while your performing your wifely duties, and bound the konigswolf, if I might bring him some *comfort*. Like I said, males love coupling. Their bodies sometimes *rise* to the call, even when their heart is distant."

Gerwalta's hands curled so tightly into fists beneath her cloaks, pearls of hot blood pooled under her fingernails. "You wouldn't."

"Would it grieve you if I claimed your beloved's virginity, leaving him bonded to me?" Helga mocked. "Leaving him *in love* with me?"

"You hate me, sister, but you hate werewolves more. Enough with your empty threats. You would never *touch* a lupine with anything but derision."

Helga claimed the space remaining between them. "You're right, I wouldn't. But now that you've confirmed with your anger what my spies reported to me, I have all the evidence I need to kill Andreas Baron." She leaned in, whispering, "with complete legitimacy."

Gerwalta wanted silver. She wanted to kill Helga where she stood, but the consequences facing Helga were the same ones forestalling Gerwalta.

Helga backstepped her way down the stairs. "But don't worry, little sister. I'll make it look like an accident. After all, I can't have the satisfaction of killing you later if I expose your sins and get you banished now, can I? In fact, you should thank me for disposing of the powder keg that the konigswolf represents. Go to your *rightful* husband. I have things to do, and I cannot depart until you are riding your husband inside that tent out there. I should return to the castle by morning with a glorious wedding present."

With that, Helga left.

Gerwalta didn't move. Couldn't move. Couldn't force her feet to obey. What to do? *What to do?* Did Helga mean it? Even she would know the dangers of killing the pack's king unprovoked. Even if it was made to look like an accident, rumors and unrest would plague the lot. Was Helga the kind who wouldn't care, as long as any arising crisis gave her opportunity to hurt her own little sister.

Of course, she was.

Stepping forward would be the same as walking Andreas to the gallows. Retreating upstairs, the same as if she slew him herself.

She lifted a foot...

...and pivoted.

Gerwalta dashed up the stairs, across the throne room, to the base of the tower. She had no silver to mold stairs, but she didn't need. With a flex of her legs, she rose into the air, ascending. She couldn't flee through the bailey, of course. The wedding guests would have their eyes fixed on the door leading from the castle, ready to cheer her emergence and escort her to the tent where Mehmet waited. The only way she could get to Andreas in time was if she flew, and the only way to get out of the castle unseen was through the tower.

She only hoped that Helga did not realize what she'd done until it was too late, and that when she got to the packlands in the valley below, she could convince Andreas to run for his life.

TWENTY-EIGHT

She found him in the field, alone, chopping wood by the dim light of a small blaze he'd built for utlity.

He would know she was there; such was the nature between wolfsretters and lupines. The konigswolf, however, gave her arrival no pause except to still a single moment, before reaching to the pile of lumber beside him and picking up another log.

"Go away."

"Herr Konigswolf, you must to listen to me."

Swing. *Thwack!*

"Helga is coming. She means to kill you."

Thwack!

"You must flee now. Make for Navarre. Seek sanctuary with Karahan."

Thwack!

"Why aren't you moving already? Andreas!"

He raised the axe overhead, but this time, before he could bring its weight down upon the log he'd positioned, she rounded on him. Gerwalta pushed her arms to his biceps and her stare to the depths of his soul.

"Did you not hear what I said? Run, Andreas. Save yourself."

The tremor in his arms could have been because of any number of things: the weight of the blade frozen in an odd position, the lure of swinging forward and pushing her away in the process, the temptation to drop all and claim her lips....

His words were hoarse. "Save myself for what? I have lost you. What have I to live for?"

"What have you to live for?" She motioned vaguely to the

trail that led back to his homestead. "Every wolf who calls this valley home, that's what. The land that you and your pack have tended for generations. The hopes of a mate who will give you strong daughters and handsome sons. You have everything to live for."

The wolf threw the axe to the ground as he turned away. "I thought so too when I jumped off that boat. I told myself I would live for only them, for my pack. But what am I now? I am no king who can lead. I am pup who followed a moth to the flame and was burned in the fire."

He turned over his shoulder, looking toward her, but not at her. "You should leave, Frau Faust. If your sister is truly coming to kill me, perhaps it is a mercy to us both. You can move on with your life, and I can stop treading endless still waters in mine. Go, Gerwalta. Go home to your mate."

She stepped up behind him, putting her hand on his shoulder and leaning her chin against his back. "I need not go anywhere to see my mate. He's right here."

Andreas turned, grinning. "Pretty words, but you already have a husband, do you not?"

Another three steps to circle him. Gerwalta laid one hand on his chest, and the other behind his neck, pulling herself up to him. "I only proposed to him because I was angry at you for pushing me to be Matron. A foolish act of momentary insult. The moment Helga said she was coming to kill you, I knew I'd rather be the cause of your death than the one who costs you your life. If you're prepared to die either way, at least die in my arms, Andreas. I pledge myself to you and only you. I am *your* mate, forever."

Her eyes closed as she drew herself to him, but moments from his lips, his words stilled her.

"I will ask one last time, and you must be certain: am I who and what you want forever, knowing what it means for us both? If we do this, I will be *bound* to you."

The wolfsretter paused, pulling back just enough to frame him in her vision. "I know what I want."

He grinned. "Do you?" Andreas's left hand circled around, finding the curve of her backside and filling his palm with it. Meanwhile, his right hand crept up her ribs, drifting lithely, until it found the swell of her unbound breast beneath the cloak, closing over it, squeezing it in the most delightful way.

Oh, sweet agony.

Gerwalta's hands clutched at the collar of his jacket, holding herself as even the teasing of her breast weakened her knees. His head tilted like that of a puppy when she unwound herself from him, and she saw the concern weigh in his eyes. Was she again changing her mind? Would she deny him? But apprehension turned to appetite when she drew in a deep breath before letting it out in a gentle push. The magic that summoned her cloak ebbed, dissolving the garment into nothingness.

His eyes clung to her naked form, even as the dew of night began to fall upon her. She veritably stalked him, each step languid, her hips swinging as she navigated the uneven forest floor.

"It's you, Andreas." Gerwalta's hand cupped his cheek. "I only want you."

It was such an odd reversal: she, the one raised to contain and hide, presenting herself to the world red cloak-first, to be without it in his sight. He, from a people who treated nudity as common fashion, obfuscated from sight, suddenly struck dumb by her exposure.

Andreas leaned in, treating her to a taste, a mere brush of lip on lip, a tentative first step in the dance that lay before them. Gerwalta raised her other hand, holding his face in her grasp.

"Andreas Baron, Konigswolf of the Schwarzwald Pack, walk in night and hunt by moon with me. Offer me your fealty, and I will offer you my fidelity. Do you accept me as your bride, and will you consummate these, our vows, with your body in kind?"

He blinked. "These are the same words you said to Mehmet."

"The vow is not binding until the union is consummated."

"You mean you have not…." His words died away. Andreas took her face in his hands, drawing her lips to his. "I accept. Even if you *had* been with him, I'd accept. My love has no qualifications."

Gerwalta gasped as the konigswolf swept her from her feet, carrying her with all the ease of a bear lifting a twig. "Is there not some lupine custom you wish me to uphold?"

"We don't use words." He walked her away from the shattered, split pile of logs and toward a patch of untouched snow.

"We take action."

Frost bit her skin as he laid her upon the ground, a contrast to the heat building within her. Andreas's eyes stayed locked in hers as he pulled off his coat and let it fall away, soon joined therein by his shirt, his breeches, his boots. Her eyes had feasted on his form before, but never with so much anticipation. He paused over her, taking a moment to breathe before falling to his knees.

"The snow?" He said, curling one hand behind her neck and pulling her lips to his. "Does it bother you?"

She let the act play out languidly, slowly using their connection to draw him back. "I am a dark one; it causes no offense." Her head flattened, her long auburn hair pooling underneath and providing something in the way of a pillow. "Besides, I find myself quite warm."

Andreas's weight settled over her, molding the winter landscape beneath to her form. He laughed into her neck as he nuzzled. "We may melt the whole forest before we're through."

His mouth explored her, moving with aching clarity down her neck, dotting kisses across her chest, until he wrapped his lips around the rise of her breast. Gerwalta threw her head back, sucking in breath, even as he moved his attentions from left to right.

"I will make you happy, Walta," he mumbled as he found his way back to her mouth, demanding her kiss. His body shifted, leaving his manhood crested upon the pulsation of her desire, teasing her with promise. "I swear it."

With one last look, he sought permission. Gerwalta suppressed her frustration, wanting him to take what was so clearly his, but understood that the next moment would seal his heart to hers. He could never walk away.

She nodded, preparing herself for the initial discomfort her sisters had harked on about behind folded hands. Andreas's hips rolled with aching slowness, as the pressure of his entrance pressed in on her. Gerwalta bit her lip; the stories had not been wholely false, and she suddenly wondered if the enjoyable part of this practice had all been a lie. The konigswolf let out a slow moan, pausing when he was fully sheathed within her. With a deep breath, the tightness of her frame eased, and yet, he did not move. His head stay buried in the crux of her neck and shoulder.

"Andreas?"

No answer, no movement save for his breathing.

"Andreas, are you all right?"

His head jerked up, revealing feral eyes. *Lupine* eyes. Eyes that had found prey and sized it up for eating.

"I... I love you." He'd said it before, but never like this. Never with such... awe. His hand rose to stroke back her hair. "Walta, I love you."

"And I love y—Oh. *Ohh...*"

Her words stilled as his passion unleashed. Suddenly, their exchange transformed from serene and sacred to ferocious and animalistic.

And she found she quite liked it.

Andreas's hands curled under her, clutching her shoulders from behind. He used her as an anchor, pulling himself deeper with each thrust. And with each thrust, a grunt, a growl, a heated pulse of his lupine nature. Gone was the anxiety and the discomfort. Gerwalta fought her own nature that screamed at her to dominate this man, this creature. The woman within her knew there was so much more promise in ceding control.

He waxed and waned, the cycles of the moon playing out between her thighs. They ceased being separate creatures as she felt the shift. It seemed impossible; a wolfsretter didn't *bond,* but the emotions that invaded her as he worked into her... What else *could* it be called but bonding?

And suddenly, she realized: love. It was love that was swelling up within her.

In a blink, the physical grabbed attention away from her emotions. Her insides coiled, even as Andreas pushed into her so hard, he moved her across the ground in the process of claiming her.

"Walta, I'm...."

But his words cut off as she called out, her body reverberating with feeling. One moment, every muscle within her clenched as though struck by lightning, every nerve electrocuted. The next, her body went limp, a sense of euphoria flooding her from head to foot. It was everything she had felt the first time, but more so and deeper. Within a few more strokes built to a crescendo, Andreas growled, almost howled, before falling atop of her, destroyed by his own efforts.

They rested there, in the snow under the trees, as though eminent danger did not grow closer by the moment. Andreas's arm hooked out to gather her close as he rolled onto his side. He turned to kiss her forehead, folding her arms in between them. His hands worked the tangles of her hair as Gerwalta recalled her cloak into being, untying it at the neck and using it as a blanket to cover them both.

"It is done, then," Andreas huffed, struggling to catch his breath. "Now what?"

Gerwalta pushed herself up on the palm of her hand and reached for him with another. She leaned in, brushing a kiss to his lips. "Now, we run."

TWENTY-NINE

Triberg had not impressed Mehmet, that was for certain.

As he awaited his bride, he recalled his initial impression upon arrival. Was this what passed for a fortress in these parts? One measly tower that didn't rise but five floors? A scattering of odd, mismatched buildings trapped into a compound by the presence of irregular stone walls hardly tall enough to keep out a squirrel, let alone a vampire? A throne room that would be lucky to hold fifty people, and a courtyard that struggled to hold two hundred?

Venice hadn't suited him either, frankly. At least the Doge's Palace was large enough to host a proper party, though. If there was one thing Mehmet had learned from the laity of Istanbul, it was that: largess demands authority. Authority demands power. Power demands whatever it wants.

If Schloss Wolfsretter did not demand authority, then he would have to seize it through ruthlessness, cunning, and guile.

All of which would be aided by wedding Gerwalta Faust. As a *kushan,* a hood who could fly, she would become her bloodline's next Matron. As a fourth daughter and barely into her birthright, she was young enough to be brought to heel. He'd oversee her furthering education and have her eating from his hand. It did not hurt that she was an attractive little thing. He was so going to enjoy stripping her of her innocence.

If only she would come down from her quarters in this poor excuse of a castle to let him do as much! He'd put off on the trip to Triberg, using concern for her mother's approval, until he was certain her family and her lands had enough potential to exploit. He did not favor his bride's schloss, but those silver mines which ran through the dominion of the House of Red? They were worth the arrangement.

And it hadn't been a lie, what he told her; there hadn't been a *kushan* born in the House of Night for decades. If he could return to barter children with the potential: he'd rule both east and west, even if by proxy, achieving the goal that fool Bernhard Dreger had planned and failed at.

The air inside the tent shifted, a slash of winter darting through the space heated by the brazier burning within. *Time to pull back on the* masque *of innocence*, he thought.

"You made me nervous, Gerwalta. I was beginning to fear that you'd changed your mind."

When he turned, however, he found not his betrothed, her red hair falling languidly over her milky white shoulders, but her eldest sister, the reincarnation of a northern goddess.

Helga held a silver staff poised to strike, but he stayed his reaction. She might have causes that had nothing to do with him. No such luck. Within moments, she had the weapon kissing his throat.

"Are you party to her betrayal?"

Mehmet blinked his confusion. "Whose? What?"

"Gerwalta, you fool! I have just heard back from my spies in Venice. They say that not only did she openly declare Andreas Baron her mate, but that *you* assisted her in escaping the city in the aftermath of the coup."

Was that the way of it? Sister spying on sister? Helga must have known the Matron's fourth-born posed a threat to her claim on the throne, then. She'd want to take her down, and if that happened *before* he'd consecrated their union, all the work and sacrifice of these last months would be for naught.

Mehmet lowered his masque, pushing Helga's sword away with a delicately placed finger tip. "Escape is a bit of an overstatement, Frau Faust. I *isolated* her."

Helga posture softened. "Isolated her? To what end?"

"To exploit her, of course." He held his hands aloft, indicting their surroundings. "You do not seriously believe I would compete to win this, do you? To be son to the House of Red and have a fourth-born daughter as my bride? No, my ambitions are a bit *bigger*." He dared a step forward. "As I believe yours are, too."

"I wish to be Matron of the House of Red," she snapped, dropping the staff in a huff of frustration. "That is no secret."

When she backed into the central post holding the tent up,

Helga dropped the sword.

Mehmet stepped into her, drifting a finger over her chin. "No, *bigger*." He focused on her lips.

The muscles of her face tightened, but she did not back away. "What are you doing, Herr Mehmet? I am the sister of your betrothed."

"And where *is* my betrothed?" he asked, already knowing the answer.

Helga's throat twitched as she swallowed. "I know not."

"Of course, you do. *I* do. She's gone to Baron. As disgusted as I was by their romance, I do not think it false. Their attraction was evident to all who saw them. I wouldn't be surprised to learn that he's defiling her even now."

A smile ticked up on Helga's face. "You would have cause for retaliation if so."

"Yes, I would." Finally, some progress. "But surely I'd want more for enduring such an insult than the head of the konigswolf." He drew a line down her chin, her neck, tapering off right above her breast. "I have big plans, Helga. Far bigger than the Schwarzwald, though it's a start. What about you? How big can you dream?"

"I already have a husband."

An obstacle, but not one that couldn't be overtaken. "He should accompany me to the packlands tonight, but he should know the mission will be dangerous. Killing a whole pack is not for the faint of heart."

Helga's chest rose and fell with increased effort. "I will send for him directly."

"Good. Then I will gather my silver and make my way immediately. Tell me, Frau Faust, where will I find their encampment?"

"The pack shares a farmstead in the valley. It is over the river and through the woods."

He kept their eyes locked as he kneeled, picking up the weapon she'd abandoned. In his hands, the metal transformed, closing in on itself, thickening, condensing, until where a staff had been, only an axe remained.

"Tell your mother I will return with Baron's head and her daughter in chains."

Helga cocked her head to the side. "You will let Gerwalta live?"

"Of course. Killing the pack will make every lupine fear me. You and I killing your sister together, however? That will make *every dark one* fear *us*."

RED AND THE RESTORER

RED ORIGINS

BOOK THREE

ONE

Never did Gunda Faust allow grays to streak outwardly across the bold colors of her declarations. Oh, in her heart, her spirit often rebelled against the injuries her position forced upon those around her, but not even her own husband had heard her doubts regarding their eldest daughter. Helga did claim many traits that would make her a powerful leader: intelligence, cunning, determination, even beauty... But woven into the cord of her demeanor ran an undeniable thread of sadism. Gunda would be the last to propose violence was without place in the policing of wolves, but extreme acts should be born of extreme circumstances. Helga lusted for blood not to nourish power, but to quench a thirst for pain.

She'd managed to rule the wolves, but in short order, she'd lose her family's loyalty, and where would that leave things? All her children in the ground, that's where. Gunda shuddered when she thought of any of her progeny coming to violent ends. A matron demanded respect and obeisance, but that didn't mean she held no love for her children. Gunda treasured all five, from fierce Helga to reserved Gerwalta.

And then the news came from Venice: Gerwalta could fly. By the traditions of their kind, it was a sign that it was the youngest child, not the eldest, who would follow Gunda unto the throne. Helga wouldn't cede for tradition's sake, however. Her youngest, so often overlooked, would now find herself on the sharpened end of her eldest sister's sword. Perhaps the wolfsretter of the House of Night to whom Gerwalta had betrothed herself would help keep her from harm. It wasn't the match Gunda would've chosen, but it was a good match for a child she suspected would be reluctant to sink to cruelty.

A knock on the door pulled the Matron from her reverie.

"Enter."

Helga's head poked through the chamber door, bringing Gunda to her feet. "What? What has happened?"

When the door swung farther, revealing Gerwalta's intended,

Mehmet, in Helga's wake, the Matron knew.

"She refuses to enter the tent." Gunda nodded in the shadow of her own presumption as the other two crept in. "Never fear, Herr Siyah, nerves about the joining aren't uncommon and quickly remedied. I'll find my erstwhile daughter directly and assure that she performs her marital duties posthaste."

The two young people exchanged a look of confusion.

Gunda arrested herself on the spot. "There is something more."

Helga looked to her clenched hands. "Yes, Gerwalta didn't claim her bridegroom, but the situation is more dire than nerves. What I mean to say is..."

The Ottoman wolfsretter assumed the rest. "It appears she has betrayed our vows and your clan, Matron," he announced. "She has run into the arms of the königswolf."

The news hit Gunda in the gut and threw her off balance. "Impossible. No wolfsretter of the House of Red would do such a thing."

"Yet, it appears to be so," Helga resumed. "No one in the schloss has seen Gerwalta for nearly an hour. Maximillian just returned from the packlands, reporting that the königswolf is also unaccounted for."

"But that doesn't mean... It's not as though Gerwalta would..."

Or would she? Truth be told, Gunda had suspected some festering secret behind her daughter's eyes. When Gerwalta had returned from Venice proclaiming she'd arranged her own marriage, Gunda had surmised that her youngest had pulled an excellent coup, working some secret conspiracy. Could it really be the secret she'd been hiding was that she was in love with a lupine?

Each of the Matron's knuckles cracked in succession as her hands tightened into fists. "Find them."

Both Mehmet and Helga dipped their heads, the latter saying, "And what shall we do with them?"

"Bring them both before me in chains," Gunda declared. "He in silver, she in iron. I'll have the truth of it from their own mouths."

Mehmet stepped forward. "Matron Faust, if I may? You are entertaining a great many guests, and it is possible that Gerwalta hasn't committed any act of the flesh with the lupine. I'd suggest a small party of men for this mission. Perhaps this can be contained silently, and men will not be missed as much from the festivities. It may still be possible to seal our union and merely punish the wolf without any inside the grounds being any the wiser tonight."

She chewed on that a moment, discerning the taste. "Yes, perhaps. Helga, send the men, your brother included. My order otherwise stands but advise them to be discreet upon their return. Once I have the truth of it, I'll decide how to proceed."

TWO

Pulling on Andreas's hand had as much effect as yelling at the wind. There was no arresting him. Unless she wanted to cause him injury.

Honestly, breaking one of his legs became more tempting by the moment.

"Andreas, stop! I cannot go before the pack like this. I haven't any clothing!"

That at least made him slow a fraction as he glanced back at her over his shoulder. "Yes, and I approve wholeheartedly."

"You approve?" Enough of this foolery. She wouldn't cede their lives on the altar of his amusement. Gerwalta sped her steps, placing herself between him and the path back to the pack's farmstead, her arms stretched out wide. "What part of 'we need to run with haste for our very lives' didn't you grasp? We haven't time to visit the pack for a social farewell."

At last, he stopped. Andreas fixed her with feasting eyes, raking over the contours of her unclad form. "Exquisite."

She fell in on herself, attempting to cover her treasures. "You may be a wolf, Andreas Barron, but you are still such a man."

"It is no sin for one to appreciate the beauty of his mate."

"It is if it comes at the cost of her life." She pressed on. "That Helga hasn't already arrived is a slim blessing. I love you. I've given myself to you, but will you treat that so gallantly as not to heed my warning?"

He stepped forward, closing the space between them. At first, Gerwalta thought he may mean to take her again—he'd already attempted once. Instead, Andreas's gaze softened. He took up her hands in his, raising them to his mouth to kiss the back of her knuckles.

"Love, hear me," he begged. "I am the königswolf. If I leave my pack without proper ceremony, the consequences for them will be manifold."

"You were prepared to leave them without ceremony when we were in Venice," Gerwalta argued.

"Then I had already been away from them for nearly two moons. A third would snap my tether with them, letting them decide upon a new king. But now…"

"If you left, there would be no one to represent them against the Matron." Gerwalta cut him off. His sad eyes told her she'd surmised the consequences. "There needs be a new king ere we depart. But, Andreas, in our current circumstances, that can happen only if one of your pack defeats you in battle. Your pack loves you. None would dare."

"Do you forget so quickly, love?" he asked. "There is a new packling, one who harbors quite a dislike for me."

"But to leave him in charge against my family would… He'll drive them into silver swords for certain!"

Andreas turned back towards the village. "Once Gerhart is king, a king's honor will comply him to do what is in the best interest of the pack. He'll protect them."

"And if he doesn't?"

Despair contorted the beautiful brow of her beloved. "Then we are all dead."

THREE

Andreas met Wilhelm's eyes across the shorn field. A momentary smile faded as Gerwalta stepped from the tree line in his wake.

Wilhelm dropped his pitchfork and stumbled forward. The sheep, awaking with the dawn, would have to wait for their morning meal. Andreas hesitated, wondering what he would say when they were close enough for words. Many times he'd imagined a foggy future in which his beloved would be his mate and mother of his pups, dreamed of their bliss and resilience in the face of adversity to their coupling, but he'd never anticipated the ignition of the battle they were sure to wage. Now, staring down its nose, he wasn't sure how to confront the beast of their reality.

Whatever the next few minutes held, they were only the first of the forever in which they'd always be in violation of not only Dark One ways, but of their very nature. If Andreas couldn't gain the understanding of his own pack—of his own second—what hope did they have?

Gerwalta, clutching the edge of her conjured red cloak in an effort to conceal her nudity, drew to a stop at his side.

"He is wondering if I am stalking you. Quickly, take my hand."

Andreas didn't allow his gaze to break from his second's as he complied. "There is such hate in his eyes."

"It is for me, not you," Gerwalta assured him. "We should expect nothing less."

"We should hope for so much more." Andreas licked his lips. "Whatever happens, know that you are my priority. I'll protect you."

She pulled his hands to her lips, even as it forced some view of her flesh beneath. "I vow the same."

By the time the two parties had closed the distance, Wilhelm boiled. "Mein könig? What goes on here?"

So few words, but what they said was so much more. They spoke of confusion, anger, betrayal, desperation. Heartbreak.

Abandonment.

Andreas assumed the confident mask of the ruler. "Wilhelm, gather the pack."

"You cannot possibly mean to say that—"

"Wilhelm!" Andreas more growled than spoke. The wolf raged within him, a command now, not a request. His second would have only two choices: comply or defect. "Now say I."

Forever gathered in a dew drop as Andreas waited. Finally, Wilhelm acquiesced. With a pivot, the lupine within him took control, letting out a high, wallowing howl. Soon enough, the others began to come into view, moving with haste from whatever daybreak errand they'd been about. Some still carried the implements of their tasks. A washboard, a basket of eggs, a butchering knife...

His pack... He loved them each. Some he'd grown up with. Some, grown older under. Some had grown under him. To be their könig had been his joy, his privilege. But now, he'd be their greatest regret.

"I have an announcement." He resumed hold of Gerwalta's hand, pulling his beloved under his wing. "I've chosen my mate, and it is she."

Several of them flinched. Others looked ill. A mother with her young pup in her arms covered the boy's ears, as though the act would keep the evil of the world from soaking his thoughts.

"Mein könig, you cannot be serious." Wilhelm voiced that which Andreas knew they all thought. "She is one of them."

"She was one of them," Andreas declared. "And now, she is my mate."

As he'd predicted, the Wehr pack defector stepped forward. "I knew it would come to this, and now, Andreas Barron's arrogance and betrayal to the pack will cost us all." Gerhart turned to the others, addressing his words to them. "You know their law: a wolf who tussles with a wolfsretter is subject to death. And as it is our king who has committed the crime, we all will bear the punishment, all because he took satisfaction up some red bitch's skirt."

"How dare you!" Gerwalta was out of Andreas's grip and charging Gerhart ere he could recall her, her finger drilling into the lupine's chest, her nakedness forgotten. "How dare you betray your fealty to the wolf who spared your life."

"You mean when you wanted to kill me?" Gerhart pushed right back, but Gerwalta didn't falter. Even now, with daggers being thrown her way from the glare of every wolf, his love stood firm.

It was an accusation for certes, but one she wouldn't eschew. "Yes, when I wanted to kill you. You owe him your breath, and you use it to speak ill against him."

Wilhelm's mate Lisi, came between them. "The matter of who owes who what is of little consequence," she said. "You may love Andreas, and if he has mated you, the same is true for him. But Gerhart is right, it matters not. Your mother will use this as an excuse to bring down harsh judgement on us all, for they'll come for Andreas, and we, his pack, will be duty bound to fight for him."

"Not if I am no longer king."

Wilhelm swung about. "Sire, you don't mean to have one of us challenge you?"

"I do, and I expect it immediately. According to my mate, Helga implied a mission to either corrupt or destroy me. Gerwalta had come to warn me."

He let them stitch together the threads of the implied: and so my solution was to stop playing lovers' games and make her my mate, firm and true. There was no call to pour salt upon their wounds.

"Helga won't come alone. A team requires coordination, planning, time. Perhaps even the Red Matron readies herself for my destruction and yours as I speak. I am your king, and as such, it is my duty to protect you from all dangers, even if the source of that danger is me. One of you must challenge me, and once defeated in battle, exile me so that the Reds shall have no cause to exact vengeance on you."

Suddenly, Gerwalta's eyes went wide. She'd thought through the ramifications of his intentions then. "But Andreas, without a pack, you'll go mad."

"Not immediately. I'll have three moons for us to find a new pack."

"And who will take in an exiled king with a wolfsretter whore for a mate?"

Andreas would give credit to Gerhart that he didn't flinch as the back of Gerwalta's hand connected with his chin. Perfect. It would raise the wolf's ire all the more, playing right into Andreas's plan.

"As a dark one, I am many accursed things, but I am no whore. I've taken but one man to my bed, and it is and will ever be only your king."

Andreas had chosen his mate well. She was more shewolf in spirit than any lupine he'd encountered. Pride burned in his chest as he stepped forward, peeling off the clothes he'd only just put back on in the woods not a half hour before. "One of you will challenge me, by god, for it is your only path to salvation. Now, step forward, or I will demand—"

"I challenge!" Gerhart stepped into his role just in the nick of time. The scrappy, southern wolf stepped forward, teeth bared even in his layman form. He mirrored the king, undoing his clothing, preparing for battle. "You are an embarrassment of a wolf and a sham of a king, and it will be my honor to assume your mantle."

No sooner were the two ready to bare fangs and assume their fur than they all heard it: a battle horn from the mountain.

Andreas turned to Lisi. "My last orders as king are these: first, and with much haste, clothe my bride. Second, secure the pups and what shewolves can be obligated beyond their care, prepare a defense."

Lisi looked for a moment as though she may refuse, perhaps even argue, but all knew that any delay invited death going forward.

"Yes, my king." Lisi curtsied, took Gerwalta by the wrist, and escorted the children and the shewolves to the farmhouse.

Only the men remained.

Andreas turned out his hands, cracking his knuckles. "Wince I am defeated, you must make haste to exile me and let the Reds know I am no longer of the pack."

"Don't forfeit, Andreas," Wilhelm said, "or the transfer of kingship won't take."

He knew this. It wasn't a simple thing to become königswolf.

To mock battle wouldn't do. Andreas could also not merely cede. Gerhart must defeat him.

Andreas gave one last solemn nod. "I won't yield, but for the sake of every member of this pack, Gerhart, you had better force me to my surrender with great urgency."

The two wolves cried out as they let their power take them, making fur of what had been flesh and fang of what had been jaw. The hulking forms stared at each other, unmoving save for the curl of their lips over long, gleaming teeth.

Until finally, one twitched.

Gerhart was the first to charge, but Andreas was the first to draw blood.

FOUR

Lisi made haste delivering Gerwalta to the main farmhouse, a structure not insignificant in its size, and shared by several of the families that made the pack. The shewolf's muttered curses ended with, "A wolfsretter, on mine own hearth. The enemy at the gate, indeed," when she threw open the door of a wardrobe to sort through its contents.

Gerwalta tempered her instinct to argue. "I don't want to be the pack's enemy, Frau Kosner."

An acidic stare landed on her with scorching effects. "You became that when you let him bed you," Lisi spat. "What were you thinking, seducing a wolf? Don't you know that you've ruined him now? That he can never love another?"

"Neither can I." Never mind that the balance of the seducing had been on the wolf's side. Gerwalta caught a dash of white and pale yellow cloth that flew through the air. "Andreas is the man I love. The only man I'll ever love."

"Honeyed words, but you aren't a lupine. Your heart is fickle." Lisi turned to help the wolfsretter pull the frock down over her arms. "There, you are dressed. Now, if you'll forgive me, I need to see to our defense against certain death by your family. I advise you to stay here until someone comes for you. Andreas would hate if his blushing bride was harmed in the melee of battle, and I cannot guarantee your safety, Frau Baron."

Lisi left even as that term cracked open Gerwalta's heart. Frau Baron. True, Gerwalta had become Andreas's mate, but for some reason, in practical terms, that meant she now had a husband. In the eyes of all dark ones, Gerwalta was now Andreas's wife. Though why the wolves expected her to take on his name and not the other way around was a queer notion. She wasn't Frau Baron: he was Herr Faust.

And Herr Faust had another thing coming if he thought his wife was going to sit idly by while danger threatened. The wolves had a saying, 'mate before pack.' It was time for her to uphold her duty:

defend her spouse from the greater threat, her clan. Above any wolf, Gerwalta knew the tactics and the weaknesses they evidenced, and by consequence, how best to defend against them. Surely, the pack wouldn't be so foolish as to turn away that kind of intelligence.

Right, then, time for war.

Gerwalta stepped down to the floor, gathered up her red cloak, and threw it over her shoulders. Let there be no confusion when her family arrived if she was among the enemy. She'd chosen her side, and it was with the wolves.

"You mustn't stand all in a group!" Gerwalta called out as she approached. "Wolfsretter raid tactics rely on the pack bunching together. You must spread out."

Lisi was the first to turn, the senior pack shewolf's eyes gaging wide.

"What is this now?" another of the women asked. "Think you can spread yourself for the king and then we'll all do the same? Go away, little red hood, or we're as liable to hurt you in the battle as the others."

Gerwalta ignored the remark and pressed on. "I have as much right to fight as you. My mate is my home, and you are his pack. I stand where my heart, not my blood, tells me."

The three other females exchanged looks before they began a slow pace in different directions. That was, until Lisi snapped at them.

"Where are you going?"

A shewolf with straw-colored hair and a blanched complexion fumbled. "The königinswolf ordered us to…"

Lisi's eyes squeezed shut. "She isn't queen-wolf, Esther. How could she be? She's not a wolf at all!"

Another of the females came to Esther's defense. "But she's Andreas's mate."

"And a wolfsretter!" Lisi rolled her eyes, clearly not understanding how her packmates could forget.

"You are right." Gerwalta turned. "I am no queen. I wouldn't assume any privilege as such. But I know Andreas loves each and every member of this pack. Please, I beg you, I know my family. For something like this, the hunting party will be small. Four warriors at most. Four on four are fair odds, but only if pitted evenly. Your lupine instinct to isolate one fight, four-on-one, isn't the best strategy."

Esther turned on Lisi. "Maybe she's right. When's the last time our pack was raided like this? None of us were alive then, I'm sure. If what Gerwalta says is true, then…"

"Now, now, is my wife's little sister spreading rumors."

The shewolf's words stopped as the rambling bass of a mighty male voice broke their ranks. The red-cloaked wolfsretter, chest plated with silver, carried a sword the height of half his body. A thick, burly black beard had grown so long, the ends of it had been braided. He held his weapon at the ready, and with a strong swing and good fortune, he was close enough for it to land among their throng.

The shewolves took their fur, an act which held both good and bad. Now Gerwalta couldn't directly communicate with them, but as wolves, they were more formidable foes.

"Coaching the mutts on defensive strategies?" he continued as he trod closer. "So it's true, then. You've forsaken your own to be another lupine bitch."

"Alexandre!" Gerwalta threw herself between the shewolves and Helga's husband. She cocked back an arm, ready to throw blows, though what her fist could do against a sword, who knew. Gerwalta reminded herself that she didn't have to hit Alexandre: she just had to throw him off balance and seize the silver. As a woman, it had stronger allegiance to her than him. "I don't want to hurt you, but I will if I need to."

Alexandre stopped where he was, grinning. "But the same isn't true for me. Besides, your mother only said we aren't to kill you. She didn't say you needed to come back with all your limbs intact."

That Helga's spouse held the same contempt for Gerwalta as did his wife came as no surprise. No doubt Alexandre had also begrudged Gerwalta's ability to fly, a revelation which displaced the first-born daughter as heir apparent. He'd be delighted to do anything that corrected things, for certes. But why would Helga trust her husband to capture her? Surely her plotting sister would want to see through the deed herself.

Unless...

Why had a sole male been sent ahead and alone? Because he was a superior warrior? Hardly. To negotiate a truce? Wolfsretters didn't negotiate with wolves. There could be only one reason: because Helga was playing someone she thought a pawn, someone she wanted cleared from the game.

Poor Alexandre.

Alexandre spoke, bringing Gerwalta back to the moment. "Come quietly now, and I'll only kill one of these bitches. A man must have a little fun."

"According to my sister, you are a man who has quite a few little things."

A look of confusion glossed over the brute's face before wide eyes signaled clarity. "I satisfy my wife."

"Is that why she sent you here to die? Because she finds you so... satisfying?"

His face screwed up. "What are you talking about?"

"My sister is many vile things, but she isn't a fool. She would know you'd be no match for me," Gerwalta said. "Helga means for me to kill you, and while I'd not aid my sister's ambitions, I will protect my pack."

"Your pack?" Alexandre threw back his head and barked a laugh. "How rich! Fine then, little red shewolf, come get me if you think you can."

Gerwalta shifted as a flash of brown fur flew past. She barely had time to register the shewolf's movement before Alexandre was on his back, his sword a few feet away. She had less time still before the shewolf went flying back through the air, pushed away by her beastly brother-in-law. Lisi yelped as she crashed to the ground, but Gerwalta didn't turn. She couldn't let the distraction go to waste. The moment Alexandre's body surrendered, she lunged for the sword. By the time he turned on her again, Gerwalta was belly-down on the ground, eye-to-eye with her brother-in-law, the blade of the sword pressed to her palm. Later she'd tend the injury of its lick into her flesh, but the moment the metal heeded her command, the blade receded, forming a three-pronged dagger in its wake.

"You're a fourth daughter and a fifth child no one wanted. You wouldn't dare strike me down. Helga will—"

She waited no more. With a role, she was on her feet. Before Alexandre could manage to move his hulking mass the same way, the blow was delivered.

A crimson stream shot from Alexandre's chest in triplicate as the silver clawed in. Even as the life fled her brother-in-law's eyes, Gerwalta felt the metal twist and curl, his last attempt to reclaim its control. Too late and too little came of the effort. Within moments, the male wolfsretter went limp, his body kissing dust and snow.

Gerwalta gave herself a moment, then turned to the wolves. "The others will be upon us soon, and they won't make the same mistake of coming alone. Prepare. I'll attempt to find out more."

No time to waste. With a kick off the ground, she was airborne. Not too far off, the hunting party came into view. Three men, all of them her clan: her father, her brother Maximillian, and another of her brothers-in-law, Helmut. Coming up the rear, the mastermind herself, Helga.

There were still guests at the schloss from the wedding that had never happened; surely amongst them were any number of finely gifted hunters the Matron could've called upon. That the three approaching were males of her own clan confirmed what Alexandre had said. She was to be brought back alive. That gave the wolves a power they didn't know they had.

Gerwalta brought herself back to ground and turned to the shewolves. "Three males, all of them of my clan. They have been ordered to capture me, but they will kill you if you get in the way. I shall not abandon you, but if one of you comes into imminent danger, you will give me up to save yourselves, is that understood? I escaped the schloss once, I can do it again."

Or at least, she hoped so.

FIVE

The farmhouse bell heralded the inevitable: wolfsretters were in the packlands, uninvited. Andreas fought past the instinct to abandon battle and run to the defense of the shewolves on the western ridge. He would need to trust in them to hold off the raid until Gerhart had gotten the better of him. Trust them, he lectured himself. Trust your Gerwalta.

His Gerwalta. Had he known when he'd risen with the moon that the night would end with her in his arms? And when the bond of their mating set in… He'd loved her before, but nothing compared to the intensity in the wake of their mating. Before, his heart smoldered. Now it blazed, a fire which fueled his every thought and gesture.

Gerhart's body slammed Andreas into the ground and back into the moment.

Lupine language in wolf form was not that of poetry. It communicated grand notions, overarching thoughts. Gerhart's growl was unmistakable in its meaning, however.

Surrender.

Andreas hadn't time to right himself before the wolf formerly of the Wehr pack was upon him, his teeth closing over the base of Andreas's throat. He reared up, his bottom half twisting to find purchase of the ground. Andreas almost righted himself when Gerhart pivoted and pulled, dragging him some distance before finally clenching his jaw.

No pain had ever been more welcome, for in it a king would be born. Andreas whined, a high-pitched sound meant to signal his surrender. Within moments, he felt it: the mystical ebb, the animalistic trophy that he'd claimed when he'd become königswolf just two years before. It fell away from him now, leaving him weakened but happy. Finally, for he didn't know how much longer he could withstand the attack. Now, as soon as Gerhart released his hold and Andreas recalled his flesh, the new king could proclaim him exiled and remove the reason for the wolfsretter to attack the pack.

As soon as he let go...

Why wasn't he letting go?

"Gerhart..."

Pain turned to panic as Wilhelm's voice eked through Andreas's thoughts. Air... He couldn't get enough air.

"Gerhart!"

The axis of the world shifted as black fur streaked through the air. Andreas gasped, spinning over unto all fours, reclaiming his flesh. His hand flew to his throat. Puncture wounds, but luckily, over his collar bone, the highest alone in soft flesh. He'd heal in a week or two, if he kept the wound clean.

If he was still alive...

Andreas shot to his feet, turning to see what had happened. His eyes found the pair just in time: Gerhart crawling out from under Wilhelm's paw. Wilhelm had interfered, but did he wait long enough? Was Gerhart now king?

Both wolves took on their lay forms, as the younger pup spun on the pack's second.

"How dare you interfere!" Gerhart bellowed. "He was mine to destroy!"

"That wasn't the arrangement," Wilhelm snapped back. "You were to defeat him fairly in battle only. You took victory. You are now königswolf, we all feel it."

"And is it your role, Wilhelm, to decide my mind?" Gerhart's arm lashed out as he pointed an accusing finger at Andreas. "He brought the wrath of the wolfsretters upon us all, just so he could bed a whore."

Rage filled the fallen king. He drove forward, his hands up and ready to strike. "Call my mate a whore again and I'll wear your entrails as my skin."

Instead of take the bait, Gerhart put up a hand. "Stop!"

And he did. Not because he wanted it. Not because he willed it. But because Gerhart had commanded it. Because Gerhart was king.

Before Andreas had too long to ponder on the consequences of that truth, Wilhelm was between them.

"As second, it is my duty to bow to the king's demand, but it is my duty to call him out when one of his decisions is in his own interest instead of the pack's." Accusing eyes shifted to Andreas before they turned back. "The wolfsretters are coming and they'll want Andreas dead. But if you deny them their own justice, they'll take the punishment out on all of us. Exile him now, Gerhart, and let him carry their rage away in his wake."

Conflict warred across Gerhart's features. The king threaded his hair, tugging at the roots. Finally, after some hemming and hawing, he turned on Andreas. "You must never return."

Andreas nodded. "Now do it, Gerhart. I'll thank you for it."

"You'll thank me?" Gerhart laughed. "I'm not saving your life today, Andreas. I merely forestall your death. Without a pack, you'll slowly go insane. The wolfsretter will have your blood then, there is nothing to stop that."

It was a truth Andreas couldn't argue, but he had to have faith that he and Gerwalta would find a pack willing to take them in. First, however, this one must be saved.

"Wilhelm," Gerhart said, turning to the second. "Go immediately to the front line; meet the wolfsretters and tell them I am king and that Andreas Baron is no longer a member of this pack."

Wilhelm snapped straight as a board. "Yes, mein könig." Which upon, he made to leave.

"Oh, before you go, Wilhelm?"

The second turned.

A sinister smile waxed over the king's face. "If they refuse to accept this as grounds to withdraw, give the order to the shewolves and a howl to arms: kill on all on sight, starting with Andreas's unholy mate."

"What? No, you cannot—"

Andreas doubled over as Gerhart's fist connected with his gut. "You have your wish, Andreas. You are hereby exiled."

All the air rushed from Andreas's lungs as the magic was

made so, and he was left alone, wild to the world.

SIX

It wasn't two flicks of a lamb's tail before the other wolves took their fur and followed in Wilhelm's wake. Gerhart waited to be last, allowing himself one more menacing glare at the fallen king before his flesh rippled and his maw grew long.

Alone, it came down upon Andreas: the emptiness, the utter sense that he was alone in the world. Packless. Exiled. It was what he'd asked for, but he couldn't have anticipated how it overwhelmed. Discouragement melted into his marrow, a sense that he'd taken the first step toward his own doom. And very well, he might have. But then, the lupine turned on himself, lecturing.

"Gerwalta still needs you," he said, leaving unspoken *even if the pack does not.*

The pack. He could do nothing for them now but leave and hope the Matron quickly squashed Gerhart's rebellion without casualty.

The blood on his chest had already begun to dry, the puncture wounds won in battle ebbing in their intensity. Taking his fur again risked exasperating their severity, however, as the shift from man to beast would reshape his body. He had to get to Gerwalta and he had to do it on two feet. Resolve infused his spine. Andreas turned, prayed, and ran.

Fur and red cloaks marked the sparring warriors from each side just beyond the farmhouse. Andreas narrowed his eyes, trying to discern which side held advantage and learn where his beloved stood. Desperate eyes raked the ground, searching. Dizziness crushed him as he tried to advance, sending Andreas to his knees just as he heard someone call out his name. He turned his eyes to the sky just as Gerwalta lowered into view.

A frown flitted across her face as she laid hands on him, feeling out his wounds. "You're injured."

He nodded with some difficulty as he captured her hands

with his own. "Gerhart defeated me fairly, though he also tried to kill me. It will heal."

Given that Gerwalta's expression didn't shift, Andreas guessed this came as no surprise to her. "He lunged for me the moment he was in sight, but Helga and the men of my clan arrived just in time to draw him off. Helga and he are squaring off now, I suppose. I hope with words and not violence."

"He's a fool if he challenges your sister."

"He's a brave and bold king," Gerwalta said. "Helga wasn't given leave to kill anyone else in the pack or she'd have done it without coming into view. She saw me leave; as soon as her line pushed through the pack, they will follow the direction I flew. Are you safe to move? We must make haste."

"I cannot take my fur without reopening my wounds. I'll have to go on two feet, but I think if I... Gerwalta!"

She hadn't waited for him to finish his thoughts. Instead, Gerwalta hooked the lupine under the arms and lifted off. Soon, his feet skimmed the tops of the trees as she whisked them over the valley. For the first time, Andreas truly grasped why a wolfsretter who could fly was such a threat. He was terrified out of his good senses. Surely, she recalled that lupines feared heights?

"Forest... High... Air... Fall..."

"I would never drop you, love, but I cannot go far like this," was her reply to his ramblings. "Do you have a cache of clothing somewhere?"

Gerwalta changed course just as the sun kissed the horizon. The crimson fingers of dawn reached out and stung his eyes. He pointed toward the waterfall that rose above the village, too terrified to speak.

She bobbed her head. "Good, because it is morning and laymen tend to notice flying women carrying naked men about."

They took the laymen's roads. If Helga's hunting party managed to catch up, apprehending them would be more difficult with witnesses.

"We have to figure out where to go."

Andreas's words broke her from her thoughts. Gerwalta kept her pace strong as she could without looking like she was running away. "I already know where we're going: Navarre. Karahan is going to pay me back what he owes me by giving us sanctuary."

She jerked back as Andreas took her hand and pulled. "I've a little more than two months," he said. "Two months to find a pack that won't only accept me but will also accept a wolfsretter as a mate. We cannot spend it hiding out with vampires."

"You'll only be able to go mad if we are still alive. Until we get out of any area my mother holds influence if not control over, no pack will be safe. Navarre isn't ideal, but it's ruled by the Casa de Amarillo and they detest the House of Red. A pack under their guard is far more likely to be accepting of..."

"The packs of Iberia are itinerant, religious zealots!" Andreas said, cutting her off. "Insofar as either of us heed the church, we are both Protestant. They may not kill us for our mating, but they'll never offer us a place in their realm."

She ground her teeth until it sent pain shooting into her temple. "Where else would we even have a hope? Unless you want to try for the Americas, in which case we'll need to figure out how to conceal your lupine condition during the... What is it, two months it takes to get there? You are no longer a königswolf, Andreas. You won't be able to keep your laity form during the full moon."

Anger infused his tone with gruff. "Do you not think that I'm aware that I'm no longer king? I've sacrificed my pack and my position for us, Gerwalta. I know that in your customs women rule, but can you add that to my balance and for once, just let me decide our course?"

Her face grew taut with rage. "This isn't about me being a woman, this is about strategic thinking! We can flee to neither wolf nor wolfsretter—not immediately, anyhow. We need an impartial and powerful ally before we approach anyone. And sacrifice? Do you think I've made no sacrifice?" Her arm lashed back in the direction of the village. "I just killed one of my own clan to save members of your pack. Now, my sentence is the same as yours: death. Merciless, unconditional death."

Her admission managed to still his tongue. Andreas took a

step back. "I'm sorry, I didn't know."

His apology also softened her resolve. Gerwalta crossed her arms over her stomach. "It was a thing required."

"Even, still..." Andreas drew a deep inhale and pushed the air out through pursed lips, even as the gesture tickled the pain. "Gerwalta, love, I understand what you are saying, but I think it best to try for England. If we can find Stephen's pack, they would take us in to settle the life debt if nothing else."

"But England is no small country, Andreas. Do you have any idea where precisely he might be?"

Andreas's chin dropped into his chest. "I've had no word from my brother since parting ways in Nuremberg. But please, Walta," he looked up, the biggest set of puppy eyes she had ever seen set in his face, "consider my reasons, and that there is truth in what I say."

She turned then, refusing to be manipulated by emotions— his or hers. In the wider scope of consequences, she couldn't deny that Andreas's plan held advantages. Stephen and his pack formed of stolen seconds from across the Holy Roman Empire wouldn't be alive if not for their mercy. How could they be turned away? But Gerwalta also knew that the Isles were the Verdant Realm, overseen by the House of Green. The Reds were infamous for their strict character, but the Greens were renowned for their incorporation into the politics of the laymen around them. They could travel no easier through cities there than they could through the forests, and that would be if they knew where to go when they landed in some English port.

"Perhaps," she admitted finally. "But at least with Navarre, we know our destination. What if we were to go there first and ask Karahan to use his contacts to find Stephen's pack for us? Vampires can travel thrice as fast if properly motivated."

"And what would we motivate them with? We haven't any coin of any realm."

"If I can get my hands on more silver, I can create any realm's coin. Grand churches often have plenty."

The rigidity of his features softened, though Andreas refused to yield. She drew a deep breath as she realized she must take her own advice. She was mated to a wolf, and among their kind, it was the male who made decisions. She would need to submit to Andreas on some things on occasion.

Even if he were wrong.

"I've made my best argument and yield to your counsel. What say you?"

Hands on his hips, Andreas chewed on his thoughts. "To Navarre. For a start." He grimaced. "Well, that wasn't so bad."

Confusion drew her eyebrows down. "What wasn't?"

"Our first mated row." The lupine closed the distance between them, his hands settling on her hips and his lips, to hers. The kiss was gentle, tentative. "And our first reconciliation. I've heard rumors that such events are made more grounded by an act of the flesh…"

Heat swept through her body. "Perhaps when we've put more ground behind us."

He nodded as he again brushed a kiss. "Let us go then, and put, as you say, 'some ground behind us,' so that later, I can put some ground beneath us instead."

Her knees threatened to revolt, but Gerwalta lectured her body into submission. She nearly changed her mind when, turning to continue up the road, his palm flattened against her backside.

She had thought their lovemaking may be unbalanced, both as the dominant sex of their kind and thus, out of harmony. Reality was proving a keen teacher, however. They would both demand dominance in the marital bed, and by such measure, both come out on top.

In all the glorious ways possible.

SEVEN

A crimson staff of twilight sunset fell across her closed eyes, bringing Gerwalta Faust back to the world of the living. A heavy weight across her hips and a warm body behind her brought a smile. Waking up beside one's beloved truly was a delight. More delightful still when one's beloved proved an amorous beast once... aroused.

Though it was not without consequence. Her hips were sore. Her lips, swollen. The grass stains present on both palms and knees would probably endure for some time. Yes, they'd both lost a good deal to be together, but certain things they'd gained counterbalanced their sacrifices.

Truth be told, it may actually be a gain.

Andreas would continue to slumber under the last rays of light unless she woke him. As tempting as it may be, she knew he needed rest. His recovery from the injury he'd sustained amazed her; she didn't think a wolf unmoored from a pack could achieve such progress in a week. The flesh wounds had vanished, leaving only marred skin and bruises. Whatever miracle had caused it, she'd not demand payment for blessings. Andreas, on the other hand, reveled in it. Each day, he seemed to grow less somber and more... well, drunk on her love. It was almost like he had a secret he was concealing, some wonderful surprise he'd spring on her to blow her away.

But what could that possibly be? They'd both escaped the Schwarzwald with their lives and not much more. If he'd managed to find out some gift for her, he had grifted in from laymen in one of the villages they passed. They both agreed they needed the silver to trade, but that they wouldn't take more than necessary. She didn't therefore think it likely he'd stolen just to flatter her.

Gerwalta rose, pulling on the laity clothes they'd stolen from a drying line a few days back, and worked the silver she'd siphoned from a church in Friedberg back over her arm. Its gentle embrace renewed her. Of course, sleeping in Andreas's arms did have some cost: her silver must be shoved off lest it burn him in intimate moments. Now with it back on her person, she strode off into the forest, hoping to find some woodland creature to make their evening meal.

Not a quarter of an hour into her quest, scattered amongst mighty pines, deer grazed. A young buck died with haste and mercy. Of course, they couldn't consume the whole thing between the two of them, but Gerwalta refused to take one of the smaller does. It was early spring now, the time of nature's renewal. Likely many of the females were with child, and hungry though she was, what kind of hunter would strike down pregnant prey?

Gerwalta let her legs collapse beneath her as she withdrew the silver-made-spear from the spent creature's chest and made of it a blade to clean what they needed from it, when a familiar voice floated down from above.

"You don't eat it raw, do you?"

The deer was forgotten as she turned the blade skyward. Gunda Faust descended with utter care, meticulously lowering herself until her feet impressed upon the dewy, newly sprung grass, and continued.

"I ask," her mother said, "because I wonder how many of our traditions you've forsaken already. Tell me, do you cook the meat, or have you taken to pulling it bloody from the bone as does your lupine mate?"

Gerwalta weighed her options. She could run, but even she didn't think herself capable of besting her mother's speed. Even flying she would be at the mercy of pulling Andreas's weight. She might be able to land her blade in her mother's chest, but the chances that Gunda wasn't wearing her own silver plated beneath her tunic were slim. Her only solution, therefore, was to play out the scene and hope a solution or advantage emerged.

"We need not give up ourselves to become each other's," she said, keeping the blade between them nonetheless. "I cook it; he eats it raw, but I doubt you've tracked us so far and so long to ask culinary questions. What is it you want from us, Mother?"

"Your obeisance." Gunda's grin flattened. "Andreas Barron will return with me to Triberg. Whether that is in chains or in pieces depends on you."

"Andreas has no cause to return to Triberg. He is no longer king. He was fairly defeated in battle and exiled; no one in the Schwarzwald has any claim to him."

One of Gunda's eyebrows quirked. "And you do?"

"I am his mate. I am the only one whose claim matters."

Gunda blew out an exhale through pursed lips, her eyes turned to the ground. "Why are you intent on making this so difficult? This wolf has lain with you and his heart can never be turned, but that doesn't mean you need share his fate."

"You never were particularly keen on the non-political and emotional aspects of marriage, were you? No, you weren't. Then how could you possibly understand that my heart is just as bound as his?"

"This is youth and romanticism talking, both of which fade with time." When again Gunda raised her eyes, it was with such tenderness in her gaze that it forced Gerwalta to take a step back. "Only honor survives the grave. Only family and power preserve you from it. Please, daughter, I would have you live, even if in exile. I wouldn't wear my own blood on my hands."

The tiny part of her that had always preened itself for her mother's acceptance and approval nearly took control, but Gerwalta shoved it down. "You would have me return when we both know I slew Alexandre? Even if you managed to somehow twist the truth and pin the death on the wolves, which, knowing your tactics, you've no doubt already conceived, do you think your first-born daughter will let your fourth-born live?"

"I don't even know if she'll let me live."

Another mental blow which challenged Gerwalta's balance. "What do you mean?"

"You brought an asp into our home. Mehmet is twice the snake Helga is, and they brood in their shared mayhem," the Matron explained. "I beg you, forfeit Andreas's life and let me save you, because someday soon, you may need to save me."

Gerwalta's hand flew over her face, as though a foul smell had crept into the air. "Chasing me down, then... It's not about recovering me. It's not even about punishing Andreas. Both are just mechanisms to save yourself."

"If I'm not successful in returning you both to court, mark my words, Helga will come, and what mercy I am willing to show will render me a saint in comparison."

"I don't need saints, and I don't need you." The younger wolfsretter turned to leave, now confident that a dagger wouldn't land in her back when she did. "Follow us no more."

Gerwalta had only managed two steps when it happened.

Silver rope encircled her ankles. She fell, flipped, tried to command the metal to yield, but it would not. It stayed, immovable. In moments, another lash of silver twisted itself around her wrists, trussing her like an animal to be taken to market.

Or a wolfsretter to be taken as prisoner.

"There's no use struggling." Gerwalta looked up from the ground upon which she lay to see her mother, the end of the cording wrapped around her hand, stalking toward her. "This is blood-claimed silver. It heeds only my command."

But the silver Gerwalta wore under her clothing had no such limitations. No sooner had she bid it, however, then she felt it siphon off her, running down the cord that bound her to her mother.

"Did you really think you could rebuff me with your own supply? I am a matron; you are an insolent child. Your will can never best mine."

"And yet, I had the will to follow my heart instead of your command, didn't I?" Gerwalta flexed, writhed, pulled, all in a futile effort to free herself. "Let me go before..."

But it was too late. A swish of leaves, a snap of twig, and a mat of fur flew from the foliage.

Gunda let go her hold, but it was only to form a blade intended for the werewolf flying straight for her.

EIGHT

He reached out for her the moment he knew himself awake but found her not.

One eyelid cracked open to confirm that what his hand had found was true; Gerwalta wasn't where she had been when they'd fallen asleep at dawn. Mayhap she'd ventured off to hunt? It was a wolf's duty to provide but such was a wolfsretter. Not that he begrudged the game she'd managed to capture. Gerwalta was a gifted huntress, and Andreas, a lupine of tremendous appetite.

He stretched out long, his limbs going up then akimbo, before the former king turned on his side and folded back in on himself. The breeze blew across his face, bringing him insight into a shift in the weather. So far, they'd been fortunate to encounter agreeable conditions. It had rained one day, but only lightly. Now the air smelled of heat and moisture and a tingle of unresolved winds. There would be lightning soon, and he'd need to get Gerwalta somewhere safe until it passed.

"Gerwalta?" Andreas called out, his eyes closing against the wane of slumber. "Love, there's a tempest brewing. Are you near? We'll need to leave soon."

His ears sorted through the sounds of the forest, of the stir of deer catching the last bit of grass before bedding down. Of the owl flapping its wings in a nearby tree, it too shaking off the last vestiges of sleep. Of the mouse already scurrying. Of the...

Andreas shot to his feet and pulled in a series of rapid, short breaths, turning in a slow arc. Three-quarters through his rotation, understanding came to him. The lupine didn't dwell to consider strategy or consequence. His mate was in peril, and if his senses could be believed, it was because their escape hadn't been as successful as they hoped.

He jumped, took his fur, and landed on padded paws, eating up the forest floor. Andreas's heart raced. His fear upset the balance of man and beast within. If Gerwalta was unharmed, he would fight to free her. If she was injured or worse, then the cloak of the Matron wouldn't be the only red to spill across the forest today.

It seemed to take forever for him to reach the clearing. Gerwalta lay on the ground, both her wrists and her ankles bound. As the profile of the scents processed, the aroma of blood was undeniable. She moved, so she still lived. Thank God, then he need only free her. The silver cords which ran from his beloved to her maniacal mother's grasp would burn like hell when he hit them, but if he was lucky, he'd knock them hard enough to loosen the Matron's grip.

He didn't see the blade until he was already sailing through the air.

"Andreas, no!"

His beloved's words cleaved his soul. No, he couldn't leave her. He couldn't let her go on alone. They'd suffered too much, given up too much to be together, for it all to end so soon. All this occurred to him in the flash of a moment, but what could he do? A second or two more, and he'd fall upon the Matron's blade. Gunda Faust was a seasoned warrior, an expert huntress. She knew precisely where to hold her weapon so that it would strike deep into his heart when he landed upon it. And in that moment of accepting his fate, of recognizing he was powerless to change it, Andreas understood how to survive.

The Matron meant to strike down a wolf.

But if a man fell upon the blade instead, her position was all wrong.

Andreas forced his body through the quickest transformation he'd ever experienced and paid the cost. His nerves sizzled, his head pounded, his muscles contorted and spasmed. The lupine didn't know where the pain he'd pushed himself through ended and where that caused by the Matron's weapon began, but he did know this... He wasn't dead.

Given the torment he now experienced, perhaps this was the worse fate.

"Mother, no!"

His arrival must have created a circumstance that allowed Gerwalta to break free from her bonds. Soon, her body covered his, bringing Andreas back to his purpose. He did this to save her, to protect her, to protect his family.

Only when his mate wrapped her hands around the hilt of the dagger buried in his shoulder and yanked it from its corporeal bedding did he understand where he'd been struck. A shoulder... Good. That would heal. But given that the injury was silver-born, it would take some time.

If they survived this, their journey just became all that more difficult.

"Move and I'll finish the beast off, put him out of his mercy."

It was the Matron who spoke, but her words had the opposite effect. Gerwalta laid herself over his writhing body, bringing to Andreas's mind a fresh litany of fears. He had to quell the pain, bring himself under control. If his flailing did her damage, he'd never forgive himself.

"Kill us both or let us be," Gerwalta declared, "but I'll not yield."

"Mercy!" His own words sounded like those of another, his voice hollowed by pain, even as his shaking began to subside. "Matron, mercy for her."

"I am attempting to be merciful!" Gunda snapped. "A month spent in the dungeon, a flogging before the court, but she'll live."

Hot tears streamed from the corner of his eyes as Andreas shook his head. "No, not just for Gerwalta," he said. "For... For our child."

A chill settled over Andreas's body as Gerwalta shot to her feet. "What?"

Andreas looked up, seeing the faint embers of twilight's fade dance across her face. "You are with child. Three or four days now, but still."

Gerwalta's hand slid down over her midsection. "I'm... Oh, Andreas!"

But as his mate fell to her knees and threw her arms around his body, difficult given his inclined position, the Matron reminded them that her task was left undone, and she demanded satisfaction.

"Impossible!" she hissed out through clenched teeth. "You only consummated a week ago. There is no way for it to … How could you possibly know?"

With Gerwalta's aid, Andreas pushed himself up, using the side uninjured in the attack. In moments, she had conjured her cloak and pulled it off, using it as a compress for the wound. "I am a lupine; I noticed the change in her scent."

Gunda remained incredulous. "Something which you've concealed from her only to conveniently blurt out when I've arrived to remedy your crimes?"

"I've been waiting to tell her. I didn't think that Gerwalta should carry the burden of knowing until she was safe."

Gunda's silver siphoned back under her sleeves as she bit her bottom lip. "A child… It cannot be. What fate would it have? Half lupine, half wolfsretter? Our laws forbid this. Neither fold would claim it."

"It wouldn't matter if she were to be half suckling pig, Mother, we will claim it," Gerwalta said. "Hate me if you must, wish me ill, but our child has committed no wrong. Will you condemn it too? Will you condemn me along with her?"

Gerwalta had never known her mother to be the kind who shuddered, but that didn't change truth. Gunda Faust veritably vibrated, the fingers of her weapon hand flexing, opening, flexing, opening. Vexed, she paced the forest floor.

"Mother?" Gerwalta took a hesitant step forward. "Mother, please. Do not destroy your grandchild and kill an innocent child merely for the fact that its parents erred in your eyes."

Gunda's gaze flew up, even as her chin remained tucked into her chest. "A lupine is never innocent."

"But a wolfsretter is." Gerwalta motioned behind her back, asking for leniency in her remarks from her husband. "Our child is as much of your bloodline as it is Andreas's. Would you destroy a wolfsretter thus?"

The salve of tenderness applied, Gerwalta waited, unmoving, frozen in her pose, for the sentiments to sink into her mother's skin. After a few moments, it came: the change, the resolution, the shift.

"I would not." Gunda lifted her head. "But your sister would."

Gerwalta nodded solemnly. "Is she with you on this hunt?"

"If she were, you'd already be dead."

A stark truth, but the truth nonetheless. Gerwalta licked her lips. "Tell her I died, mother. Tell her you killed us both and burned the bones, your rage so hot it wouldn't allow patience enough to return us."

"She'll never believe that I let go a chance to humiliate you both. I need... I need proof."

Andreas asked, "What would it take to convince her?"

"Nothing short of a body." The Matron's eyes focused on the wolf's leg. "Or perhaps she'd concede with only part of one."

In a flash, Gerwalta covered Andreas. "No. No, absolutely not. He couldn't possibly—"

"I'll do it."

Gerwalta shot a dagger's stare at her mate. "You will not."

"I will too, Walta." Andreas hobbled in the Matron's direction, past his wife too stunned by the act to attempt to pull him back. Raising both hands, the left still shaking, he looked at them in turn before dropping his right side. "This paw does less for me."

Gerwalta attempted to part them. "Mother, don't you dare. This is too high a price. Too high!"

"If it buys us our freedom and our pup's life..." The lupine stepped in closer, around his mate. "Take it, Matron. Fair payment: my paw for her heart." He nodded in Gerwalta's direction. "Though the favor of balance would still lay with me."

The Matron eyeballed the offering, her lips tight as she peered at something it seemed she didn't quite believe. Gunda summoned silver, shaping in her hands a blade in the shape of the crescent moon and as long as her forearm. She passed one more look up to her daughter. "You concur?"

Gerwalta's wet eyes belied her resolute exterior. "I do."

Gunda took Andreas's hand in hers as she pivoted, giving her the proper angle from which to strike. "The blade would cut cleaner through a narrower juncture. Perhaps if you took your wolf, Andreas. Yes, that would do better. Take your fur, and I'll take your paw, and in doing so, give you both your freedom."

The birds of the forest, only just settled in for the night, fled their nocturnal harbor and took to the sky.

NINE

Karahan jumped from the table the moment Gerwalta's form slipped into view. "Lady Baron, you are positively glowing this evening."

Andreas took a step back, allowing their host to dote upon his wife. At first, the werewolf had questioned the vampire's fervent attentions, but had simply come to recognize in the five miraculous months in which they'd been guests of Lord of the Dracule that Karahan was, at heart, a family man. That held even if he'd recently employed Gerwalta's services to trap most of his.

"But now, you are flushed," the vampire continued as he guided Gerwalta toward the table. "Are you feeling well?"

The blush that blew across Gerwalta's cheeks when she met his eyes matched Andreas's own. "Oh, quite well."

Karahan followed her gaze, and upon seeing the smirk on Andreas's face, cleared his throat as he lowered her into her chair, Gerwalta supporting the swell of her stomach with her own hand.

"Master Baron, any further pain?"

Andreas held up the absence of his hand in response to Karahan's question. Where once there had been a paw, now only a scarred stump remained. In the end, it had bought them their freedom, and what more can he ask than that? Still, how would he love to have had run his fingers through Gerwalta's long, auburn hair one more time.

"Every day, it aches less," the lupine said. "Thank you for your concern."

He nodded, turning back to his cup of tea. Another thing he'd learned of vampires. Yes, they required blood to maintain life, but they were also great fans of drinking any liquid in general and did so at grant lengths recreationally. This he observed again as they sat for their evening meal; a dish of stewed rabbit which Andreas gulped down joyously, even if he did think the game was somewhat overcooked. And by overcooked, he meant cooked. Better for Gerwalta, he supposed, and beggars couldn't be choosers, could they? After some conversing and recounting the news among the laity of the day—apparently there had been some upset in the French court regarding their finance minister—Gerwalta and Andreas exchanged a look, nodding to each other that the moment had come.

"Lord Dracule," Gerwalta began.

"Please, Lady Baron, do call me Igor."

She grinned despite the interruption. "Very well, Igor. Andreas and I wanted again to offer our greatest thanks for your generosity since we arrived. If not for your kindness, we aren't certain where we could've gone."

Igor raised his glass in salute. "A debt was owed, one I've repaid with joy. Your company has been very welcomed in this land with sparse amusements."

"Be that as it may, your hospitality has far exceeded repayment. You've treated us as honored guests, catered not only to our needs, but many of our wants as well. It is something for which we'll be eternally grateful."

The smile faded from Igor's face. "I sense a pivot forthcoming."

Here, a hesitant Andreas took up. "Shortly after we arrived, I hired an emissary to seek my brother in England, to inquire if he would have us. Early this morning, word arrived that that emissary not only located Stephen in the north of that country, but that my mate and I would be welcome to join their pack."

"Join their pack?" Igor repeated the words as though their echo would bring clarity. "I'm sorry, I'm afraid I don't understand, where has my hospitality failed that you feel driven away?"

Gerwalta turned to Igor, crestfallen. "Our decision is in retaliation to nothing. We think merely of the welfare of the babe. A wolf needs a pack."

"And yet... here Andreas is, without one." Igor brought up an uncertain gaze to Andreas. "Please understand that what I'm about to say is only born out of my concern for you both. For you all. Given Gerwalta's condition and your incapacitation, you cannot think it wise to travel such a great distance."

Gerwalta wrapped her hand around her mate's, squeezing it as though she might squeeze the words from his tongue. "The fact that I am so far along is precisely the reason we feel it wise to go soon. Andreas has avoided the lunacity that customarily claims exiled wolves by virtue of our child. The magic that binds a pack has bonded him and our babe to save them both, but who knows if it'll endure after the birth, or if the same will be true of our child."

"And from a practical position," Andreas added, "even among dark ones, not all births are successful. If, Lord forbid, there should be a complication with the delivery…"

His words tapered off, but Gerwalta was a wolfsretter, a creature born of rougher materials than those from which sentiment were fashioned. "If the baby doesn't survive, we don't know how long the effects of lunacity can be avoided," she added. "And if I do not survive, at least I'll go to my grave knowing that Andreas and Brünhild have a pack and family to keep them safe."

"I told you, love, I don't care for that name," Andreas cooed. "Besides, we do not know if it is a girl."

"It is a girl," Gerwalta persisted.

"If that is your wish, then." Igor stood and buttoned his jacket. "I'll have the servants ready what supplies they can and arrange for trusted men with proper knowledge to escort you to England and see that you are settled there properly."

Andreas rose to his feet in kind. "That is very kind, but we must make our way alone."

The vampire guffawed. "I don't understand why you would refuse so generous an offer, and from such a prestigious member of the dark one community. Many would be honored."

Andreas bowed, his disfigured arm resting against his abdomen. "Indeed, we are honored, but both Gerwalta and I are aware that our safety depends upon our ability to be covert. A werewolf and a wolfsretter, the latter visibly expecting, traveling in comfort with the aid of a prominent vampire's retinue would attract attention. The more hands that reach out to assist us lead to more tongues that might disclose our existence."

Igor took the explanation in full before nodding. "Then I will accompany you personally."

Gerwalta clicked her tongue. "You don't mean to leave your own daughter behind in Navarre alone, do you? Igor, you yourself said that Inga's penance is being served only by virtue of your regular visits at the monastery at which you've left her."

The vampire planted balled fists on his hips and sighed into his chest. "Then at least accept my best wishes and prayers for your safe journey?"

Gerwalta grinned. "I would never refuse that. Please know that I'll always look back at the months we were here as some of the happiest in my life. Your debt, sir, is paid in full."

"No, Frau Baron, I fear it is not."

TEN

Someone touched her, and it wasn't someone she knew.

The moment Gerwalta's eyes flew open, she jolted up, ready to dismember whoever had the audacity to push his fingertips into her person. The woman was of small carriage, with olive skin and a gaunt face that went white at the sight of her. Gerwalta's senses reached out for silver but were left wanting. None was near. Only as rationality rose up within her did she recall that no silver was kept in the chamber she shared with her lupine husband.

The husband who, in fact, had just placed himself between her and the stranger dressed in red.

Was it her clan? Had they come for them? Her eyes went wide, her heart raced.

"Gerwalta, it's only the midwife. Be calm."

Her spirits ebbed as she gained perspective. Yes, there was a stranger, but the woman was of the laity. Both Igor and Andreas stood near; if this newcomer meant her harm, either would have her throat out in moments. Midwife? Had they lost their...

"The baby?" Gerwalta pushed herself up in the bed, her back against the wooden headboard as she ran hands over her abdomen.

Andreas prostrated himself at her side, reaching up to pet her hair with his remaining hand. "The babe is well. But you swooned, and we wanted to be certain you were too."

Swooned? What kind of wolfsretter swooned? But then again, as she searched her memory, she couldn't recall what had led to this moment. She'd been walking back in from the gardens when she scented something burning upon the air. That drew her to one of the hearths in the castle; if the laity staff were in danger from some breakout of fire, she wished to help. Then suddenly, smoke, as thick as it was black, blinded her.

She must have been overcome.

"And Igor?"

Gerwalta passed a look to the man she normally welcomed in her presence. But the moment seemed much too intimate for the oversight of a vampire.

Andreas shrugged. "He insisted no one he was unfamiliar with personally was to be anywhere near you." The werewolf leaned in. "And you think I'm overprotective."

"You would be as overly protective if you had my centuries of experience in court politics," the vampire mumbled. "And it is rude to speak of someone present in third person."

"It was not our intention to snub, Igor."

Igor was unimpressed by good humor. Any further discussion on the matter, however, was interrupted when the midwife said something in that peculiar mix of tongues the locals spoke. The vampire was kind enough to translate.

"As best she can tell, both mother and child are fine," the vampire reported. "But she wishes to hear the same from Gerwalta's own lips."

If the baby was well, she'd soldier through anything. But there was something upsetting her. Something that needed addressing. "I am... I am monstrously hungry."

Andreas and Igor cracked smiles, as did the midwife when Igor made the words plain to her. The small woman bowed and left.

"She's going to stop by the kitchens on the way down," Igor said. "They'll send something up directly."

Andreas sat at the edge of the bed, taking her hands to his lips. "Walta, love, what happened?"

She tried her memory. "I'm not certain. I smelled smoke, I followed..."

"Smoke?" Andreas turned to Igor. "Has there been any fire reported by your staff?"

"None, and surely a wolf could detect it on the air better than could I."

"How bizarre..." Gerwalta searched her thoughts for some

better clue until her groaning stomach stole back her attention. "Andreas, I really am quite famished. Are there no victuals at the ready?"

He laughed. "Soon, love. Marta only now just... Walta? Walta, where are you going?"

At least he was wise enough not to attempt to coax her back into bed. Andreas had learned early in their pairing the pointlessness of arguing Gerwalta out of her decisions. So, when she swept past him and out into the hall, the only thing the lupine could do was follow, as did the vampire, though out of concern or merely for the entertainment, she knew not.

It wasn't as much her thought as her nose that led her out of their suite, down the stairs, through the small hall where oft they dined, and into the part of the castle used by the servants. The scent of laundering intensified, as did a handful of others that didn't interest her. On, on and on Gerwalta went, seeking out the aroma that tickled her senses and made her mouth water.

The moment she entered the kitchens, she saw it. Manna. Lorded over by one, single servant. The bald layman looked up when she came to a standstill before the carcass he'd been butchering. He spoke no German—no one except Igor and Andreas did—but he had originated from a region north of Navarre and Gerwalta had discovered a fortnight before he spoke French.

"Madame?" He asked, dropping his cleaning knife on the table and giving her his full attention.

Gerwalta swallowed back the saliva building in her mouth. "What animal is this, Antoine?"

He glanced over the skinless, headless, footless thing between them. "Ox, madame. Freshly slaughtered not an hour ago. Cook was thinking to use it to—"

She heard no more as the sound of her own pulse sped. Gerwalta attacked face-first. The moment her teeth hit bone and blood filled her mouth, she felt it: relief. This, yes, this was all she had wanted. With another bit, she filled her mouth and found her heaven.

"Walta, love?" Andreas's hands settled on her shoulder. "Are you—"

She couldn't explain from where the feral growl that left her mouth had come, nor could she have made such a noise on command. The only thing she knew was that another wolf was near, and she had no intention of sharing.

Her mouth went slack in the echo of her own thoughts. Another wolf?

Gerwalta's hand flew to her mouth as she fell back. "Good lord, what am I doing?"

Igor, his step tenuous to avoid the early morning sun coming in through a nearby doorway, expressed the same query.

Andreas, however, was not as stumped. "You're craving fresh kill. It's very common among expecting shewolves."

"But I'm not a shewolf." Gerwalta stated the obvious. "I'm not a... Oh, Andreas, what is happening to me?"

Igor balanced his chin on his balled-up fist. "Remarkable. I'd always had the theory, but to see it in practice... Simply exceptional."

The wolfsretter pulled out of her husband's hold. "What, Igor? Do you know what's happening to me?"

"Well, to make it plain, you are carrying a wolf. Or at least, something that's wolf enough to make lupine demands of your palate. Antoine," Igor directed his words to the butcher, "I wonder if we might beg for a smaller knife Frau Baron could use? She may have a wolf's appetite, but she lacks one's teeth."

"I'm fine." Her next words muffled as her lips wrapped around the creature's hindquarter. Only when she nearly injured herself ripping off a morsel did she acquiesce and reach for the little angled blade the butcher had procured for her. No sooner had she touched it than she felt it... the sear of pain, the jolt of lightning made solid.

Gerwalta called out and dropped the blade, even as Igor with his vampiric speed caught it before it hit the ground.

"It... burns!" she gasped, dropping it in an instant.

Andreas was on Antoine in a moment. "How dare you?"

Only, the poor man, speaking not a lick of German, understood only two things. The pregnant woman's husband was angry, and he was also a werewolf who'd just sprouted very lupine fangs in a very red face.

"Unhand my servant, Andreas." The vampire remained completely calm. "Antoine did nothing but hand your wife a blade."

Andreas took a step back, though his heaving chest demonstrated his continued disquiet. "You saw how Gerwalta reacted. He must have done something to—"

White as a sheet, Gerwalta interrupted. "Antoine did nothing. The blade is silver, and silver burns wolves. Silver burned me. Am I—?" Her trembling arms crossed over her stomach as she turned and fled, the knife falling to the floor. She didn't wait to see if Andreas pursued her but hoped not. Should he ask her what was wrong, she knew her words would dig a dagger into his heart as much as if she had stabbed him herself.

ELEVEN

When the wind shifted, Gerwalta scented the vampire on the wind.

"I hope you don't take offense, Igor, when I tell you that I wish to be alone."

The vampire leaned against the wall beside her, just out of reach of the sunlight coming in through the open window. "I hope you don't take offense that I intend to ignore your request."

Planting her hands, she pushed herself back a bit, landing her in a less precarious position. "I assure you, I am well. Or will be, if given a little space."

"Are you certain? You are, after all, sitting on a window ledge four stories off the ground."

"You forget, I can fly."

"To fly is a choice. You could equally choose to fall. In fact, I don't doubt the thought has crossed your mind. Oh, not the intention, though few in your situation would blame you. But I don't think you are the kind who gives up so easily."

Guilt pulled up the hairs on the back of her neck as she surveyed the patch of ground beneath her with its dry earth and stones.

"You can speak at ease with me, Gerwalta," Igor continued. "Tell me, what are your thoughts?"

"My thoughts?" She managed her feet, despite the awkward gyrating required by her belly. "I crave raw meat and silver is poison to me. What do you think my thoughts should be?"

"That you don't understand what you are anymore, let alone who."

His accuracy hit her hard, making her blink in surprise.

Igor grinned as he offered her a hand and helped her to navigate her way off the ledge and back into the building. "Don't forget, unlike lupines and wolfsretters, vampires aren't born dark ones; we are dragged into this world by makers, sometimes against our will. The first time I thirsted for a good man's blood, I was just as confused and perplexed as you're likely feeling now."

"And what did you do about it?"

"I found a monk in a dark corner of an abbey and drank my fill."

She didn't know if Igor had meant the statement as a jest, though the light tone suggested it, but she couldn't bring herself to find its humor.

"That is different," Gerwalta persisted. "What you were driven to do was necessary to continue living. But this... I can tolerate and perhaps even understand craving unusual food. When Zelda was expecting the first time, she briefly had a taste for pine sap. But I am a wolfsretter; silver has answered my call since I stepped out of my sacred fire. Now it turns against me, as though I was nothing more than a..."

She cut herself off.

"Nothing more than a werewolf," Igor finished for her. Her guilty eyes confirmed it. "There is no sin in the fear that you'll assume another's weakness. But I'm certain your current condition isn't your condition at all; it's the child's. For the moment, her blood is your blood, thus the inversion."

"But does that mean my child... my child...will be harmed by the very element which gives me strength? How can such a child possibly thrive in our world?"

The vampire shrugged. "Perhaps it cannot."

"Igor!"

"What? I'm not saying the child will die. I am merely saying that, perhaps, the kind of life you'll give your daughter will need to be very different from what you and Andreas envision."

Gerwalta shook her head. "If she is susceptible to silver in utero, there is no way she'll thrive without a pack. Survive, perhaps, but I don't believe it'll be good for her. For the moment, she and

Andreas have bonded, saving him from lunacity nonetheless, but if something were to ever happen to him... Wait!"

Gerwalta stopped in her steps and turned to her host. "You said 'daughter' distinctly. Are you... Do you have anyway of..."

"It is my belief that you carry a girl," Igor confirmed. "I suspect Andreas knows as well, but so many men want of men simply because they are men. There is no scent of anything male about you. Except occasionally on your person when you come from your room too hastily."

She fought the blush filling her cheeks.

Igor gently nudged her with his shoulder as they walked. "Stop. There is no shame in partaking of the blessings marriage affords."

"I've no shame. Only..." She exhaled, preparing to unravel the last layer of her unease for the vampire to examine. "Do you know why I rushed from the kitchens just now? Because for the first time, I realize what a selfish thing it was for me to wed Andreas. I don't mean because it took my mother's heir from her or the king from his pack. There will always be another to fill that void. But..." Her hands smoothed down over her child just as the halfling kicked within her. "She will be the one who truly feels the consequences of our apostasy. What right did I have to create such a tempest of an inheritance for so innocent a creature?"

"Frau Baron, vampires are not soothsayers. We cannot see the future, but I cannot believe fate would so haphazardly marry your fortunes only to turn a blind eye to the fruit of your union. Don't think of the legacy you'll leave as a burden. You are two creatures who defied the bigoted traditions of your people to embrace something bigger than rules and races: your love. Would that all children could claim such lofty pedigrees, I feel this world would be a much better place."

At that, the vampire offered his arm. "Now, I've not had much experience with expectant mothers, either as a human or a vampire, but I do recall, one is to indulge their appetites. If your daughter wants fresh meat, let's make sure she gets some before Antoine cuts that ox into something fit for cooking. I'm quite certain we can procure a knife made of lesser metals."

She accepted his arm. "Was Andreas terribly disturbed when

I rushed out?"

"Not so much as Antoine."

"But why?"

"Because he was left alone with Andreas."

TWELVE

The messenger clutched the letter in one hand while vaguely holding out another. Inga considered killing him. She'd killed others for less insolent misdeeds than expecting payment. In addition, who asked payment from a nun? True, Inga wasn't a member of the order. She was hiding out here, pretending to make penance as her father demanded, waiting out her sentence until Igor thought she'd suffered enough or until a better opportunity made itself clear.

But must that include payment for services like some common pauper?

At last, she huffed and pulled a gold coin from the small purse tied at her waist, slipping it into the messenger's hand. "Meet me here again before dawn, in case I have to send a reply." Bodies created problems, no matter how much blood you drained from them.

"Of course, Sister, it would be my delight."

With the boldness of a musk ox, the merchant took up the hand Inga used to take the letter and kissed it. Some men enjoyed tempting the sisters. The insolent cur indeed flared temptation within her, but not the sort for which he hoped. She'd let him live tonight, but she might take something more precious than his blood come morning.

The moment she was out of sight of the main hall, Inga broke the seal—the one that had been hers not even a year ago—and unfurled the parchment. The sliver of the moon above provided light, though her sensitive eyes needed even less than that to make out the writing.

I write to acknowledge the receipt of your letter and to tell you for the discussions here at court upon its deliberation. Indeed, you still have friends among the courtesans. Messina di Grecchi in particularly spoke at some length in favor of your petition. However, it is my decision as Doge which I write to share with you.

Your request for a pardon of your crimes against Venice

has been denied. This isn't to say that you might not one day find yourself in our illustrious Republic, but at present, the injury caused to influential members of the court at the fangs of your guests, the Ravens, as well as the significant uptick in deaths caused by their ravenous appetites and the subsequent suspicions of the laity of our presence, mean that the wounds are still too fresh to be cut again. In a few decades, I'll reassess if enough time has passed and enough of the hatchet been buried that you may once again—

"Damn you, Massimo!"

Inga threw the paper on the ground and proceeded to stomp it, a flattened effigy of her former lover-turned-usurper. How dare he? How dare he? A curse upon the court of Massimo Brunneli. Didn't he remember that it was she who elevated him to the role of her royal consort? And now, he was offering favors to her even to consider if she may return in a few decades! What was she supposed to do until then, while away her existence in pestilent Navarre?

It wasn't that Basque country was without charm, but it wasn't Venice. It wasn't at the core of everything fashionable, powerful, and delicious.

It wasn't, frankly, good enough for her.

THIRTEEN

Only the cracking of bones and scrapping of plates broke the silence.

Helga wore a mask of indifference, a dam behind which her frustration built. Across the table, Mehmet's face curdled, the black hood pushing bits of boar about his plate before finally dropping his fork and huffing.

"Can you Germans eat nothing but pork?"

No one spoke, for the Matron sat at the end of the table. Instead, they left it to her to dictate a reaction to the ungracious, overstayed guest.

Gunda took time working through a mouthful of meat. "We are hunters, Mehmet, and what this land provides to us in this season is boar. If you don't like it—"

"It is haram," he broke in. "Unclean! The House of Night doesn't partake of pig, for it was commanded—"

"I won't force you to eat our food." Gunda recaptured control of the conversation with brisk tones. "If you are to be one of us, you must partake like one of us. Or are our offerings and hospitality not enough for you?"

His expression flattened as his head dipped into his chest. He could not take another night bound in irons as punishment. He needed to woo Helga behind closed doors to keep her favor and that was not done from the dungeon. "My apologies, Matron, it wasn't my intention to... Forgive me."

An acidic glare stayed fixed on his as Helga leisurely drew a pull of her wine. Wine he would not touch, because it too was forbidden. Finally, the platitudes came. "No insult taken, Herr Siyah." The dripping, fatty meat slid off the fork and into her mouth. "But so as not to further upset you by forcing you to dine with us at this unclean table, you have my permission to leave."

Anger boiled beneath the surface, threatening to break out across his face and his speech. Mehmet clenched his teeth as he pushed out from the table, bowed to the Matron, and gave Helga one last reproachful scowl, as if to say, you see, this is what I was talking about.

His footsteps could not be fast enough. He wanted to hit something, to yell at the top of his lungs and vent his fury. He'd gambled when he'd left for Venice, aiming for a path into the House of Red... an outcast, exiled. He'd never considered that he may lose his bet and end up without a wife, without a clan, and worse, without power.

In short order, Mehmet found himself outside the castle, through the baileys, and out the east gate. He jumped, smacking Andreas Baron's severed hand, hung on the outer wall of the Schloss as a warning to any other wolfsretter-fancying lupines. It swung on an arc behind him as Mehmet threw back his head and bellowed into the night.

"That smug, arrogant, ungracious... bitch!"

Passion trumped wisdom, and the moment the word escaped his lips, Mehmet threw his hands over his mouth. He had to stay focused, stay contained. Helga was his last chance at redemption. By now, his story had filtered out to all the European houses, the betrothed fiancé of the Red Matron's fourth daughter, abandoned at the tent. Even dark ones loved gossip. He was wed, but unwed. Trapped into a marriage that had never been consummated, and thus, in an odd limbo between the two. He couldn't arrange another marriage unless either his fiancé died or the matron of her clan absolved his obligation. Gunda Faust would not allow the latter, and had refused to secure the former, choosing to exile her daughter instead and only slay the wolf with whom she sinned.

Helga must become matron, release him of his obligation to Gerwalta, and accept him into her clan, or the only choice left to him would be heading east into the Caucasus. Or worse still, the New World.

He'd rather die.

But after the bold acts of setting up her husband to be slain, Helga refused to advance on the throne. "I know my mother and the mood of the court," she'd said, "and I will act when I am certain I can do so with my family's support." So again, Mehmet was obliged to wait on the determination of willful women. With a huff, he schooled his features and turned back to the castle. If he hoped to keep that chance alive, he needed to be ready to entertain Helga when she called upon him at dawn. Mehmet took one last look at the swinging hand, offering the slain lupine's hand a silent curse, when he saw that there was no hand.

But there was a paw.

Mehmet blinked. Rubbed his eyes. Looked again. Saw the same.

Impossible. That's all he could think. Impossible. Once a werewolf died, even if it should happen whilst he was in his fur, his body—or any portion thereof—reverted to a laymen's form with the rising of the sun. It did not change postmortem. It could not change.

Unless...

Unless, perhaps, the wolf from whom the paw had come...

...wasn't dead.

Helga waited until the sun peaked over the edge of the horizon and the rest of the household had descended into sleep to sneak into Mehmet's room.

"My love..." He stood to greet her, arms open.

Helga delivered punishment in the form of an open hand across his cheek. "Fool!" she growled as he spun. "She can kill you, you know? My mother will throw away your life as easily as a pebble in her boot. If you die, then everything I've sacrificed for us will have been in vain!"

Clutching the patch of skin which bloomed blue, Mehmet rose to his feet. "What you have sacrificed? You gave up a husband you didn't care for and a sister you detested. I've abandoned my homeland and my chance at marrying an uçan, all to prostrate myself before your beast-loving, lying betrayer of a mother."

"Lying?" The accusation came out of nowhere, a cannonball which hit Helga's walls and left a hole. "What are you talking about?"

Mehmet turned and crossed the room to where a basket lay atop a table. Whatever he drew from it was no bigger than a fist but concealed inside a slip of cloth. He laid the object in her open hand, helping her to pull off the wrapping.

"A paw?" Her face screwed up. "But... the nerves and vessels are dry. This isn't a new injury. Or is it a natural wolf, not a lupine at all?"

"It is werewolf, but as you say, not a new injury."

She turned the ghastly object over in her hand. "A severed limb this old should have reverted to a laymen state by now. How is it still like this?"

"It is not how you should ask," Mehmet said as he took the paw back, wrapping the linen back about it and hiding it away. "Rather, ask me whose paw it is."

All Helga had to offer was a blank stare. "I don't understand."

Mehmet closed in, playing with the buttons of the red hood's tunic. "Do you think your mother's betrayal of her house and clan would put the court on your side?" He lowered his head, pulling kisses up her neck, before pausing and turning his head. "Why is the hand your mother brought as proof of Baron's execution suddenly a paw if its owner is dead?"

Helga tilted her head to the side as Mehmet's hand slipped under her tunic. "That is Barron's hand?"

"His paw, his hand." Mehmet laughed. "Don't you see, Helga? This is it. This is what you needed to finally seize the throne."

But her heart refused to accept it just because it was a convenient turn of events. She could believe Gerwalta's betrayal; the youngest daughter of the clan had always been the least fervent in her loyalties. But her mother, the matron herself?

Mehmet pressed a hand to her cheek. "Do you not believe me? If you want, we can go now outside the outer walls. You'll see Baron's hand no longer there."

"I believe it is his, but how would we even begin to convince my siblings and my father? My mother will merely say it is not so, and they wouldn't dare to call her liar without better proof than a magically shifting paw. It could be anyone's paw."

Mehmet's eyebrow arched. "What sort of proof?"

Her breath hitched as he picked her up and walked her to the bed, her legs weaving around his waist. "We need him. But my mother wouldn't let any one of us go without cause, and trying to keep such a secret, she will not be eager to give leave."

The wolfsretter of the House of Night was dark in all the beautiful ways his bloodline allowed. Black eyes, tanned skin, curly ebony locks. He looked like the midnight sky made flesh as he hovered over her on the bed. "Matron Faust refuses to release me from my marriage contract with Gerwalta, and in doing so, she's given me all the reason I need to go. I am only attempting to win back my bride."

"But where will you go? You don't even know where to find them."

"Of course, I do. She will have gone to the only place that would put her under the aegis of someone as powerful as your mother. She's gone to Karahan, and Karahan is in Navarre."

She buried a laugh into his neck. "As if you are privy to the movements of so illustrious a vampire."

"I am not, but I did not squander my time in Venice. I have ears in the court. I've been told that the new Doge recently received a message from Karahan's daughter, Inga, from Navarre. He will not be far from her, I can guarantee it. I will go there under the guise of reclaiming Gerwalta, and instead drag back Baron in chains."

Yes, that could work, Helga thought. "Then leave come nightfall. But for now—" She bucked her hips up, joining them together in their bedroom dance. "—your night belongs to me."

FOURTEEN

Few were the men who could truthfully claim they had surprised a vampire with their approach, fewer still that were left alive to tell the tale.

Mehmet Siyah of the House of Night nodded when their eyes met as though they were old friends. Igor's hands clenched so tightly, he wondered if his fingernails would be bloody should he lift his hand. The petite señorita he'd been charming followed his gaze, in the act of giving Igor an eyeful of that beautiful neck stretched long. His fangs burst forth of their own volition. He'd been foolish to go so long without feeding, but he feared what might happen if he left Andreas and Gerwalta unprotected. So far, he'd succeeded at keeping their presence concealed from other dark ones. If anyone understanding the significance of that child should learn of its imminent birth… He hesitated to think of the devious sort of aged vampire that would like nothing more than to have a youth-bestowing blood creature in his stable.

Igor leaned in and took the peasant girl's hand, raising it to his lips to lay a gentle kiss. He bit back his desires, both for the blood and for her body, and mumbled his apologies. "A moment, dulcinea, but someone needs to see me urgently."

By the time he'd made his way across the partially filled tavern, Mehmet had settled himself at a table, his black cloak pooling around his person.

Igor assumed the seat across from him. "The locals would think you a priest if you had a white collar and any sanctity to speak of."

"Do you say that because I am a Muslim?"

"No, I say that because you are a scoundrel." Igor leaned forward. "It has been two centuries since this land was taken back from the Moors, but be warned, Siyah, some have not let it go. I doubt as though Andreas Baron will take your arrival well, either."

The wolfsretter wove his fingers together as he planted his elbows on the table. "You give away your secrets, Karahan."

"I give away nothing you don't already know," Igor replied. "There would be no reason for you to be here unless you knew."

"I respect that you aren't the type of man who—what is this saying, beats around the bush?" Mehmet lowered his hands and leaned forward. "Are they still in residence?"

"Yes, and if you know anything of my reputation and capabilities, you would do best to take that answer with you to Constantinople. You tried playing the situation with the Ravens to your advantage and failed. Take what remains of your pride and crawl back in search of your imaginary lost pack of the Golden Horn."

The smirk across the other man's face flattened. "They are real, and someday they'll slip up and trust in someone or something they shouldn't. And when they do, the House of Night will be there to smite them and their anathema queen."

Igor rolled his eyes. He'd never understand the rigidity that lupines and wolfsretters alike had about the agency of the two sexes.

"Nevertheless, I've abandoned that quest, and sought more... fruitful opportunities."

Mehmet moved with a speed the quickest vampire would appreciate. One moment he sat, relaxed and nonchalant. The next, he'd drawn—or given the talents of his kind, perhaps, created—a silver blade out of thin air. The dagger plunged into Igor's left hand, severing flesh and bone.

The laity about them revealed themselves for the cattle they were. The herd was spooked, and spooked herds ran. Within moments they were alone.

Good, fewer witnesses that way. Perhaps that had been the hood's intention. Igor had underestimated Mehmet's schemes once; he was not eager to do it again.

Igor looked up to Mehmet who, a credit to him, wore smugness instead of surprise. No doubt the wolfsretter thought such an act would have more of an effect, or he'd not have undertaken it. "What is it you're after now?"

"The wolf. You'll deliver him to me tonight or the next cut will be to your spine."

Straight-faced, Igor examined the inflicted hand. The pain was minimal. The blood loss, insignificant. "What claim is it you believe you have to him?"

"Gerwalta is my wife by contract if not yet consummated in flesh, and that wolf practically stole her from our marital bed. Don't pretend you're unaware that by our laws that is a capital offense."

What an annoying little pissant. No wonder his own clan had sent him packing.

"I know what your laws state, but they came to me seeking sanctuary. Why would I betray them like that?"

Mehmet folded his arms across his chest and sat back in his chair. "Remind me what it was that you originally went to Triberg to inquire about? Some sort of safekeeping of your shame?"

Every nerve in the vampire's body pulsed. "You wouldn't."

Mehmet rubbed his chin. "Tell me, Karahan, why should the wolfsretter be the guardians of the vampires' refuse? What offense did the Ravens ever commit against us?"

"Even you couldn't be that foolish. If the Ravens go free, the first person on their kill list will be the wife you claim you want to rescue."

Mehmet's eyes went wide. "Did I say anything to imply I cared what becomes of Gerwalta after my use of her passes?"

Igor swallowed down his hate. Rage would not serve him now. "If the Ravens are released back into the world, it won't only cost the dark ones dearly. They'll mobilize their alliances in the east and attempt to overthrow the laity courts, just as they had been working towards before. Thousands, perhaps millions will die." Keeping his anger from boiling over grew more difficult with each word. Clutching the edge of the table, Igor's fingernails splintered wood. "Are you so blinded by your own ambitions that you'd release death upon humanity? The Matron looked the other way and let Barron go, why can't you?"

"It is you, not I, who will determine if that comes to pass."

Igor shook his head. "I won't give up Gerwalta."

"But the wolf? Come now, what would she need him for? I imagine by now, she's taken his seed." Mehmet drew a lazy pattern over the table, even as Igor's jaw dropped. "Let's not pretend that she's a shy and reserved woman. I had anticipated that my wife, properly wooed, would be overtly encouraging of bed sport and wolfsretters are known for their bountiful fertility."

As though lightning had struck Igor's body, his spine went rigid. "Have rumors spread?"

"Rumors would suggest something happened to know about. You've been playing the long game on this one. I know why you conceal her, and I know why you risked all to extract the two of them from their clan and pack and why now you've brought them here to guard. That baby's blood... It would be quite valuable to the right vampire, wouldn't it?"

Curse the eastern hoods and their access to ancient knowledge. "A single drop more precious than that of ten laymen."

Mehmet stood. "I'll be in the vicinity of this tavern tomorrow at this time. Produce the wolf and I'll let you keep Gerwalta."

"And the babe?"

Mehmet swished his hand through the air dismissively. "It has no place in our world but the grave. Do with it what you like." The wolfsretter turned to go. "I make for Triberg tomorrow, and it will either be with the wolf, or with word to the Matron that your contract to house the Ravens is void. The choice is yours."

When Inga's father arrived just as the sun crested the sky and the chants of morning prayer had echoed away, she knew there was something wrong.

The vampire leapt to her feet when he burst into her chamber, having just laid off her habit for the day. "What has happened?"

The words never came. Igor crossed the chamber, pulling her into his arms, her cheek pressed to his chest.

"Father, you are worrying me," she muttered. "It is already dawn. I was about to smoke into the catacombs for the day. Come with me, or hurry home before it is too late."

"It may be too late already. What he says and what he intends to do may be two very different things."

"What who will do?" The words made little sense. "If someone is threatening you, let me leave this place to stand at your side."

Igor's eyes went wide as he pulled back, staring at her like she'd just said the most ridiculous thing imaginable. "No. Stay here. Don't leave the monastery except to go to day rest until my return. Drink from the sisters if you must, but don't leave. I'll be gone no more than a fortnight. I should be able to do it in that time."

"Do what? Father, what is going on?"

"The less I tell you, the safer you are. I just... I feared how much he knew, for he shouldn't have known of any of it, but he somehow did."

"You're not making any sense."

Igor kissed her forehead. "I know, love, I know. I promise, one day I'll tell you. For now, stay and pray. Pray especially for me, that I can save us all from the mess I've made of things. Just know that I have solutions in the works, a way to assure that we'll endure and that you and I both will still be alive to see the end of this. I promise, Inga, all will be well. Just trust me."

"Of course, I do, but I still have no idea what you're talking about."

He squeezed her shoulder. "To your rest, and I to my labor. I love you, and I'll count the moments until my return and our reunion."

And with that, her father smoked out of sight.

FIFTEEN

Why were wolfsretters not partakers of grand literature?

It wasn't that they were an illiterate culture by any means. Gerwalta, like her siblings before her, had been made to learn letters and numbers, as well as French, Latin, and Greek. While the shapes of the Roman tongue had always escaped her mastery, she had read books, but never without intent. All the Faust children studied Machiavelli (in French, as it were) in some depth. But never had Gerwalta had the opportunity to read something merely for pleasure.

At least if their departure for England had been delayed until after the baby was born, Andreas spooked by her fainting spell, she could fill the time with so, so many books.

She lowered the copy of the German translation of Don Quixote Igor had gifted her and sighed as the swell of her belly began to dance. A hand placed against it landed just in time to receive a swift kick.

"Definitely a girl," she said to herself. "And definitely eager not to be in there anymore." She observed the room around her at large, trying to recall the last time she'd felt at ease anywhere else but here. "I can sympathize, little bug."

Thoughts of her child and her longings for the forest flitted away as Andreas swept into the room, a mask of apprehension on his face. She tried to shoot to her feet, but what ensued instead was a comical balancing act between the realm of the possible and practical. She finally achieved a standing position after several modifications to both style and form.

"Is something the matter, love?"

Bless her mate, he didn't say a thing about her awkward composure. "Igor has left."

"Left? To go where?"

"He wouldn't say." Andreas turned to peek back into the hall before closing their door. "He said he would return within a fortnight, and that we were to remain here and to be certain that we didn't venture outside the castle, not even at night and not even on its own grounds. The laity staff remain to serve us, but the castle has no lord."

The great dragon whose presence warded off any interloper had flown. But while that seemed at face value to open them to danger, Gerwalta had to remind her spouse of the obvious. "We've been here for months without the least sign of danger. No one knows of us. Well, except for the laymen in Igor's employ, but surely you don't fear their disloyalty. It would cost them their own livelihoods, not to mention in all likelihood, their lives."

"I don't fear the servants; I question the intentions of the master."

An odd pang tightened in her abdomen, making Gerwalta bend slightly. "Igor? But he's been nothing but hospitable and welcoming since the moment we arrived."

"True, but have you noticed how concerned he is that we'll be seen, or how he never asked about our decision to leave and why we never acted on it after your silver sickness?"

"I presume he wishes us to stay to provide distraction. Have you noticed how isolated he is? Vampires favor grand cosmopolitan cities because of the excitement and activity. The village barely tops Triberg in those ways. I suspect he's here until the consequences of Venice shake out, and he's starved of entertainment. Even if his reasons are selfish in that way, Andreas, there is no crime in enjoying the company of guests. Surely, you're not saying that Igor is plotting in the shadows against us? To what end? We can offer him nothing."

Andreas's eyes cast down Gerwalta's frame. "He has made himself overly interested in your comfort and the baby's wellbeing. He has never treated me poorly, but he often only addresses me as an afterthought. I have to wonder if..."

"You suppose he has some cruel intention for our child." Gerwalta cut him.

"I don't know that it is cruel, but I don't know that it necessarily involves us," he said. "Gerwalta, have you ever asked yourself why the asenaic and his mate we met in Venice never arrived in Triberg?"

"We don't know that they didn't," she countered. "Mehmet said that they were on their way, that they were awaiting my wedding festivities to slip into the packlands without the Matron's notice whilst all in the schloss were distracted. And then you and I... well, mated and fled right after that."

Andreas shook his head. "I cannot be without my doubts. We do know that it was Igor who helped them flee Constantinople. We've only Mehmet's claims of that. It's made me wonder why a vampire would care what happened to an asenaic?"

Doubt furrowed her brow. "You're attempting to build castles out of field stones."

"And what of the Doge?" Andreas continued, undeterred. "Bianca? Inga? She went by both names, depending on who was concerned, as I recall. She is here in Navarre somewhere; I've overheard the servants mention her, but Igor never has. Don't you find that bizarre?"

What she found was this sudden suggestion of conspiracy inconvenient. Why must wolves always circle prey? Why could they not just attack head-on? "Perhaps vampires just keep their own counsel."

Andreas shook his head. "Something isn't adding up. Gerwalta, my duty as your mate is to protect you and our baby at all costs, and I'm no longer certain this is still the best place to do that."

In an instant, Gerwalta cupped her hands over his sole remaining one. "Then we go."

"Just like that? I say I've a suspicion and you resolve to let go your own?"

"It is the most efficient way to address your concerns. Besides," she said, "even if I don't share them, I trust your insight. You were a king. Perhaps only of a small pack in the Schwarzwald, but that made you privy to seeing things others wished you not to. If your instincts tell you something is afoot, then it may be."

"Then we go tomorrow at dawn," he said, pushing a kiss unto her cheek. "I'll see what provisions I can scrounge up; you do the same. We must travel light and with the sun, so that if Igor is indeed planning something, he'll be powerless to pursue us."

That part, however, seemed wrong to her. "As impacted as we will be by my condition, isn't it best we travel at night, when we are stronger?"

Andreas lifted his missing appendage, gesturing as though his left hand was still present. "I am a wolf without a paw and you are a wolfsretter who cannot control silver. Outside of our ability to scent and see better than the laity, night gives us little advantage now. Besides, in the day we'll have an easier time blending in among other travelers."

"And our destination? Does it remain unchanged?"

Andreas nodded. "Yes, we need to make England, and soon. Our child will come with the next full moon."

SIXTEEN

The vampire was so predictable. Or better yet, he was so manipulatable.

Mehmet knew the moment he suggested the Raven's jars could be expelled from the custodianship of the House of Red that the thought would fester in Karahan's head. What a shame that vampires couldn't simply kill off their misguided progeny. Not only did it esure their mistakes would come back to haunt them, it also gave others a weakness to exploit. Mehmet found a gathering of large boulders not far from the entry to Karahan's property, a place where shadow gave him cover, and waited.

Night passed, and the black hood had begun to think he'd miscalculated. He was about to bed down for the day when he heard it: his betrothed's voice approaching.

Wonderful, he thought. Late, but still as predicted. Now that the cat had run, all Mehmet need do was wait to see the mice scurry.

And that was the thing about mice. They always scurried.

"Andreas!"

He jolted awake at the sound of his name. "What? What is it? I'm awake. I'm awake."

Gerwalta, through some laborious twisting, maneuvered herself on to the bench beside him. The hay cart wasn't the finery his mate deserved, but in pressed moments and with no other options, it was the one Andreas could offer.

"You're sleep deprived and overly taxed from doing too much with too little time." She took the leather straps from his hand. "Go, rest. I'll drive some distance."

Though he surrendered the horses to her, his mind still

rebelled. "I'll lay down, but I'll stay awake."

"How do you propose to do that? You can't even stay awake sitting up." She jerked her head to the bed of grass behind them. "I'll rouse you when I stop midday to water the horses."

"And if there is any danger…" His voice trailed off, even as he crawled over the wall of the hay bin and began to pull and push the dry grass to suit his comfort.

"What danger could there be? Even a highwayman wouldn't be so cruel as to attack a woman in my condition."

The cart emerged from a patch of low-rise forest. Mehmet pulled his silver from concealment beneath his cloak, used it to tip the arrow shaft, and nocked it onto the string of his bow.

Pull, aim, release.

Direct hit.

His feet flew, eating up the ground. Blood scented the air. Lupine blood. The arrow vibrated with each flail Baron made, its head buried deep in his left thigh. The wolf wailed, screamed, bellowed… all driving the horses to distraction. The two meager beasts bucked, throwing the frame of the cart onto which they were attached flying.

Gerwalta grabbed a sword from the hay and swung out before her, unleashing the shocked creatures who wasted no time in running off. As his betrothed turned to aid the wolf, Mehmet saw it… the evidence of her advanced condition. Until that moment, he thought he didn't care what happened to her, nor did he take any offense for her infidelity. But seeing the proof made plain, anger flared within. Mehmet detested her not because she had betrayed him, but because she had betrayed her own kind.

"Traitor!" He pressed on with lopped steps as the balance of his silver formed the scimitar in his hands. "Befouled and wretched creature!"

Gerwalta spun, all the color from her puffy face fading at the sight of him. "You!"

She left her mate to bleed, knowing the shot that had landed must be painful, but not deadly. That didn't mean that Mehmet had missed his target. With silver embedded beneath the lupine's skin, Andreas Baron would find taking his fur impossible. The wound was calculated only to keep him human.

"How dare you!" Gerwalta shouted.

"How dare I?" Mehmet returned, raising the sword. "How dare you? You leave me at our wedding fire to open your legs to this putrid creature? You killed one of your own clan to protect his dirty pack? You Jezebel. I should slay you both for this treachery."

The lupine struggled to turn over, anchoring himself on all fours, looking for a moment very much like a layman imitating the wolf he could become. And then Mehmet saw it: the reason he struggled to find balance.

In addition to the arrow wound, of course.

"Missing a paw, Andreas?" Mehmet mocked. "Don't fret. We have it waiting for you back in Triberg."

Gerwalta stopped dead where she stood. "Andreas, run!" The red hood raised her sword, ready to strike if Mehmet came closer. "Stand down. I will kill him before I let you drag him back in chains. That is your plan, isn't it? Use him to implicate my mother, give Helga all the evidence she needs to kill two birds with one stone."

"You're as wise as you are depraved." Mehmet lifted his silver. "You could have been an empress among my people and yours, and you gave it all away to become this cur's bitch. You don't deserve a reprieve, Gerwalta. You die now."

The wolf called out as Mehmet swung and his love fell to the ground. Moments later, the black wolfsretter turned his attention back.

It took only one hard knock upon the head to render him unconscious. His massive body would take hours to drag back to town.

Luckily, somewhere near, there was a cart with two horses ready to go.

SEVENTEEN

Hunger sparked by the delicious scent took Inga's body hostage.

Blood had been spilt. Fresh, warm, oozing blood. Blood that would slake her thirst and fuel her powers and drive her to the edges of carnal satisfaction.

Blood, blood, blood...

Her fangs dropped into place of their own volition even as she steadied herself against a wall. A hand shot up to hide the evidence of her condition, even as one of the sisters rushed past her.

"Sister Maria Dominga?" Inga forced her teeth to retract just as the small, young nun came to a stop and turned. "What has happened? Is it one of the sisters? Someone is injured badly."

Maria Dominga grinned. "You truly are blessed by the Creator. His gifts are strong in your veins."

Not as strong as they would be if I drank you dry.

No, penance. You are here to do penance. Venice has rejected you, you have nowhere else to go. Father will find out if you kill anyone, then you'll end up just like the Ravens, sealed in silver until the end of time.

Igor was fair, but once one of his children crossed a line, he was also cruel. The paterfamilias of the Dracule bloodline could have easily exchanged favors with that of another and had Vlad and his sycophants killed. Instead, he'd forced them to endure, deprived, powerless, alone to contemplate their misdeeds until at last, they surrendered to the sun or just faded away encased in silver.

"A traveler found a woman on the side of the road," Maria Dominga continued, bringing Inga back to the moment. "Poor thing is beaten something dreadful, stabbed and left for dead. It is only by some miracle she survived. Mother Superior and Sister Maria Inez are doing what they can, but the injuries are quite..."

Inga's thoughts turned to the benefits of magnanimity, of how proud her father would be if she could offer aid in the face of utter temptation. Perhaps even proud enough that he'd think her debt to the laity balanced and allow her to leave the convent.

"I'll help." She drove forward, past the nascent nun. There was no need to inquire where the beaten woman was; a vampire's thirst drew her to wherever that glorious liquid pooled over fresh wounds.

Maria Dominga scurried after her. "Yes, perhaps our Lord will continue to work miracles through you. Perhaps you can help save her."

The moment Inga saw the bruised and bloodied creature, however, she knew that even God would be challenged. The sisters had stripped the woman of her clothing, allowing access to wounds that started at the top of her head and continued down to her ankles. Patches of red and blue bloomed across her arms, her legs, her back. Red hair, matted with dried blood and dirt, hung in clumps. Black eyes floated in a swollen mask of pain above a busted lip and bloody nose. Just beneath one breast, Inga saw where a section of skin was missing. Stabbed wasn't quite the right word, for that would imply a blade had entered her person. Whomever had tried for that had missed, cutting down the poor creature's side but not entering the body cavity.

And how she bled...

In the oddest of all circumstances, that wound, unlike the others around it, looked singed. Had whatever rapscallion that attacked her burned her as well? A pregnant woman? If Inga knew the bastard's identity, she'd personally rip off his arms and filet his gullet.

"Rosaria!"

The vampire snapped to attention at the utterance of her alias. "Yes, Mother Superior?"

"Clean cloths." The elderly nun's eyes and attention had already turned back to the victim who, Inga would credit, was doing her best to breathe through the pain. "Whatever happened, it has the baby thinking it might be time to exit. Inez, ask the other sisters to pray. After we dress the wounds, her fate will be in bigger hands than ours."

The battered creature on the table muttered something, but the language was neither Basque nor Spanish. Mother Superior, who only could hold a passable conversation in the former, leaned in. "What dear?"

"She's speaking French," Inga informed while translating. "She's asking if anyone has found her husband."

"I see." Mother Superior paused from cleaning the side wound to push the woman's hair off her face. "Tell her, Rosaria, that we didn't know to look but we'll send word to the village near where she was found to inquire. Tell her to give us a name and a description of him."

Delirium transformed the woman's words into something not entirely intelligible. Inga translated what she could. "His name is... Wolfson? He's missing a..." Inga paused to ask if she had properly understood, then continued when the woman managed a nod. "He only has one hand. The right one."

Mother Superior grimaced. "Was that before or after they were attacked?"

But the answer would have to wait. With a groan, the woman sighed and slipped into unconsciousness.

"Just as well." Mother Superior rose to her feet, gathering up a handful of saturated rags before dropping them into a dish of crimson-stained water which she shoved into Inga's chest. "She won't need any translating while she's out. Get fresh cloths and hot water and hurry."

Inga stood transfixed. The blood... it was just there, in her hands. Diluted in water, perhaps, but still fresh, still warm even. Her father hadn't given her leave to drink from the nuns, but was someone under their care that different? All she had to do was...

"Rosaria!"

"Yes, at once." Inga turned and ran as quickly as she could without spilling the bowl's contents, and without attracting attention. When she found herself outside, the light of a half-moon beaming down, she couldn't quite remember how she'd gotten there.

The stars danced, reflecting against the blood-laced water. Tears formed in the corner of her eyes. It was barbaric, beneath her, but how long had it been? Her father fed her his own blood on his visits.

It kept her alive, the secondhand life in his veins stolen from others infusing her body with just enough strength to endure, but she'd been starving for months. Igor split hairs; the victim being treated inside wasn't of the monastery. If she drank, Igor would consider that a violation of his trust. But how could he learn of this? What evidence would there be if she partook of this fortuitous offering?

Inga squeezed out the rags, thickening the brew, before tossing them aside. The sweet and savory scent pulled at her senses as she lifted the bowl, bringing it to the rim of her bottom lip. The bouquet... It was different somehow, more tart. But blood was blood was blood, and she hadn't had nearly enough of it in so very long. She tipped up the bowl and...

"No!"

An arc of red shone for a flicker of a moment, catching the rays of the moon above. Inga fell to her knees, pressing the grounded liquid into the dirt, willing it to soak into the soil more quickly. She wouldn't betray her father. She wouldn't quench her thirst with the spilt blood of an innocent mother-to-be. She wouldn't become the monster they all had said she was.

Determination stiffened her steps and quickened her pace as she resumed a place at Mother Superior's side, a pile of clothing in her hands. The beaten woman had come to—conscious but trancelike. She'd either been trained to hide injury or had been injured enough in her lifetime to know how to masque pain. It was a warrior's tactic, but what kind of woman would receive such an education? The laity did not send their women to battle.

It was then that the terrible thought entered Inga's head. Had the woman said her husband was named Wolfson, or that he was a wolf's son?

All the color drained from Inga's face as she leaned in to whisper into the woman's ear. "Are you of the dark, child?"

Mother Superior raised an eyebrow. "What are you saying, Rosaria?"

"I am asking if she was attacked after dark," Inga lied. French wasn't Basque, nor was it Spanish, but the tongues twisted together and the best way to conceal the truth was to be in the proximity of it. "If it was day, she might have seen who did it."

Even through busted lips and looking out of bloody, swollen

eyes, Inga heard the condemning admission. "Oui, je suis de la nuit."

Inga rose, knowing what she must do, but hating all the same that it must be done. Her father had forbidden her to seek any dark one. Not only vampires, but wolves and wolfsretter alike. Igor's faith in her was so shaken, Inga wasn't sure if he'd believe that a wolfsretter had by chance been brought to her convent. Perhaps he himself had even arranged it, the whole story of his needing to journey suddenly a prologue to a test, a way to see if Inga could be trusted to follow his edicts while he was afar.

She wouldn't fail so easy a test.

When Mother Superior finally deigned to raise her eyes, Inga took the woman under her influence, pushing away her own thoughts. "In the morning, you'll send this woman away from here."

Mother Superior nodded. "Yes, that would be best."

"We'll do what we can to assist her, but she'll be made to leave as soon as she can walk."

The nun's faith was strong, but her mind was weak and easily reshaped. "She is recovering with remarkable speed. A merchant caravan is leaving north tomorrow. We can ask that she be given a place amongst them."

Inga hated herself, now more than ever. "And if anyone is to ask after an injured woman brought here, we'll say she passed away. You'll instruct all the sisters that this is what we'll say."

"We shall say we buried her in the graveyard."

Yes, that would do nicely. "You'll have to be certain the groundman digs a grave then. Her battered clothing should be buried there, and any silver she was carrying."

Little lines formed on Mother Superior's brow. "There was no silver."

What kind of wolfsretter went about without silver, especially while expecting? No wonder she had been bested. In her condition and without any weapons, she would have been an easy kill.

Inga gave one last resolute nod. "And my father will never know I was in the same room with her, nor that I even knew of her presence."

The nun nodded. "As if you were never here."

EIGHTTEEN

The castellan came at dawn, just as Gunda had taken off her silver and readied herself for bed. "Can it not wait?"

Therese hesitated before saying in the smallest voice she'd ever used, "I don't think so, your grace."

As the Matron entered the throne room, a slurry of scents washed over her. Blood, sweat, silver, and agony combined to tell a story of suffering. The stench of spoiled meat suggested a wound from a beating that had either been allowed to fester, or freshly opened before it could properly heal. Soon, the source of the stink became apparent. The hobbled lupine wore shredded rags and his own filth for clothing. What concerned Gunda wasn't the fact that a werewolf had been dragged into her presence as a prisoner when she had given no orders for one to be taken. Rather, it was the fact that every member of her clan was present. Both her daughters who remained in Triberg, her son and his wife, the one son-in-law left alive, her husband… And in the midst of them all, holding the silver chain which bound the wolf, the horrible snake who'd slithered his way into her court, the wolfsretter from the House of Night.

Her heart seized. Had he succeeded in tracking down Gerwalta?

Gunda drew to a stop as she focused in on Helga and Zelda standing on the dais, her eyes narrowing. "Who dared to call for a clan gathering in my stead? And why is this one—" She slung a hand in Mehmet's direction. "—returned without Gerwalta? Is that not why he left, to find her?"

"Indeed it is," Mehmet said, turning slowly, "but as it turns out, I found something of greater value than a betraying bride. Would you like to see, Gunda?"

She stomped forward, prepared to give the insolent interloper a lesson with the back of her hand for referring to her in so informal a fashion, when he tugged on the chain and spun the wolf around.

She was ruined.

His eyes were swollen. Deep cuts around his face and neck still glistened with fresh blood. He'd been beaten so closely within an inch of his life, not even his own mother would know the sight of him. But Gunda did.

It was the missing hand that gave it away.

As all the color drained from Gunda's face, Helga stepped to the front of the dais. "Correct me if I'm wrong, Mother, but this is Andreas Baron, is it not? The same Andreas Baron who you said you tracked down and killed? Whose hand you brought back as a trophy? He does appear to be very much alive."

Gunda took one piteous look at the wolf before stumbling toward her eldest. "Helga, please, you—"

No sooner had she gotten the words out than the two male members of her bloodline closed in, taking her by the arms.

"Gunda Faust, I find you guilty," Helga said, passing judgement. "Not only did you lie to us, but you aided and abetted a criminal lupine to escape justice. In doing so, you have become a betrayer. The sentence for such betrayal is death."

Gunda drew in a deep breath, the initial shock turning over into anger. "How dare you! I am the Matron of this house, and it is at my discretion who is punished and for what."

"Your discretion put you in league with our enemies." Her husband's face... Heartbroken. Injured. Forlorn. "Why, my Gundy? Why did you do this to us?"

"I did nothing to you. To any of you." Gunda's head lashed to the right. "Can you not smell the conspiracy cooked up by this usurper? Or did any of you, as did I, write to inquire of the Matron of the House of Night as to why he was purged? Insubordination and insurrection, that's why. Disobeying orders and trying to seek out a pack everyone knows was killed off a century ago!"

Helga bellowed. "A convenient lie and at a desperate moment. We can believe nothing that comes from your lips. You will wear your scarlet v in blood, and you will bear it with shame, Betrayer."

"I'm not the only one who has betrayed this bloodline." Gunda turned to her power-hungry daughter. "But I am the only one who did it for the right reasons."

Helga's face curled into a smile. "Sealed by her own admission."

"As someday, you shall be sealed by yours," Gunda said. "My crime is that I discovered I loved my children more than I loved power. I only wish I could say the same of them."

Perhaps due to the indirect derision, Maximillian's grip tightened on her arm. "Who'd have thought, my own mother a betrayer? Why? Gerwalta chose her fate willingly, knowing the consequences."

"Perhaps she did," Gunda said. "But her child did not."

The others' eyes widened just as a ripple of understanding went through the room.

"The child will never come to be," Mehmet proclaimed, and she watched with disappointment as the others expressed their relief. "I stabbed it in its mother's womb with silver. The child has been slain."

Gunda buried her head into her chest, trying to hide the tears, even as she shook with silent sobs.

Helga clicked her tongue in disgust. "To the dungeons with her," she said. "To the dungeons with them both."

Moist earth, fungus, the filth of dying creatures...

Moonlight pulled open Gunda's eyes, but it was the scent in the air that stained her dreams with blood. She sat up without urgency. What good would it do to hurry? She was trapped in this tomb of a dungeon. An ability to fly did one little good when imprisoned underground.

Nothing to do but sit, wait, and imagine her impending death.

Then came the sound of metal clinking in the darkness, pulling her gaze into the shadows.

"They've chained you."

"Not in silver," Andreas Baron muttered through swollen lips. "They were wiser than that."

"Of course, they were. I am a Matron. Even if I couldn't touch the silver, if I could see it, I'd control it." She crossed her legs to gather what comfort she could. "They must have been frustrated when you threw yourself over me and took the beating meant for me."

"I owed you my life, what else would I do?"

"Let me die," she said shortly, matter-of-factly. "Let me receive the just punishment for the crimes I myself have committed."

His eyes went to the floor. "Are you angry that I intervened?"

Gunda couldn't help but laugh. "As if that matters now." When she grew somber again, she asked it… the very question of which the answer would legitimize her suffering. "Gerwalta?"

Andreas's eyes lifted. "You heard what Mehmet said."

"And I know you're a mated wolf and would have no reason to live if your mate and your baby were dead," she said. "You weren't my first königswolf, Andreas Baron, even if you were my last."

"Be that as it may, Gerwalta is not a wolf. The bond I have with her… I don't think it works that way."

The Matron said nothing, but she did raise an eyebrow in suspicion.

Andreas's face bunched up, as though he were frustrated to have his secrets revealed. After a moment, he heaved a heavy sigh. "I cannot sense her wellbeing. I wouldn't even know that she still lives, except I know that our child endures. A wolf can sense these things, sense when a close member of his blooded kin passes from this world, no matter the distance."

A queer sense of relief flooded her. It hadn't been until that moment that Gunda Faust herself understood the depth of her concern. "And your brother? Is he still alive?"

Andreas ignored her question, asking instead, "Why aren't they just killing me? I've openly committed the greatest crime your kind prescribes for mine. Even Gerwalta tried to warn me the fate in store if I committed myself to wooing her. Now it is come, why am I unpunished?"

Gunda's strategic mind drew up the likely reason without much work. "Because, Herr Baron, you did not commit the greatest crime, I did. A wolfsretter who loves a wolf... Well, it's an embarrassment, yes, but at the end of the day, her injuries are only to herself and her reputation. But a matron who helps a wolf flee justice? That is why you are still alive. Or should I say... for now."

The lupine shook his head. "I don't understand."

"I am to be executed," Gunda continued. "They await the full moon, when your nature will force you to fur and fury. And then they'll let you lose on me. You see, Andreas, you are the way I die."

She said all this with amusement, and perhaps that's what it was now, amusing. The one thing Gunda knew it wasn't, was avoidable.

"I won't," the wolf suddenly declared. "You saved Gerwalta and me both. As much as I detest you for all the slights you've committed against my people, I refuse to be the cause of your undoing."

Gunda laughed. "Herr Baron, if there is mercy in your soul, I pray that you will be the very thing which ends me. The alternatives will not show me your compassion."

NINETEEN

The last time he'd been at Schloss Wolfsretter, Igor had observed every form of decorum. He sent ahead a messenger to ask formal permission to call. A gift befitting the head of a prominent clan was secured from Munich and presented upon arrival. He'd dressed in his eastern finest so as not to offend the Matron's sensibilities and deferred to her preference in every matter.

Today, Igor observed nothing. He didn't even wait for the gate to be lifted. The vampire became smoke, winding his way around tree and rock, up the mountain from the village through the mist, straight into the heart of the Faust court. He lingered in the shadows until the throne held an occupant, before materializing, fangs bared. "You aren't Matron."

On the throne, the figure wrapped in the traditional red cloak and holding a silver staff glared down at him. "Who are you to say who I am in my own court?"

It took only the space of these words for others in the chamber to rally. He was surrounded, axes and swords and staffs all made of or topped in silver hovered a hair's breadth from his person. The blond woman on the dais, however, took a great amount of leisure in rising to her feet.

"Oh, I know who you are by name," she said. "Goran Karahan, Lord of the Dracule. But what place you think you have in supposing you've any power in this court is presumptive. I am Helga Faust, thirteenth matron of the House of Red. Now, state your business or I'll order your head from your body."

"Try, and I'll delight in personally removing the skin from your exsanguinated corpse."

The red hood bristled. "You have some nerve, Lord Dracule, threatening me in my own court."

"And you've some nerve claiming it as yours," Igor snapped back. He had no time for insolent children. "I come to reaffirm the terms of the contract I made with Gunda Faust last winter."

Helga's eyes rolled to the side, as though looking in the air for answers. "I know of no such agreement."

"Your mother did. She—"

His words cut off as two of the males of the court, one the elder version of the other, raised their silver blades to his throat.

"My mother," Helga said, spitting out the word like a curse, "no longer rules this clan. She lost her position through betrayal, and as such, all contracts she made on behalf of the House of Red are now defunct."

Igor bristled. "Is that the way of it then?"

The wolfsretter nodded. "It is."

"Then bring me the six silver jars. They are my property."

"I'm sorry, but I cannot do that."

"Cannot or will not?" The vampire raised an eyebrow. "Watch yourself on this, Frau Matron. I am attempting patience, but I've never been renown for it."

In a single, swift motion, the wolfsretter leapt from the dais, landing a sword's length from Igor as documented by her suddenly-wrought blade. "This court is aware of the role you played in harboring criminals whose life and fate were forfeit by the weight of their crimes. As such, we could demand restitution, even vengeance. But we did not. We decided to bury your sins with my mother's tenancy and move on. Don't tempt me to reconsider."

If they thought swords would dissuade him from his errand, they were sorely mistaken. Igor glared as he reached out and curled his fingers around the end of Helga's blade. With two steps, he guided it through his ribs, passing just under his heart, all while not flinching a muscle in pain.

Though his blood trickled down over the silver, his countenance remained unwavering. "This is all the effect your weapons have on me." He opened his mouth just as four gleaming fangs sprouted from his gums. "Would you like to see how mine treat you?"

For a spell, Helga stared at the dripping wound on his stomach before pulling back her sword in one rapid pull. The silver flooded its form, melting back into a staff.

"Fine, then," she huffed. "Have it your way."

Igor snapped his fangs back from view. "My property?"

"Maximillian will retrieve the jars." With two snaps, both the men at Igor's sides dropped their weapons, the younger of the two skittering off. "Tell me, Lord Dracule, can I have your word that, without business between us, you'll leave this place and never return?"

"Do I have your word that your clan in turn will not seek me out?" His eyes drifted to the Turk standing at the edge of the room.

Helga flashed an acidic glare at Mehmet before spinning back. "None under my command shall approach you again. If ever the House of Red and the Dracule Bloodline meet, it will be a dark day for us both."

A few minutes later, with the six jars pushed into a large sack and slung over his shoulder, Igor traveled a more conventional route: he walked out the east gate. It was then, on the edge of the bridge that carried one from the keep to the inner bailey, that Igor heard a whimper. With a shift of the wind and a scent upon the air, his senses confirmed it: Andreas Baron was here, and by the sound of it, suffering.

The vampire had given his word, and while the wolfsretters threw such things away at their convenience, a Dracule did not. There had been no fresh scent in the throne room of Gerwalta. In fact, there had been no scent of her anywhere near Triberg. But where would she be if not here?

His feet and heart rebelled. He thought of the baby Gerwalta carried, of the promise of its blood, of the possibilities it held for him and Inga both. An asenaic's blood could sustain a vampire beyond his allotted five hundred years. Igor could still be in the world to assure his demon progeny passed from it, and Inga could be his companion.

But it was more than that selfish care that kept him. Igor tolerated Andreas, but he liked Gerwalta. More than wish her no harm, he felt an urge to protect her. Perhaps because that had always been his lot: to foster young women exploited by families who didn't value them. He thought of Inga, of how he'd taken her into his clutch and under his protection after Vlad had discarded her. Each time Vlad discarded her. Gerwalta was no less deserving of compassion.

If he dropped the six silver jars, turned, and fought his way into the dungeons, he knew he could defeat any defense the House of Red mounted. But at what cost? Any one of them could melt the jars weighing down his sack and release evil back into the world. How many other lives would his malevolent sons take, just so he could save one wolfsretter?

Igor closed his eyes and whispered a prayer that Andreas's suffering may not be too great. And with that, he left all thoughts of the Barons behind.

TWENTY

Wilhelm knew something was unusual when Herr Minster's cart was heard winding the way up from the village into the packlands, Lisi's form visible even from afar on the bench beside him.

The second-in-command of the Triberg pack had to bite his own tongue to keep his mind focused. His nature called on him to take his fur; four legs would move faster than two along the road. But what would the laymen think of that, seeing an oversized wolf closing in only to shift back to a mortal form to converse politely. And, oh, also the man he would become wouldn't have a stich of clothing on.

Lisi had left for the village at dawn, taking their daughter Jelena; a supply of linen was said to be coming into the market that morning. Little wolves grew fast and sometimes it seemed that Lisi made new unmentionables nonstop. That, or repairing ones their son had torn in his excitement over being old enough to shift. (Lisi made the stiches looser in his things to allow a cleaner, more repairable break.)

Upon approach, his wife's face spoke of nothing but frustration. It was then that Wilhelm felt his heart race a second time. Where was Jelena? Oh, no, what had happened to their child?

Herr Minster drew the cart to a stop, pulling on the reins enough to get the single horse to listen. "Herr Kosner." He tipped his cap.

"Herr Minster." Wilhelm aided his wife in her descent, a needless accommodation for someone of preternatural ability but necessary to keep up the rouse that there were, in fact, no dark ones of any kind. "Lisi, did something happen? Where is…"

She laid a hand on his heart. "Jelena is in the back." She grimaced. "With her."

"Her?" Wilhelm turned to the loose hay in the cart, trying to see over the top into the blanket of pale yellow. His sense of smell did nothing to inform. Did the hay cover the scent? "Who?"

Just at that moment, his adorable little Jelena's head shot into view, bits of hay sticking out of her hair. "Hello, Papa."

Relief flooded his soul. "What are you doing back there, little lamb? And who is with you? Did you bring back one of Herr Minster's puppies?"

The children had been on him for two weeks, ever since Frau Minster had asked Lisi if the family would be interested in adopting one of his bitch's litter to "chase all those wolves people are always saying are up in those hills near you."

Wereolves didn't need dogs. Try telling that to the children.

Jelena's eyes went wide. "No, Papa, but I would love that an awful bunch. Jacob and I promise we'd take care of her."

"Lisi?"

The voice drew away Wilhelm's adoration of his incorrigible child and set his teeth on edge. The smile on his face melted, the need to use caution in the presence of laymen, dangerously on edge of being ignored. "Jelena, come down from there." Wilhelm pulled his wife behind his back.

Lisi swerved between her husband and the cart. "Wilhelm, hear me out."

"She cannot be here." His whisper came out as more of a growl. "She's Andreas's ma… An outsider."

"She is also days away from giving birth," Lisi shot back.

Wilhelm's eyes went wide, until he recalled that, indeed, enough time had passed since the day the wolfsretters attacked the packlands for a proper brooding.

Herr Minster, having maneuvered to the back of the cart, paused. "Frau Kosner, didn't you say this was one of those Faust girls?" He scratched his head and turned eyes on the ground. "Always thought they were a bit bluer than traveling by merchant caravan, but that's the way she came in. You sure we shouldn't take her up the hill? Her family would want to—"

Lisi turned on the laymen, pouring honey into her words even as she cut him off. "She married Andreas Baron, Herr Minster. You remember Andreas, don't you? My cousin, strapping farmer? I'm afraid the Fausts didn't accept the marriage and she and Andreas decided to find their fortunes elsewhere. But she's come back to stay with us..." Lisi carried her gaze over her shoulder to her husband, growling, "...at least until the baby is born."

Wilhelm crossed his arms and huffed. "Fine, then."

The males were the stronger in body of their species, but when it came to will, the bitch always ruled. Besides, it was never a good idea to infuriate the shewolf you shared a bed with unless you were eager to not share a bed with her.

Defeated, Wilhelm rounded the cart, expecting to find the Gerwalta he remembered from eight months before, only with a significantly larger waistline. As it turned out, he was to have his second surprise of the morning.

"Saints help us. What happened to her?"

The voice he recognized, but the face... He'd always thought of the youngest Faust child as mildly handsome, even if she were a wolfsretter. Ivory skin, bright, intelligent eyes, and apple red hair. The hair was still red, but everything was some disturbing color of black or blue. Only one eye looked up at him out of a face made dough, the other swollen shut. Her clothes were those of an everyday woman; no fine, imported, and costly fabrics here. Gerwalta was dressed like them: as a farmer would be. As Herr Minster reached down, Wilhelm did the same.

Gerwalta's black eye turned up on him. "I fell down."

If there was one thing Wilhelm knew for certain, it was that whatever misfortune had befallen Andreas's mate, that was the last possible truth. How did a creature who could fly become injured by a fall?

They were in trouble. On one side of the barn, all the members of the pack who believed turning Gerwalta over to the wolfsretters was best. On the other, all those who believed she should be given sanctuary until the baby was born, then turned over. On the former side, all the males of the pack. And on the other...

"If you give her to the red, the baby is as good as dead," Lisi surmised, her statement bringing nods from the shewolves. "You can believe what you like about Gerwalta, but her child is one of us and holds no fault for the misjudgment of its parents."

"It is only half wolf," Jacob Fitz, Lisi's brother, shot back from across the barn. "We don't know what it will be like. What if it cannot take fur? What if it doesn't heed the full moon? What if it—"

"What if it has horns and a duck bill and gobbles at the moon instead of howls?" Esther, Wilhelm's own sister, jumped in. "It doesn't change the fact that it is an innocent baby. We are many things the laity are not, but murderous of children for the sins of their fathers? That has never been our way."

Michael Fried coughed a laugh. "It isn't our way to give comfort to our overlords. The child is half wolfsretter. We'd raise a spy in our very midst. And what of the mother? How do we know this isn't some ploy to embed Gerwalta Faust—"

Lisi rolled her eyes. "Gerwalta Baron."

"Gerwalta Faust," Michael insisted. "The wolfsretter bitches don't defer to their husbands like our women do, and that is only one of the many ways in which they are different. It's unnatural, is what. Besides, you cannot tell me that you honestly believe she sincerely loved him. Then why did she abandon him and come here, half-dead and alone?"

"Because my mate is dead."

All the wolves shot to their feet as the ragged, swollen creature wrapped in one of Lisi's sheepskins hobbled into their midst. Her suffering made itself known by every twitch in her face with each step. When finally Gerwalta reached their throng, she dropped to her knees, her eyes trained on the floor.

"An interloper to my clan did this to me, all to get to Andreas, to drag him back here."

"Such manure!" Michael scoffed. "Why would a wolfsretter drag a convicted wolf back anywhere? Why wouldn't he just kill him where he stood?"

"Because it is easier to move a living body than a dead one," Gerwalta said. "My mother pursued us after we fled. She would have killed Andreas, only she discovered I was with child and it moved her heart. She… She cut off Andreas's hand, used it to claim the kill."

All the wolves felt it then: the shiver that overcame them when remembering the sliced-off appendage mounted outside the Schloss gate. They'd been told it was Andreas's but they refused to believe it but couldn't be sure. He was no longer of the pack; would they know if he passed, or would had those bonds been eternally severed?

"The wolfsretter from the House of Night captured Andreas to prove my mother's lies. After that, though..." The woman's face curdled like milk left to lay, tears streaming down over flushed flesh. "I tried to tell him. I said his love would kill him, and now it has. Andreas is dead, and it's all my..."

The words after that tapered off. Lisi closed in, wrapping Gerwalta in her arms, pulling her forehead to her shoulder. Wilhelm surveyed the room and found on each lupine's face the same reaction. Disbelief. Not in Gerwalta's story, for its plausibility melted well into the mold of their reality. Rather, it was for Gerwalta herself. A righteous wolfsretter, a daughter of the House of Red, openly weeping for one of their own. Openly showing weakness before a pack.

A wounded animal baring her injuries before predators inherently bent to hate her.

Gerhart, königswolf, cleared his throat, rising from the milking stool on which he'd sat listening. "I don't care whether this red-blooded pig lives or dies."

The shewolves bared their teeth, but Gerhart held up a hand, silencing them all.

"But her sin," he continued, drowning all the growls, "wasn't against us. A fact is a fact, however. She is the mate of an exile, and having left with him, accepted his punishment as her own."

"Don't be ridiculous," Lisi snapped as one of the other shewolves came forward to assume her place. "Gerwalta didn't know that is our way. And what could she have done if she had? Would you have let her stay with us as a packling?"

"Of course not." The king's tone bordered on anger. "She is not, cannot be one of us. I do not wish the child harm. Believe me, I do not. But I am king, and as king, it is my duty to protect this pack from threats of any nature. A child who could very well turn the power of the enemy on us from within... That isn't a risk I am prepared to accept."

Lisi's face went red. "You cannot be suggesting that…"

"Enough!" Gerhart spun. "It is their nature. Even when their heart softens… Look at what happened to Andreas!" he barked, letting the second woman go. "Their hate burns, but their love poisons. I won't have this among us. Wilhelm!"

The second, roused from observation, stepped forward, even as he examined from a sideways glance if his mate was well. "Yes, mein könig?"

Gerhart waved a hand dismissively. "Take this traitorous whore to the Matron. She isn't our bitch to whip."

"But she'll die if you—" Esther barked.

"Enough!" Gerhart spun, his chest puffing, his eye bulging, his voice full of brimstone. "This is the king's command! Now, Wilhelm, obey!"

Wilhelm looked once at his wife, then to the king, and at his wife again.

It was all very good for Gerhart to spite Lisi, but it would be Wilhelm who'd be sleeping with the pigs come morning.

TWENTY-ONE

As Zelda's feet slammed the stairs of the wall leading to the gate, Gerwalta closed her eyes against memory. How distantly in the past it seemed now, that day when Gerwalta herself rushed to defend the Schloss from the intentions of the königswolf. How could she have known then what fate had in store? If she could go back to that day and refuse her mother's orders to accompany Andreas on his mission, all this could've been avoided. If she had asked to join in her cousin's conspiracy when it had been discovered instead of killing him over it, she'd be far from here, perhaps raising a child already. A child whose legitimacy wouldn't be questioned by her clan. A child whose birth wouldn't bring so much death.

Zelda grinned. "My, my. What have we here?"

Wilhelm cleared his throat. "Frau Faust."

"Herr Kosner." Zelda surveyed her bruises and cuts with mild disinterest. "What a pretty present. But she looks somewhat... used up. What happened, did the pups have some fun with her?"

Beside her, the wolf bristled. "Frau Faust, your sister is weary and beaten and days away from giving birth. Show some compassion."

So the pack's second had been on Lisi's side of the argument? How interesting.

"Shall I just kill her right here then?" Zelda pulled the lever that allowed the gate to open. "If only the Matron hadn't said I'm not to harm her should she show up."

Gerwalta stepped forward, a prisoner being transferred, until her body jerked back.

"I don't care what Gerhart says," Wilhelm spoke into her ear when her back pressed against his shoulder. "You chose one of us over all of them. Die with honor, die without fear. Die like a wolf."

His words warmed in a way she hadn't expected any to. "Thank you, Wilhelm, but I knew where this road led when I set out on it. Give Lisi my thanks, tell her all is fine."

"How can you say that when they mean to kill you?"

Gerwalta took two steps forward. "Because I've no fear."

The gate slammed back into place the moment they were through, and even though she could no longer see him, Gerwalta felt Wilhelm's tenderness as they crossed the outer and inner bailey.

At midday, the hall stood empty. Her family and most of the servants would be upstairs or in the other buildings of the complex, sleeping away. Zelda shoved her sister down on the floor of the throne room, using a pair of iron shackles to secure her to one of the ornate pillars.

"Wait here in silence, or I'll make you wait in the dungeon while you scream."

She needn't ask wait for what. Gerwalta knew. The Matron. Not her mother who, no doubt, was condemned and overthrown the moment Andreas had been revealed to be alive, but for Helga, who at this hour would be in bed, high in the tower in the Matron's chambers.

Water dripped in some distant corner, reverberating off the stone walls. Bells rang in the valley; their song crawled up the steep hill. Her bladder disobeyed commands and emptied itself beneath her. Nothing to be done for it, unfortunately. A mouse squeaked as it passed, pausing to sniff her toes. She proved even below its interest and it skittered off.

She shifted, her bones aching. As a nascent, she'd been trained to keep her body under her command, to separate the physical from her consciousness. Pregnancy had made her both wonder at the body's capacity for change, but it also made her feel like an outsider in her own skin. Even now, as she attempted to ignore the way pain shot up her back and down to her toes, she hoped the suffering proved worthwhile.

Suddenly, feet pounded up the hall. Sound became sight as Gerwalta, eyes trained on the floor, noticed a pair of pointed slippers come to a halt on the ground before her.

"Well, well..."

Pain shot through her body as Helga fisted her hair and yanked Gerwalta's head up.

"Little sister," Helga hissed. "What big eyes you have. What big ears. What a mouth. Every part of you is as swollen as that hideous gut of yours." Gerwalta cried out as Helga whipped back her neck. "Someone has had a go at you, haven't they?"

"I suspect he had a go at you as well." Gerwalta's soft words still lacked no courage. "Mehmet's scent is all over you."

"Is it any sin for a Matron to share a bed with her husband?"

"Husband?" As much as her swollen eyes could allow, Gerwalta squinted. "But I killed Alexandre."

"Ah, an open admission of one of your many crimes." Helga petted her sister's matted red hair. "Not that I needed it, but it does make killing you a little more... defensible."

"Kill me if you wish," Gerwalta spit back, "but spare my child. Our law has no sanction to execute a child, even if it is born of one of us and a lupine."

"Do you think that matters? No righteous wolfsretter would allow such a creature to survive."

"The House of Night would," Gerwalta said.

Just then, Mehmet strolled into the throne room. "Oh, I'm sorry, Gerwalta," he said, taking a position at Helga's side. "That's actually not true."

"But... in Venice, on the ship. The lupine and her mate, the asenaic..."

"What asenaic? Ahmet was a stupid wolfsretter who raped a lupine. A sick thing, really, that mating bond of theirs. Made the shewolf fall in love with the man who forced her innocence. Don't worry, he was properly punished after we parted. After that, she saw no point in going on and took care of herself, saving me the work."

"But you said that... I sensed another wolf. I..." Terror struck at her as the tie of the deception loosened in her mind. "She was pregnant. The wolf I sensed and sometimes didn't sense... It was a baby." She looked up at the interloper with angry eyes. "So she's dead."

Mehmet leaned down and stroked one of his long, bony fingers down her cheek. "That's what I do to betrayers. I kill them. But you?" He shook his head. "That beating I gave you in Navarre should have killed you both. I stabbed you, but even that didn't work did it? Here you are."

How could she not have seen from the beginning what a loathsome creature he was?

"My question is why?" he said instead. "It isn't to save your mother, and you must have known we'd kill your mate after he served his purpose. So, tell me then, Gerwalta, what was it that forced you through all that pain and suffering, just to have more pain and suffering?"

All emotion drained from her face. "I'm here because he is my mate, and because I cannot live without him."

Helga leaned in, bringing herself inches from Gerwalta's face. "Don't worry, you won't have to." Then rising, she turned to Mehmet. "Take her to her old chambers and lock her inside. Tonight, her bones burn with the wolf's."

TWENTY-TWO

Gerhart hadn't been a bad königswolf, but that didn't mean he was a good one either. He didn't, for example, ask for an invitation to enter the bedroom after giving one gruff knock.

"Lisi Kosner!" He growled her name like an insult. The king burst in, his cheeks red, his chest puffing. "What is the meaning of this?"

Lisi finished folding one of her son's shirts and placed it into the sack. "The meaning of what, mein könig?"

"Don't treat me as a fool, woman! Every mother in the packlands is readying their children for a journey, all saying that you are the one who gave the order." The king took two more steps forward, planting his pointed finger into her chest. "I am king. I alone can order the children the leave the farm."

"You've no argument from me, your majesty," she mocked. "I ordered nothing. I merely told the mothers of the pack and only the mothers that I was sending Jelena and Jacob into the forest for a few days with my sister and invited any who wished to do the same to have the children ready by twilight. No one is under any obligation to—"

"Don't you think I see what you're doing?" Gerhart interjected. "You're going to try to free Gerwalta, and where will that leave me? There's no way you and a few other lunatics can take on the whole Red clan!"

Lisi placed the sack on the foot of the bed, next to a nearly identical one she'd packed for her daughter earlier. "There are more members of our pack than there are wolfsretter in the schloss. With Gunda Faust in the dungeon, Gretchen serving in Ravensburg, that leaves only four in the castle. Both the Matron's father and brother are on patrols, and they'll pursue a group of juvenile wolves breaking off from the packlands more than they'll worry about any of us."

"And all four can draw a blade or arrow of silver into existence in a blink and kill you dead," Gerhart countered. "Is that what you want, Lisi? To send the children back and have them return orphans? And for what? To rescue a wolfsretter?"

"I would never put my life in danger for the likes of Gerwalta Faust, but the baby she carries… It is an innocent pup, Gerhart, one that sadistic Helga will take much joy in torturing before she finally kills. Even if Andreas has been exiled, it doesn't mean we can stand idly by while the Reds destroy his child."

"But how can you justify risking the shewolves, the mothers of this pack, to save one bastard child?"

"Because the child is a lupine," she answered. "Don't tell me you didn't sense it, smell it when Gerwalta was here."

The king's façade began to crumble. "I won't sanction war against the wolfsretters."

"My intention merely is to force a negotiation to free the pup and only the pup whence it is born."

"And just how would you negotiate?" Gerhart asked. "It is full moon! Yes, our lupine strengths will be at their greatest, but all of you will be unable to reclaim your skin. You'd need a king with you to serve as mediator."

"I agree," Lisi said. "My question now is, will that be you, or must I ask Wilhelm to challenge you?"

The king wolf recoiled at the mere suggestion. Wilhelm was a beloved son of the pack, one they'd known for years and respected. Second to three kings, and while a mild soul, capable of vicious animalistic terror. In short, a foe not to be easily trifled with.

"He will do it if I ask it of him, and he will win. Do you know why? Because his love for us in his strength, while yours is only hate. The only reason you won against Andreas was that he was so desperate to lose," Lisi said. "You know you'd never have defeated him otherwise."

An inferno raged in Gerhart's eyes. "Is that what you think? Well, then, we shall see, won't we?" He turned toward the door. "You have your wish, bitch. We are going to the Schloss. And there, I will kill Baron once and for all."

TWENTY-THREE

Gunda had never felt sympathy for a wolf, and the emotion didn't fit well. If she had silver, she'd put Andreas Baron out of his misery. Or perhaps, put herself out of her own.

"Must you make so much noise?"

"I am going moon mad. I can feel it." Andreas's bloodshot eyes rolled her direction. "This is how I end. The full moon comes and I am bound in silver. My body is driven towards fur, but the metal repels my ability. My mind cannot take it."

It had been an act of cruelty to hold a wolf prisoner. When Helga had visited towards evening, wrapping a layer of blood-claimed silver around his bonds, she'd become the devil herself in his eyes. With the rise of a gravid moon in the midnight sky, every bone and muscle in the wolf's body broke and tore, only to fall back to his layman form again and again and again. Add to that the fact that the silver also burned away large portions of his flesh, and there was no wonder how much he suffered.

"I'm going to die without ever seeing my child." The wolf let out a jagged sigh as his eyes turned back to the ceiling. "How will he go on, when I am gone? Who will care for him?"

"My daughter, your wife, of course," Gunda snapped. "Or do you think your mate unequal to the task?"

"No, but... My child needs a pack. He needs..."

They both stilled their tongues when the dungeon gate flew open and a shadow of a man paraded in. Apart from his olive skin, everything about Mehmet was black. His cloak. His eyes. The hair and beard that helped conceal his features in the dark. His heart. His soul.

His ambition.

"Matron."

Gunda hated him. Not because of the kind of person Mehmet

Siyah was, but because he represented every quality she had tried to instill in her own children. Each had fallen flat on some key criteria, and only now she managed to be thankful for that. In his wake, her second-born daughter Zelda and her husband, Helmut, followed. Zelda pushed a key into the lock of Gunda's cell, letting the door swing open.

Mehmet reached for the link of the chain that kept Andreas secured. "Hungry yet, wolf?" he asked, pulling Andreas to his feet. "I do hope so. It's time for your last supper."

When Andreas opened his mouth, more moans than words emerged. "Kill me if you will, but I won't die a murderer."

"Oh, I think you'll find yourself more tempted than you might suppose," Mehmet said.

"Mother." Zelda swooped in, taking a key to the chains tying Gunda to the wall and unlocking them.

"Don't call me mother, you foul child. Not when you've forsaken me like this."

"Very well, then. Gunda," Zelda corrected. "Recall your cloak."

Fisting folds of red fabric, Gunda took a step back. "What?"

"You won't drag your bloodline down as you die. Disrobe and go to your death without clan."

"But I..."

"Now!"

Zelda's tone allowed for no margin of disagreement. Gunda took one last look at her arms, her tunic, imagined herself reaching back and throwing the hood over her head. Then, she closed her eyes, and made it disappear, leaving her only in the soiled, laymen-made garments.

She hadn't truly felt defeated until this moment. But like the wolf and she agreed, what did it matter, when you were about to die?

"Finally." Zelda tugged on the chain, pulling her mother along.

At first, Gerwalta didn't understand what she was seeing. It was almost like when she was a child and her father shaved off his beard. It amazed her that the man she'd called Papa and played with every day could suddenly look like a different person yet be the same. It was the first time Gerwalta could remember seeing her mother without her cloak, and it didn't pass her over how much smaller it made the woman who had loomed so large in her memories. In the outer bailey, her mother had been tied by all fours, outstretched on the ground. She was a skeleton that merely clung to its meat.

Gunda's weary head rose, catching sight of her daughter. The Matron's stony resolve ebbed into sadness. "In the end, it was all for naught."

"Walta!"

Gerwalta spun and felt all the wind rush from her lungs. Andreas, bound in silver chains, no doubt blood-claimed to prevent any attempts at heroics, fell to all fours when he saw her. At first, she thought because the moon was pulling him inevitably towards his fur. Only then, she realized that as high as the moon was, he should already be in it. The horizon bisected the sun, but it was dipping fast. The full moon already had begun to claim the sky.

"Walta, fly! Go!"

She shook her head. "I cannot."

His face went suddenly blank. "Then we are all lost. Ah..."

"Silence, dog!" Mehmet's foot landed square in Andreas's ribs.

"No!" Gerwalta pulled, lunged, strove, but Helga's restraints proved too strong. With every effort, all she gained was frustration, until Helga slackened the iron chains, letting her fall to the ground.

"Oh, take heart, little sister," the new matron cooed as she kneeled at her side. "You'll survive the night. You see, I've decided that you shouldn't die alone. I'll let you hold your baby to your chest when I burn you. But mother..."

At that moment, the statement was broken up by Andreas's tortured screams.

The sun had disappeared.

"Withdraw the silver!" Gerwalta begged, her open palm

slapping down on the packed dirt. "You're destroying his mind, keeping him in flesh like this."

Helga just laughed. "That's the point. A few more minutes, I think, and then, when he's nearly mad with the effort, we'll let him loose on Mother."

"You heartless, cruel, bi—"

But Gerwalta never got the word out. It was cut short by her own groan as her body seized and a spasm wrenched her.

The smile on Helga's face evaporated. "How very convenient."

Zelda, standing nearby, spun. "What is?"

Before Helga could say anymore, Gerwalta cried out again. How was it possible? This couldn't be the baby coming. A first delivery took hours if not days. This pain had come from nowhere and was already akin to the worst of what she'd seen her sisters go through.

Zelda swooped in, bracing her arms under Gerwalta's and lifting her to her feet. "She shouldn't deliver for several weeks, at least. I don't have a birthing chamber prepared."

"Fool, her child is half-lupine. Their waiting time is less than ours. Of course this baby would be born sooner than a wolfsretter."

As Gerwalta's screams erupted for a third time in as many minutes, she was joined by Andreas.

"It is your own blood!" he shouted across the bailey. "You heartless beasts, how can you treat your own blood like this?"

"I'll do what I can in the time we have to prepare." Zelda began to move Gerwalta back toward the castle.

Gerwalta did what she could to plant her feet. "Please, if you won't let me say goodbye to my husband, at least let me say goodbye to my mother."

"What cause, little sister? You'll both be dead come morning."

"Then what cause to oppose?" Gerwalta mumbled. "Please, Zelda, you are a mother too. Would you deny your daughter this?"

Zelda's expression soured. Sucking on her own lips, she turned her eyes to Helga. "Matron?"

Bit by bit, Helga's muscles tightened, until finally, she huffed and took Gerwalta by the hair, pushing her down to her mother on the ground. "Make it quick."

Gerwalta paused only a moment to nod at Helga before crawling close to her mother. "I want you to know, I forgive you."

"Gerwalta, I—"

"Shhh—" She wrapped her hand around Gunda's where it was tied to a stake. In an instant, her mother stilled and her eyes went wide. Gerwalta leaned in to kiss her cheek. "I send you my love. Do you understand?"

The relief of leeching the silver off her skin lasted only a moment as Gerwalta felt another convulsion come on. She fell forward, her fingers digging into the earth.

"Take her away!" Helga commanded. "Mehmet, cast the chain so you can take shelter inside, then release the lupine from his bond. We'll return to kill him as soon as he's killed my—"

The orders stopped as Gunda unbound rose to her feet. "You don't mean me, do you, daughter?"

The new Matron fell back to see her predecessor on all fours, a silver sword in her hand. `

She pulled back the weapon, ready to take on any who would dare approach. "I raised you better than this. If you want me to die, you kill me."

Gunda grinned. "The moment I touch the silver, it will obey me. I am Matron. Remember, Mother, you brought this on yourself."

Then, everything seemed to happen at once.

Helga charged. Gunda swung. Gerwalta called out. Mehmet pulled back the silver chain, forcing Andreas to howl.

And the pack?

They poured into the courtyard from every direction.

TWENTY-FOUR

With all her focus on the executions at hand, Helga had forgotten the most critical part of being Matron: to protect everyone not a wolf from everyone who was.

That included the wolfsretters.

Fur flew in every direction, driving the ill-prepared House of Red to the edges of the courtyard. Outside of the chain made of Mehmet's blood-claimed silver, no one had a supply upon their person. No one, it seemed, except Gunda.

At least that means the wolves will target her first, Helga thought.

"Everyone to the keep!" she called out, waving her hand and running for the doorway.

"Helga!" Mehmet tugged back on the chain, even as Andreas Baron phasing between his two forms in dizzying succession pulled and writhed. "Help me. I cannot come through them."

Helga pushed the last of her clan through the schloss door before turning one brief moment to lock the black-cloaked figure in sight. "My name is Matron."

No sooner had she turned than the wolves reached Mehmet. The chain fell to the ground, and its form lost definition as he pulled it all in, sheltering his body from both fang and claw.

Finally, Andreas could take his fur. And that would allow him to take his revenge.

Never but in her worst nightmares had Gunda imagined the scene before her. Her family fled, closing the door to safety, closing the door on her. All around, wolves driven to fur by the moon encircled. On the ground beneath her, Gerwalta clutched her rebelling body and called out for her husband through the pain.

The wolves had followed the fleeing parties as far as the door, but the moment they were out of sight, they refocused. It didn't take a wink for them to surround her, all circling, the pack moving like water, bearing fangs, growling, but awaiting their king's order.

What to do? She could fly herself to safety; of that she was pretty certain, but would the wolves protect Gerwalta or destroy her? Carry Gerwalta along? Impossible. As much as the pain was causing Gerwalta to thrash about, the feat would prove too daunting and dangerous. Surrender to the wolves and hope they showed mercy? Why would the creatures she'd spent her lifetime subduing and oppressing show her a kindness? And even if they at least came to Gerwalta's aid, Gunda was no fool. Her family hadn't really fled; they'd retreated to gather weapons. It wouldn't be long before Helga led a charge back into the courtyard, silver at the ready, to destroy them all.

"Stay back!" Gunda threw herself over Gerwalta, brandishing the sword. "I'll kill any who comes for her."

At least if the wolves fell upon her, she'd die fighting and she'd die quick.

No sooner had the words left her mouth than the new king-wolf approached. A massive beast, black fur with a brown undercoat, looked poised to kill. Gunda leaned in to whisper into her daughter's ear. "If you survive this day, run as far as you can and carry my love with you wherever that is."

The king snarled, Gunda shouted, and they both lunged. They hadn't reached each other, however, before they were both knocked back into the ground. Gunda shook away her confusion as she pressed callused hands down, pushing herself up.

Andreas Baron, his lupine form far stronger than his mortal one had looked, stood sentry before her.

His body ached. His heart pulsed. His mind vacillated between man and beast. But this he knew… the king and his pack were here to save the child, but they weren't here to save Gerwalta. In fact, with labor under way, assuring Gerwalta's welfare wasn't even necessary.

Lupine infants had come into the world from dead mothers before. Even werewolf women died in childbirth. If Gerwalta didn't survive... Well, then, there was a way to free the babe, as gruesome as that was.

Man.

Beast.

Man.

Beast.

The beast within demanded that he protect his pup. The man longed for his wife. Both Andreas's natures agreed, however, that either outcome demanded proximity. With bounding leaps, ignoring both the agony of a body beaten bloody and the torment of a mind poisoned by silver, Andreas had crossed the bailey. A ring of wolves, all his old pack led by their new king, surrounded his bride and, to his surprise, Gerwalta's mother. Gunda could have saved herself if she wanted. She could fly, after all. Had Gerwalta not gone into labor, perhaps she could as well. One look at the fierce pose the former Matron struck told him, however, that Gunda had no plans to sacrifice her daughter to allow for her own escape.

But Gunda couldn't protect Gerwalta and take on Gerhart. Andreas would save Gerwalta, then, but the best chances for that success would be greatly aided by saving her mother first.

The pain ebbed and Gerwalta finally opened her eyes. For the last several moments, she'd been blind, relying on nothing more than the sounds around her. She knew she was surrounded by the wolves. She knew her mother was near. She'd known her clan had fled the courtyard.

They'd return with weapons. She understood this, because Gerwalta had never stopped recognizing what a realistic outcome would look like. She'd known from the day she'd run off with Andreas that it was the first step towards her own death. She never expected, however, that the path would lead back to her own front door.

To her husband and her mother, working together, to defend her against the wolves.

She pushed herself back as the melee ensued but took some relief in the fact that the pack didn't attack. Rather, the battle seemed only to be between Andreas, Gunda, and Gerhart the King. Why were the other wolves waiting? Why didn't they join in? Why weren't they falling collectively on her, who had backed herself unprotected against the wall?

Then it hit. Because the king was fighting with an intention to kill, and Andreas refused to yield. Andreas was fighting back. Not just for her. Not just for their daughter. He was fighting to win back his pack.

And with the pack on their side, how could Helga and the others triumph against them?

"Mother, fall back!"

Gunda shook her head. "No, he'll be over—"

"FALL BACK!" Gerwalta repeated. "It is a challenge. Let Andreas fight." Let him win. "The pack awaits the outcome, and the magic cannot happen if you interfere."

Gunda dropped her sword to her side and turned. "Why would he want to—"

"Because he's trying to save us both. He—"

A red cloak flew down from above, landing just behind her.

Helga's silver blade bit into Gerwalta's neck. "Fall back into the keep with me now, or you'll die before you can scream."

Broken, beaten, malnourished, and on the edge of madness, Andreas fought like he'd never fought before. Perhaps because of the love he now had for another. Perhaps because the only alternative at this point was death.

Gerhart was a worthy opponent, but that wasn't a surprise. After all, he'd beaten Andreas before. But on that occasion, Andreas had wanted to lose. Tonight, he needed to win.

At last, the black-furred wolf yipped when Andreas's maw took his throat. Power surged through his body as the pack's loyalty shifted. Andreas didn't waste a moment. He turned just in time to see Helga pulling Gerwalta back into the keep at the end of a silver blade.

With one mighty yelp, the werewolves fell in behind him.

"Hurry!" Gunda Faust shouted as she joined the pack's ranks. "To the tower with Gerwalta, Andreas. The pack and I will secure the stairs so that no other may breach."

Helga drove forward but had barely managed the throne room when the wolves burst through the doors. She spun, the blade's point drifting away. Gerwalta saw Helga's hand outstretch and threw her weight forward. Her teeth dug into her sister's soft flesh, drawing blood. Drawing temptation.

Fresh meat. Fresh kill.

The silver blade clanged on the floor, its ding bringing Gerwalta from her hazy bloodlust just in time for another pain to bend her in two.

"Animal! How dare you?" Helga called out, pulling her bleeding hand into her chest. "Now, you die!"

Gerwalta fought past the pain to reach for the blade. The moment her finger brushed it, the locus of her agony shifted from her center to her limbs. She flopped unto her back, using her feet to push her body away from Helga's approach, knowing it was no use.

Helga salivated as she reached her feet, her silver staff drawn from reserves painted against her person. She lifted the instrument back in the air, and then... fell back as two wolves moved into attack.

Gerwalta had no time to react. Before she could even manage to roll onto her side, someone had their arms braced under her shoulders from behind and was pulling her to her feet.

"We make for the tower!" he said.

"Andreas." Joy. Utter joy. "You defeated Gerhart. You are king."

"And you, my queen." He kissed her forehead as he swept her up into his arms and began to cross the room. "Our little lamb picked an auspicious moon to be born under, didn't she?"

Gerwalta laughed. "You finally admit it's a girl."

"I pray that it is, so she can be every bit the shewolf her mother is."

At the base of the tower, Gunda stood. "Hurry!" she waved them on.

Andreas came to an abrupt stop. "There are no stairs."

"Gerwalta will make them of the silver that sits there." Gunda pointed at the large metal disc of a floor that surrounded a central pillar.

The wolf gently placed his mate on her own two feet. "She can't. The silver doesn't listen to her now. It burns her."

Before Gunda could get a word of question in on that, Gerwalta stepped into the stairwell. "I'll make it listen, even if it kills me."

Gerwalta fought her own body, even as it broke and betrayed her. Her knees turned to dough, her heart became a drum in her ears and her sex. One hand shot out, bracing the wall, steadying as much as she could. The other encircled the shifting, bulbous belly she'd watch grow for the past eight months.

Not yet, my love, she begged of the child within. Just a little longer. Just let me get to the top of the tower.

But the ruined wolfsretter was to learn her first lesson in motherhood: it isn't the way of things for the child to obey the parent.

They were almost there. A few more steps, and they'd be safe. Andreas held her up as another labor pain struck. Or it could have been that he held on for his own support. Wolves didn't favor heights, and Gerwalta fought with all her strength to keep the stairs solid beneath her feet.

"Walta?" he yipped.

"I... will... not... let... us..." The seizure gripped her, her womb constricting, driving fire into her gut, crushing her determination.

Gerwalta doubled, pushing her hands out in front of her, catching the edge of the steps.

Andreas breathed a sigh of relief as the stone landing held them up. He stopped on the stair above, turned, blanched. He was so gaunt, so unnaturally wane and weary in a way she'd never seen any other lupine. Gerwalta had never known a werewolf had the capacity to become beleaguered, but that had been before she and Andreas had been forced to flee, running the length of God's green earth just to keep their own lives. He pulled Gerwalta to her feet. Or tried, for the pain still held her captive, and even her strong will proved incapable of resistance.

"Walta, please," he begged, gently coaxing her. "Just a little more, my love. We're almost safe."

Her words were more cries now than voice. "I'm coming."

The wolf found her a shade of white lighter still and assumed it, even as he whisked them into the first room he came to: the Matron's bed chamber.

"I am sorry, Walta. This will hurt."

Without warning, her husband managed to heave her up, pulling her into her arms, even as the bolt of anguish sunk into her again.

"Andreas!" She squeezed shut her eyes against the suffering, seeing red without the benefit of sight.

"A moment more, love. And… look, we are here."

Gerwalta took what relief she could from the cool sheets beneath her thin, torn frock. Andreas knelt at her side, pushing pillows drenched in her sister's scent under her back. "I don't know what comfort I can offer but ask it of me and I'll do what I can."

"Just promise me that you'll do whatever it takes to make sure our child survives."

The lupine wrapped her frail hand in his paw, drawing Gerwalta's white-knuckled fingers to his lips. "I swear to it."

The tender moment passed as the ache of labor lit her body on fire. Gerwalta dropped Andreas's hand, planted her palms flat against the bed, threw her head back, and screamed.

"The baby is coming."

These words not from either of them, but from a third who had just entered the room.

Andreas teetered on the edge of shifting. "If you try to hurt her now, Matron..."

"Cease your fight, cursed wolf!" Gunda Faust snapped, even as she closed the door behind her and worked to move what heavy items the room offered in front of it. "Do you think I fought beside you below just to kill you up here. Now, step aside, unless you know how to birth a baby. Guard the door. Helga will make her way here soon enough."

The emotions cycled through the lupine's face. Anger, spite, frustration, and finally, acceptance. "If another member of your clan enters this room, I'll tear them limb from limb, just, please, protect my pup."

The Matron sat on the bed, wrapping Gerwalta's hand in her own. "When the pain comes again, push."

Gerwalta shook her head as the tension ebbed. "The labor just started. It cannot already be time."

"Wolves' pregnancy is shorter, and their labor quicker still. Prepare daughter. You're about to experience the worst pain you've ever felt, and the quickest ever forgotten."

No sooner did the words fall from Gunda's lips than the pain came upon her again. Gerwalta bit her lip, biting down so hard, her teeth were soon stained with blood. "There is something wrong!"

"All mothers think so, but a child is a miracle, and those come with no small amount of sacrifice and pain."

Gerwalta lashed her head side to side, grunting her words. "No... something... is... wrong."

Gunda softened, rubbing Gerwalta's knee as the contraction tapered off. "I'll look. Try to relax. I promise, I'm not going to hurt you." She lifted the frock, discerned the situation, and lowered it again, giving Gerwalta a smile. "All is well. Now, I need to gather something to swaddle the babe in. Breathe."

Gerwalta was either too weary to hear, or too trusting to answer.

Gunda stood, catching the unspoken attention of the wolf. She waved him aside, out of Gerwalta's earshot. "The baby is breach."

"What does that mean?" Only, then, he passed into an expression of resolve. "It matters not. I'll love her, no matter what she is."

The fallen Matron exhaled frustration. "Breach means the baby is turned the wrong way, and I fear that Gerwalta has already pushed her into a place where I cannot correct it."

"So you're saying..." The wolf's eyes verily spun. "What are you saying?"

"I'm saying that you have a choice to make, Herr Baron. I can save your daughter, or I can save mine, but I cannot save both."

Suddenly, the choices balanced on the end of his tongue. "How? Gerwalta is my mate, what is my life without her? But my daughter is pack." He looked up, the weight of the world in his eyes.

Gunda wrapped a hand over Andrea's shoulder. "You are a king, Andreas. You need to make a king's decision. But truth be told, it may be too late for my daughter. The look of her..." She bit back a tear. "I know what death looks like when it creeps into a woman's face. But your child could survive." She turned somber eyes on the wolf. "If you are willing to make the sacrifice."

In short order, the Matron explained the plan and left the fate of all in the werewolf's hand.

His eyes closed in the wake of his decision like the axe of the executioner. "I know what I need to do then."

Gunda nodded, prayed for the Almighty's forgiveness, and set about her task.

TWENTY-FIVE

It took nearly an hour for Helga to gather enough silver from around the castle to form the stairs and make her way to the top of the tower. Gerwalta had retained the customary pool at the top, an attempt to delay the pursuit. That's all it had done, however. Delay. With her bow staff in hand, she led the charge up the stairs.

Gerwalta would pay for this. Never before had one single wolfsretter committed so long a litany of crimes. Mating a wolf would have had her sister exiled, but this? Her body and baby would be sliced into steaks and roasted over a fire and fed to the dogs. Her bones would bleach in the Black Forest until the end of days.

Each step mirrored the anger rising within her. Kill the wolf, cut the baby from my sister, rip Gerwalta's heart from her chest. As to her mother, Helga could go either way. If Gunda submitted, she'd gladly offer her a quick, painless death at a more convenient time. But if she got in the way... Both Alexandre's and Maria's graves testified that Helga was willing to do what was necessary.

In the tower, Andreas wore more blood in lieu of clothing. He sat on his heels, looking at the carnage staining his hands, rocking back and forth. On the bed, Gerwalta stared, glassy-eyed, in Helga's direction. Something about this didn't make sense. Why wasn't he running? Why wasn't she crying out? Surely Gerwalta must know this was the end for all three of them. And where was their mother? Had Gunda fought to bring them to safety so hard just to abandon them at the first opportunity?

Then Helga relaxed her eyes, taking in the larger picture. Gerwalta's tan frock was stained red. Certainly birth came at the price of some bleeding, but this was... This was...

This was more than birth. This was death. Gerwalta's body was practically torn in two.

Helga took a step back. "You... You killed my sister."

"Shh!" Andreas Baron pushed a crimson-stained finger to his

lips with his one remaining hand. "You'll wake the baby."

A curl of sickness worked through Helga's gut. She took survey of the room. "Where is my mother?"

"Dead." The corner of the wolf's mouth ticked up.

"But how did you..." Suddenly, Helga put together the clues. So much blood. More than one person's? "You ate my mother."

"Yes, and I must say, wolfsretter is far sweeter a meat than even I imagined. But I found one that is sweeter still." He pushed a finger into the edges of Gerwalta's ravaged corpse. "Had to claw at it to get to it, though."

The statement landed on Helga like a physical blow. She'd been prepared to kill anyone who stood in her way, but seeing this before her... Even her stomach turned. "You've gone mad."

"No, Frau Faust. I'm actually quite clear, perhaps the clearest I've been in months. Your scheming and treachery cost me everything. My pack, my bride, my home... I wouldn't let you have my child. She rests now with her grandmother." He tempered a laugh. "In the belly of the beast."

Helga threw a hand over her mouth to stop the revulsion of her innards. "You ate your own daughter?" Even her iron constitution threatened to break at the thought. "If one ever needed proof of why we are necessary to your existence, you've given it for centuries to come. You are truly a monster."

"You say that, but all you had to do to prevent all of this, was love your sister and your family more than power. But if you think, now that I've gotten a taste for your flesh, that I would stop, then—"

But he never got to finish his sentence, for Helga had had enough. The eldest daughter of Gunda Faust breathed in her power, and breathed out her revenge, driving the blade on the end of her staff deep into the lupine's heart.

Blood bubbled on his tongue as the eerie smile stretched across his face. Andreas managed one last, longing look at the dead woman on the floor before him, then turned his eyes up to his slayer.

"Thank you, Matron."

TWENTY-SIX

She needed to fly, but not yet. From the top of the mountain with the vantage of the schloss, Helga or the others need only look out to see her figure darting across the moonlit sky. The moment Gunda had been able to make the ground, she did. Then, it was just a question of how fast could her feet carry her.

Gunda tried to remember the last words her daughter and the lupine had said to her.

"When you come to Navarre, find Igor, the vampire you knew as Goran Karahan. He'll take the child and keep it safe."

Andreas Barron had looked down at his daughter, and she could see all the lupine's strength engaged to keep from crying. Even she had problems not weeping. She didn't care what happened to the wolf, but she was a mother. To know that you'd never see your child again, that you'd be gone from this world and rely solely on the best intentions of others to raise it and keep it safe...

"But why would a vampire raise a child born of a wolfsretter and a lupine? I could raise her. I can keep her safe."

Andreas smiled. "You'd try. I know you would. But both lupines and wolfsretters will want her dead. She is safe with neither. I had hoped that..." His chin dipped. "It doesn't matter."

"Very well, then. I'll take her to Karahan." The sounds of feet pounding up the tower steps told them time had run out. "Quickly, give me the babe and do what you must. I... I cannot watch it be done."

What kind of mother could? Even if it created a story that Helga would all too readily buy and keep her from thinking the baby survived, inducing her not to look for it, what kind of mother could watch her youngest child be ripped apart by a werewolf?

The vampire looked at the bundle in his hands, then up again at Gunda, then to the bundle again.

"They told me you could be trusted. They said you would care for it."

"I..." Karahan's words cut off as he broke into a smile. "Did they say why?"

She shook her head. "But I would ask you to do more than that. I would ask you to kill it."

His eyes snapped up from the child. A wave pulsed through his face, pushing away his amusement. "Why would you come so far, protect it, spend up all your silver to procure the services of wet nurse after wet nurse, all just to bring it to me and ask me to do something you yourself could have?"

"Because she is my blood." Gunda fought back the tears, fought back the exhaustion threatening to topple her. "And I will not... cannot force myself to do it. Andreas and Gerwalta entrusted me because they thought I would have mercy enough to bring the baby to you to raise. But I've more mercy than they realized, because I know how a child born of our two lines can find harbor in neither. There will be no place for her in this world. I thought that you might consider..."

Karahan closed his eyes. "I would never kill a child," he growled. "I would never take the life of an innocent."

"But she could never..."

"She will!"

Gunda jumped back, the wave of his anger a physical blow against her body.

"She may not have a place with wolves or hoods, but I am neither of these things. I'll protect her from everything, even your bigotry and hopelessness."

Gunda nodded, lowering her arms to the side. "Then I've done what I came to do. I'll leave you, Herr Karahan."

"Not so fast, Frau Faust."

The wolfsretter paused in the doorway.

"What you ask of me is no small thing, and while I'll raise

Gerwalta's child as if she were my own, it isn't done solely out of the kindness of my heart. You will need do something for me."

She turned, her chin buried in her chest. "Yes, Lord?"

"The silver jars holding my own errant sons," he said, "I retrieved them from Schloss Wolfsretter when I understood you had interlopers in your house. They aren't safe with me, however. My longevity makes it necessary for me to restart with some regularity. I cannot be responsible for relocating the jars with each move. Vlad wasn't without his supporters, and they will use those times of readjustment to free him if the jars if I did."

"And how could I aid that?"

"By taking them and putting them someplace safe."

TWENTY-SEVEN

Zelda wiped the last of the blood on to her cloak as she took a place at Helga's side before the unlit pyre.

"Everything settled?"

Zelda bobbed her head. "The surviving wolves have been rounded up and expelled back to the packlands. Wilhelm Kosner is the new königswolf. He has been detained to bear witness."

Wilhelm? Yes, that would work very well indeed. He'd been Andreas Baron's second, then Gerhart's. He was used to taking orders and doing as he was told. Oh, and Helga would be giving orders and demanding obeisance for some time to come. The pack had to be punished for their insurrection. Had she a choice, Helga would've ordered them all killed. They deserved it, for certes. But even a new Matron understood that little power was gained in death. She'd fortify her rule better by allowing the pack to live but making the legend of their oppression one that wouldn't soon be forgotten. She'd raise her own daughter to be a matron every bit as cruel and ruthless as well. It would be her legacy. Ten generations from now, the pack would still be suffering for this revolution.

"Bring him into the courtyard after we've mounted Gerwalta and Andreas's bodies onto the spits." She pointed at the silver structure she herself had created. Burial was too dignified a process for such traitors. The order was passed back into the schloss even as Helga continued. "Speaking of which, are they almost ready?"

"Helmut is putting the corpses unto the litter now. It is funny, though..." Zelda's voice tapered off.

"I doubt anything regarding this is funny, Zelda."

"No, of course not, Matron. My apologies. What I meant was, it is peculiar," the third-born daughter amended. "Are you certain the wolf claimed that he ate the baby?"

"You saw the way Gerwalta's body was left in shreds. A child was ripped from that womb by force, I have no doubt of it."

"But, Matron, we found the babe still intact."

Helga spun. "What?"

"A little boy," Zelda said. "He was dead, of course, though I cannot say if that was because of something that happened before Gerwalta died, or if he simply suffocated in the womb afterward. His hand slipped out from the visceral when Helmut moved her body."

Helga bit her tongue. If the child had in fact not been clawed out of its mother, then what was the wolf playing at, saying he did?

If only the dead could speak...

"The child is dead then? I am agreeable to that. Light the pyre. I want the first thing Wilhelm Kosner to see when he emerges is me, standing before the spitted, burning body of his fallen king. I want that image seared into his brain so deep, it is still fresh on the minds of his great, great grandchildren. Let no packling or member of our clan ever forget: it is a crime for a wolf and a wolfsretter to love, and death to all who break this sacred law. None goes unpunished."

Helga watched as the flames grew hungry, burning through the fuel. And when the fire reached the smallest of the three bundles atop the pile, she smiled.

None goes unpunished.

None.

www.ingramcontent.com/pod-product-compliance
Lightning Source LLC
Chambersburg PA
CBHW011123190726
48289CB00012B/2882